THE
PROPHET
OF QUEENS

GLENN KLEIER

The Prophet of Queens
Copyright © 2021 by Glenn Kleier
www.kleier.com

Released through:
Liberum Press/BANTAM.CT

Hardcover ISBN: 978-1-7364174-3-0
Paperback ISBN: 978-1-7364174-2-3
eBook ISBN: 978-1-7364174-6-1

First Edition: June 12, 2021
Printed in the United States of America
0 9 8 7 6 5 4 3 2 1

Cover design by Antonio M Del Esporti M da Rocha
Interior design by TeaBerry Creative,
and Stewart A. Williams

Media Inquiries:
PO Box 703 Bantam.CT 067509998

*"All that's necessary for evil to prevail
is for people of conscience to do nothing."*

—UNKNOWN

ACKNOWLEDGMENTS

As I write this, America is suffering one of its darkest times in living memory—a medical, political, and social clash more divisive than any crisis since the Civil War. I cling to the belief that new vaccines, and a new national awakening will see us through...

The Prophet of Queens was a challenging project. And while the distractions of current affairs made finishing it more difficult, the pandemic gave me the incentive to do so. All the same, I couldn't have reached this point without the help of many smart, generous people to whom I'm deeply grateful:

—First and foremost, my family, who traveled this long road with me from start to finish. My beloved wife—first and last reader, my go-to for wisdom and critiques. My two sons, who kept me sensitive to the changing times and offered insights and contributions far beyond their years.

—My editor, Sulay Hernandez, who I had the good fortune to meet during her stint at Simon & Schuster, now performing her editorial magic at Unveiled Ink. A truly brilliant, gifted lady. In the course of our work, she's become a dear friend.

—My agent, Al Zuckerman of Writers House, who provided valuable input early on.

—The wise lady who masterminded the labyrinth of the book's internal layout, Tara Mayberry, of TeaBerry Creative. Tara, you are a consummate professional, I can't thank you enough for your expertise and unfailing good humor.

—The great cadre of beta readers who perused the final draft and offered helpful thoughts: Debbie Heald, Bella Ellwood-Clayton, Catherine Garrett, Jose Diaz, Gina Karasek, Maryam Gehad Ali, and a special thanks to Debbie Coverdale, who made a number of smart, spot-on contributions.

—And my friends and acquaintances who patiently supported me through this glacial process. Not forgetting Dr. Arielle Lester, a heroic healthcare provider in this pandemic, who graciously gave technical advice for a medical issue in the story.

To all of you, my love and appreciation, always.

Glenn

January, 2021

PART ONE

CHAPTER 1

The course of history took a detour today. Not that anyone realized at the time.

Scotty was in bed when it began, deep in a dream smiting evil after a late night of online videogaming. Until his mind cleared, and he realized the wail he heard wasn't in his head, but Homer yowling in the front room. Homer wasn't neutered, Scotty couldn't afford to have it done, and thinking some alley cat must be in heat somewhere, he tried to block the noise with a pillow.

But the wails continued. He'd never heard Homer so upset. Sliding from bed in his boxers, he raked his dark hair from his eyes and stumbled out of the bedroom to see his big orange tabby facing the shadows of the living room, hackles up.

"What is it, boy?"

The cat growled low, riveted.

Scotty stole toward him past a small closet, bath, and kitchenette on the right. The living room was spacious, especially for a second-floor walkup in this old part of Queens. Hazy shafts of light filtered through the blinds of a large window in front—only window in the apartment. In the left corner stood Pop's old tube TV and VHS player.

In the right, Mom's big umbrella plant. In between, set back from the window and facing it, the couch Scotty had bought on craigslist. And abutting the couch from behind, one end of a long table he'd salvaged from the streets for a computer desk.

He went to the door and switched on the overhead. All looked just as he'd left it last night.

But Homer insisted otherwise.

A rat? Scotty scratched his scraggy beard. A damn big one to frighten a tomcat. No point calling Samood, his worthless super never picked up and took days to respond. If Scotty hoped to sleep tonight, he'd have to deal with this himself. He turned to the coat rack and grabbed the umbrella with the pointy tip, only to be frozen by a sound unlike any he'd ever heard. Loud, deep-pitched, ominous. He saw no apparent source, as if the air itself bellowed. He staggered backward, and the noise ceased. Inched forward, it returned. Like throwing a switch.

"Jesus." No rat, more a monster growl from some horror flick. He felt the hairs on his neck prickle. Again he advanced, again the same. Damnedest thing he'd ever seen. Except, he couldn't see it. An invisible boundary of some kind.

He raised the umbrella and made for the front of the room, when suddenly the growl warbled into screech. He froze again, and Homer tore for the bedroom, claws raking hardwood. Still, nothing looked out of order. Radiator, smoke alarm, TV, computer. Scotty snatched his phone from the desk to call 9-1-1, but had no bars.

Finally, the shriek dropped to rumble, the rumble faded, and his phone was working again.

He edged to the window and parted the blinds, peering down on a street pot-holed and strewn with litter. Quiet. He went to his door and squinted out the peephole at the hall. Also quiet. He turned the knob and stuck his head out, met by a musty, cold draft. The halls here were unheated, lit by sallow milk-glass globes layered with bug carcasses, walls sloughing pea-green paint, linoleum floors worn through in high-traffic areas. And no clue to the source of the noises.

3

He returned to the bedroom, jumped into jeans and a T, and called to Homer under the bed, "Gonna check on the neighbors."

The cat peeped out. *Hey, don't leave me here alone.*

Scotty nodded, Homer jumped into his arms, and trading the umbrella for a leash at the coat rack, Scotty rushed downstairs to stop in front of the first door he came to. Apartment 1-B, Mrs. Steiner. Like a grandmother to him these past months. A note on her door read in tidy script: *At the Center today.* The neighborhood Family Services Center where she volunteered. Mrs. Steiner lived alone, and when out, left word so neighbors wouldn't worry.

Scotty was thankful she'd missed the disturbance. Not forgetting, she was allergic to cats.

He crossed the hall and rapped on 1-A, Mr. Zola. No answer, but the man was near deaf. Detecting a rattle of dishes inside, Scotty moved on to the Valenzuela family, 1C. They had nothing unusual to report. Likewise, Mrs. Ngato, 1D. And lugging Homer back upstairs, Scotty was baffled to learn from the two families on his floor, they'd heard no strange noises, either. 2D was vacant. He slung the cat over a shoulder and climbed the ladder to the hatch, scoping the roof for anything out of the ordinary. Nada.

Homer suggested, *Maybe they're doing road work outside.*

They headed downstairs again, pushing out the building's front door, hinges screeching, down the steps to the sidewalk into a bright, crisp day. Scotty shielded his eyes to scout the area for construction. None to be seen in this woefully neglected neighborhood. To the left of his brownstone sat another just like it, empty and for sale as it had been since the economy tanked. One of a dozen such rundown rubberstamps lining the street. Scotty fastened the leash to Homer's collar, set him on the sidewalk, and they struck off to check the rest of the block.

As he passed people, Scotty asked if they'd heard anything unusual. Most ignored him, or simply squinted at Homer on the leash. Those who bothered to respond shook their heads.

GLENN KLEIER

At the corner, Scotty came across a boarded-up storefront plastered with old flyers. One stood out fresh, and he slowed, smiling to recognize a black-and-white photo from the vintage film, *Metropolis*. The iconic face of the sexy female robot, encircled by an orange ring with a diagonal bar struck through it. Emblazoned beneath the ring in orange letters was the acronym, *R.U.S.T.* And under that, the phrase: *Rescue Us from Science and Technology.*

Scotty lost his smile. The worse the economy, the more he saw of this. So many people were out of work and desperate, crushed by forces beyond their comprehension, seeking refuge in things irrational. He felt bad for them. And fortunate to have a job, lousy as it was.

Snatching down the flyer, he tossed it in a trash can and pressed on. Around the corner were more abandoned stores, and he took a right into the alley, feeling Homer strain against the leash.

You sure this is a good idea?

Scotty had forgotten how desolate it was back here, the reason he seldom used his building's rear entrance. He continued, and soon came across vagrants rooting in dumpsters. A man with tattered clothes shuffled into his path and extended a grimy palm creased like a road map. Scotty asked him, "Happen to hear any weird noises this morning?"

The man shook his head, wiggling his fingers. Scotty could ill afford it, but fished out his wallet to give him a single. More hands materialized, Scotty's wallet quickly emptied, and he backed away apologizing to those who went without, figuring he'd gotten off easy.

The alley ended at a pawn shop, the last store still open on the block, and Scotty headed home none the wiser. No work crews, machinery, or anything else to account for the noises.

Homer squinted up at him. *So what the hell did we hear this morning?*

"Damned if I know. Maybe the sounds were all in my head. Like your voice."

The cat shrugged, and they returned to the apartment.

Scotty fixed them breakfast and took his to the couch, determined

5

to get his weekend back on track. He'd hardly settled in to watch reruns of *Rick and Morty* when he heard a new sound. Metal rolling on metal from the street below. He peeked through the blinds to see a moving truck double-parked, tailgate up. Behind it stood a young woman in jeans and a ribbed pullover, hands on hips, hair short and flipped. Scotty's age, about. A ballerina or model, judging by her figure. Though not established in her career, else she wouldn't be locating here. A new tenant on his floor, he hoped.

Sighing, he could feel her left-swipe him already. The only hits he ever got on his dating app were porn come-ons.

Scotty detected the pungent scent of liver, and turned to see Homer puzzling up at him.

What now?

"An addition to the neighborhood, I think."

The cat vaulted onto the windowsill to nose aside the blinds. *Hot damn, dude, a babe. Quick, go lend a hand.*

Scotty rolled his tongue along a cheek, and Homer snapped, *Un-uh, no waffling, you made a deal. Remember what the guru says?*

Last summer, Scotty had signed up for an online course at self-helpguru.com. *100 Steps to Success.* He'd paid his fee and taken the pledge, and Homer wasn't letting him out of it.

Step #19: Extend yourself, and the unattainable
shall come within reach.

Before Scotty had a chance to extend himself, however, out the back of the truck leaped a tall, wide-shouldered guy. *Métal Urbain* T-shirt, jeans, man-bun. He gave the girl a squeeze with a tattooed arm, and they began moving things into the vacancy down the hall across from Scotty. Scotty toggled from window to peephole, noting only women's clothing and paraphernalia. Through his door, he heard the girl call the guy "René." Finally, they emptied the truck, René drove off, and the girl retired to her apartment.

Scotty felt a paw tap his leg. *Now's your chance, get your ass over there.*

But the girl had to be exhausted, and faced a ton of stuff to sort out. Scotty went to his computer instead and opened his daily log, recording the events of the morning while still fresh in his head—as the guru also advised.

Homer leaped into Scotty's lap, read his entry, and cried, *What? You're passing off this morning as 'one of those things?' It sounded like the Second damned Coming to me!*

"Whatever it was," Scotty said, "we're none the worse for it. Come on, let's play The Game."

The videogame he and Homer were playing last night. And almost every night. The Game was the only aspect of his life Scotty felt he had control over.

Homer snorted, hopped down and trotted off, and Scotty's stomach knotted. Cats possessed perceptions beyond those of humans. And never before had Homer turned down The Game.

CHAPTER 2

S cotty threw on wrinkled khakis and a button-down shirt as Homer sat watching on the bed.

So, the cat growled, *you just gonna abandon me?*

"You know I can't take off work," Scotty said. "No worries, I got a plan."

Homer did not look assured. Yesterday, Sunday, at precisely 10:00 AM, the terrifying noises had returned. Scotty had awakened into a repeat of Saturday. Homer howling in the front room, Scotty entering to freakish thunder and whine, another frantic search, no apparent source, over in minutes. Exactly like before.

What's the plan?

Scotty headed to the kitchen, stuck a donut in his mouth, and ferried cat food, water, and litter box into the bedroom. Closing Homer inside, he wedged a towel under the door (broken latch). If the noises came back, hopefully the cat would remain in the room, the disturbance out.

But Homer wasn't used to being confined.

You can't do this, dammit, he whined from behind the door, *it's against fire code!*

8

"What choice do I have?" Even if Pop weren't pissed at him, the old man wouldn't let Scotty's sister, Ivy, keep a cat. To Pop, pets were parasites. Mrs. Steiner had allergies, and Scotty didn't know his other neighbors well enough. He'd toyed with asking the new girl as an excuse to meet her, but didn't want to start off by imposing. "Just chill, you sleep all day anyway. Tonight I'll open that can of *Fancy Feast* I saved for you."

Telling himself all would be well, he slipped off to the bus stop.

The subway was a quicker commute, but Scotty hated it. Like catacombs down there. Three transfers and fifty minutes later, he arrived at Webster and 180th in the Bronx Northside—removed enough from his old Bronx Southside neighborhood to avoid running into Pop. Midway up the block stood Schlompsky's Grocery. Two stories of yellow brick and glass, store on the 1st floor, offices on the 2nd. Unchanged since Leonard Schlompsky Sr. built it in 1956.

Scotty kept the books for the six-store chain. Assistant bookkeeper before his superior died of an embolism three months ago at the desk Scotty now occupied. The promotion came with no raise, and while Margo promised to hire help, so much for that. The job was high stress, low pay. Scotty had always dreamed of doing something creative with his life, but accounting was a practical profession and a lifesaver for a Bronx Business College dropout in a recession.

He pushed past glass doors papered with the day's specials, inhaling the scent of citrus, returning the "hellos" of the checkout ladies, trudging upstairs.

The 2nd floor was an open mezzanine at the front of the building, packed with metal desks under fluorescent lights. It ran the width of the store and overhung the main floor to look down on registers and aisles through a glass divider. Against the divider in the far corner sat Leonard III's office. His walls were also glass, but shuttered, blinds always drawn. Scotty had never seen inside the office, but heard it contained TV monitors connected to cameras throughout all the old coot's stores. A command center from which he could surveil operations, addressing concerns by phone, or directly to a store over loudspeaker. Bent stick of a man, first to arrive, last to leave, often heard, seldom seen unless really pissed.

Scotty answered to general manager, Margo Boggs. Plus-sized, mid-forties, she ran operations from a glass cubicle on a platform dead center of the floor. Her "watchtower," she called it. A strict Jehovah's Witness, she wore her religion on her sleeve and everywhere else. Gold "Jehova" earrings, necklace, bracelet, lapel pin; "Jesus" stickers on her car. As a practitioner of faith-based management, she kept a bible on the corner of her desk like a loaded pistol. Once, Scotty foolishly let slip he'd quit his religion, and she'd been gunning for his soul ever since. To Margo, followers of any faith but hers were doomed to hell. And especially so the unchurched.

Scotty's desk adjoined Reggie and Zing's, who faced each other. Scotty's office friends. Apart from Mrs. Steiner and Homer, Scotty didn't have close friends.

He draped his jacket on his chair and slid in, returning the men's greetings.

Reggie Watson, the company's meat & deli manager. Forties, big black guy with one of those faces frozen in frown. He could've played pro ball but for a bad knee.

Zing Li Po, produce manager. Thirties, Asian-American, small-statured. A community college graduate, and he liked to flaunt it.

The men were busy at their keyboards, bickering as usual, this time about last night's presidential debate. Margo forbid politics in the office, so the two spoke in low voices, stifling their lips and facial expressions, quite good at it. How ventriloquists might argue.

"Shackleton's a pinko," Reggie muttered. "Karl Marx in a skirt. What's she know about creating jobs? Never worked a day in her life, daddy gave her everything."

"Filby's a sock puppet," Zing replied. "Religious Right's up his ass working his mouth."

They turned to Scotty, and Reggie asked, "Who you think won?"

Scotty made a show of switching on his computer, getting to work. "No idea. Didn't watch."

Zing exhaled. "Pathetically apathetic."

Not apathetic, resigned. The system was hopelessly rigged. All the gerrymandering and vote suppression; the constant deluge of insidious false facts. Getting involved was a waste of time.

Zing paused to study Scotty. "Damn, dude, you look like hell. You sick?"

Scotty preferred to keep personal issues to himself. But this latest complication had nothing to do with finances or females. "There's something really weird going on in my apartment," he confided, and unspooled his tale of loud growls and whines mysteriously confined to his living room. Noises only he and his cat could hear, as if behind a sound barrier.

"That's some strange shit, all right," Reggie gave him.

Zing asked, "What do you know about your building? Its construction?"

"Not much." Scotty subleased from a woman who'd vacated to tend an ailing sister abroad. "The neighborhood's old. The building must go back a century or better."

"In that case," Zing said, "you never know what's buried under it. Or in the walls. Rusting systems. Plumbing, electric, heating ducts."

"Doesn't sound mechanical to me," Reggie said. "Growls and whines, that's a restless spirit."

Scotty wasn't inclined toward the supernatural, but Reggie's words gave him goosebumps.

Zing said, "Before we go all spooky, how about a *rational* explanation? Microwaves. Microwaves can cause all kinds of creepy crap. Maybe there's a dish out of whack somewhere."

Those saucer-shaped transmitters were everywhere on towers and buildings in Queens. Even Reggie had to concede, "That storm last week could have knocked a dish loose. Get one aimed at your ass, it'll cook the shit outta your 'lectronics."

"Not to mention your brain," Zing added. "Like living in a microwave oven. Better find it and report it before you're bleeding out the ears."

Microwaves. Why hadn't Scotty thought of that? He felt relieved—aside from the brain part. Eye out for Margo, he hopped online. She couldn't see his screen from her office, but she liked to roam. Uncannily light-footed for her size, liable to sneak up behind.

A Google search supported Zing's theory, halfway. A single microwave beam couldn't account for what happened, though *two* might. A phenomenon known as a *moiré effect.* Beams crossing paths at just the right angles, combining to create a mutant wave with peculiar audial and/or visual properties. One other qualifier: for a moiré to occur, the beams needed clear lines of sight to their point of intersection.

• • •

Scotty stopped to buy cheap binoculars on his way home, arriving at his building and entering the foyer to see a new name taped on its row of mailboxes.

2-D, *K Kraft*

His heart lightened. Karen? Kathy? Kelly?

No time for that now, he raced upstairs, held his breath, and opened his door to find...

Things just as he'd left them. Quiet. Bedroom door closed. Yet, *something* didn't feel right. And heading to the back room, sure enough, he spied Homer under the bed.

Scotty hauled him out and sat with him.

"Microwaves," he told the cat.

Homer blinked, and Scotty explained, "According to Zing, microwave dishes are out of position somewhere, beaming at us. When waves line up, they cause weird noises and stuff."

What are we supposed to do? Wear tinfoil hats?

Showing Homer the binoculars, Scotty slung him over a shoulder and left the apartment, climbing the ladder to the roof, picking his way through a patchwork of tarred cracks and seams. He made for the right front corner above their living room, giving the surroundings a three-sixty. Between the binoculars and the cat's sharp eyes, he identified dozens of dishes.

Yet a thorough search revealed none directed their way, and they returned home flummoxed.

If not microwaves, what?

Reggie's spirit theory sprang to mind, but Scotty refused to go there. And though exhausted, he spent a restless night.

CHAPTER 3

The conference room sat on the 29th floor overlooking 57th. Fine art on the walls, plush carpet, long teak table with cushy seating for thirty. But the attendees did not look comfortable.

A well-dressed woman took a seat next to another, grumbling, "Why the fire drill, Shonda?"

Shonda brushed back dark hair and shrugged. "I got here at 6:00, and the directors were all in the crisis room teleconferencing. Whatever's up, it's not good."

Endicott, Percy & Moore Communications was one of four firms handling public relations for the Ellen Shackleton U.S. presidential bid. As the race entered the home stretch, hours and nerves were stretched, too.

"*God,* I loathe politics," the first woman spat. "Constant damage control."

"Vicious, sleazy, and the bastards don't pay their bills."

On the other hand, a Shackleton victory would mean huge cachet for EP&M and its strategists. Like Shonda.

The table filled, and five younger attendees entered to stand at the back of the room, notepads poised. The first woman asked Shonda, "Your new crop of interns?"

Shonda, who also served as intern supervisor, nodded. "It's all hands on deck."

"Who's the fashion plate?"

"Kassandra Kraft. Great pedigree, but she's shown me shit so far. I don't see her making it to the balloon-drop."

EP&M's internship program was a high-pressure process, candidates steadily winnowed until the survivor earned a permanent position. But the firm didn't typically include interns in senior-level meetings like this.

Abruptly the room fell silent as in walked Franklin Percy, last living partner of the firm, trailed by four men and a woman. He withdrew files from an attaché and passed them out.

"I'll get straight to it," he said, eyes stern behind glasses. "We're shifting focus and tactics."

Met by groans, he raised a hand to still them. "As you're aware, the election will turn on the battleground states of Ohio, Pennsylvania, and Florida. We've known for months the Republican National Committee's planning something big, and last night we finally got word." His voice sharpened. "The weekend before the election, they're going to unleash a ground assault in all three states. And on a scale unlike anything we've ever seen."

He yielded the floor to a colleague.

"For the past several months," the woman explained, "a number of megachurches across the country have been building secret armies of volunteers. Tens of thousands. They plan to ship them to the swing states the last week of the race in a massive get-out-the-vote for Filby. We haven't the forces or time to match it, and all things considered, the strategy could damn well work. We need a Mother of all Bombs, and we need it fast."

Group-mumble. Then a man down the table offered, "We've still got the debates. Shackleton carved Filby up in the first, and it moved the polls. She'll do it again."

The spokeswoman replied, "It moved the polls where she's *already* ahead. Barely a ripple in the swing states. This requires a targeted response. Something with teeth."

"Wait a minute," another man snapped. "Churches supporting a political candidate? That's bullshit. That violates all kinds of rules and regs."

"No question. And there'll be plenty of lawsuits—*after* we lose the election."

Percy took the floor again. "The Democratic National Committee is putting every think tank on this. I don't have to tell you what it would mean for us if *we* carry the day. I want a plan to beat the threat. Nothing's off the table, money's no object."

Shonda asked, "Who's behind this ground assault scheme?"

CHAPTER 4

The Reverend Penbrook Thornton had been at his desk since before dawn. His custom every morning but Sundays, never enough hours in the week for the head of the world's largest Evangelical church. Especially these days as Thornton approached a goal he'd been working toward for more than three decades. A goal on which he'd wagered his entire ministry.

And it would all come down to the first Tuesday in November.

Noting the time, he snugged his tie, pushed back his chair, stood, and stretched. His secretary would have arrived by now, ever-prompt, and he buzzed her on the intercom.

"Morning, Ms. Willoughby. How are you this fine gift of a day?"

"*Morning, Reverend. Feeling blessed, as always. Can I freshen your coffee?*"

"Thanks, no. I just wanted to say I'll be out on the overlook if you need me."

"*Very good, sir.*"

Thornton crossed the room in the loping strides he'd acquired as a young man in a very different line of work, wingtips clacking on

17

white marble. Reaching a wall of glass, he exited a door onto a rooftop terrace, stopped at a rail, and filled his lungs with brisk air. Though his office was in the penthouse, it was nevertheless designated "First Floor." Here at Decalogue Tower, floors were numbered inversely, in homage to the Ten Commandments.

Before him lay a spectacular view. In the foreground was a park with a tall hill known as Chapel Mount. Beyond sat the Tabernacle of the Church of the Divine Message, the heart and hub of the City. The Tabernacle was more massive even than St. Peter's in Rome, dazzling in the morning sun. Its dome was pure-white Penteli marble, topped by a golden cornice and statue of the Ascending Christ. For a brief time, the Tabernacle had the largest seating of any church in the world—until Thornton found out and removed just enough pews to preserve his decorum.

The City's streets radiated from the church like spokes of a wheel, past alabaster offices, shops, hotels, restaurants. Townhall displayed the Commandments, and at Christmastime, a crèche. Police and fire stations served with compassion. The hospital and sanitarium combined state-of-the-art technology with spiritual healing. Elementary and high schools wove God and prayer into the curricula. There was a divinity college, country clubs, airport, bus station. And in the suburbs, new homes and apartments sprang up by the day. Every day but the Lord's.

The City of God was a rare bright spot in the recession. Over the years, Thornton had attracted to town some of the nation's largest Christian businesses, helping the community thrive and grow to more than 70,000 residents today.

The City had also been spared most of the problems plaguing the rest of the country. Thornton credited that to founding his community upon fundamental Christian principles, incorporating it as a private township in conjunction with the Church. No alcohol sold here. No nightclubs, gambling, rock concerts. No R-rated movies at the cinemas. No provocative radio or TV programming, no adult bookstores or massage parlors or profane literature at the libraries.

And by extension, as Thornton had famously predicted, no crime.

Well, no *serious* crime. Minor offenses attributed primarily to teens, prone to mischief as they were. Scuffles, shoplifting, truancies, runaways. Not forgetting the most irritating infraction in his sparkling-white City. Graffiti. And yet there was a matter concerning City juveniles that was dire, indeed. Something that weighed on Thornton's soul like a millstone—

"Sorry to disturb you, sir," Ms. Willoughby called out the balcony door. "Reverend Durban is on the phone."

Durban. Another unpleasant problem.

"What's *he* want?"

"A meeting. He says it's urgent."

CHAPTER 5

Scotty sat at the back of the bus, head in hands as he lurched homeward. Not only were the noises in his apartment continuing, bizarre new developments had deepened the mystery...

Two days ago, Scotty returned home from work and opened his door to the sharp scent of tobacco. Sweet, like from a cigar or pipe. Scotty didn't smoke. Nothing else looked out of order. The bedroom door was closed, towel in place, Homer mewling inside. He felt his pulse race, and snatching up his umbrella, he marched to the front of the living room.

But as he rounded the couch, something crunched underfoot. Scattered across the floor and throw rug was white dust, along with tiny crystals of some sort, no bigger than an eighth inch. Rough, cloudy-colored. Rock salt, it appeared. He snatched one up and examined it closely. Had he been burgled? All else proved normal, save for the cat under the bed in a pouting ball.

Homer growled, *The noises again. Twice this time, 10:00 and 2:00. Do something!*

Scotty almost called the cops. But with no signs of forced entry, what would he tell them?

Furious, he cleaned up the debris—angrier still to find some in Mom's umbrella plant. The plant was the one thing he owned that still tied him to her. He'd so carefully nurtured it over the years, now *this*. Picking out the crystals, he'd mulled a shortlist of suspects. All long shots.

Pop smoked, yes. But cheap cigarettes, not a pipe or cigars. And he had no key. Nor did Ivy, Scotty's sister who lived with Pop. Neither had ever visited him here, Ivy forbidden. Besides, this kind of stunt wasn't in their natures. Pop had interacted little with Scotty during his childhood, why start now? And while Ivy was mischievous, she wouldn't do anything to upset Scotty. Not on purpose, anyway.

Scotty's super, Samood, had a key. Scotty wouldn't put anything past that cockroach. But never having even met the guy, he couldn't imagine why Samood might want to force him out. Scotty was low maintenance, and his apartment was a sublet.

Of course, the intruder could have picked Scotty's lock. But to what end? Nothing here was worth taking, everything a relic. If someone were venting a grudge, who? Scotty had no enemies he knew of. Well, his boss, Margo. But why go to this trouble when she could abuse him at work? If only he could discuss things with Reggie and Zing, but they were out on rounds all week. He went online and ordered a spycam, rush delivery...

Wednesday night, Scotty had come home to see a package awaiting him in the foyer. The spycam. He'd carried it upstairs into his apartment with renewed hope, relieved to see things apparently undisturbed. All the same, Homer was under the bed again.

Thunder and wailing, 10:00 and 2:00. Whatever's haunting us, it ain't goin' away!

But now, Scotty had a means to solve the mystery. Taking the package to his desk, he opened it, and Homer jumped up to sniff a self-contained, battery-operated mini camera, complete with a removable USB card for storing video. Scotty set it up next to his monitor, aimed it at the front door, and switched it on. A little red light began to blink, and Scotty smiled at Homer to say, "Let the bastard try salting us again."

Assuming cameras can record a spirit...

Tonight, as Scotty's bus reached his stop, the cat's words from last night nagged him. Scotty wasn't prone to premonitions, yet as he neared home, staring up at the darkness of his window, he felt a chill track his spine. He stole upstairs, held his breath, and pressed his ear to the door.

No sound, save the thumps of his heart.

But entering, he detected a foul stench. Not tobacco, a burnt, acrid smell. And flicking the light on, he gasped. Mom's big umbrella plant lay toppled on the floor. Nothing else looked out of place, far as he could tell. The bedroom door was shut, Homer complaining on the other side.

He raced for the plant, but rounding the sofa, his legs flew out and he landed hard on his back. When finally his head cleared, he sat, jolts of agony shooting through his spine and left ankle. And turning to the plant, he swore. Seared onto its back side was a ring of scorched leaves. Like someone had pressed a flaming hoop against the foliage. The kind circus animals jump through.

He let out a cry. The plant was his birthday gift to Mom when he was six. He'd sneaked out of his room at naptime, took his savings and wagon down to Schlompsky's, and picked it out. A twig in a pot. Mom was beside herself when she found out, scolding, hugging, weeping. And thereafter, she'd cherished the plant the way she had him. His last, personal life link to her, thriving in his care all these years, tall, wide, lush and full. Now, *this*.

Struggling to his feet, he heaved the plant upright, aggravating his back and ankle, gaping in disbelief at what he'd uncovered. Aside from spilled soil and leaves, a hodgepodge of pebbles, prunes (or maybe dates), a skid mark of red grapes (what he'd slipped on), corncobs, a small statue of an angel, and a bible, face-up and open.

And oddest of all, lying across the bible was a six-foot-long wooden pole with a crooked end. A shepherd's staff. Gray and weathered, grain splitting along the shank, charred on the tip.

Like a scene from *The Exorcist*.

He removed the staff to find it stout and old. The bible lay open to the *Book of Exodus*, the tale of Moses leading the Israelites out of bondage in Egypt. Mom used to read him bible stories, this a favorite. Every Easter they'd watch Demille's classic, *The Ten Commandments*.

Scotty set down the staff and picked up the bible, flipping to the front. Not the Vulgate edition he was raised on, a Gideon King James. He turned to the first page to see a simple, handwritten inscription. *For Joseph*. He frowned. *Joseph* was Scotty's given name. Joseph Scott Butterfield, Jr. Not that he ever went by Joseph, or Joe, or Junior. Pop was Joe.

He swapped the bible for the statue. Dark, heavy soapstone. An angel kneeling in prayer. Palms pressed together, haloed head bowed, wings wrapping like a hooded cloak.

These odd religious elements. Was the bible displaying *Exodus* by chance, or to send a message? But *what* message? The bible was a Rorschach. No matter what passage you turned to, you could extrapolate some sort of personal meaning. Was Margo behind this, after all, punishing Scotty for giving up his faith? But she couldn't have done this alone, she was at the office all day.

Homer wailed from the back room. Scotty hobbled over, using the shepherd's staff for a cane, opened the door with a grunt, and staggered in.

The cat gaped at him from under the bed. *What the hell happened to you?*

"Our intruder dumped garbage on the floor and knocked over Mom's plant. I slipped and nearly broke my neck."

Finally, we get a break.

"Not funny."

The spycam, I mean. It was switched on, right?

In all the turmoil, Scotty had forgotten. He about-faced and limped to his desk, excited to see the camera's red light blinking. Homer joined him, and Scotty removed the USB with shaky hands, inserting it into his computer port. A few clicks of the mouse, and a black-and-white video of his living room door appeared on the monitor. No audio, Scotty couldn't afford that option.

He fast-forwarded to the end, never seeing the front door open. No sign of anyone or any movement whatsoever, the plant wasn't visible in the frame. He ran the video again.

Nothing.

"Makes no sense, Homer. There's no other way in but the door."

Maybe spirits don't need doors.

Scotty felt his back spasm. Swearing, he reoriented the camera toward the plant this time.

"There's got to be a *rational* explanation."

The cat shrugged. *Is madness rational?*

CHAPTER 6

Scotty awoke with a stiff back and swollen ankle. In no shape for work, but he had no choice. Having lucked into his job last spring after Pop kicked him out, he'd yet to accrue any vacation or sick days. Nor could he afford to take off and have his pay docked. Or, God forbid, give Margo a reason to can him.

He rose in pain, showered, dressed, shut his unhappy cat in the bedroom, and snatching the bible his mysterious visitor had left, he hobbled downstairs using the shepherd's staff for a cane.

As he boarded his bus, the driver stopped him. Seems passengers were spooked by the shepherd's staff. But it passed inspection, and Scotty took a seat in the back, given wide berth. He spent the commute immersed in Moses. The story came back to him in a rush, in Mom's sweet voice. A tale of trials, perseverance, and triumph:

Many years ago, God's Chosen People, the Israelites, were held as slaves in Egypt by an evil Pharaoh. God raised up the Prophet Moses to lead them from captivity, but the Pharaoh's army trapped them on the shores of a sea. All seemed lost until

25

Moses raised his staff over the waters, God parted them, and the Israelites escaped. And when the army followed—

The bus braked at Scotty's stop, and he made his painful way to Schlompsky's, explaining his injuries to Margo as a fall in the shower, the shepherd's staff as an antique he had lying around. He expected no sympathy, and got none. And doddering to his desk, checking to ensure Margo was occupied, he continued reading:

...From the Red Sea, Moses led the Israelites to Mt. Sinai, where God gave them Ten Commandments and a holy Covenant: obey the Commandments, and reap everlasting blessings in the Promised Land. Yet Moses never shared in those blessings. God, in a pique of anger over an infraction Scotty had always thought petty, condemned Moses to everlasting exile—

Abruptly the keyboards around Scotty went silent, and he froze. Reggie and Zing weren't here to serve as lookouts today, still out on rounds. A husky voice behind Scotty barked, "What's so important we let it interfere with our work?"

Scotty felt flesh against the nape of his neck, and his nose filled with the scent of Shalimar and gym locker. He cringed, girding for the Wrath of Hell. But Margo's tone changed.

"A *bible?*"

He turned to see her frown over his shoulder and snap, "If you seek answers, the Good Book is where to find them. Just *not* on my clock."

Face afire, Scotty slipped the bible in a drawer.

Margo started off, stopped, and tossed back with a raised brow, "I won't write you up this time. But I expect to see you at Kingdom Hall services Sunday."

Jehovah's Witnesses preferred the term "Kingdom Hall" to "church."

She strode away, the keyboard crickets resumed, and Scotty

shuddered. As a boy, he'd endured church twice a week for years, enough religion to last a lifetime. And though he'd abandoned his faith, he hadn't quite rid himself of its grip. The idea of suffering one of Margo's revivals made him ill. Fresh brains for her Jesus zombies.

CHAPTER 7

With the election nearing, weekends and overtime were compulsory at EP&M. The pace was hectic, pressure palpable. Especially for the firm's dwindling field of interns, for whom the screws of the job-selection process were tightening.

Four days ago, EP&M strategist Shonda Gonzalez had given her interns a final assignment. Each was to create a battle plan for the Shackleton campaign—a comprehensive response to the opposition's pending swing-state ground assault. Concepts were due this morning, and those interns whose ideas passed muster would polish them to submit as written proposals Monday, determining who advanced to the final round.

Kassandra Kraft was first in the room, a small, windowless space with a table and five chairs. She took the seat immediately to the right of where Shonda always sat. If Shonda stuck to form, presentations would proceed clockwise, and Kassandra would go last.

She popped a Tums, watching her colleagues straggle in looking as nervous as she felt.

28

Finally, Shonda arrived, setting a Red Bull and iPad on the table to say, "Okay, people, let's get to it. Nutshell pitches, five minutes each." And clicking a stopwatch, she turned to her left.

Bobby Driscoll. Kassandra had sized him up early on as her likeliest threat. A Dartmouth frat-boy. Blond, good-looking in a toothy sort of way. Cheery, with a default smirk. He had a thing for her, and though not her type, she gave him just enough encouragement. An ally could be useful.

He began, "Our target demos in all three states are the same. White, thirty-five plus, high-school grad, mid-to-low income, conservative Christian. In short, Walmart shoppers. That gives Filby a big leg up. He draws his army from the same demos, and most swing-state voters will identify with them. The only way for us to fight that is head-on."

"Let me stop you right there," Shonda said. "We don't have the human resources, much less the right credentials, to go toe-to-toe against Evangelicals. Filby's got a lock on the God angle."

Bobby was undeterred. "Our target voters have other gods we can exploit. *Celebrities*. Sports figures, movie actors, country-western singers. Shackleton draws support from big names that skew the right demos. Election week is dead time for celebs, like a national holiday. My idea is to line some up and send 'em to the swing states, put 'em in hospitality suites near the polls, use 'em as bait to get the vote out. In return, they get VIP tables at the inaugural balls."

The other male intern interjected anxiously, "You can't do that, it would violate FEC rules. Undue voter influence."

"It's a gray area," Shonda countered, adding to Bobby, "Regardless, it's old hat. But you're thinking straight. See if you can give it a new wrinkle."

Bobby sat back with a smirk, and Shonda added notes to her iPad, moving on.

Kassandra took another Tums.

The second intern appeared rattled, slow off the mark. And with good reason. Her proposal was simply to run TV spots of Shackleton in church; meeting with religious leaders; making speeches to religious groups to shore up her spiritual credibility. It fell flat, she trailed off, and Shonda looked to the next apprentice.

"I like the TV approach, too," he said with forced enthusiasm. "I propose we create vignettes of Shackleton talking to everyday Christians about their shared faith and principles. Hype her integrity and honesty—"

Shonda cut him short. "The far right is hammering Shackleton over her divorce and alleged affair, not forgetting those rumors of wild party days in college. We can't win that battle."

The man went red. It would be back to the drawing board for him.

Kassandra's turn. She breathed a sigh. Bobby appeared her only threat. She ticked through her plan: a strategy to offset the Christian Right by marshaling a Christian Left counterforce. Before Shonda could raise the obvious objection, Kassandra addressed it.

"Yes, right-wing Christians outnumber the Left in all three states. But my idea isn't to target all three. I propose we key on Pennsylvania. It's a toss-up with the largest proportion of Christian Left. Assuming we hold onto the states already projected for Shackleton, Pennsylvania gives us the deciding electoral votes—"

Shonda broke in, "Again, not a new idea."

Kassandra smiled. "Except for this twist: we send volunteers to every Left-leaning church in the state, every Sunday from now till the election. They stand outside touting Shackleton, signing up supporters, passing out literature, arranging rides to the polls."

Shonda paused. "Not sure the DNC hasn't already considered that and passed for legal reasons. Better run it by Mitch, first."

Mitch, EP&M's legal counsel and political adviser.

That wasn't a "No," and Kassandra felt encouraged—save for the fact that Mitch was a busy man, and the weekend was here. What were the chances a lowly intern could get through to him? He might not respond till Monday, when formal submissions were due, forcing

Kassandra to cobble a contingency plan to be safe. *If* she could come up with one.

Everyone filed out of the room except Bobby, who stopped to offer, "I'm auditing a conference call with Mitch this afternoon. If you want, I'll run your idea past him for you."

Sometimes interns were invited to sit in on calls as part of the firm's instructional program. But protocol required them to be flies on the wall. Bobby was sticking his neck out. And it wasn't as if he could steal her idea, Kassandra had just made it a matter of record.

Yes, an ally could be useful.

CHAPTER 8

Reverend Penbrook Thornton sat at his desk putting final touches on tomorrow's sermon. He rechecked the clock as it ticked toward his appointment at the top of the hour—a critical meeting he was *not* looking forward to. His gaze turned reflexively out the glass wall to the adjacent park and hill, coming to rest on the little clapboard church that graced its summit. Chapel Mount. The church where he'd preached his first sermon thirty-four years ago, restored and on the National Register of Historic Places, complete with bronze plaque.

The chapel held profound significance for Thornton. Even now he'd retreat to its sanctuary when seeking the Lord's guidance in crucial matters. It was there in the chapel that he'd found his calling. There he'd met and wed Doris, and baptized their children, Paul and Sarah. And it was there, in its little hillside cemetery, he'd laid them all to rest.

"Excuse me, sir," a bubbly voice on the intercom interrupted, *"Reverend Durban is here."*

Thornton sighed, smoothed his thick, silver hair, folded his hands on the desk, and settled into a repose he'd long-ago perfected. "Please show him in," he replied. "And now go enjoy the rest of this gorgeous day, Alice. Bless you for coming in on a Saturday."

"A labor of love in the service of the Lord, Reverend."

What a treasure, Ms. Willoughby. He'd be lost without her. His longtime personal secretary, friend and confidante. At his side all these years, despite their shared tragedy.

Thornton and Durban also went way back. They'd begun their respective ministries about the same time, meeting when Thornton formed the Coalition of Christian Conservatives (CCC). Decades they'd worked together, yet despite Thornton's good-faith efforts, they'd never forged a friendship. Perhaps because Durban's church hadn't enjoyed the blessings of Thornton's.

These past several years had been especially testy. Durban's position as internal liaison for the CCC required him to ferry confidential information to and from members, and especially to Thornton, who chaired the CCC. It forced the men to meet frequently, aggravating the friction. At least today, Thornton had home-field advantage.

The door opened, and in stepped a tall, thin man in a gray suit. Hooked nose, glasses. Henry Durban, ThD, director of The Righteous Way Ministries, Andover, MD.

"Hello, Hank," Thornton greeted him, rising, smiling, extending his hand.

The man came forward to accept the hand, not the smile. Placing his briefcase next to the chair, he sat, planted his elbows on the armrests, and tented his fingers.

Thornton sank back in his chair, letting the man own the moment. No point forcing civilities.

Durban glanced around, not that he hadn't been here many times before. The office was a showcase of Thornton's credentials. Bookcases thick with religious tomes, many bearing his name. Walls a scrapbook of diplomas, theological doctorates, civic and charitable awards; news and magazine articles, photos of Thornton golfing, dining, ribbon-cutting with the wealthy and powerful. How far he'd come. How close he was to achieving the vow he'd made so long ago.

Turning again to the little church atop Chapel Mount, he thought back to the night of the holy vision that launched his journey…

Thornton was a young man early in his ministry at the time, his congregation but a handful. Evening services had concluded, his flock gone home, and he left the chapel to stand alone on the hill under a full moon, gazing out upon what was then merely wilderness valley.

Like so many ministers in those days, he feared for his struggling church. A dark time in America, fundamentalism under relentless attack from the Left, religion in decline. God was barred from government, public squares, schools. Society had given over to secularism, gay marriage, feminism, hedonism. Many a conservative Christian leader had lost faith.

But in the stillness of that night, in the depths of his desolation, Thornton touched the gold cross of his lapel pin and whispered a prayer. And as God had done before in such moments of trial, He blessed Thornton with an epiphany. It sprang fully formed in his mind—a means to save not only his ministry, but America's soul. *A Great New Awakening.*

The vision came to Thornton in two parts:

First, he saw before him stretching out in grand detail across the valley, a city gleaming like ivory in the moonlight. A model society founded on the bible's guiding principles, man's laws bowing to God's. A City that would serve as a shining example of applied theocracy.

Second, Thornton saw with perfect clarity how to restore the country to God's good graces. He and fellow Christian leaders across the land would join forces to rebuild government from the ground up. Together they'd work to remove secular bureaucrats, politicians, and judges, replacing them with men and women of God. Town by town, city by city, state by state, all the way to Washington.

And now these many years later, Thornton was in sight of his goal. Twenty-five days from today, his handpicked-and-groomed candidate,

Republican Senator Roger Filby of Kansas, would face off against Democrat Governor Ellen Shackleton of New Jersey for the presidency of the United States. Should Filby win, Thornton would stand behind him in veiled gray eminence, using the City of God as a holy template to create, at last, one nation *truly* under God—

Durban cleared his throat. "Brooks," he said in the tinny voice that doomed his televangelical dreams, "as you know, the past few weeks I've been shuttling among the Council members gathering perspectives. And to put it bluntly, the sentiment isn't good."

He was referring to the Council that governed the CCC. Twelve clergymen representing the Big 12 U.S. Christian denominations: Evangelical, Pentecostal, Catholic, Baptist, Lutheran, et al. Though the law barred religious institutions from the pursuits the CCC was awash in, Thornton and colleagues had successfully masked their activities behind a Political Action Committee, taking advantage of disclosure loopholes to divert funds from Church coffers while evading detection.

Indeed, God had blessed their efforts. The CCC had not only captured many state legislatures over the years, it was close to controlling the U.S. House *and* Senate. Albeit, the balance was unlikely to shift this election cycle.

Then there were the many judgeships the Coalition had acquired, including six Supreme Court justices—all Catholic, but reliable conservatives, nonetheless. And now Thornton was poised for his crowning achievement, within a whisker of uniting all three branches of government under Christ's banner.

But as Durban pointed out, "We're losing ground in the polls. The debate was a fiasco. Filby's gaffes, his slips of the tongue. Late-night TV is having a field day."

Thornton assured, "He'll do better next time. We've got a battery of forensics coaches working with him. And let's not lose sight of our ground assault in the swing-states."

Durban shook his head. "No guarantees in any of that. The consensus on the Council is, it's time for the 'Nuclear Option.' And we want you to use it *now.*"

Nuclear Option. Code for the explosive video Thornton kept locked here in his desk drawer. A political weapon-of-last-resort, certain to take Shackleton down.

Thornton crossed his arms. "The Council knows my position."

"Yes. And it's time you set aside your scruples for the greater good. It's not only our dreams for the country, Brooks, our very *Churches* are on the line. Need I remind you, it was *you* who put us in this position."

In pitching his plans to the Council years ago, Thornton had sworn on the bible that they and their Churches would be shielded from the prying eyes of the IRS, media, ACLU, atheists and other enemies of Faith who'd surely go after them if their scheme were discovered. Such a calamity, God forbid, could strip their Churches of their exemptions and put them all on the hook for decades of back taxes and penalties. They'd be bankrupted, the Christian conservative movement in America, crushed. The end of the CCC, Thornton's ministry, his Tabernacle, his City. The end of his holy Crusade.

Thornton replied, "Back when we entered into our agreement, there was no risk. Who could have foreseen these new laws working their way through Congress?" Laws that threatened to make Super PACs transparent and expose participating members. "The Constitution grants free political expression to the rest of the country, even corporations. If *all* people are endowed by our Creator with inalienable rights, why are we of the cloth excluded?"

All the same, the public had grown tired of PACs and Dark Money abuses, pressuring Congress to act. The reform bill was scheduled for vote next year. Republicans opposed it, Democrats favored. And if Democrats kept their slim majority in the House this fall, as expected, the bill would pass, rip the veil off the CCC, and catch Thornton and colleagues with pants down.

But, as Durban noted, there was a way to stave off catastrophe. "A presidential veto is our only hope. Filby *must* win in November. And you, Brooks, have the power to guarantee it."

Last winter during the primaries, a follower of Thornton's TV ministry who'd attended college with Ellen Shackleton, sent him an old VHS. The only copy in existence, she swore. When Thornton viewed the tape, he was stunned. And revolted. A terribly disturbing video that would surely destroy Shackleton, if it got out. Thornton wanted no part of a sordid exposé, and believing the Council would concur, made the mistake of informing them.

Instead, they saw the tape as a godsend, demanding Thornton take it public. He'd refused, and locked the tape away in his desk where it remained to this day, smoldering like a radioactive ingot.

Durban pressed, "The time has come. The Council wants action, and we want it *now*."

"The Council knows my position. The tape's off the table."

"And what will it take for you to put it *on* the table? Our foray into politics was *your* idea. You swore we'd never be up against this wall. Well, here we are."

"Have faith," Thornton replied. "God didn't lead us this far to abandon us."

"I *have* faith. Faith that the Lord helps those who help themselves. God gave you that tape for a purpose. If you haven't the faith to use it, you'll have to answer to the Council yourself."

That gave Thornton pause. There hadn't been a meeting of the full Council in years. Stressful, unpredictable affairs bristling with hubris, hidden alliances and agendas that could easily derail his plans. To date he'd held the Coalition on task with patience and diplomacy, and without compromising his principles. Last time he'd given in to temptation, long ago, it cost him his family. But he could see in Durban's eyes, the Council wouldn't accept a refusal in absentia.

If Thornton had any hope to defuse the situation, he'd have to plead his case in person.

CHAPTER 9

Whatever was haunting Scotty's apartment, it seemed to have granted him a reprieve.

Last night he'd limped home from work to find everything quiet and undisturbed, including the cat. No strange smells or objects, and as Homer reported, no bizarre noises.

Today the same. And it being Saturday, Scotty was home to appreciate it. Not that the calm lulled him into thinking his ordeal over, he was simply grateful for the breather. And once the clock safely passed 2:00 PM, he left for a nearby hardware store, picked up a new latch for the bedroom door, and returned home to fix it.

Finished, he and Homer headed to his computer and jumped online, logging into the extraordinary videogame he'd been obsessed with since a boy.

R U God. Short for *Alternate Reality Earth, Universe,* **God.** The most popular, enduring simulation game of all time, if past its heyday. Not for Scotty. He held the world record for continuous successful play. It was his only claim to fame, though he reaped no personal glory, playing under a pseudonym. The game was single-player, and each *RUG*rat, as enthusiasts were known, was given an entire planet to manage. Their own, simulated, working-equivalent of contemporary Earth. Scotty called his, *Scottworld.*

Players presided over their worlds as God, ruling their populaces as they coped with disease, weather, war, terrorism, and other trials and crises. Like God, players were omnipotent, able to step in and perform miracles, rain manna, smite evil.

But unlike God, they lacked omniscience. No way to know how the wonders they worked might unfold.

And as everyone soon learned, divine intervention was a tricky blessing to apply. No players proved able to sustain their worlds indefinitely. None but Scotty. Of the thousands of *R U God* planets conjured into pseudo existence over the years, his was the longest surviving. *Scottworld* had been thriving since he launched it a decade and a half ago. He was a legend among gamers, his anonymity adding to his cachet. Unfortunately, there was no money to be made from playing. Scotty didn't even benefit from bragging rights, performing under the alias *Infinitiman.*

No matter, he was in it for his love of the game. Homer hopped into his lap, and leaving their problems behind, they escaped once more into the virtual realm. Scotty was a bit anxious about what they'd find today. Seldom had he neglected his planet so long, used to addressing issues before things could spiral out of control. But with all the distractions lately...

He moved his cursor to the game's icon, a disembodied eye enclosed within a triangle—like the Great Seal of the United States. Clicking, he brought up a familiar blue-and-white-marbled globe that filled the screen, and suddenly he and Homer were plummeting into its atmosphere, swooping over the northwestern hemisphere to the East Coast and New York City, their customary starting point. A gleaming, bustling city far removed from their tawdry reality.

First stop, One Times Square. Scotty liked to check the electronic ticker that tracked across its façade, a great source of breaking news and updates on hotspots and flashpoints around the planet. He hovered invisibly out front, noting a situation that required attention:

Rhomboids staging protest in Paris.

Homer flitted his tail. *Bullheaded bastards are at it again.*

Yes. Trouble had been brewing on the Continent for some time. Established populations were clashing with immigrant ethnics, and Scotty had been working to quell it. The *Rhomboïdes,* as they were known in what used to be France, were the worst agitators. A faction of mostly young, white, Euro-nationalists spoiling for a race war. Scotty had smacked their noses before, obviously not hard enough.

The ticker said demonstrators were gathered on a hill above Paris, preparing to march on the city. Armed police awaited, and if recent events were any indication, it would not be peaceful.

"We'll see about that," Scotty said. Exchanging nods with Homer, he punched controls and zoomed back into the stratosphere, speeding across the Atlantic. In seconds he was over the outskirts of Paris above a hill topped by a large, white-stone, multi-domed church. The Basilique du Sacré Coeur de Montmartre. A crowd had assembled below the cathedral on a sloping lawn. Young adults mostly, sporting the battle badge of the Rhomboids—maroon armbands with a yellow rhombus in the center. They shouted and waved placards espousing their peeves, in French. Scotty didn't speak the language, but he'd seen it all before.

The lawn sloped up to a stone wall topped by a terrace, the church towering behind. The Rhomboids had commandeered a flagpole on the terrace to fly their banner. In front of it stood ringleaders with bullhorns, exhorting the mob to their cause: the deportation of non-Europeans.

Scotty sighed. He attributed the longevity of his planet to squelching extremist ideologies. Political, religious, social, Right/Left, he made no distinction. An equal-opportunity mole-whacker. But having taken his eye off things, he'd let the threat escalate. He could see bottles of liquid in some hands, rags stuffed in the tops.

"What did we use on them last time?" he asked Homer.

Earthquake.

"Right. We shook 'em up. Let's try something flashier."

Scotty controlled *R U God* from a dashboard at the bottom of his screen—levers, dials and buttons arranged in an Art Deco-like design. Manipulating dials, Scotty aimed his cursor at the flagpole on the hill, targeting its tip. And giving Homer a wink, he punched a button. Instantly a lightning bolt burst from a clear sky, blasting the flag to oblivion as thunder rocked the hillside and people screamed and cowered. Before they knew what hit them, Scotty sent a storm front sweeping in, unleashing a torrent, everyone scrambling for cover.

Homer purred, *That put the fear of God in 'em.*

Scotty hoped so. Maybe this time it would stick. Of course, he could have made his point clearer by parting the clouds and declaring his displeasure in a thunderous voice. But that wasn't his style. He liked to keep his godhead down, careful to mask his meddling behind natural phenomena. To reveal your divinity was a mistake other RUGrats made, taking the game at face value, Are You God? It was a dare few players could resist, using their powers to impose personal worldviews, politics, and theologies on their subjects, lording over them, basking in the adulation.

Until, ultimately, their worlds self-destructed.

It had occurred to Scotty early on that given the real world was failing so badly under God's Hand, how could a mere mortal do better? So, he didn't try. His success wasn't due to planning or forethought, but to a strategy he'd simply stumbled upon when first he discovered the game.

He was a boy at the time, fleeing the loss of his mother, bitter over a senseless death he was helpless to prevent. He'd concluded that the God who took her so cruelly was no God for him, and he'd bowed out of his religion. Not that he stopped believing in God, Scotty just didn't like Him. And he did then what he did now when overwhelmed. He fled to *Scottworld,* where he could vent his angst on the types of institutions and attitudes that had cost Mom her life.

Homer pawed at the screen. *Not everybody got the message.*

One Rhomboid leader staggered to his feet with a bullhorn, defying the storm to re-rally his troops. Scotty grunted and maneuvered his gunsight round to the back side of the terrace. Dialing down the amperage, he directed his cursor at the seat of the man's pants, punched a key, and sent another bolt zapping. The man leaped in the air, cried out, and scampered off, holding his ass.

Scotty and Homer howled with glee.

CHAPTER 10

The third day in a row with no strange disturbances in the apartment. Not a peep.

Scotty lay on the couch with Homer watching the noon news, hoping against hope their torment was finally over. He saw nothing new going on in the world today. Recession, unemployment, crime—all on the rise. As he grabbed the remote to change channels, his apartment door-buzzer went off, startling him. Visitors here were a rare occasion.

Homer yawned. *Bill collector?*

Scotty limped to the intercom and pushed a button. "Yes?"

"Hey, Snotty, let me in."

He couldn't believe his ears. Hitting "Enter," he rushed out into the hall to hear the front door creak open, and footsteps skip up the stairs. He couldn't believe his eyes. Months since he'd seen Ivy. Blonde hair short and sassy now. Skimpy skirt—bet she caught hell from Pop over that. And as she rounded the stairs in makeup Pop would also despise, Scotty's heart faltered.

Mom.

Ivy leaped into his arms like when she was little, squealing,

43

wrapping him tight. Christ! *Breasts.* She was nearly as tall as him, too—Pop's genes, the ones that had skipped Scotty.

Down the hall, a door opened and Scotty's new neighbor, K. Kraft, slipped out, looking chic in a burgundy pantsuit and beret. She glanced over, did a double-take, and Scotty felt his face redden. This wasn't the introduction he'd had in mind.

Still clinging, Ivy turned and waved, and the woman raised a quick hand before gliding down the stairs, front door shrieking.

"Well-well-well," Ivy murmured. "Who's the sophisto?"

"New tenant. Haven't met her yet."

Setting his sister down, he flexed his ankle. Ivy was the image of Mom. Same impish grin, wry and dimpled—braces-free now. He waved her inside.

• • •

It surprised Ivy how large Scotty's apartment was. Neater than expected, too. He was such a slob at home, Pop always on his case.

"Can't stay," she said, shedding her jacket. He hooked it on a rack by the door, and she noted an odd object hanging next to it. "What the heck is *that?*"

"A, uh, a shepherd's crook. Gift from…someone."

"And *this?*" She pointed to a leash on another rung.

"You'll see."

He led her toward the couch, hobbling, and she cried, "Jeez, what'd you do to yourself?"

"Slipped and fell. It's nothing."

Curled in a corner of the couch was a big red tomcat, and Ivy let out an *ooh*, gathering him in her arms. He didn't seem to mind.

"Where'd you get him?" she cried, plopping down. She'd always wanted a pet.

Scotty joined her, smiling. "Found him here the day I moved in. Must have gotten inside when I left the door open. I asked around, and no one claimed him. I call him Homer."

"Hey Homer," Ivy cooed, rubbing his round belly. He stretched and purred. "Don't tell me you walk him on that leash like a dog?"

"He's smarter than he looks. More dog than cat."

Ivy could have sworn Homer gave Scotty a scowl, and laughed.

Scotty said, "He not only heels, he fetches." Digging around in the corner of the couch, he produced a fur-covered plastic mouse, warning, "Watch the claws."

Displaying it to Homer, Scotty called, "Here, boy—*mousie.*"

Instantly the cat was engaged, ears back, fixated. Scotty fired the toy across the room and Homer shot off, trotting back seconds later, spitting the mouse into Scotty's hand.

Ivy hooted, and Scotty said, "Pop doesn't know you're here?"

"Thinks I'm at Mass." Pop always made her go, while he didn't.

"So how's he getting on?"

"Same. Spends his days with Jim Beam and Hawk News, cussing the world. But I do my chores, keep my grades up, and we get on."

Hawk News. Ivy had watched in despair over the years as the right-wing news network sunk its talons ever deeper into Pop.

Scotty asked, "Does he…ever mention me?"

She avoided his eyes. "I'm really, *really* sorry what happened."

Scotty failed to reply, and she snorted, "For Pete's sake, I thought it was a stupid videogame. How was I to know? *Blue Angels?*"

"You shouldn't have been in my room on my computer. How'd you get my passcode?"

"May the Force be with you? Please!"

He sighed. "You did me a favor. I should have left years ago."

"So how you doing? Other than your foot."

"Good. Good."

He didn't *look* good. Scotty was dearer to her than anyone in the world, but honestly, the way he kept himself. Circles under his eyes. Hair brushed with an eggbeater. Wrinkled T-shirt, stretched-out jeans, socks with holes. And those nasty, nasty whiskers. She gave them a tug. "Jeez, *shave,* will ya? You look like Rasputin junior." She'd taken AP Russian history. The only reason Scotty had grown a beard was to hide behind it, like his hair. Somewhere underneath all that scruff was a nice-looking guy. "You seeing anyone?"

"A shrink."

She jabbed him in the ribs with an elbow, and he grunted, "Too busy with work. You?"

"Pop keeps me on a short leash. Afraid I'll meet a guy I like—not that I will."

There were some things she kept private, even from her brother.

"Then you've had plenty of time to work on your college shortlist."

"It's short, alright. BBC."

Bronx Business College. Scotty's tone sharpened. "Dammit, Ivy, you *promised*. You're *not* going to that schmuck hole. You're gonna get a legitimate degree."

That was her dream, too, and that's all it was. Pop, who never went past high school, thought BBC highbrow.

"...You apply to those schools we talked about. American, Washington, the others. Don't worry about tuition, we'll deal with that later."

"Yeah, the *rest* of our lives."

His face clouded, and his voice fell. "You've got a real shot at a scholarship. Your grades, your college boards. Regardless, I'm setting money aside."

Who was he kidding? He'd been employed less than six months at a zippo job.

"Scotty, it's fifty bucks an application. We can't even afford *that*."

But seeing him darken, she relented. "Okay, okay, I'll get a list together." And giving Homer a pat, she stood. "I'd better go."

"Not till you meet Mrs. Steiner. She'd never forgive me."

Scotty had mentioned his neighbor in texts and brief chats. The "grandmother" Ivy never had. Pop's parents had skipped out on him when he was a toddler. All he had left of them was his birth certificate with their names. Ivy had met Mom's parents only as a newborn, at

Mom's funeral. There were photos of them holding her. Kind-faced. From Idaho. They'd passed on.

Ivy bid Homer goodbye, grabbed her jacket, and Scotty ushered her downstairs, stopping at 1-B. Before he could knock, the door opened to engulf them in opera music and the scent of cinnamon. Greeting them was a petite, gray-haired lady in a long coat, buttoned up. Ivy assumed the woman was about to go out, yet she wore indoor slippers. She held a pie, thrusting it into Scotty's hands. Apple crescents grinned up through windows of golden, cross-hatched crust.

"I've been watching for you," the lady said, voice soft, eyes magnified by wire-rim glasses.

Scotty's face puzzled. "Thanks. But what's the occasion?"

"A little treat for all you do for me." She turned to Ivy. "And who's this lovely young lady?"

"My sister," Scotty said. "Ivy, meet my good friend, Mrs. Steiner."

Ivy extended a hand, but Mrs. Steiner pulled her in for a hug, gushing, "I've heard *so many* wonderful things about you, Ivy."

Ivy returned the compliment, and the lady beckoned them inside.

"Can't stay long," Scotty told her as they entered, "Ivy's on borrowed time."

"You've time for a slice of pie, at least."

Mrs. Steiner noticed Scotty's limp. "Gracious, what did you do to yourself?"

"A little fall, nothing serious." He glanced around, frowned, and said, "Man, it's cold as a meat locker in here. What's with your heat?"

"No idea, it's been like this all week. I'm waiting to hear back from Samood."

Scotty handed Ivy the pie and headed for the living room radiator. Mrs. Steiner's floor plan mirrored Scotty's, but the similarity ended there. 80s-era decor in mint condition. A divan with needlepoint pillows, facing a TV. A mahogany dining set, matching sideboard, a bookcase filled with psychology tomes. The walls were full of framed photos featuring Mrs. Steiner in younger years, and a kind-faced man with playful eyes.

Scotty looked up from the radiator to say, "I'll be back," and hobbled out the door.

Ivy followed Mrs. Steiner to the kitchen where the oven door was open, burner on, a small table and chair pulled close. Sitting atop the table were a cup of tea and a newspaper. The only other person Ivy ever knew to get an actual paper was Pop.

"Scott is such a sweet boy," Mrs. Steiner said with warmth. "Always there for me." She began to fill a tray with plates, cups, napkins and cutlery.

Ivy felt a sadness pass through her. Scotty had been more father to her than Pop. Reading to her at bedtime. Helping her with her homework. Nursing her when sick. "I worry about him."

"How so?"

"Ever see him with any friends? A girlfriend?"

Mrs. Steiner said nothing, and Ivy added, "He's a recluse. Growing up, he spent all his spare time in his room, online. His only friends were videogamers—and a few in his head."

The woman's brow knotted, and Ivy assured, "He outgrew the imaginary friends. But it used to drive Pop nuts."

"We all have our coping mechanisms," Mrs. Steiner said, patting Ivy's hand.

Scotty returned with a wrench and towel, and proceeded to bleed the radiators.

Mrs. Steiner poured milk and cut the pie, telling Ivy, "Scott is so proud of you. He says you're an avid reader with an encyclopedic memory. Only sixteen, and graduating high school in the spring."

"I skipped a grade in middle school."

"And I understand you're going to college. What would you like to study?"

"Still working on where, but I'm interested in poly-sci, foreign relations, and history."

"My–my."

They carried things to the dining room table, and Scotty joined them. Ivy felt heat emanating from the register.

"The pie's *amazing*," Ivy said. Scotty agreed.

Mrs. Steiner beamed and turned to Scotty. "Have you met our new neighbor yet?"

His eyes lit. "Not exactly."

"Kassandra Kraft. Pretty little thing."

Scotty seemed wistful. "What's she do?"

"Didn't say, we just spoke in passing." Mrs. Steiner gave him a wink. "Why not take her a slice of pie and introduce yourself? She could stand to fill out some."

He said nothing, and Ivy gestured to the photos on the wall, asking Mrs. Steiner, "Are these pictures of you and your husband?"

Mrs. Steiner's smile broadened. "You know, when Arty and I first met, he looked a bit like Scott." She pointed out a snapshot of a bright-faced young man in a flowered shirt, longish dark hair and scruffy attempt at a beard, the stem of a carnation between his teeth. Behind him, out of focus, was an ocean of people on a hillside. "Woodstock," she said.

Ivy leaned in closer to the photo. Indeed, Arty had the same blue eyes as Scotty. Except Arty's were dancing, and he was grinning in every shot. Scotty seldom grinned, and always behind a hand. His crooked teeth.

"How'd you meet?" Ivy asked.

"In a paddy wagon headed to jail. We were arrested together."

Ivy squinted, assuming she was teasing.

Mrs. Steiner explained, "Spring of '68, SDS protests at Columbia."

Ivy knew. The nationwide activist movement, SDS. Students for a Democratic Society.

"...The school was conducting weapons research for the Defense Department, and students occupied campus buildings to demonstrate. They rounded up seven hundred of us."

"Peaceniks," Ivy said with awe. "I learned about the 60s in social studies. You went to Columbia? What was your major?"

"I wasn't there long enough to major in anything, but I always thought psychiatry would be a fulfilling career. Arty and I fell in love, dropped out, and moved in together. Such idealists."

"But you helped stop a *war*. Demonstrations go nowhere nowadays. We raise our voices, and the opposition shouts us down and sends in riot control." She felt her face heat. "You watch, it's all coming to a head. If Shackleton loses, there'll be *another* Civil War, bloodier than the first!"

Mrs. Steiner patted Ivy's hand, and Scotty sighed and stood. He and Ivy gave out hugs, promised to visit again soon, and rushed off, forgetting the pie.

• • •

Scotty walked Ivy to the subway, and the nearer they drew, the quieter she became.

"You're not getting sentimental about me, are you?" he teased.

She punched his arm hard, called him a jerk, and skipped off down the steps to the platforms, shouting back, "See you next week. If Pop isn't wise to me."

Scotty's arm still stung on the way home. Albeit, his ankle and back were better. He no longer needed a cane. He was feeling better about his plans for Ivy, too. If, in fact, the problem in his apartment was behind him, he could now devote himself fully to her tuition. A second or third job might do it. Nights, weekends. Ivy meant everything to him. Whatever it took, she *wasn't* ending up like him.

But the moment he opened the door to his apartment, his hopes vanished.

Once more, Mom's plant lay overturned, cat crying under the bed. Furious, Scotty did a quick search to find nothing else out of order. Rushing to the spycam on his desk, he removed the memory card and slipped it into his computer, hands trembling.

On screen appeared a silent, black and white video showing the plant upright and seemingly untouched in the dimness of the living room. Scotty wished now he'd left the blinds open. Imbedded in the bottom left corner of the video was a timecode. He fast-forwarded until, at the 2:01 PM mark, the plant abruptly toppled. Scotty backed up to 2:00, resumed normal speed, and watched in astonishment as one instant the plant was there, the next hurled violently over as if by some invisible force. He replayed the recording in slomo, leaning in close. Yet he saw nothing to account for what happened.

"Holy shit! *Holy, holy shit.*"

Rising on unsteady legs, he crept to the felled plant. Now, in addition to the ring burned onto its back side, branches were broken. No marks on the floor or the walls in the corner behind.

He staggered to his room and collapsed on the bed. These attacks felt personal. Yet nobody but Pop and Ivy knew the plant's importance to Scotty, and no way either were involved.

Homer hopped up beside him. *Face it, man, Reggie's right.*

Much as he tried, Scotty could muster no argument. Mom had also viewed life through a supernatural lens. He rolled over and stared at the ceiling, mind hurtling back decades to his first encounter with things spiritual. A *traumatic* encounter he'd never gotten out of his soul...

Scotty was five or six at the time. Surely Mom had taken him to church before, but *this* visit seared his memory. They'd entered through the vestibule, Mom holding his hand, leading him down the main aisle toward the altar. A huge, somber old church. Must have been a weekday, the nave was nearly empty. Scent of candle wax and stale incense. Lofty arches and stained-glass windows. Surreal. Intimidating.

When they reached the communion rail, his eyes fell upon the figure central to all this pageantry. A realistic, life-size statue of the crucified Christ, suspended in space. Scotty froze in his tracks, screaming. Never in his young life had he seen anything so terrifying.

He thought it a *real* man. Naked, contorted in agony, bleeding from countless wounds. He tore for the exit, his only other recollection that day was of Mom trying to comfort him on the bus home.

And in the coming years as his religious instruction unfolded, he was unable to resolve his phobia of church, careful to keep those feelings to himself. Despite Mom's convictions and his best efforts, he never could embrace her Faith. The same Faith that eventually cost her her life...

Scotty's thoughts returned to the problem at hand.

What the hell was going on? How much more could his poor plant take? How much more could he and Homer take? Unless he solved this crisis, and soon, he'd be forced to move. But to *where?* His rent-controlled sublet was one in a million, not forgetting his security deposit and prepaid rent he'd forfeit. On his salary, he'd end up in a dump far from the transit lines, forced to find a roommate. The thought of losing his solitude sickened him.

Yet he sensed things were only going to get worse.

CHAPTER 11

If Margo was upset with Scotty for missing Sunday services, she seemed no crankier at work today than usual. Regardless, she was off his list of suspected intruders. Scotty had come to a reluctant decision he chose not to share with Reggie and the sardonic Zing.

Mom had always told him, especially toward the end when she grew weak, "God is a jealous God with a long memory. Keep the Faith, and even in your darkest hour, He'll be there for you."

Well, no. Scotty's darkest hour came soon after in a waiting room at a Bronx Hospital, Pop slouched drunk in the next chair as Ivy came into the world, and Mom departed. Mom's promise and Scotty's pleading prayers aside, God had abandoned him. And in return, filled with anger and bitterness, Scotty shucked his religion. Only to haul it back out last night and dust it off.

Not that he didn't believe in God, exactly, he simply didn't like Him. Scotty embraced science. All the same, science said to keep an open mind to *all* possibilities. Suppose then that Mom's God was real, and His patience with Scotty's faithlessness had finally worn thin. Were these demonic events in Scotty's apartment God's punishment?

Much as he wanted to rule that out, he couldn't, and it left him feeling way over his head. Apart from the religion of his youth, he'd no exposure to the supernatural. Especially the sinister side—horror movies and graphic novels excepted. If forced to delve into this Unknown, he'd need professional help. And unable to sleep last night, he'd gone online looking for it.

To his surprise, many such services were available. Paranormal consultants and investigators, psychics, mediums, crystal ball gazers, and on. Yet he knew enough to know you didn't apply an occult fix to a spiritual problem. What he needed here wasn't *Ghostbusters*, but *The Exorcist*.

Lunchtime found him outside Schlompsky's on the phone, pacing the sidewalk, jawing with the Catholic Archdiocese of New York. Getting nowhere. Mere mention of exorcism drew choked responses, and he was passed from one person to another like a collection plate. No one wanted to hear about restless spirits, much less arrange to have them expunged.

Of course, Catholicism wasn't the only religion to perform rites of exorcism. It was, however, the industry gold standard, in the business a thousand years longer than its closest competitor. Scotty refused to give up, and at last he found a sympathetic ear. An aide to the New York archbishop. An elderly woman, by her voice.

She listened to Scotty's story, then said, "Sorry, Mr. Butterfield, I'm afraid you don't meet Church standards for the services you seek. We get so many requests, a huge backlog, and just one priest to handle the entire Northeast."

"I swear I'm not crazy," Scotty insisted.

"No, I don't believe you are. But the current wait is a year or better, and frankly, as these matters go, yours sounds trifling. A minor, mischievous spirit, I suspect."

Scotty moaned, "It may be trifling to the Church, but it's terrifying to me and my cat. There's got to be *something* I can do."

"You might ask your pastor to drop by and bless your apartment."

"That works?" Scotty didn't have a pastor.

She paused. "Truth be told, once a spirit settles in, it can take some effort to dislodge it. Special prayers and rituals."

Whatever it took. "Where can I find the prayers and rituals?"

"Sorry, they're not available. The Church keeps a tight lid on Her rites of exorcism. A dangerous business, not to be dabbled in. Only a specially trained priest can conduct the rite, and only with the expressed permission of the bishop."

"Even a minor case like mine?"

"I'm afraid so. You might try praying to St. Michael the Archangel, patron saint of exorcism."

Thanking her for her time, he skulked back to work, flustered and depressed.

• • •

Scotty continued in an anxious mood on the bus ride home, arriving at his apartment to find his forebodings borne out. He opened the door to a noxious reek, fumbling the light on to see his living room a *wreck*. As if a tornado had blown through. Chairs, lamps, bookcase upended. Cushions torn, stuffing everywhere. Magazines, papers, CDs strewn about amid leaves of Mom's plant—toppled *again.* Many personal possessions were clawed and chewed almost beyond recognition. Including, to his dismay, the spycam and its memory card.

If not the work of a demon, it certainly smelled of it. A demon enraged by Scotty's delving into exorcism, either marking its territory or scaring the piss out of Homer.

Shutting the door behind him, Scotty entered to detect a *second* odor. His nose crinkled at the sharp scent of burnt hair. Or *fur.* He moaned and his eyes flew to the bedroom door. Closed, but bearing deep scratches. No sound from Homer, and the latch was open. Scotty was certain he'd fastened it. Plucking the shepherd's crook of the rack, wielding it like a club, he headed for the back room calling anxiously, "Here, Homer. Here, boy..."

No response. If anything happened to his pet! The kitchen and bath were also ransacked. He pushed open the bedroom door and stared into the gloom, surprised to find the room undisturbed. Dropping to his knees, he held his breath and peered under the bed.

Two shiny eyes glared back.

CHAPTER 12

"Sit," Shonda Gonzalez said, eyes never leaving her computer screen. Kassandra sank into the cool black leather of a chair, facing her department head across an aircraft-carrier-size glass desk. The office was equally spacious, well-appointed. Just what Kassandra envisioned for herself here someday.

Endicott, Percy & Moore was the crème de la crème of PR firms. Kassandra had fixed her sights on it long ago, pursuing a dual poli-sci/public-relations degree at Vassar, graduating with honors last spring. And now she was but *two* competitors away from realizing her dream. The deadline for proposals to counter the GOP swing-state assault was yesterday morning, and the only other female intern had missed it, bowing out. Kassandra was in high spirits, exhaustion aside, confident her well-honed plan would propel her into a face-off finale next week.

At length, Shonda sat back, folded her arms across her chest, and stared out the window. She asked, "How long did you work on this?"

Kassandra smiled. "Nonstop till I turned it in. Thank God for energy drinks."

"Did you develop any other concepts?"

"No. I believe in this."

The woman turned to her. "I told you to run it by Mitch before resubmitting."

"Right. Mitch signed off on it."

"You spoke with him?"

"Uh, no. I left messages and emails, but got no reply. Someone on the team ran it past him."

Fellow intern, Bobby Driscoll, had come through for her, bless his frat-jock heart. He'd presented her plan by phone to Mitch, EP&M's legal advisor, who'd green-lighted it. That hurdle cleared, Kassandra was confident of getting Shonda's approval, and it would be on to the next round in the competition. At which point, she was also confident she'd find a means to dispatch Bobby, the likely front-runner.

Shonda replied, "Well, whoever pitched your plan wasn't clear. The DNC is already pursuing the same strategy. Mitch knows it, he wouldn't have you duplicate efforts. If you'd taken time to explain it to him yourself."

Kassandra felt her jaw drop. "But, but Mitch wasn't available—"

"I don't care if you had to track him down at home and camp on his doorstep. If you're going to succeed at EP&M, you've got to be clever *and* resourceful."

Like Bobby Driscoll.

Face burning, Kassandra started to defend herself, but trailed off. She dared not mention Bobby, having no way to corroborate his subterfuge, expecting to be terminated on the spot.

Nevertheless, Shonda bent back to her keyboard, and Kassandra slunk away crushed and panicked, left with precious little time to cobble together a new plan.

CHAPTER 13

Awakening from a fitful sleep, Scotty swatted his alarm clock till it shut up. He wrinkled his nose at the stench of Lysol, urine and burnt fur still strong in the air. It had taken him hours last night to clean up the mess, but thankfully neither the piss nor fur were Homer's. The cat had been safe behind the bedroom door, describing what occurred on the other side as a tirade of snarling, growling and destruction that began at 10:00 and continued until 2:00.

Scotty was at wit's end. Demon or no, he had to work today, forced to leave Homer alone again. Rising, he called to him under the bed, got a growl in response, stuffed himself into clothes, dragged to the living room, and sat on the exposed frame of his tattered couch, staring at Mom's plant. It looked worse in the light of day, upright and back in its corner. It *might* recover if Scotty could shield it from further assaults, but he'd nowhere else to put it, it needed sun.

He surveyed the rest of his belongings. Nasty scars on the old tube TV and VHS player (guilt gifts from Pop last spring after he'd kicked Scotty out). Deep gouges on the table/desk as if it had hosted a rodeo. Luckily Scotty's computer tower was under the table. Its files were intact, including the novel he'd been hacking at since high school, unable to come up with an ending. *R U God* was also protected, being an online game.

But many other items were ruined, and Scotty had no hope of replacing them soon. No insurance. Not that he'd grounds for a claim. He'd no evidence of forced entry, no way to prove he, himself, wasn't responsible. And he wasn't about to touch Ivy's college fund, paltry as it was.

His greatest worry at the moment, however, was Homer. Whatever nightmare had unleashed its fury here yesterday, surely it wasn't finished. Scotty had no choice now, he *had* to move out. But all he could do before leaving for work was stock food, water and litter box in the bedroom once more, promising Homer he'd be safe.

Homer wasn't buying it, still holed up under the bed.

• • •

Another tedious day crunching numbers. Scotty couldn't concentrate. He so wanted to confide in Reggie and Zing, but something told him it was a bad career move for Schlompsky's bookkeeper to come off insane. He masked his agitation as the seconds dripped slowly off the clock, at last making his way home...

To find Mom's plant upended again. More broken branches, spilled soil. Nothing else looked disturbed, the bedroom door secure, Homer mewling inside. And righting the plant, Scotty strained his back and ankle once more.

CHAPTER 14

Reverend Penbrook Thornton sat at his desk in his office, two-finger typing Sunday's homily in concert with the tick-tock of the grandfather clock.

Thornton took special care with his sermons, an important means to expand his ministry. His words reached not only his congregants, but many thousands more nationwide via CFN, the Christian Faith Network he'd founded years ago. Today's programming was about to begin, and as he reached for the TV remote beside him, he heard a *pop.* A little gold cross cartwheeled across his desk and spun to a stop in front of him. His lapel pin, its clasp broken.

He groaned. The pin was a priceless heirloom. He'd no idea where it came from originally, but it had seen Gramps safely through World War II, after which Gramps gave it to Ma when she married Pa, she, in turn, pinning it on Pa when he took his guard job at Whiteville Correctional. Upon Pa's retirement, both pin and guard job passed to Thornton, for whom the little cross continued its good blessings. Not only did it save his life one stormy night, it launched his ministry.

Ms. Willoughby's cheery voice on the intercom interrupted his thoughts. *"Sir, a reporter's on the line for you. Kyle Heath. He wants to come down to do a story."*

Thornton didn't recognize the name, rolling his fingers on the desk. The media hadn't always been kind to him. Mainstream media, anyway. For many Liberals, the City was their greatest fear made flesh, a Fundamentalist theocracy operating openly and prosperously in America.

Years back, the ACLU/separation-of-church-and-state crowd had brought suit to negate the City of God's charter. The case was tied up in the courts, now at the Supreme Court, exactly where Thornton wanted it. Six current justices owed their seats to Thornton and his CCC. Even so, the Court appeared divided, the case resting on thin Constitutional ice, and with a decision nearing, Thornton's City could ill afford any negative publicity.

Thornton asked, "What media?"

"Hawk News."

Ah, that was a different matter. The Hawk news juggernaut held Christianity in proper regard. Thornton was a frequent guest on its shows, one of their go-to authorities on religious matters.

"...We don't have Mr. Heath on file, but he sent me his bio, and I forwarded it to you."

Checking his computer screen, Thornton saw the photo of a handsome, well-groomed young black man with dark hair and gray eyes. Heath's vita described him as a junior correspondent at Hawk with a Doctor of Divinity degree from Harvard. A bit Leftist for Thornton's tastes.

"Bless you, Ms. Willoughby. Please put him through."

Picking up, he boomed, "Penbrook Thornton here, nice to make your acquaintance, Mr. Heath."

"An honor, sir. Thanks for taking my call, I know you're busy."

Thornton chuckled. "God's tasks are many, but I've always time for my friends at Hawk. How may I help?"

"I'll be brief, Reverend. We're working on a story about spiritual counseling to air end-of-month. We think our audience would be interested in the methods you use at your Christian Family Research Institute, and we'd like to drop by for a visit."

The phone felt moist in Thornton's hand. "What's the thrust of your story?"

"We want to give viewers a Christian perspective on the treatment of mental illness; compare the benefits of spiritual healing to pharma-based psychiatry. We feel counseling centers like yours get short shrift, and we'd like to interview you and Dr. Neuhoffer."

Dr. Phillip Neuhoffer, director of the Institute. Indeed, the Institute's methods were poorly understood outside of Evangelical circles. The American Psychiatric Association, comprised of secularists, as it was, had little knowledge or regard for faith-based therapy. Numerous times the APA had denied accreditation to Thornton's Institute, forcing it to operate unlicensed as a private center. That, coupled with rumors of youth problems in the City, led reporters to come sniffing on occasion—only to be stonewalled by Thornton and his buttoned-up congregation.

Thornton had good reason to fear the media. For years now, a segment of City youths had engaged in self-destructive behaviors. Marring their bodies with piercings and tattoos. Cutting, burning themselves, indulging in premarital sex. And *most* devastating, some had taken their own lives, and in far higher numbers than the national average for municipalities this size. An enormous embarrassment for a community of professed Christian values.

Fortunately, the City's crime rate didn't include incidents of suicide. Suicide itself wasn't a crime. Not even a civil offense. Still, it was a grave sin. A deeply disturbing failure of faith that grieved Thornton to the core. Evil had taken root here. The Devil had come preying on weak souls, working to undermine Thornton's great achievement. And despite all the praying and preaching Thornton had devoted to the battle, the casualties mounted. He'd needed an answer, urgently, and from the depths of his desperation sprang the Christian Family Research Institute.

For more than a decade, the Institute had served as both a sanctum for the spiritually disturbed, and a means to shield the public from unpleasant issues. The Institute's patients were afforded doctor/patient confidentiality during their treatment, their names and afflictions safe from police records and court blotters—and beyond the reach of prying media.

Hawk News was no threat. Surely Thornton could count on the network to give the Institute the objective coverage it deserved.

He responded, "You've caught us at a hectic time, Mr. Heath, but let me do this. I've a meeting with Director Neuhoffer on Friday. I'll discuss this and see what I can do, and get back with you."

Heath thanked him, and Thornton hung up. As he did, a gleam from outside the window caught his eye. A sunbeam radiated from high atop the Tabernacle in the distance, flaring off the upraised, gilded hand of John the Evangelist, shining into Thornton's office to set his fallen lapel pin aglow. Thornton took the cross in trembling fingertips and studied it in the light.

An omen.

But how to interpret it?

CHAPTER 15

Scotty entered his apartment relieved to find things as he'd left them. Plant upright, bedroom door closed. As he hung up his staff and jacket, however, he sensed *something.*

The cat called out from the bedroom, *The noises again!*

Homer didn't sound too upset, perhaps growing used to the sounds. And when Scotty released him, he bounded for the kitchen. But as Scotty turned to follow, he noticed something odd on his computer screen. Gone were the swimming fish, replaced by a chat window from *R U God.* Scotty never used the chat line, so how did the window open on its own?

He hobbled over to see the window was blank save for an icon in the center. No icon he'd come across before, yet familiar. The face of God from the Sistine Chapel. Bearded, stern, wise. Under the icon appeared a red message alert, time-stamped *10:00 AM.* He opened it to read: *you have an epistle.*

But how? Scotty hadn't enabled any alerts, email or otherwise. Fearing a virus, he went to the kitchen, fetched Homer his dinner, himself a cup of soup, and returned to his computer to ponder. If a virus, it wouldn't be his first. He checked his firewall. Up and running, no alarms. Curiosity finally getting the better of him, he clicked on the epistle and up popped a message:

beware the rising moon—herald@deiknumi.kyrios

What the hell? A *riddle?* Scotty had no clue what it meant or where it came from. He didn't recognize the email address, and he knew no "Herald." But whoever this was, he was no longer online, or the browser status bar would have featured a green "live" dot.

Suspecting spam from some horoscope site, Scotty deleted the message, closed the window, and ran a virus scan. Clean. As he finished, Homer leaped onto his lap.

Enough of the crap. Let's play God.

Exactly what Scotty needed, a distraction. He hadn't checked on *Scottworld* since Saturday, a long time to leave his planet adrift.

Moments later, he and Homer were swooping into Times Square. All appeared normal, city thrumming along. But when he stopped by the news ticker for updates, he was annoyed to discover those pesky Rhomboids at it again. Homer growled.

The Rhomboid leaders were planning another march tonight, it said, and Scotty noted with alarm, the time was now well past midnight in Paris. He zoomed across Times Square to an electronics store where TVs in the window aired the march live, confirming his fears. Thousands of Rhomboids were moving down the banks of the Seine through the city, torches lighting the streets. Ahead lay *L'Office Francais de L'Immigration et de L'Integration*, defended by an armed force of federal Gendarmerie.

All the worse, a *second* mob was approaching opposite. Middle-Easterners, Africans, and other disenfranchised immigrants. Two onslaughts converging on an anxious militia in the middle. The news reported similar tensions throughout the rest of the Continent. How tonight went in Paris, likely so went PanEurope. If only Scotty had the power to wave his hand and change the hearts of his virtual subjects. But that's what made the game so challenging.

He rocketed back into the heavens toward the City of Light, descending moments later in darkness above the Seine, holding his breath. *L'Office* stood out aglow in spotlights, a large, imposing stone structure encircled by soldiers and armored vehicles. Both mobs had zeroed on it, and catching sight of each other, they erupted in war whoops and rushed ahead. The Gendarmeries stood their ground, leveling guns at the approaching threats, seconds till impact.

Homer's claws dug into Scotty's legs. *Whatever the hell you're gonna do, do it fast!*

Scotty whispered, "High school physics, don't fail me now..."

He flew over the river to the deserted Left Bank, rotating toward the conflict, working the climate controls on his screen. Instantly a breeze arose and swept across the water, condensing into cloud, reaching the far shore in a towering fog bank, like Egypt's final plague in *The Ten Commandments*, the Angel of Death. The white wave rolled over the Seine's retaining wall onto the riverfront, panicking the rioters as it engulfed them. They turned and fled, lost in the haze, zombies groping with arms outstretched, crashing into parked cars, lampposts, one another.

Scotty mopped his brow with a sleeve. He was lucky this time, he dare not lay off so long.

Homer pawed him. *Apparently, all frogs can't swim...*

Marchers had tumbled blindly over the wall into the river. Scotty rushed to unmoor dinghies from a dock, blowing them within reach until all in peril were finally safe.

"Frogs?" he asked Homer, scratching the cat's ears. "How do you like being called a pussy?"

Homer shrugged and smiled up at him. *Touché.*

CHAPTER 16

THURSDAY, OCTOBER 16, 6:15 PM, QUEENS

Scotty returned home from work, grateful to find things undisturbed again. He'd given Homer run of the apartment.

The cat greeted him at the door. *I'm starving.*

"No problems today, then?"

The noises were back, 10:00 and 2:00. Nothing more.

Scotty was thankful for that much. He could contend with the noises, and apparently Homer was adjusting.

But as he headed for the kitchen, he glanced at his computer and froze. The chat window was on screen again, the icon of God's face from the Sistine Chapel. Moving closer, Scotty saw that same, flashing red alert, time-stamped 10:01 AM.

It read: *you have an epistle.* He frowned, and clicked.

take not the bus tomorrow—herald@deiknumi.kyrios

What now, a promotional ploy for Uber? "Herald" was again offline. Fearing a spam trap, Scotty trashed the email, and this time he blocked its sender, restoring his screen to fish.

He fed Homer, microwaved ramen noodles for himself, and retired to the couch and TV. Why he bothered with the local news he didn't know, depressing. But as the guru advised,

Step #26: An informed man is a wise man.

The usual fare. Crime rising, jobs falling, protesters picketing the mayor's office over slashed education funds. And the day's top story, a deadly gas explosion at a restaurant in Chinatown.

Homer jumped into his lap, and Scotty picked up the remote. But before he could change the channel, the picture cut to a close-up of the restaurant's scorched sign: *The Rising Moon.*

Scotty dropped the remote.

That strange email he'd gotten from "Herald" yesterday, *beware the rising moon.*

Homer stared at him, and Scotty shook his head.

"Coincidence. *Has to be.*"

CHAPTER 17

Scotty boarded the bus for work with a little more spring in his step, dispensing with the shepherd's staff today, ankle and back on the mend once more. With his problems at home improved, he'd again given Homer run of the apartment, and sat back to enjoy the ride.

Until he heard sirens.

A fire engine whizzed by his window, lights flashing. More sirens, and the bus lurched to an inner lane, overtaken by a screaming hook-and-ladder. As the truck drew alongside, a car ahead jumped out of an alley into its path. The truck swerved into the bus, the bus screeched to a halt and threw Scotty and everyone else from their seats.

In the dust, screams, and panic, Scotty was badly shaken. And from more than the crash. Last night's cryptic email echoed in his head: *take not the bus tomorrow.*

Police and ambulances arrived, and while no injuries appeared serious, Scotty had wrenched his back and ankle once more. Medics whisked everyone to the hospital on standing orders of the Metro Transit Authority.

Scotty loathed hospitals. Mom's ordeal had deeply imprinted him. Though in agony, he refused treatment, signed a release, was issued pain pills, a bus voucher, and sent home in a taxi with orders to rest. He called Margo on the way, foolishly expecting sympathy.

"If you don't make it in today," she told him, "you're coming in tomorrow. I don't care how sore you are, we've got inventory to finish. Noon, and not a *second* later."

Tomorrow was Saturday, but Scotty swore he'd be there, and Margo left him with a dial tone. He popped two pills. Margo was the least of his worries. Whoever sent him those warnings about the restaurant and bus was either responsible for the disasters or at least failed to prevent them. But how was it possible to stage such things?

The explosion at the *Rising Moon*—people *died.* Not an act of terrorism, according to the news. A buried gas line. Rusted, rupturing. An *apparent* accident. And the bus crash. Scotty had watched it unfold in real time; a chain of events seemingly too complex to be orchestrated. Not that Scotty knew a thing about staging terrorism.

On the other hand, how on earth could anyone foresee these events? And why involve Scotty? He felt he was going mad.

Dropped off at his building, he popped two more pills and hobbled upstairs in the throes of confusion. His apartment was quiet, no odd scent, the plant in its place. Homer greeted him at the door.

You're home early. Christ! You look like a train wreck.

Scotty limped inside and shut the door. "That epistle last night? Dead on. My bus crashed!" Noting the clock close to 10:00, he added, "And unless I miss my guess, I'm due another email."

He shuffled to his computer and sat with a groan, waking his desktop, restoring the two emails he'd dumped last night. He unblocked their source, too: *herald@deiknumi.kyrios.*

Hardly had he finished than the air rocked with thunder, and Homer tore for the bedroom. The roar changed to whine, the whine trailed off, and the chat window appeared with the icon of God's stern face and the flashing epistle alert. Steeling himself, Scotty opened a new riddle:

> in the legend of a diamond
> tomorrow at the strike of two
> a foul deed shall claim a life
> —herald@deiknumi.kyrios

Another ominous prediction. But what the hell did it mean? Distraught, Scotty happened to notice on his browser's status bar a green dot next to the email link. *Herald@eiknumi.kyrios* was still live. Hurriedly he typed a response:

> who are you? what do you want?
> —sbutterfield@webgab.com

Long minutes, then:

> behold
> i am the paraclete of the lord
> hearken to his word

Scotty called up an online dictionary:

> **Paraclete** [pare-uh-kleet] noun
> (archaic) a biblical term for one who intercedes between God and man.

No more enlightened, he fired back:

> why are you doing this? what do you want from me?

Again the answer was a while in coming.

> you are the chosen one
> ordained to carry forth the lords will

Scotty blinked. What the hell did *that* mean? Was Herald recruiting an accomplice? Then again, what if this *was* the work of an evil spirit sent to punish him? Hands quaking, he pecked:

> why tell me terrible things i can do nothing about? i want
> no part. leave me alone.

A lapse, and a reply:

> by the lord are you empowered
> to change what will be

Scotty begged:

> for godsakes how?

He waited. And waited. Finally, the shrill whine returned, causing him to jump. It gave way to thunder, then faded, and the link went dead. By his computer clock, ten minutes had elapsed from first thunder to last.

Still shaking, Scotty stood and paced, favoring his ankle. What did Herald mean, *ordained to carry forth the lords will?* And what was Scotty to carry forth? He didn't want to be chosen, or ordained, or carry forth anything. All he wanted was to be left alone!

CHAPTER 18

Reverend Penbrook Thornton exited the backseat of the car with his briefcase, telling his driver, "Thanks, Mark, I'll call when I finish. Could be awhile."

"Very good, Reverend. I'll run by the jewelers and get your lapel pin fixed."

Thornton thanked him, and Mark tipped his cap, and drove off.

A driver was one of the few privileges Thornton allowed himself. A necessity, actually. He hadn't driven a car since the night of the accident that took his family. Irrespective, he wasn't a man of pomp and show, like his "prosperity gospel" colleagues. A driver was efficient, enabling Thornton to apply travel time to work. The same reason the Church kept a small jet and pilot on call for him. Beyond that, he lived modestly. His home was no different than most in the City, other than the convenience of its location on Tabernacle grounds, a housekeeper, and cook.

Inhaling the scent of autumn leaves, Thornton strode the walkway to the Christian Family Research Institute, air fresh in the morning sun. The center sat removed on a manicured lawn amid mature spruce, oak, and elm. Three stories of white-marble towers, turrets, and spires. A sedate, soothing environment in which to heal the aggrieved mind and soul.

Or so one would think. Sadly, that hadn't been the case for many patients. After two and a half decades of operation, and more-than-generous funding, the CFRI had a spotty record.

A guard in smart blue uniform met him at the entrance, smiling. "Welcome, Reverend," he said, opening the door.

Thornton clapped the man's shoulder. "Morning, Sam. How's Sally and little Sammy?"

"Everybody's good, sir, thanks."

"And how are things at the Institute these days?"

"Also good, Reverend."

Thornton always made a point to ask the guards about conditions. He wanted to make clear his concerns that patients be treated with compassion. Smiling, he quoted James 5:14: *Is anyone among you sick? Call for the elders of the church and let them pray over him, anointing him with oil in the Lord's name.*

The guard grinned. "Amen."

Thornton continued into the atrium, past statues and artwork featuring idyllic themes. The sound of his shoes on the terrazzo carried him back many years to a very different place a hundred miles to the west. Whiteville Correctional Facility, in Hardeman County. A young prison guard at the time, Thornton had walked The Walk—as the prison's perimeter circuit was known. A desolate beat where he'd acquired his faith listening to bible tapes. And where, ultimately, his faith had saved his life.

At the far end of the atrium stood a reception center where another bright face greeted him. He waved, and bypassing elevators for the grand staircase, he took a right down a hall decorated with murals of Eden. Inside windowed rooms, he saw clinicians in blue attire supervising youth activities—arts, crafts, bible classes. The hall ended at an office with a brass nameplate on the door: *Dr. Philip K. Neuhoffer, PhD, Director of Psychological Services.*

Thornton entered, and a woman rose from her desk to offer a cheery, "Morning, Reverend, the doctor's expecting you."

She showed him through a second door into an impressive suite unchanged since Thornton's last visit. Tall windows wrapped a large corner octagon with a desk facing the center of the room. The walls bore awards and certificates of merit. The bookcases held reference materials and Neuhoffer's own published works.

"Welcome, Brooks," Neuhoffer greeted him from the desk, beaming. "Good to see you."

"Hello, Phil," Thornton replied, shoes sinking into thick carpet. "Please, don't get up."

Too late. Neuhoffer stretched across the desk to offer a hand, gesturing Thornton to a chair. He waited until Thornton settled before retaking his seat, then said, "You're looking well."

Thornton knew otherwise. He'd seen the fatigue in his mirror this morning. The election. His concerns about the Institute. "I could use a vacation," he admitted, unable to recall his last.

"My professional advice? Two weeks in the Caribbean. A celebration cruise, post-election."

An appealing idea. Only eighteen days more. It felt an eternity.

"How's the family?" Thornton asked.

The doctor nodded proudly. "Joan was just elected secretary of the Tabernacle Outreach Program. She's thrilled."

"Quite an honor. Please convey my congratulations, I know how hard she's worked. And didn't I hear your daughter received a scholarship to an Ivy college?"

Thornton had met the young woman on occasion at church services and functions with her parents, but couldn't recall her name. Likely because he'd never been able to engage her in conversation. Very unusual-looking child, and exceedingly shy. Come to think of it, he hadn't seen her in years.

"Stepdaughter," Neuhoffer corrected. "She's doing well, thanks."

Thornton preferred to see high school graduates continue their education in town. The City boasted a top-notch University. "I trust she took along her bible. Important to keep one's moorings against the tides of temptation."

Neuhoffer assured him she had. "I'm eager to get to our discussion," he said. "I've news I think you'll find encouraging."

Withdrawing two blue binders from a drawer, he handed one over. Thornton sighed inwardly. *Another* report. *More* numbers.

The doctor seemed to read him. "I won't take your time parsing figures. Peruse them at your leisure—on your cruise. But let me highlight a few points before I get to my recommendations. I believe we have the solution we've been searching for."

Thornton noted the cover. *15-Year Statistical Analysis/CFRI Case Histories.* Had it truly been that long?

"What I have for you," Neuhoffer said, opening his binder, "is a comprehensive analysis of all adolescents admitted to the Institute since we opened."

A clinical scrapbook of the enduring nightmare that had begun during the City's big growth spurt. Thornton flipped through. The report began with accounts of smoking, foul language, prurient clothing, tattoos, piercings, et al. Which led to drug and alcohol abuse, promiscuity, homosexuality, and on. It reminded Thornton of a sermon he'd given on the situation at the time, warning that a venial sin corrected is a mortal sin averted. Prophetic.

The promiscuity spawned out-of-wedlock pregnancies, out-of-town abortions, and disastrous attempts at self-abortion, some costing the lives of the mothers. The homosexuality, drugs, and alcohol led to a host of other maladies and misfortunes. And then, the ultimate failing.

Suicides.

The Institute was Thornton's desperate attempt to solve the emergency. He'd lured Neuhoffer away from a tenured professorship at Peabody Divinity College, Ohio, to set up the CFRI. But to his frustration, it hadn't proven the solution he'd prayed for.

Neuhoffer said, "I direct you to page 241. A breakdown by age and psychological disorder of every patient who engaged in self-terminating activities, successful or otherwise."

Thornton skimmed, noting, "The majority of cases are classified as 'sexually disordered.'"

"Correct. Not a new finding. Victims of sexual disorders are eight times more likely to attempt self-termination than victims of other disorders. Understandable. Sexual confusion results in greater emotional stress and instability. Self-loathing, depression, impulsiveness. Suicidal triggers. Note page 254. Here you'll find the ages of all sexually disordered patients at time of first admittance, followed by case result. Notice anything?"

Thornton squinted at the page, and Neuhoffer had to point out, "The younger the age at admittance, the more likely the subject to complete our program."

"Complete? As in *cured?*" Thornton knew better.

"Admittedly, cures are rare. But younger patients appear more amenable to our methods, demonstrating improved survival rates over older subjects."

Scanning, Thornton couldn't see how Neuhoffer reached this conclusion, and said so.

Neuhoffer replied, "The correlation isn't readily apparent. We treated so few young children. But viewed over time, the data is compelling."

Thornton was neither psychologist nor statistician, he was an autodidact via Christian-based correspondence courses. As ever, he had to take Neuhoffer at his word.

"The upshot is," Neuhoffer said, "we've identified a new course of action. Knowing sexual disorders lead to self-destructive behavior, I believe we have a mechanism to improve survival rates. As you're aware, our approach has always been to have our schools identify problem teens and refer them here for treatment. But my data suggests we're reaching subjects too late. The answer is to recognize their disorders at an earlier age, and intervene sooner."

Intriguing. "At what age are sexual disorders detectable?"

"Symptoms can appear as early as three or four. The idea is to begin therapy before the affliction takes root. Not only can we hope to save more lives, we may finally be able to cure victims of their disorders altogether."

Thornton's heart leaped. This time Neuhoffer had spared him the highbrow psychology to lay out a seemingly practicable course of action. Dare he hope, the miracle he'd prayed for. "But how do we go about identifying these youngsters? We can't screen every child in the City."

"No. The answer is to involve the community. Educate the public about what to look for. The signs are rather evident once pointed out. We can prepare pamphlets, announce the program during Sunday services. Conduct adult training sessions. Enlist the help of our children in the schools."

"Use *children?*"

"Certainly. Children must be taught to recognize these threats, too, for their own protection. They're our first line of defense. Who better to notify parents and teachers of questionable behavior in playmates?"

Thornton pressed a hand to his heart. "Turn our children into spies and informants?"

"No. *Lifeguards.* To keep an eye out for others wading into dangerous waters."

The reverend leaned forward. "I need you to be very clear on this, Phil. You're telling me, these troubled lives can *truly* be saved."

Neuhoffer took a breath and sat back. "Let me share a personal experience," he said. "One very close to my heart." He turned to gaze out the window. "I never told you, but my stepdaughter was once headed in, shall we say, the wrong direction. I saw signs at age six. A reluctance to engage with the opposite sex. A preoccupation with masculine interests. I took it on myself to work with her, applying some persistent tough love, and I'm pleased to say she's now leading a godly life. Given the data I just showed you, I firmly believe if I'd waited to intervene, the outcome would have been very different. God knows if she'd have even survived."

Indeed, Thornton had never met anyone as unusual as Neuhoffer's stepdaughter.

The doctor turned to him. "Yes," he said with conviction. *"I can save these children..."*

Thornton was so taken by the good news, he didn't realize until on his way home, he'd forgotten to mention the Hawk News interview. He called back to make arrangements.

CHAPTER 19

As he recuperated at home, Scotty was online, frantically researching *deiknumi.kyrios*.

deiknumi *[dike-noo-me] verb. (Greek) A term commonly found in ancient manuscripts of the bible, meaning "to point out," "to show."*

kyrios *[kee-ree-ose] noun. (Greek) A term for master, lord, or god.*

But a thorough search of email domains turned up no trace of *deiknumi.kyrios*. Which made no sense. To function as an email core protocol, the address had to be registered with the Internet Assigned Numbers Authority. This address wasn't. Hours of effort, and Scotty still had no better idea who—or what—the mysterious Herald was.

A rumble of thunder jolted Scotty in his chair. *2:00 PM.*

His chest tightened as the sequence of sounds played out, and then a new epistle alert flashed in the black window of his screen. He hesitated, and clicked:

that you may know the lords will and obey
this night a crane shall descend on the wind
to strike frogs neck

Grimacing, Scotty replied:

i don't understand

He waited. One minute. Two. He sent another message:

hello?

Nothing.

At length, the whine returned, nearly costing him his seat again. The thunder rose and ebbed, and the link went dead.

Scotty jumped on craigslist to spend the rest of the afternoon combing for a new apartment. He soon found, however, his finances limited him to Bronx apartments and multiple roommates. Firing off inquiries regardless, also mentioning his cat, he popped more pain pills and retired to the couch and the local news, fearful of what he'd learn tonight. And his eyelids grew heavy…

St. Thomas Aquinas Elementary, seventh-grade history class. Today's lesson: The Revolutionary War as Experienced in the Bronx.

Scotty had trouble keeping his focus, eyes wandering to that redhead with the pigtails. Until a grip on his ear yanked him from his seat to the front of the class, shoving his face into a pull-down map of modern-day New York City.

"There," barked his teacher, her gnarled finger tapping a point on the map. Scotty saw a strip of land tailing from the Bronx out into the waters of Long Island Sound. "What's that say?"

"Th-Th-Throggs Neck," Scotty managed over the snickering.

"And what name did General Washington know it by when the redcoats landed there in October 1776?"

"I-I-I dunno."

"I just told the class," she snapped, giving his head a whack. "Frog's Neck!"

Scotty bolted upright on the couch in a sweat, rubbing the back of his head. It was dark outside, a storm raging. Inside on TV, presidential candidate Roger Filby was bloviating in an ad. *"Jobs, jobs, jobs,"* the man cried—when abruptly the station broke to live news.

A scene of bedlam. Tangled scaffolding and trusses.

A breaking-news headline read:

Construction crane falls from building in Throggs Neck

CHAPTER 20

SATURDAY, OCTOBER 18, 9:42 AM, QUEENS

The sun was well up when Scotty awoke on the couch, TV on. He looked to see news of the mangled crane, and groaned. Not a bad dream, after all. At least, no reported casualties this time.

He sat up wincing, his back the worse for this sorry bed. Unlike the news was reporting, Scotty knew it was no accident. Herald was a terrorist. There could be no other explanation. Scotty felt panic. What was Herald's purpose in sending him warnings disguised as riddles? Riddles he hadn't the ability to solve. He felt trapped inside an episode of *Black Mirror*.

He'd no choice, he had to notify the authorities. What complications would *that* bring him? The clock read *9:45*. Fifteen minutes till a new message of looming catastrophe, no doubt.

Homer leaped to the arm of the couch and cocked his head. *Dude, I'm starving!*

Scotty rubbed his neck and back and rose on unsteady legs. Despite his worries, he had to be at work by noon. *God*, he hated his job. At least he had time to wait for the next message of doom and call it in to the cops. But he had to be careful what he told them, or he could implicate *himself* in whatever new plot Herald was hatching.

He fed Homer, dressed, grabbed a pop-tart, and headed for his computer to see if he'd gotten any responses to his apartment inquiries. Not a one.

The clock ticked to 10:00, and Scotty girded himself as the thunder and whine arrived. Then silence, and once more the window with the Face of God and flashing alert popped on screen.

An epistle from the Paraclete. Scotty clicked it:

> in the legend of a diamond
> today at the strike of two
> a foul deed shall claim a life
> which you are empowered to spare
> behold, and obey

Same message as before, but with two new lines added: "*which you are empowered to spare; behold, and obey.*"

The email bore an attachment, and Scotty opened it warily. Step-by-step instructions how to prevent another tragedy. Unless he followed Herald's orders to the letter, someone would die.

Another dire prediction, yet different than those previous. This time, Herald warned of a misfortune surely *impossible* for any human to plan and execute. No act of terrorism, *an act of God.*

Scotty trembled, in turmoil. If Herald were, in fact, a messenger of God, why communicate over the Internet, of all methods? To *Scotty*, of all people? And yet, how could Herald foresee the future without the aid of an all-knowing deity? Scotty had no choice but to skip work again today. Were he to call *this* in to the cops, they'd no doubt think him insane.

Afraid to speak with Margo, he emailed her an apology, blaming his injuries from the bus accident, swearing he'd be in first thing tomorrow. Whatever the outcome of this prediction, he was done. God's Will or not, Herald would have to find another chosen one.

Grabbing his black hoody, Scotty sucked up his fear, and hobbled out the door, leaving his shepherd's staff behind. If he'd any hope of saving the poor life at stake today, he couldn't afford to attract undue attention.

He stopped at an ATM to withdraw the last of his petty cash, and caught a bus to 161st and River, arriving by 12:30 PM. In front of him stood massive Yankee Stadium. Game three of the American League Championship Series was underway, fans streaming in, vendors hawking. It was Scotty's first time here. He'd always wanted to attend a game as a kid, but Pop thought it frivolous when you could watch free on TV. Pop was right about the expense; a standing-room-only ticket nearly drained Scotty's wallet.

He passed through Gate 2 into the crowd, slowing to check his phone. Multiple messages from Margo. He ignored them to review Herald's orders. Never had he felt more fear or pressure. He'd scant minutes to pull off this absurd feat—assuming he wasn't stopped and arrested first.

He pressed on. The instructions took him to the field-level food court, where he worked through the bustle toward the home-plate-end of the stadium. His objective was a ramp leading to the seats above the Yankee dugout. The *Legends* section. Locating it, he held back, anxiously studying the security guards at the entrance. Big, brawny. His phone shook in his hands as the clock ticked down. And when at last it read 12:52, Scotty inhaled and made his move.

Adjacent to the ramp was a first-aid station. He headed for it. The door was open, as promised, and he burst inside calling out, "Help, come quick! *Heart attack.*"

A man and woman in EMS uniforms sat at monitors. They jumped to their feet, snatched medical bags, plucked a defibrillator unit from a recharger, and asked in unison, "Where?"

"This way," Scotty cried, waving them on, and he hurried back out the door.

As he and the medics approached the ramp, two guards cut him off. But the EMS lady stepped up to declare, "Medical emergency," and the guards let them pass. So far, so good.

Scotty led the way up an incline, through a tunnel. As he burst out into the open air of the stadium, however, he skidded to a halt, ankle howling. Suddenly exposed to the vastness of the arena, he felt lightheaded, disoriented.

The medics pressed him, precious seconds wasting, and finally, he spotted the Yankee dugout. Pointing to the section above, he yelled, "024B. *Hurry*," and took off again. The medics chased after down a flight of steps, where Scotty pulled up puffing. The seats were packed with raucous fans, bottom of the third, Yankees up, one strike, three balls. But no sign of trouble.

The medics looked around, then turned questioning eyes to Scotty. He rechecked his phone, frantic.

"Legends Section, 024B. Row 8!"

They zeroed in. All appeared normal. Until, down on the field, the batter swung at a fastball, clipped it, and sent it careening straight toward them. Scotty gasped, but the ball came so fast, there was hardly a chance to react. It swerved away toward a young man in Row 7, who ducked, and a gray-haired gentleman behind caught it square in the chest with a sickening *thud.* He slumped, face white, ball resting in his lap.

The Jumbotron caught it all, and the crowd uttered a collective gasp followed by eerie silence. Play on the field stopped. The medics gawked at Scotty, then leaped into action, people making way, Jumbotron zeroing in. The female medic ripped open the victim's shirt, searching with a stethoscope.

"No pulse," she told her partner, motioning for the defibrillator.

The stadium was quiet as death while she positioned the electrodes, and Scotty cringed when the woman called, "Clear." She pulled the trigger, the stricken man convulsed, and the crowd groaned and held its breath. Scotty, too.

Still, the man sat limp. Scotty's heart beat for the both of them.

The medics tried again. This time the man bolted upright, his eyes popped open, and he gawked around in confusion, color returning. The stands erupted in cheers. Players doffed their caps and waved. And Scotty felt faint.

Using the celebration as cover, he limped up the stairs, down the ramp, and made his way outside to catch his breath, and a bus home.

CHAPTER 21

Scotty limped into his building, ankle and back raging, upstairs into his apartment, leaning against the door to close it, closing his eyes. He felt a tap on his leg.

You didn't stick around for the game?

All Scotty wanted was for this to be over. Over before he lost his job, if not his mind. He was now broke, broken, and surely in trouble with Margo. Dragging to his computer to read her replies to his email, he found instead a black screen with a blinking epistle. He opened it:

> you are ordained for a special mission
> await word from the lord tomorrow morning

No "Job well done." Not even a thank you. Lord or no, Scotty wasn't waiting around tomorrow for another epistle, he absolutely *had* to be at work. Afraid to read Margo's messages, he went to the couch and collapsed, exhausted to his soul...

When he opened his eyes again, it was dark, and Homer was sitting on his chest staring down at him like a buzzard.

"All right, all right," Scotty grunted, pushing to his feet, lumbering for the kitchen, Homer on his heels. But something told him to check his computer first, and he detoured.

No epistle this time, but *dozens* of emails. Never had he gotten so many in one day. Mail from nearly everyone he knew, including Reggie and Zing—and a new message from Margo.

He opened Reggie's email first:

Carnac the Magnificent! How'd you do that?

Confused, he opened the email from Zing:

what the hell u doing at game? ur all over the news, bro! margo's pissed.

Crap. *The Jumbotron.* Scotty swallowed, bracing for Margo:

Hope you enjoyed the game, Butterfield.
Miraculous recovery.
Just in time to pound the pavement next week.
You're fired.

A wail filled the room, and Scotty jumped—only to realize, it was him. He wailed again. What now? He'd no hope for a new job with this blotch on his record. His plans for Ivy's college, what would he tell her? Thanks to the Lord, he'd lost all of what little he had.

He slumped to the kitchen and spooned out the last of the Fancy Feast, telling Homer, "Enjoy, buddy, it'll be dry cat chow for the both of us from here on."

Back in the living room again, he collapsed on the couch and snatched up the remote.

Zing was right, the stadium story was all over the news. Scotty watched crestfallen as the video played in slomo like a bad dream.

Batter at the plate, pitcher delivering, ball slicing off the bat, streaking for the stands in a laggard blur. The camera zoomed in as the one fan ducked and the second took the hit. Then the image froze, and the focus shifted to the medics—and Scotty, standing beside them. The picture moved closer, and Scotty grimaced to see his face highlighted in a circle. He turned up the volume.

"...*an as-yet unidentified young man who called paramedics to the scene before the accident even happened. Whoever the psychic is, he saved the life of longtime Yankee fan, Jimmy Salem...*"

The Jumbotron cut back to the batter, who struck out.

CHAPTER 22

Scotty was at the library with Mom. The one on East Kingsbridge where she took him on the bus every Sunday after Mass. A place more spiritual than church.

They walked the aisles hand-in-hand, choosing books for the week, browsing adventure and excitement and knowledge. Mom had always read to him, introducing him to worlds of wonder far removed from their humdrum life. But as she lifted him to a high shelf for a special book, his fingers closing on *Through the Looking Glass*, he heard the Jabberwocky snarl and Mom cry. He felt her snatched from under him, her hands let go, and he plummeted to the floor.

…coming to rest on his back in front of the couch.

He shook himself awake as the dragon's snarl continued, and the Cheshire cat fishtailed past him, headed for the bedroom. The snarl gave over to whine, and Scotty pulled himself up, limping to his computer to see an alert flashing beneath the icon of God's flinty glare.

Absolutely not. Scotty was done. Not that he didn't want to see victims of Fate spared, but it could no longer be at his expense. This had to end. Now. He clicked on the epistle:

make sunset before midday
or the city will lose its head

No idea what that meant, Scotty shot back:

find someone else, i'm out.

A long pause, and:

you and no other are chosen to carry forth the lords will

Reply:

carrying forth cost me my job. i'm broke. i quit.
leave me alone.

No response. Scotty sat staring, hoping for another pink slip. The ten-minute window was about to close when at last there popped on the screen:

have faith
the lord will provide
hearken to his call and you shall be blessed
one-thousandfold

It came with an attachment, but Scotty wasn't biting. He folded his arms tight on his chest till the whine and thunder returned and ended, and the link died. Telling himself his ordeal was over, he went to fetch himself and Homer breakfast.

Scotty dawdled over a bowl of Alpha-Bits at the kitchen table. *Make sunset before midday or the city shall lose its head.* How the hell did you make the sun set before noon? And regardless, didn't the city lose its head all the time? New York!

Damn these insipid riddles. Why didn't the Lord speak clearly? How much better off humanity would be without bible babble.

Behind him, Homer paused his munching. *For chrissakes, open the damned attachment.*

Scotty stared into his bowl. Cereal letters had arranged themselves in the milk to read *DO NOT.* Or was that *DONUT?* Swearing, he pushed back his chair.

Herald's attachment was brief. Instructions to solve the riddle. Scotty was being ordered to Brooklyn, immediately, to a church in Sunset Park. This morning at 11:54, the mayor of New York would be assaulted by a madman as he entered his house of worship.

Scotty jumped up, freaking. The instructions identified the "madman" by his clothing, but there was little more to go on. What was Scotty to do? He'd no experience in matters like this, dealing with a crazed attacker. He needed time to think, but had none. It was already 10:40. To make the deadline, he had to leave *now.*

Homer padded over to ask, *What would the guru say?*

Scotty knew.

Step #33. Be guided by your aspirations, not your fears.

Scotty certainly had no aspirations to be a hero. Not in the *real* world, anyway. When overloaded by reality, his fallback was Sci-fi and computer games. He'd no capacity to confront a *real* madman. Yet once more a life hung in the balance, all the weight on him.

He was about to despair when, like an epiphany, the solution came to him.

CHAPTER 23

"*I said,*" René repeated in French accent, "try the brioche. *Superb.*" Kassandra Kraft took a bite and washed it down with a sip of mimosa. Another bland Sunday brunch at René's favorite bistro. He raised a tattooed arm to toast her.

She shouldn't be here. Tomorrow, she and the two remaining interns were to present honed strategies for blunting the Far-Right ground assault. The clock was ticking, and still, Kassandra had nothing. Nor was René helpful. No head for business or politics. An empty head of hair.

Over his broad shoulders, a TV above the bar aired a sports clip from Yankee Stadium. Kassandra stared vapidly, then squinted to see a fan in the stands struck by a baseball—only to watch him swarmed immediately by EMS. As if the medics had been standing by on alert.

But how was that possible?

The picture zoomed in on the face of a bystander highlighted in a circle. *Good Lord,* was he that dork in the apartment down the hall from her? She couldn't be sure.

René tossed his hair, turning to see, asking, "What is it?"

"Damned if I know."

CHAPTER 24

SUNDAY, OCTOBER 19, 12:07 PM, QUEENS

Scotty lay on his battered couch in old exercise sweats he'd never worn for that purpose, surfing news channels, Homer curled on his belly. The Yankee Stadium story continued to air. To Scotty's relief, he hadn't been identified publicly so far, still clinging to his privacy.

Homer yawned. *You've finally done something interesting to put in your journal.*

Indeed. Scotty couldn't deny that it felt good having helped that poor spectator. Never in his life had he accomplished anything he was especially proud of—*R U God* notwithstanding. But now, it weighed on him that the hour Herald predicted for the attack on the mayor had come and gone, and he'd seen no word on the news yet. If harm came to anyone because he'd ducked his orders, how could he forgive himself?

His doorbell sounded, and he jumped, causing Homer to bolt.

Rubbing scratches on his stomach, Scotty went to the intercom. "Yes?"

"Are you accepting visitors, or do I go through your agent?"

Crap. Ivy was onto him. He buzzed her in and waited in the hall as she bounded upstairs, her face aglow. Hopping into his arms, she wrapped her legs around him.

"My hero!"

Grunting, he trucked her inside. She shucked her jacket to reveal an *Honest Ellen for President* T-shirt.

"The media's calling you *Guardian Angel*," she said. "That baseball video's got millions of hits on YouTube. No one's ID'd you yet?"

He shrugged. It wasn't like he was a known commodity outside the old neighborhood. Not that he was much noticed inside, either.

"The beard," he replied.

She touched her cheek where he'd kissed her. "Even Pop didn't recognize you."

Scotty shifted his weight to his good leg. "You didn't rat on me?"

"And have Pop guess where I was *really* going today?"

He hung up her jacket, and motioned her to the couch. She hesitated, eyeing its shredded condition, looking around. He'd forgotten how things had changed since her last visit.

Her brow furrowed. *"Holy moly,"* she cried, "you let a mountain lion crash here?"

"Long story."

She bunched up a blanket on the couch and flopped on it. He offered coffee, she declined, and he sat beside her on the hard frame.

"So," she said, looking down at him with an arched brow, "How'd you pull it off?"

"What?"

She gave him a slow, annoyed blink, and he replied, "It's complicated."

"I'll *try* to keep up."

Breaking news on TV saved him, and he raised the volume.

"Just in—an attempted attack on New York mayor Andy M. Beard a short time ago as he attended church in Brooklyn."

Attempted. *Thank God.* The story showed video from a bystander's phone: well-dressed people entering a stone church with red doors. Commotion, confusion, plainclothesmen swarming, people shouting, shaky and blurred. But knowing what to look for, Scotty made sense of it. A man in a pea-green jacket had surged for the mayor, immediately overwhelmed and subdued.

> "No word so far from Mayor Beard, who was unharmed. His assailant has yet to be identified, but a source tells Eyewitness News the mayor's security detail was tipped off just in time, apprehending the suspect when he made his move. Stay tuned."

Scotty leaped to his feet and pumped his fist, shouting, "Woo-hoo!" But feeling Ivy's eyes, he sank back to the couch.

After an uncomfortable pause, she demanded, "What the *heck's* going on?"

He lay his head against the backrest and stared at the ceiling. To bring anyone else in on this insanity had to be a mistake, especially his kid sister. But how could he put her off now? Ivy was a bull terrier once she set her teeth. And Scotty so needed to get this off his chest. To confide in someone. To know, once and for all, he *wasn't* nuts.

"I warn you," he said, "you're not gonna believe me."

She folded her arms, and he told her everything. The strange noises in his apartment that came out of nowhere, and no one else heard. The ever-more-bizarre incidents that followed, including the objects left on his floor—bible, angel statue, shepherd's staff and assorted debris. His qualms about an evil spirit, and his frustrated efforts to exorcise it.

Ivy scoffed. But her eyes grew concerned when he told her of the cryptic emails sent him by the Paraclete, explaining what a Paraclete was. How Herald would contact Scotty each day at 10:00 and 2:00, predicting events that unfolded with chilling accuracy. The deadly restaurant explosion. Bus accident. Toppled crane. Yankee Stadium.

Frowning, she said, "Most of that stuff sure sounds like terrorism. But I gotta admit, I've no rational way to explain the baseball thing."

Scotty wrapped up with the latest warning, the attack on the mayor today—and how Scotty handled it with a call to 9-1-1.

"No way the cops would ignore a threat like that," he said. "I passed along the details and hung up before they could trace the call." He'd seen *CSI: New York.*

Ivy gaped, searching his face. "Who else knows?"

"No one. Not even Mrs. Steiner." He dropped his gaze. "I was supposed to work yesterday but called in sick to make it to the stadium. Margo saw me on the news...and canned me."

"You lost your job? *Oh my God,* what will you do?"

He sighed. "Herald said to have faith, and I'd be rewarded a thousandfold. Unfortunately, I think he meant in the *next* life."

She shook her head. "I'm not buying Herald the Paraclete."

Ivy was nowhere as steeped in superstitions as Scotty had been at Mom's knee. And while Pop forced Ivy to attend parochial school and church, that's as far as he went with it.

She continued, "If Herald's so supernatural and all, why's he use a chat line? What about talking snakes and burning bushes? For crying out loud, why not appear to you in person?"

Scotty cringed to recall the burnt ring of leaves on the back of Mom's plant. Nor was he keen on snakes. "I couldn't believe it, either," he said. "But the fan at Yankee stadium hit by a baseball? How the hell do you fake *that?* That was the clincher for me. Who but God knows the future? Fortunetellers? Astrologers? Herald is five-for-five, for chrissakes."

"So why use you as a middleman? God could stop these things with a snap of His fingers."

"Damned if I know. Why use a nobody like me at all? Not that it matters anymore, I quit."

Ivy's phone rang, and she plucked it from her jeans. *"Crap.* Pop. He's been on me like chewing gum."

"You better go."

"Not on your life." She stuck out her chin the way Mom used to. "I'm hanging around for the two o'clock show." Standing, she rubbed her palms together. "Whaddya got for lunch?"

• • •

As the hour of 2:00 neared, Scotty hoped to put Ivy's skepticism to rest. But he had to prepare her for possible disappointment. Closing Homer in the bedroom, he grabbed Ivy a chair at the computer next to his, and told her, "You realize, if Herald accepted my resignation, there may be no show."

"In which case," she snapped, "I'll believe you made it all up."

He sighed. It was the top of the hour. He warned her about the noises, and for once, he welcomed them when they came.

"*Jesus,*" Ivy cried, grimacing as the thunder rolled. "Nobody else in the building hears?"

"No." Importantly, *Ivy* heard. He wasn't crazy after all. Maybe. The whine took over, then quiet.

Scotty directed Ivy's wide eyes to the monitor where the fish were chased away by a black screen and lone, flashing epistle alert.

He hesitated. "I don't want Herald thinking I'm still party to this."

Ivy elbowed him. "I want to know the future. *Open* the fortune cookie."

She didn't yet realize the burden of such knowledge. A weight Scotty preferred not to bear again. Although he'd no other way to prove Herald's miraculous foresight.

Moving his curser to the icon, he clicked, and up popped:

you have angered the lord

"Uh-oh," Ivy said.

Scotty wet his lips and pecked out:

how?

Reply:

> you alone are the chosen one
> you alone must fulfill the lords will
> i am for no other eyes but yours

As if Herald might hear, Scotty whispered nervously to Ivy, "Is he upset because I sloughed off the last assignment to others? Or because I brought you into this?"
"Or both?"
Hurriedly he typed:

> i'm broke. i can't do this anymore. anoint someone else

Herald:

> accept the will of the lord and tomorrow at noon
> you shall be compensated one-thousandfold

Ivy grinned. "Not the next life. You get your reward *now*."
Herald sent a follow up:

> 2-7-4-9-6

Scotty and Ivy exchanged puzzled glances, and Scotty typed:

> explain

Herald:

> new jersey pick5

"Holy crap!" Ivy gasped. "It's a lotto number."

Scotty felt faint. He'd never played the numbers, but was well aware jackpots could range in the *millions.* New Jersey held drawings every day at noon. If Herald was shooting him straight—and so far he had—tomorrow at this time, Scotty and Ivy's money worries might be over.

"Manna from heaven," he whispered, raising trembling fingers to the keys.

Ivy grabbed his arm, screwing up her face. "What God bribes people to do His bidding?"

"All Gods. Isn't that the point of heaven?"

"I'm sorry, but Herald smells more like a Nigerian Prince."

"But he knows the future. Who but God knows the future?"

"Let's see some ID, first."

"How do you mean?"

"I mean, make him show himself."

"Here? In the apartment? *Live?"*

A frightening thought, and Scotty saw apprehension in Ivy, too.

"On screen will do," she said. "This is a chat line, does it have video and sound, too?"

It did. Scotty mulled her suggestion. Giving the Paraclete an ultimatum didn't strike him as wise. "And if he refuses?"

"What have you got to lose?"

A damn loaded question.

At the risk of angering Herald and the Lord further, Scotty inhaled and typed:

time we talk face to face. show yourself on screen.

He angled the monitor so Ivy could no longer see. She objected, and Scotty said, "If Herald doesn't already know you're here, let's keep it that way. No worry, I can video him on screen for you."

She didn't like it, but Scotty wasn't arguing.

They waited. And waited, trading frowns. Still no response. At length, the harsh noises returned, and soon all was as before.

Scotty squared the monitor, displaying a school of fish again.

Ivy looked worried. "What if I cost us the jackpot?"

"We've still got the lotto number."

"If the Lord doesn't change it. Assuming you *do* win, and cash in, does that say you accept Herald's terms? He owns you?"

Scotty wasn't sure.

Ivy checked her phone and jumped up. "Gotta go, Pop's *really* pissed now. I'll call from school tomorrow after you buy the ticket. Don't forget the numbers, *2-7-4-9-6*."

No way he would.

They went to the coat rack. As Scotty helped her into her jacket, suddenly there came a banging on the door. Scotty stiffened. Ivy, too.

Herald...

From out in the hall came a thundering voice, "NYPD—*open up.*"

Scotty saw his fear reflected in Ivy, pulling her aside to fumble at the bolt as the command repeated, louder, fist pounding.

Scotty opened, and heavily armed men in SWAT gear burst in. They hurled him against the wall, frisking, cuffing, sweeping him out into the hall. Neighbors gawked through cracked doors, and Scotty saw Ivy led out un-cuffed, arm in the grip of a steely eyed cop.

"Let her go!" he cried. "She's got nothing to do with anything."

The cops paid no heed, marching them downstairs past Mrs. Steiner, her frail voice protesting, outside past Kassandra on the sidewalk, into separate squad cars, and off.

CHAPTER 25

Ivy was never so terrified in her life. The police confiscated her phone and thrust her into the cage of a squad car, hurtling along, siren blaring. She begged an explanation, but the two officers in front ignored her, one reading her her rights.

If this was divine retribution for their insolence to the Lord, Ivy blamed herself. She'd put Scotty up to it.

The car raced across Queensboro Bridge to Manhattan, past City Hall, down Park Row to 1 Police Plaza, pulling into an underground parking garage. Ivy was taken to an elevator, up two floors into a small, windowless room. The room had a lone table and chairs in the center, a full-length wall mirror on one side, video cameras in the ceiling corners peering down like vultures.

The cops sat Ivy on the side facing the mirror, where she waited anxiously for what seemed forever as the men stood guard. Finally, a middle-aged man and woman arrived with a younger, sober-eyed woman in tow. All wore suits and carried briefcases.

The younger woman leaned into a cop, and whispered, "Minor?"

He whispered back, "Her only ID is a library card. Says she's sixteen, from the Bronx, a senior at Mt. St. Ursula."

104

The cops left, closing the door, and the others took seats opposite Ivy, studying her.

"Dr. Susan Grayson," The younger woman introduced herself. "Office of Children and Family Services." She gestured to her associates. "Detectives Greer and Reese, NYPD Emergency Services. You're Ivy Butterfield, yes? Joseph Butterfield Jr.'s younger sister?"

"*Scotty*," Ivy snapped. "We didn't do anything. *Let us go.*"

Grayson pursed her lips. "I won't sugarcoat it, Ivy. Scotty's in serious trouble. If you want to help him, you'll help us get to the bottom of this."

The three opened their cases, took out pads and tape recorders, and turned on the devices.

Grayson said, "Tell us what you know about Scotty's involvement in the attack today."

"That thing with Mayor Beard? *That's* what this is about?"

The three scribbled in their pads, and the woman replied, "That *thing* with the mayor, yes."

Ivy felt her face heat. "But Scotty wasn't involved. He called to warn you. For God's sake, he saved the mayor's life!"

"We have a record of the call, made from your brother's phone. It doesn't explain how he knew of the attack. What's his connection to the suspect?"

"He doesn't know the suspect, there *is* no connection."

Ivy's heart raced. The truth of how Scotty came by his information was a sure ticket to Bellevue. But in the absence of an excuse, Scotty was implicated. She opted for half-truth.

"He had a-a-a premonition. That's how he knew. He's got, you know, second sight. He sees the future. Sometimes."

The three stared at her. Grayson said, "You're saying Scotty's clairvoyant? A psychic?"

"More or less."

The woman traded exasperated glances with her colleagues, and Ivy hurried to add, "This morning wasn't his first time, either.

Yesterday at Yankee Stadium, that video all over the news? That guy whacked by the baseball? Scotty saw it coming—he saved *him*, too. Check it out. The 'Guardian Angel' is Scotty. Let's see you make a conspiracy outta *that*." She stood, snapping, "I've told you all there is, I'm done. I demand to see my brother."

Grayson rose, too, telling her associates, "If you've no more questions, I'm releasing her."

Ivy couldn't believe it. "And Scotty?"

"He's in other hands. I'll have a car take you home."

"I'm not leaving till I see him. I insist, or I'm calling our attorney." They had no attorney.

Grayson stared at her, then nodded. "Wait here."

She and the man left Ivy in the custody of the older female detective, and shortly Grayson reappeared, crooking her finger. Ivy followed her to an elevator, up several floors to another holding room with a windowed door. Inside sat Scotty, downcast, hands manacled to the table. Three plainclothesmen sat opposite with notebooks and recorders. Ivy fought back tears.

Grayson rapped on the glass, and the three men picked up their things and exited. Grayson motioned Ivy inside. "Five minutes," she told her, closing the door, standing watch outside.

Scotty perked, and Ivy rushed to throw her arms around him, tears spilling.

"I'm *so* sorry, Ivy," he moaned. "Why did I ever get you involved!"

"It's okay, they're letting me go. What about you?"

He looked relieved, then darkened again. "I got fingerprinted and mug-shot. I got a record now. They think I had something to do with the attack on the mayor."

She drew up a chair, whispering, "I know. What did ya tell 'em?"

He whispered back, "What *can* I say without sounding insane?"

"You gotta give them something, or you'll never get out. I told them you can see the future."

He looked at her as though *she* were insane, and she explained,

"I figured if they lie-detectored us, we'd pass."

He hung his head. "Pop will kill me—and ground you for life."

"So what *are* you gonna say?"

"Not the truth. Son of Sam took orders from a dog, I get mine from a Paraclete?"

"Herald's emails will back you up."

He raised frantic eyes. "Hell no, they'll confiscate my computer."

Ivy sighed. Losing his computer could be the best thing for him. When he lived at home, sometimes when he went out—which wasn't often—Ivy would snoop on his computer. He spent his life on that thing. A sad, lost little life. Links to science sites; clumsy attempts at social networking. A superhero sci-fi novel he'd never finish. A videogame he obsessed over. And a single, pitiful porn video.

A rap came at the door, Grayson at its window.

Ivy told Scotty, "I'll make Pop bail you out."

He snorted. "I'll rot before that happens. Look, I've done nothing wrong, they can't hold me without cause. I'll text you when I'm free."

"Got any cash on you?"

"Not a cent."

She reached in her jeans and handed him some bills and change. "Here, you'll need to buy the lottery ticket. I can't, I'm underage."

"How will you get home?"

"Cab. Pop will pay."

Scotty accepted it grudgingly. She gave him a squeeze, and left.

Grayson walked her to the elevator, returned her phone and said, "I'll drive you."

Ivy declined, not about to be dropped off in her Bronx neighborhood by social services.

The elevator opened and Ivy stepped inside telling Grayson, "Scotty really *does* see the future. You want proof, watch that video from Yankee stadium."

"I have," the woman replied, frowning. "Beats hell out of me what's going on. I'd help your brother if I could. Unfortunately, he's not a minor."

The doors closed and the elevator descended, Ivy alone in the company of a young black man. Scotty's age, she guessed, mid-twenties. Tall, handsome. Not that she cared.

He turned to her. "You're his sister, aren't you?"

She squinted at him, and he clarified, "The Guardian Angel."

"You a cop?"

"Reporter."

"How do you know about us?"

"I'm working the stadium story, a contact here tipped me off. Seems the mystery deepens." He handed her a business card. "Kyle Heath, Hawk News."

Ivy almost gagged. Hawk was a right-wing propaganda pipe of industrial-strength discharge.

She stuck the card in a pocket and exited into a busy lobby. Lots of shifty-looking, ambulance-chaser types in cheap suits. As she threaded through, she ran face-to-face into a scowling man with a grizzled beard and unkempt hair. He could have passed for a street person.

Pop.

He barked, "Now what the hell's he done to ya?" And snatching her wrist, he led her away.

CHAPTER 26

Reverend Penbrook Thornton sat in the backseat as his car made the winding assent up Chapel Mount. Below, the gleaming-white City played peek-a-boo through the autumn blush.

His driver smiled in the mirror. "Things have certainly changed since the night you first drove this hill, sir."

Thornton smiled back. "Indeed so, Mark, praise the Lord."

Everyone in the City knew the story, how Thornton stumbled onto this valley thirty-odd years ago. Hardly more than wilderness then. End of the road for a lost man without destination, money, plan, or hope. A young man fleeing a past of aimless circles—only to confront himself.

The car emerged from forest into an open summit, a cul-de-sac overlooking the City. Breathtaking, no matter how many times he beheld it. Source of immense pride. And humility.

The driver pulled beside a bronze plaque where a gravel path wandered down through trees.

"An hour should do," Thornton told him, stepping out into sunshine, and the car departed.

Few people visited the chapel these days, the City's famous Tabernacle was the big draw. But the little church was always

Thornton's first choice for prayer and contemplation. And today, he was seeking to bolster his spiritual spine in advance of his Council meeting next week in New York.

Following Reverend Durban's recent visit, Thornton had gotten calls from six of the eleven other Council heads, each insisting that Thornton bring his Shackleton videotape to the meeting. A transparently coordinated effort. All the same, Thornton was considering their demand. While he'd no intention of surrendering the tape, bringing it would at least show respect and goodwill, and hopefully put him on better footing to argue his position.

On the other hand, given the Council's current anxieties, Thornton feared placing the tape within their grasp might prove too tempting. A three-quarters-majority decided matters like this, and Thornton couldn't be sure he had four other votes to prevail. He needed the Lord's guidance.

He traveled down the path to enter dappled shade and the musky-sweet scent of the season. Ahead stood a small, white clapboard chapel, steeple piercing the canopy of orange, red and yellow, and his heart grew heavy. Slowing, he stepped off the path into a hillside cemetery and dropped to a knee beside three stone markers, brushing away leaves to reveal their inscriptions.

Doris Sarah Thornton, 38 years. Paul Penbrook Thornton, 7 years. Sarah Rebecca Thornton, 5 years.

Thornton bowed his head and once again begged absolution from the guilt he carried. Then blotting his eyes with a handkerchief, he rose, returned to the path, and slipped inside the chapel.

It appeared empty as his eyes adjusted to the dark. In shadow, the chapel looked just as it had when first he'd laid eyes on it. A tiny nave, scarcely room for fifty worshipers. Six sets of pews flanking a main aisle. Elevated chancel up front, altar in the center, pulpit to the left, and a few cheap, stained-glass windows. When he'd had it refurbished years ago, he'd left the windows as they were, everything else restored true to the original.

He took a rear pew and sat forward, folding his hands on the backrest before him, resting his forehead on his knuckles. And once again in the sanctity of this place, he thought back to the extraordinary night God led him here out of the storm...

That sacred evening began no differently for him than any other in those days. Twenty-five at the time, Thornton was in his fourth year working the graveyard shift at Whiteville Correctional, a medium-security prison lost midway between Memphis and this chapel. A job Pa had gotten him after Thornton flunked out of State University and slunk home to Union Springs. Pa had been a guard at the prison all his adult life, retiring to pass along his position.

Before Whiteville, Thornton had simply drifted. He'd never really applied himself, school a breeze. Until drugs and booze. While he despised his job as a guard, it was steady income for someone with no prospects. He was barely there a year when Pa passed, leaving behind only medical bills and a broken-down car. Too late, Thornton grasped the totality of his loss. He was alone in the world, no girlfriend, his mother and older sister estranged in Georgia with a stepfather he loathed. And he'd slipped into depression.

His deliverance started with a radio show. *The Gospel Hour.* He'd come across it on his drives to work, a preacher promising peace of mind through God. Having neither a religion nor a plan, Thornton took a chance and ordered the bible on tape. Thereafter, as he walked the prison's perimeter alone each night, he marched to the Word. Quickly he mastered the scripture and ordered more tapes, steadily expanding his theological repertoire, and soon he began spreading the Word to inmates. It was then that God tested his faith.

Late one Saturday night as he was making his rounds between thunderstorms, he came face-to-face with two mud-slathered escapees. All three froze. Thornton stood in the shadow of a large oak, the men in the light of a distant pole lamp. Thornton raised his quaking gun and ordered the men to surrender, but they started for him. Regulations required him to shoot if met with resistance. Nevertheless, the Fifth Commandment flashed into Thornton's mind, and he lowered his weapon. The men brandished shivs, and Thornton was certain he was done for.

But then he touched the cross pin on his lapel, and God stepped in. There came a horrendous boom, Thornton was knocked to his knees, and when finally he braved a glance, the men lay smoldering on the ground, very dead.

He staggered to the warden's office in the throes of an epiphany. No doubt God had spared him for a reason. A holy purpose, yet to be revealed. And whatever it was, Thornton was now blind servant to it. Dumping his gun and badge on the warden's desk, he got in Pa's old car and drove off in a fugue, on and on in driving rain.

How long he wandered the countryside in the dark, he'd no idea. Until at last, lost, exhausted, engine overheating, he arrived at the top of a hill and a dead end. His only shelter was a rundown little chapel, and finding it open and deserted, he curled up in a pew. The next morning, he woke to sun streaming through stained glass, and kindly eyes shining down on him—

A coarse rumble distracted Thornton from his thoughts. The sound came from *inside* the chapel. It stopped. Resumed. Stopped. Resumed.

Snoring.

He wasn't alone after all. Softly he stole down the aisle to come upon a man sprawled in a pew, asleep. The very pew Thornton had taken that night so long ago. A black man, grizzled and tattered, using a hymn book and sock hat for a pillow.

"Hello," Thornton said gently.

One bloodshot eye flickered open and found Thornton. Then the other. The man lurched upright, stammering, "I-I dint break in. Door was open, I swear."

"Of course," Thornton said. "Our doors are always open."

The man frowned. Thornton sat beside him and extended a hand.

"Reverend Penbrook Thornton. Welcome."

The man took the hand tentatively, fingers moist. "Leroy," he said. "Leroy Johnston. You the man on the plaque out front?"

Thornton nodded, detecting the sweet wisp of whiskey, an empty bottle on the floor. "Where you from, friend?"

"Atlanta. Me an' my sons. We hear you got jobs ta offer—a work-trainin' program. We come in last night an' wind up here. Boys gone to town to check things out."

Leaving Dad to sober up.

"What kind of work are you looking for?"

"Anything needs doin', we do it. We do it *good.*"

Thornton rubbed his chin. "You and your boys open to more travel?"

The man blinked. "If it takes us to a payin' job."

"And you're willing to lay off the hooch?"

The man faltered and lowered his eyes. "Yeah…"

There was a place for him and his sons in Thornton's army of swing-state campaigners. Thornton was chronically short on minorities, much needed for ethnic communities. And far be it from him, once a substance abuser himself, to sit in judgment of intemperance. The man would have time enough to dry out while training in the City. No ready access to alcohol.

The sound of a car drifted down from the road. Mark.

Thornton stood. "Tell you what, Mr. Johnston. Let's find your sons, get you all fed, fresh clothes, and a place to stay. Tomorrow, you and your boys can attend services at the Tabernacle, and we'll see about the jobs program."

Brightening, the man grabbed his hat and joined Thornton, gushing thanks. As they headed for the door, the man added, "Mind me askin', Rev'rend—what we be trainin' to do?"

"Ever done door-to-door selling? Much the same. You'll be traveling to another state to help get out the vote for Roger Filby."

The man slowed. "*Filby?* But Johnstons are *Democrats.* We Shackleton men."

Thornton turned to him. "Good wages, room and board for the next three weeks."

The man cocked his head. Then grinning, he replied, "Must say, Rev'rend, you got a pow'ful gift a persuasion."

Thornton grinned back, feeling the spiritual muster he'd come looking for.

CHAPTER 27

Handing Scotty back his wallet, keys, and phone, a detective escorted him to the rear of the police station.

Scotty felt miserable. He'd been held overnight in a tank of drunks and rowdies, little sleep, clothes rumpled and reeking. The authorities hadn't bought his story of prophetic visions. But unable to come up with charges to press, they at last set him free.

The detective let him out a back door, advising, "I'm doing you a favor dodging the crowd out front. Now do *yourself* a favor. Stop taking orders from a damned parakeet!"

And he released him into an alley.

Scotty checked his phone, the battery near dead. A dozen messages from Ivy, now at school. Pop had fetched her when she was released yesterday, grounding her, further penalties pending. She'd called the police station earlier to learn Scotty was being released, fearing it wouldn't be in time for him to buy a Lotto ticket.

No worries, two hours till the noon drawing. Scotty texted her his assurances before his phone gave out, hopped a bus, and worked his weary way toward New Jersey. Several transfers later, he was at a *Stop-n-Save* across state lines, and despite all he'd been through, he remembered the precious numbers. Just enough money for a *Pick5*, a rotisserie dog, and bus fare home. Hopefully, in time for the live drawing, ticket burning in his pocket.

• • •

Scotty reached his final stop with fifteen minutes to spare. Hurrying up the sidewalk, he spied a throng of people in front of his building. Upwards of a hundred, or so. The media must have gotten news of his arrest for the attack on the mayor. This was blowback.

Backpedaling before he was spotted, he headed into the alley behind the building. He saw only indigents back here. One recognized him and waved, but he hadn't a penny left to give. He fled to the rear entrance, fished out his keys, and ducked inside. Glancing at Kassandra's door as he passed, he ran into his apartment, slammed the door and threw the bolt, panting.

His apartment was a mess. The cops had searched it, no doubt. But thankfully his computer was still here.

Homer cried out from under the bed. The poor thing had to be traumatized and starving. Scotty opened the door and called in, "Sorry boy—bear with me, our luck's about to change."

He ran to the window and parted the curtains. From up here, the crowd looked to be in the hundreds. And *damn*—TV crews, too.

Twelve o'clock. Scotty grabbed the remote, switched on the TV, and perched himself on the arm of the couch. Tuning to the lottery, he leaned into the screen and clutched his ticket in both hands, pressing it to his lips like a sacred talisman, feeling the pulse in his fingertips.

Pick5. The moment of truth…

He whispered, "2-7-4-9-6."

The frenzied balls took forever to find slots, each number burning into Scotty's eyes.

2-7-4-9-6

It took a moment to register on him. Then Scotty sprang to his feet dancing in circles, crying, "Holy shit—holy shit—holy shit!"

Homer came out of the bedroom. *How much?*

Scotty didn't know. The TV said to consult the lottery website for details. Fatigue forgotten, Scotty hustled to his computer— only to confront a black screen and another flashing epistle, time-stamped *10:01 AM.*

Herald would have to wait. Opening a browser, Scotty rushed to the lottery site, hardly able to control his fingers. His breath came in gulps as he scrolled:

> Pick5 winning number for today: 2-7-4-9-6
> Jackpot: $351,648

Not millions, but a sizable fortune, all the same. Elated, Scotty scrolled on to read:

> Today's Pick5 total winning tickets: 3

He blinked. Of all the luck. Two other players had picked the same numbers. He'd have to split the pot. Oh well, not like a hundred grand was chump change. Insufficient to see Ivy through a top-tier university, perhaps, but goodbye Bronx Business College!

Homer leaped onto the desk for a look. *You're forgetting taxes.*

Crap. Scotty's accounting background kicked in. The winnings were a *gross* figure. Federal tax bite was 39.6%, New Jersey state tax, 10.8%. He ran the numbers in his head. Bottom line: fifty thousand... Not nearly the thousandfold compensation Herald had promised. All the same, Scotty was grateful, bailed out of disaster.

Homer pawed the monitor screen, and Scotty noticed another complication.

Under a section titled, "How to redeem your winnings," it said the New Jersey Lottery didn't have authority to issue immediate checks to New York residents. Scotty would have to allow three weeks for processing and payment. Three weeks? He couldn't afford a day's delay.

Maybe you can get a loan. You know, use the ticket for collateral.

Was that even possible? But yes, a Google search uncovered a consumer-lending source nearby that offered short-term loans against winning tickets. No doubt at predatory rates, but what choice did he have? Regardless, thanks to the Lord, Ivy's future was looking *much* brighter.

He turned next to Herald's new epistle. With his winnings, Scotty imagined the Lord would expect more of him. But Scotty had neither the heart nor energy to take on a new assignment. Expecting another problematic prophecy, he was surprised to see:

> that you may believe and obey the lord
> this afternoon shall I reveal myself to you
> for no mans eyes save yours

Scotty rocked back in his chair. Herald had granted his request to show himself!

As the realization settled over him, the quiet in his apartment loomed large, eerier for the murmur of the crowd outside. If Herald were true to form, in less than two hours Scotty would be face-to-face with the supernatural.

There came a soft tapping at his door, and Scotty froze. Herald hadn't specified exactly *when* or *how* he'd make his appearance. Scotty had simply presumed online at 2:00.

The tapping came again. Tensing, Scotty tiptoed to the peephole, squinting out into distended eyes framed by wire-rimmed glasses.

"Scotty, are you there?" Mrs. Steiner called. "I thought I heard you come in."

Scotty let out his breath and ushered her inside, scolding, "You shouldn't be climbing the stairs with your knees."

"We've all been so worried," she said, eyes fretting. She carried a newspaper and a plate of cookies. "I called the police station to learn they released you and Ivy. How is she?"

"We're both fine," he said. "Case of mistaken identity. It's straightened out now."

"I'm so relieved." She handed him the cookies, keeping the paper. Her eyes narrowed to take him in. "You poor thing, you look terrible."

He set the plate on his desk and led her to the couch. She seldom ventured upstairs, not having seen his apartment since it was trashed, and her frown deepened as she glanced around.

"Good Lord," she said, taking a seat, "the police did this? I'm so sorry for all your troubles."

"A string of bad luck," he said, then added with a genuine smile, "But trust me, things are looking up." He wasn't ready to mention the lottery yet.

"Well, you've surely been good luck for the people you've helped," she told him, handing him the newspaper. "I never took you for the religious type."

Scotty saw an article on the bottom half of the day's front page. It featured a blurry close-up of his face culled from that ubiquitous ballpark video. He opened to the headline above the fold:

Yankee Stadium 'Guardian Angel' Saves Mayor
QUEENS MAN CLAIMS TO COMMUNE WITH GOD

Feeling the blood drain from his face, he read on, distraught to see his full name revealed. NYPD must have released it. The article glossed over his arrest, depicting him as some sort of spiritual seer.

Mrs. Steiner nodded toward the window. "They began gathering early this morning. We told them you weren't here, but they won't go. They think you're a holy man."

Scotty sank to the couch. "And the rest of the city thinks I'm a madman."

She patted his hand. "You're a hero to me. I'm so proud. They say God speaks to you. Is that how you know these amazing things?"

He didn't want her thinking him nuts, too. Nor did he intend to draw anyone else into his mess the way he had Ivy. "I'm sorry," he said, "I can't talk about it."

Her eyes turned watery, and Scotty feared he'd upset her. She conjured a handkerchief from a sleeve, sneezed, and blew her nose, and Scotty realized. *Cat dander.*

She said, "I never had much use for religion, but if you've found a way to make good of it, more power to you. I just want you to know, if you need someone to talk to besides God, I'm always here for you. And now," she paused to wipe her eyes, "I'm afraid I have to go."

Scotty thanked her, helped her to her feet, and walked her out into the hall and downstairs. Stopping at the bottom for fear someone outside might spot him through the foyer, he gave her a hug, waited till she was inside her apartment, crept to the rear exit, and slipped out.

An hour later he returned the way he'd left, having secured an advance on his winnings—at an outrageous rate. And settling in, he awaited an appearance from the mysterious Paraclete.

CHAPTER 28

Ivy leaped from the bus with her backpack, racing up the sidewalk toward her brother's apartment, unable to contain herself. Scotty's luck had finally turned. A trifecta. His texts said he'd been released from jail, won the lottery, and Herald had agreed to show himself!

How many millions he'd won, he hadn't said, but Ivy ditched her last class, Pop be damned. She was coming to surprise Scotty, and hopefully in time to see Herald, too.

As she neared the apartment building, she braked. Hundreds of people glutted the street, including media with TV cameras.

"What's going on?" she asked a bystander.

The man held a sign reading, *Matt 15:30.* "We're here for the Prophet," he told her.

She saw people in wheelchairs and on crutches, others carrying children with afflictions.

Frantically she dialed Scotty. No answer. How would she get past this mob?

• • •

Scotty paced his living room, seconds wearing slowly off the clock.

The idea of meeting a supernatural being terrified him. Especially after it dawned on him, he couldn't be certain *which* side of the spiritual divide Herald hailed from. Scotty had just reviewed all the epistles he'd been sent, only to realize that Herald had never actually declared himself an angel. A "Paraclete" was simply an "intercessor." In fact, Herald never once referred to his Lord as "God." And thinking back to when all this began, Scotty recalled being convinced he was dealing with an evil spirit.

Okay, yes, the Lord's prophecies had all borne out, just like prophecies in the bible stories Mom used to read him. But as Scotty was aware from the same bible, evil forces *also* possessed prophetic powers. In the Acts of the Apostles, St. Paul confronted a woman who predicted the future—till Paul drove a demon out of her. And even now, nothing Scotty had experienced so far presented clear evidence Herald and his Lord were heaven-sent.

He watched Homer slink off to the bedroom. Had the cat sensed something? The knot in Scotty's gut tightened. Would Herald appear on screen or in person? He paced, growing queasier with each step.

At last, the thunder growled, and Scotty jumped. He crept to his computer as if it were booby-trapped, seeing the videochat up and running like he'd left it, video-capture on to record all.

He sat, his insides coiled like a spring for the eternity it took the whine to come and go. Then the screen erupted in a blizzard of distortion, and he jumped again. The picture struggled to resolve, the transmission from the other side too brilliant. But quickly it adjusted and a hint of something began to organize in the chaos.

An iridescent shape. Head, upper torso. Humanoid. And then it materialized fully.

"*Oh my God,*" Scotty gasped.

A divine creature, without question. Radiant. Magnificent. Angelic. Sublime beyond anything Scotty had ever beheld. Unlike anything he'd dared imagine…

. . .

Ivy headed up the alley behind Scotty's building, making for the rear door. No key, she tried Scotty's phone again. It went to voice-mail again. She began pounding.

At length, a dark-haired woman with a wailing infant opened the door, glaring. "*¿Qué?*"

"Sorry, emergency," Ivy muttered, bolting by, sprinting upstairs.

Scotty was slow to answer her thumping. And when he did, Ivy gasped. He was pale and sweaty, eyes wide and unseeing, lips quivering dumbly.

She cried, "Oh my God, oh my God—*Herald appeared?*"

Scotty nodded and Ivy whooped, slamming the door, brushing past. The room was a mess. The clock on the desk read *10:07.*

"Online?" she asked.

Again he nodded, and she rushed to his computer, crushed to see a blank videochat window.

"*Oh no,* I missed it?"

Scotty drifted over, and she grabbed his arms. They hung lifeless. He gaped as if in a trance.

Finally, his lips formed words, a soft whisper. "Herald is the real deal all right. But *not* what we thought."

Ivy couldn't control her excitement. "You taped the videochat on your computer, yes?"

"Assuming spirits can be recorded. But I was warned, it's for my eyes only."

"Oh no. Herald owes me, I got busted, too. We won't tell him."

Scotty looked conflicted. Ivy could see he longed to share what he'd seen, and pulling him to his computer, she drew up a chair next to his. He still seemed uncertain. She continued to prod, and at last he exhaled, cued the video, and she leaned in for her first view of the cryptic Paraclete.

Too bright at first, and she squinted. But quickly an image began to coalesce. Like a star congealing out of hot gasses. Human—head, face, shoulders. Yet unlike any human Ivy had ever seen. Surreal. Ethereal. Surely not of this world.

"*Oh my God,*" she breathed. No question, an angelic creature. Stunning beyond anything Ivy had anticipated—albeit, she hadn't known what to expect. More confused than ever, she whispered "*This is Herald?*"

Scotty didn't answer. Ivy shot him a glance, hardly able to take her eyes off the screen. He appeared glazed-over again.

The vision was surreal, but one thing was clear. Herald was *not* male. Visible from the torso up, the Paraclete was a female of extraordinary grace and beauty. Young, with a glowing complexion. *Literally.* Skin radiant, luminous. So pale it was hard to distinguish her features. Hair white gold, woven into braids, wound ornately atop her head. Breasts full and nested in a gleaming white tunic.

But by far the most distinguishing characteristic, *her eyes.* Unlike any Ivy had ever seen. Vibrant silver jewels, penetrating to the soul. The woman sat amid dazzling cloud, appearing shy. Perhaps not used to mortals.

Ivy was spellbound, hearing Scotty's voice on the video say, "*I-I-I, I don't understand. You are Herald?*"

The woman responded in a soft lilt as sweet as her face. "*I am a herald of the Lord.*" Ivy detected a mild drawl. Angels had accents? "*I bear His tidings.*"

Scotty said, "*Why me? I don't want any tidings, I've got problems enough.*"

"*The Lord has His purpose.*"

The woman lowered her eyes, and the sound of her delivery changed, turning eerily wooden.

"*The Lord thanks you for the work you've performed and the sacrifices you've endured on His behalf. You are being prepared for a special role in a Divine Plan. Complete the Missions the Lord assigns you to His satisfaction, and you will be greatly blessed.*"

She looked up. "*I am now sending you instructions for your next undertaking. In the future, we will communicate only in writing."*

Scotty blurted, *"The Lord's messages are too confusing. If you want my help, we have to talk face-to-face. I insist."*

Ivy was surprised at Scotty's pluck. The angel seemed surprised, too. She turned away as if searching for a response, then back. *"Did you just receive my instructions? Are they not clear?"*

There was a pause, and Ivy assumed Scotty was reading. Then she heard him moan, *"A tornado? Oh my God—wh-what do I do?"*

"It's all there. Go to those in the media who made public your previous deeds. They know you speak truth. Rely on them to spread the word."

"But the Lord's the Lord. He can just stop the tornado Himself."

"That's not His way. You must not question."

Scotty sputtered and dithered, and the angel said, *"I must go."*

"But what if I have more questions?"

The video ended abruptly in a black screen.

Ivy sat stunned, heart beating wildly. She turned to stare at Scotty. "Isn't it possible to create special effects like these on a computer?" she asked. "Make someone *look* angelic?"

He exhaled slowly. "It's not just her looks that make her credible. It's her prophecies. There's no computer in the world that can predict the things she does."

Ivy couldn't dispute that. "My God, we're talking to *an angel*. A real, *living* angel!"

"Assuming she's alive—in the conventional sense."

Now Ivy felt glazed. She'd never actually believed in God, much less angels.

Scotty added, "She says a tornado's coming. I'm supposed to warn people. But how? Who'll believe me?" He showed Ivy the instructions the angel had sent. "The tornado's not striking here, it's Jasper, Georgia, wherever that is. At exactly thirty-three minutes past the 20th hour. 8:33 *tonight*." He called up Google Maps on screen. "A little town north of Atlanta."

"We've time to get a warning out on the six o'clock news."

"So what do I do? Ring the doorbell at a TV station and yell 'tornado?'"

Ivy pulled out a business card she'd received yesterday in an elevator at the police station.

"I've got a better idea…"

PART TWO

CHAPTER 29

Ariel Silva and Maxwell Bach paid heavyhearted farewells to their colleagues, carrying the last of their office belongings into the elevator. As they traveled down the control tower, they looked out through glass walls upon the valley they'd come to know so well. A magnificent view of endless cornfields abutting forested foothills and mountains sprinkled with early autumn. The old farmhouse was visible a few miles off.

But as they descended, a less-peaceful scene came into view.

At the edge of the parking lot stood thousands of angry protesters, restrained by a perimeter fence topped with razor wire. Behind them in a field were cars, tents, RVs, and TV trucks. More vehicles streamed in to choke the lone access road.

The protesters shook signs and yelled through the chain-link at a dozen fidgety security guards whose only weapons were tasers and liquid mace. With the collider's inaugural run set to begin in less than an hour, the situation was sure to deteriorate.

The cause of the unrest lay two-hundred feet below the surface. A hundred-mile halo of mega-electromagnetic tunnel, circling off to the southeastern horizon and back, to meet itself directly beneath the tower. A new-generation synchrotron supercollider, vastly more powerful than any ever, about to undergo its maiden run—to the objections of demonstrators here and across the country.

Ariel had good reason to be afraid. On their way in this morning, crossing the picket line in Max's vintage Mercedes, they'd faced a barrage of swearing, spitting, banging, and kicking. And no sooner had the guards squeaked them through the gate than Max leaped out of the car to curse the crowd, nearly causing a riot. No doubt the protesters hadn't forgotten.

They exited the elevator at ground level, and Ariel begged Max, "Let's wait for the state troopers."

They'd heard the governor had called for reinforcements.

Max snorted. "The troopers hate us worse than the Dark Agers."

He piled their things in the back seat, they jumped in the car, locked the doors, and headed for the gate. The mob spotted them, howling, rattling the fence, and the captain of security ran over. Max stopped and dropped his window.

"You got a death wish?" the captain cried, wiping his brow. "Sit tight, help's coming."

"No, it's not," Max shouted back. "And the longer we wait, the worse it'll get."

Ariel said nothing, petrified.

The man swore. "For all your brains, you ain't got a lick a sense."

"Open, or I'll do it myself," Max threatened, shutting the window, gunning the engine.

The captain swore and returned to his men. An argument ensued, but finally he stepped to the gate and ordered the crowd back. It didn't budge. He punched numbers into a keypad, his men moved up raising their puny weapons, the gate shuddered and rolled aside, and Max pushed out into the fray. Ariel shrank in her seat, quaking. Once Max cleared the gate, it shut, and the crowd swarmed the car, screaming, thrusting signs at them that read:

TALAWANDA — Last stop at the end of the world

Doomsday Machine

Luke 23:34

A hulking, red-bearded man in a red-plaid shirt with cut-off sleeves pressed against Ariel's window. She recognized him, a fixture here these last weeks. His arms bore Celtic tattoos, his pale eyes fierce with hate, thick lips in a snarl. She cringed closer to Max.

The man spit, *"Deliver us from Evil."*

Max leaned across Ariel to shout back, "Wanna escape the black hole? *Get your head outta your ass."*

The man went livid, and Ariel felt faint. Had Max skipped his Valpro today? She tried to push him back to the wheel, his shoulder rigid as a gnarl of wood.

"Please," she cried.

Max straightened and budged them ahead, and Ariel watched the red-bearded man recede. He targeted her with his finger like a pistol.

The past days had been tense, but the crowd was never this large or ugly, emotions peaking with the Big Moment at hand. A moment physicists the world over had awaited for the decade it took to construct the massive collider. A moment Ariel, Max, and their roommates had devoted their souls to since taking research positions here three years ago. And now, sadly, would miss.

They cleared the melee at last, and Ariel released her breath, turning to ensure they weren't followed, bidding her career goodbye. She stared misty-eyed past the control tower to the valley beyond. No hint of the vast machinery underground, the extraordinary event about to take place.

The Talawanda Particle Collider promised to unlock secrets of the universe. But opposition had sprung up in the past year over fears it would spawn a catastrophe—a black hole to swallow the Earth. Baseless fears stoked by a right-wing political movement calling itself the "New Enlightenment." Ariel and colleagues knew them better as "Dark Agers," a mixed bag of anti-science, anti-intellectuals intent on plunging the nation into a black hole of a different kind.

Max swung onto the highway, accelerating past fields of blanched cornstalks.

"Slow down," Ariel reminded. State troopers liked to sidle up in the rows and lay for TPC workers. Max had gotten tickets before.

"Deliver *us* from Evil," he bellowed, backing off the gas.

In fact, Max had already found his deliverance. No sooner had he gotten his notice than he'd nabbed a comparable position at another collider in Europe, where the environment was less hostile to science. No such luck for Ariel and their roommates, Tia Diego and Stanley Bronkowski, who were pursuing their careers stateside. With the cutbacks in federal funding, the field of quantum physics offered dismal prospects. TPC would have been shut down entirely if not for international agreements made long ago.

Though the four were invited to attend today's inaugural run, they'd declined in a protest of their own, too upset to taste the fruits of their labors only to leave them behind. This morning while Tia and Stan packed up the house, Max and Ariel had tackled their offices. Tomorrow they'd go their separate ways.

A few miles later, not far from the town of Talawanda, Max turned into a gravel drive marked by a rusted mailbox and "for rent/sale" sign. Sixty feet back from the road sat a one-story frame farmhouse, white paint yellowed and peeling. Behind was a barn and open pasture. A sheep ranch before the economy tanked.

There was a large oak in the front yard. Past that, a doghouse. And tethered to the doghouse, Newton, the piebald mutt Ariel had adopted soon after moving here. He spotted her and his tail went like a windshield wiper. It gave her a needed lift.

Max parked behind four u-haul trailers and exited, leading Ariel past stacks of boxes and furniture to where Tia and Stan were ferrying a table from the porch.

At the sight of Tia, Ariel's eyes welled again. The little big sister she'd never had, and would miss most. Second-generation Ecuadoran, five-two (in heels), olive skin, dark eyes, chopped hair with pink highlights. If not for Tia, Ariel would have been lost her first year here, and likely never would have found herself.

Stan, she loved like an eccentric big brother. Tall, thin, disheveled brown hair. Easy-going, and a marvelous mind. But watching him navigate the steps with Tia and table was a fright—all elbows and knees, wire-rim glasses migrated to the tip of his beaked nose.

"Hey-o," he puffed, looking up. "How'd it go?"

"Ugly," Max said, taking over for Tia. "Barbarians at the gates."

Stan loathed the Dark Agers as much as Max, if less vocal about it. But Tia's hatred burned hottest of all. She'd recently had a scrape in town, narrowly escaping, still raw from it.

"Assholes," she snapped in her elfish voice.

The men set the table by other furniture and followed the women inside to finish packing, everyone to their respective bedrooms. Ariel's was at the back left corner. One window looked out onto the drive, the other across rolling pasture and hills to the north. An idyllic vista familiar to her as the face of an old friend, far removed from the Stepford Wives community of her upbringing. All that remained in her room was her bed, some overnight essentials, and a few boxes of books and clothing. The rest sat outside by her trailer, ready to load.

Inhaling, she grabbed a box and carried it down the hall, her thoughts turning to the long drive ahead. At least she'd have Newton for company. But as she pushed open the porch door, heading down the steps, she heard him yelping and lurching against his chain. She hadn't given him much attention lately with all the hubbub.

Max's voice carried out a window, "Shut that damned dog up!"

Ariel grumbled and detoured for Newton—only to brake, overcome by a strange sensation. Head spinning, she lost hold of the box and sent it and books cartwheeling across the lawn.

The spell passed as quickly as it came, and Ariel checked her phone. 10:00 AM.

The collider?

Unlikely. While TPC was by far the largest, most complex machine ever built, it was also engineered to run without detection. On the other hand, the trials this weekend were to work out bugs.

Ariel looked past the oak to the tower in the distance, picturing the sequence of events now underway. Her former colleagues would be at their stations, riveted to their instruments. While in the valley beyond, deep underground, opposing streams of hadron particles would be gathering momentum along a hundred-mile loop of massive, donut-shaped, superconducting magnets.

At its heart, TPC was a generator. The most powerful in the world. Designed to produce a staggering 10,000 megawatts, it would accelerate quantum particle streams to a velocity never before achieved. Virtual light speed.

If the test runs went well, Monday would begin the experiments Ariel and friends had worked toward so long and hard. The streams would be pushed to their limits, whizzing by in opposite directions until, at peak speed, they'd be diverted into a collision chamber and a tiny ball of antimatter plasma ten-times hotter than the sun. A head-on crash to create a micro explosion unlike the universe had seen since the Big Bang.

"Goddammit," Max barked, louder than Newton.

Ariel left the books on the lawn and hurried for the dog. Only to pull up once more, startled by a loud rumble. Thunder. Yet, not a cloud in the sky. Like the bellow of some cosmic behemoth.

The hairs on her arms rose, and she felt queasy. The thunder warbled into a piercing whine, driving Newton nuts. But *silently.* Ariel watched amazed to see the dog's mouth move without sound, as if she'd pressed a mute button. And from where she now stood, she could see it wasn't the tree he was fixating on, but an indeterminate spot midpoint, as if he were challenging some invisible foe.

No, *not* invisible…

The whine ebbed and Ariel froze. To her horror, something was materializing midair in front of her. A rippling, swirling, transparent distortion. It darkened into a maelstrom of cloud, hovering chest-high, the size of a large pizza.

Ariel gasped and sank to her knees. *The protesters were right.* Impossible, but there it was. In an instant, it would suck her, Newton, friends and all else into oblivion.

And yet, it *didn't.* The longest moment of her life. Then abruptly the specter shrank and vanished, the whine returned and segued back to thunder, the thunder subsided, and everything was as before.

Ariel collapsed on her haunches, shaking. She could hear Newton again, whimpering, chain rustling as he retreated into his house.

Behind her, a screen door banged, she heard footsteps, and Max called out, "You okay?" He appeared at her side. "What happened, you're white as a ghost."

This was no time to poke fun at her complexion. She stammered, "Y-you heard. You saw."

"What?"

"A, a *singularity.* Here in the yard, right in front of me."

The screen door banged again, and Tia called, "What's wrong?"

Max shouted back, "She fainted."

"I *didn't* faint," Ariel cried.

Tia and Stan ran to her, and Ariel pointed a shaky finger. "There, twenty feet from the tree, a spatial disturbance of some kind. And thunder. And high-pitched humming. The collider."

Stan checked his watch. "Time's right, assuming the run went off on schedule."

Max exhaled, looking to Stan. "I didn't hear anything, did you?"

Stan shook his head, and Tia said, "If Ariel says it happened, *it happened.*"

She patted Ariel's arm. "What did it look like?"

"A whirlpool of black cloud, a meter wide. Only lasted a minute."

Tia and Stan looked puzzled, and Max said, "I know what you're thinking, but whatever it was, it was *no* black hole. We wouldn't be here to talk about it."

Stan suggested, "If the collider's electromagnets are out of sync, and the beam went off track, it could have caused a spatial displacement of some kind. A phase-locked loop, maybe."

Ariel knew there were quirks of electromagnetism that could create distortions far removed from the energy that produced it. "But it changed," she said. "It started as waves in the air, then darkened into a vortex."

Tia offered, "Refracted by moisture in the atmosphere. Like a rainbow, only dark."

Ariel shook her head. "How do you explain the noise?"

"The beam splitting the air," Max said. "Same way lightning causes thunder."

"Then why didn't *you* hear it? You heard Newton. This was *much* louder."

No one had an answer.

Tia and Stan helped her up, steadying her.

Max said, "LHC had e-mag problems at startup, too," referring to the Large Hadron Collider in Geneva, an accelerator distantly second to TPC in size and power. He should know, that's where his new job was taking him. "No big deal."

Ariel pulled free. *"No big deal?* What if it hit Newton? Or me? And what about tomorrow when they go *full* speed? We've got to warn Keller."

Winston Keller, the director of TPC operations.

Max shook his head. "If it's an alignment issue, they've already caught it."

"That doesn't mean they'd detect a singularity," Ariel replied.

Singularity. A point in spacetime where intense gravitational forces distort both space and time—such as in the formation of a black hole. A phenomenon for which, so far, science had no understanding, no mathematical model to explain it. Whatever it was Ariel saw, it was exactly how she pictured a singularity.

"...TPC isn't looking for a singularity. Did LHC's problem create a spatial displacement?"

"Not to my knowledge," Max told her.

Tia said, "LHC is in the middle of nowhere, like us. If it caused a displacement, what are the odds anyone would have seen?"

Ariel whipped out her cell and began punching in text.

Before she could finish, Max snatched it, read it, and fumed, "You can't say that! Keller will have to report it to the NRC. There'll be an investigation, it could set things back months."

NRC. The Nuclear Regulatory Commission, responsible for licensing and overseeing TPC.

Ariel could barely control herself. "How petty of me—we're only talking a *black hole*."

"And I'm telling you, *it's no black hole*. You know the physics."

Tia ran fingers through her ragged pink hair. "No, *mi corazón*," she explained to Ariel softly, "it can't be a black hole. Even a hint would've been the end of us."

Ariel weighed her friends' opinions against what she'd seen. Her knowledge of particle physics paled by comparison, and in truth, what she did know argued against a singularity. But of one thing she was certain, something the others could not dispute: "The universe has a nasty habit of overturning conventional wisdom."

Stan took a long breath. "How about this? We stick around for tomorrow's run. If the anomaly repeats, we call it in before we go."

There was no pressing reason they couldn't stay another night, other than late fees on their u-hauls. Issue settled, they helped gather up Ariel's books.

Max advised, "Load everything into the trailers but your beds and necessaries, and we'll take care of the rest after tomorrow's run." He raised a brow at Ariel. "Barring doomsday."

His snark did nothing to diminish the darkness whirling in Ariel's head. Nor did it help when Stan called TPC to learn that today's test had gone off without a hitch.

CHAPTER 30

That night, Ariel and friends gathered in the living room on the floor eating takeout, watching the TV Max had dragged in from his trailer.

The demonstration at TPC was the big story on every news channel, which Max confirmed by chasing the coverage around the dial. Multiple times and from various angles, Ariel watched their car exit the gate into the thick of picketers. Eventually, state troopers did arrive, but did nothing other than observe. According to the news, TPC personnel were overnighting at the complex. Apparently, they'd also seen the video of Ariel and Max's precarious escape.

Max settled on a channel airing a live shot of the compound and crowd, cornfields sprawled with campers, RVs, and tents. TPC's tower glowed eerily in the twilight sky behind. A portable stage was set up in a field near the fence—a flatbed trailer under pole lights with a miked podium and row of chairs. The camera zoomed in on a man in bib overalls at the podium. Below and in front of him, supporters shouted and waved placards heralding Judgment Day.

Max sneered, "They'll be so bummed when the world doesn't end."

The camera panned the crowd, and Ariel saw signs denouncing science as the archenemy of religion and family values. Other signs promoted Dark-Age politicians like Republican Roger Filby, his slogan: *The Right Way to Prosperity*.

Ariel wondered, "Has Filby come out against the collider now, too?" She'd only known him to dance around science issues, avoiding controversies like climate-change by acknowledging the evidence, rejecting human cause.

"He won't risk it with the race so tight," Max replied. "It would cost him Independents. Independents aren't stupid, they support research."

Stan said, "The latest InstaPolls show TPC losing ground with Independents, too. All the fear-mongering and fake news is getting to people, even those who should know better."

The picture changed to a newswoman strolling among the campers. Ariel was surprised at the gamut of people on hand. From the well-dressed and kempt, to rough and scruffy and in between.

"I'd sooner watch football," Tia said, grabbing the remote from Max.

"Know thine enemy, " Max said, snatching it back.

The reporter approached a man spreading a bedroll in the back of a pickup, its bumper plastered with stickers. Noticing the lights, he turned. Early sixties, gray hair, a T-shirt reading:

> *"Research is what I do*
> *when I don't know*
> *what I'm doing."*
> —Wernher Von Braun

Tia snarled, *"Fool.* It means the *opposite* of what you think."

Ariel recalled that back in the days when John Kennedy was president and science mattered, rocket scientist Von Braun had pioneered the U.S. space program. He'd overcome seemingly insurmountable obstacles to land man on the moon.

The reporter called up to the protester in the truck, *"Nice night for sleeping out. Think this endless summer has anything to do with rising greenhouse gases?"*

Her crew extended a mike to the man, and he said, *"Let me clue you, lady. Science has two ways to fund itself. Either it scares up money with manufactured threats, like global warming, or it suckers you into boondoggles, like colliders promising secrets of the universe. That's how science survives, feeding off fears and dreams."*

The woman asked, *"Secrets of the universe aren't important?"*

He hooked a thumb at TPC's control tower. *"There's only one thing those bozos will discover, and it's no secret. Once they run through the billions it'll cost us, they'll decide they need a bigger smasher."* And waving her off, he went back to his business.

The reporter moved on to a group of twenty-somethings seated in front of a canopy tent. Across the front of the tent hung a banner displaying a black-and-white photo. Ariel recognized the face of the iconic female robot from the silent movie *Metropolis*. Encircling the face was an orange ring with a diagonal line struck through, and beneath that, in black and orange letters:

R.U.S.T.
Rescue Us from Science & Technology
www.r.u.s.t.com

Among the group was a bearded man in jeans plucking a guitar and singing, *"The future's here, and we're all screwed, mad cows and Frankenfood—"*

He halted at the sight of the cameras, and next to him, a slender woman rose. The reporter asked her, *"Can you tell our viewers what RUST is about?"*

The woman tossed back long brown hair to reveal the robot icon on her T-shirt. She replied, *"Science and technology are out of control, fouling the planet. We're drawing the line here."*

The reporter pressed, *"Throw out science, baby and bath?"*

"Not all *science. Science isn't evil, per se, but many of its creations are. They poison us—industrial wastes, pesticides, opioids."*

It seemed Dark Agers weren't the homogeneous movement Ariel had always thought, united instead by their various hostilities to science. Max was right. *Know thine enemy.* All the same, Max had had his fill. He changed to another news channel where a host was interviewing a physicist from the World Union of Concerned Scientists. Indeed, the physicist looked concerned.

"Science is in crisis," he was saying. *"Industries lobby the government to ignore and defund research that runs counter to their interests. PACs spend fortunes to discredit our results. The religious right preaches pseudoscience. They bury the truth under so much disinformation and ignorance, it's suffocating the planet."*

Ariel had had her fill, too. Wrapping up the rest of her sandwich for Newton, she excused herself and went outside.

CHAPTER 31

Frantic, Ariel held onto Newton, Max onto her, Stan onto him, Tia onto Stan, all clinging together in a desperate chain against the vacuum of roaring vortex—

Ariel bolted upright to find her bedclothes soaked with sweat. It had been like this all night. She blinked away the cobwebs to see the sun well up, but the clock on her phone assured her she hadn't missed today's run. Inhaling, she rose to notice Stan and Tia through the window tying down items in their trailers. No sign of Max, his trailer closed up, car gone.

Opening the sash, she poked her head out on another warm day.

"Morning," Stan hailed, and Tia waved.

"Where's Max?" Ariel asked.

"In town, gassing up. He's bringing breakfast."

Of course. Max wanted to hit the road running soon as he disabused Ariel of her singularity.

Like Stan and Tia, Max was a senior-level systems analyst with a post-grad degree—a slightly higher pay grade than Ariel's position as a junior computational researcher. Before being laid off, he'd been up for a prestigious promotion as TPC's public spokesperson/press liaison. An even higher-salaried position, and Max was especially bitter to have lost that opportunity. Now he'd be off to Boston to stay at his brother's before departing to Geneva, end of the month.

Stan was headed to Stanford, hoping for a teaching assistant position to open. While he could write his own ticket at the NSA if he wanted, having worked there straight out of grad school, he'd soured on government service. As he'd put it, "The bureaucracy has no soul."

Tia would be staying with an aunt in Omaha pending an iffy relationship with a ConAgra biologist there, and fellowship applications elsewhere. Her dad had disappeared long ago. Tough times awaited her, Ariel knew. Ariel had accompanied her to her mom's funeral two years ago—estranged sisters, lots of tears and drama. Still, Ariel regretted being an only child.

And as for her, Ariel was going to a wastewater treatment plant in Toledo as a chemical analyst. A far cry from her current position. As Max put it, "A shit job."

Stan called out to her again, "What say we get your bed apart?"

"Fifteen minutes," she told him, ducking back inside.

She showered and went through her daily regimen: contacts, light makeup, sunscreen. Ariel hated sunscreen, but not as badly as makeup. Makeup made her feel dishonest, somehow. Nor did she like the interest it drew her from strange men. But as Tia always counseled, "Think of makeup as sunscreen that protects you from the way things used to be." Ariel donned a top, shorts, ball cap and sunglasses, stepped into flip-flops, and headed for the hall.

Her footsteps echoed in a house now bare of all that had made it home these past three-and-a half years. The only real home Ariel had known since childhood. Its emptiness pulled at her as she passed through. She'd be leaving with little more of material value than when she'd arrived. No savings from her meager pay, and for all practical purposes in these troubled times, no marketable skills.

Yet, she would take away something priceless. Her time here had transformed her. Former classmates at UPenn who recalled the pale, meek geek at the back of lecture halls, if in fact anyone had ever noticed, wouldn't recognize her now. Thanks to Tia, Ariel had undergone a metamorphosis. Appearance, attitude, social acumen. Not forgetting her proudest accomplishment, seeing her work respected by the TPC community.

All the same, it was intimidating to face life alone again. Ariel's previous moves, including from college to TPC, had always been from one structured environment to another. She'd never actually been on her own, and feared she wasn't ready. As Tia always said, growth is a lifelong process, and Ariel had gotten a very late start.

Wiping her eyes, she collected herself. Sniveling wasn't how she wanted her friends to remember her.

• • •

Tia heard the screen door slam, and Stan called up to her in the trailer, "You and Ariel can take it from here, I'll dismantle her bed."

"Check," Tia said, going to the tailgate to see Ariel high-five Stan as their paths crossed. Ariel looked stunning in a yellow tank top and cut-offs, her ivory arms and legs gleaming in the sun, hair shoulder-length and shining white-gold. She'd once been modest to the extreme, refusing to appear in less than baggy blouses and ankle-length skirts. "Christian burkas," Max called them. Now she faced the world as the radiant young woman she truly was.

But as Ariel neared, Tia saw redness in her eyes, and retreated into the shadows. She didn't trust herself. Ariel would need strength as they cut the cord, and Tia had to buck up. She called out, "Put your shoulder to that headboard, will you?"

Ariel heaved, and Tia took up slack in the rope and tied off.

Leaving was hard on both of them, but it came not a moment too soon for Ariel. Even if the girl couldn't see it yet, it was time to fly the nest before Max clipped her wings again.

"Done," Tia said. And composure regained, she hopped from the trailer, rolled the tailgate shut, and brushed herself off.

Ariel asked, "Any word on your fellowships?"

Tia avoided her eyes. "Those wheels grind slow, you know."

After receiving notice from TPC, Tia had sent proposals to MIT, her alma mater, and to other big science schools. But with endowments drying up, it was a tough sell.

She asked Ariel, "How about you? When do you start?"

"Soon as I get there. Sallie Mae's on my case."

Speaking of slow grinds. Ariel had gone to college on a partial scholarship, making up the difference with loans and working part time. Her parents wouldn't help, all but disowning her. Tia and the others were more fortunate—especially Max, who came from Old Boston money.

Ariel said, "Don't worry. With your qualifications, something good will turn up."

Tia said nothing.

Stan was ready with Ariel's bed, and as they helped him lug out the mattress, Ariel raised the question Tia and Stan had been mulling all morning.

"If the electromagnets weren't out of alignment, what the heck caused what I saw?"

Tia nodded toward TPC. "The collision chamber is less than three miles away."

Ariel turned toward the tower in the distance. The collision chamber lay directly beneath it, far underground.

"Sometimes during runs," Tia told her, "colliders encounter tiny leaks in the beams as they whiz past the collision chamber."

Stan added, "They're usually of no consequence. But they *can* throw off a radiation cone."

Radiation cone: a concentrated beam of energy, like a magnifying glass focusing sunlight.

"...The farmhouse sits square in the cone zone, and we think that's what you experienced yesterday. A cone distorted the atmosphere in front of you, causing the noises you heard."

Ariel pulled up, bringing everyone to a stumbling halt.

"Radiation?" Her pale cheeks went rosy. *"Ionized* radiation?"

There were many types of radiation spanning the vast electromagnetic spectrum. From harmless non-iodized varieties—radio waves, light waves, ultraviolet waves—to increasingly lethal frequencies, such as x-rays and gamma rays. *Ionized* radiation.

"No-no," Stan assured. *"Non*-iodized. Entirely safe."

Ariel did not appear convinced, and he added, "Trust me, we've no risk of getting *Curiéd.*"

Tia winced to recall the fate of famed radiology pioneer, Madame Marie Curie. Her unwitting exposure to X-rays had resulted in fatal aplastic anemia. Ariel also caught the reference, face souring.

They got back to work.

"Whatever happened here yesterday," Tia said as they loaded the mattress, "I agree, it poses no threat. Surely no black hole. But I'd like to see for myself."

She nevertheless doubted the situation would repeat. Too many variables. And best it didn't, it would only prolong their farewell.

Tia stole a look at Ariel. After all this time, Tia still bristled to know the torment the poor girl once endured over her appearance. A victim of ignorance, superstition, and unusual genetics. Before Ariel's makeover, people regularly mistook her for an albino. In fact, she was *leucistic.* An even rarer condition. The distinction, Tia came to learn, was that leucistics weren't entirely devoid of melanin, the pigment responsible for skin and hair color. Ariel's complexion beneath her makeup wasn't pink, it was very pale. Lustrous, in fact, like fine alabaster. And her hair, brows and lashes weren't white, but platinum.

But her most remarkable feature, now hidden by blue contacts, were her eyes. Listed on her driver's license as blue, they were actually a radiant bluish silver. Unlike anything Tia had ever seen. Mesmerizing. Yet sadly, in the view of some, ominous and disturbing.

Tia's thoughts drifted back to when first she met Ariel, late spring three years ago…

New to TPC at the time, Tia had stuck her neck out to lease the farmhouse on her own. She was pressed to find roommates, trolling TPC's website for prospects, and had attracted two fellow new-hires, Stan and Max, but needed a fourth to meet rent.

At last, another response straggled in, submitted by an *A. Silva*. A new UPenn grad just accepted into TPC's program. Tia had greenlighted "him" sight unseen.

A few nights later, Tia was alone in the house reading when she heard a tepid rap at the door. There, standing downcast in the porch light, was a slender wraith in a long-sleeve blouse and ankle-length skirt, gleaming hair piled atop her head. One suitcase. The girl spoke in a soft, faltering voice, faint lilt.

"I'm, I'm Ariel Silva, here about the room."

For the briefest moment, Ariel raised her eyes, and Tia froze, fearing the girl was blind. She recovered to invite her in, taking her suitcase—surprisingly light—offering her a seat on the couch. Tia tried to make small talk, getting only "yes ma'ams/no ma'ams" in return, despite asking to be called by name. Finally, Tia showed Ariel around the house and made her comfortable in her room, where she remained even after Max and Stan returned from town.

Ariel had to have heard them arrive, but came out only when invited, eyes down. She seemed even more ill at ease in the presence of the opposite sex, addressing the men in a mumble as "sir." Max, being the ass he was, instantly sized her up for a rube. And from that point forward, he held her in contempt.

Until, that is, a few months later when Ariel underwent her transfiguration.

CHAPTER 32

They were finishing Ariel's trailer as Max drove in. He strolled over with pastries and coffee.

"Gorgeous day," he said, nodding to see everything packed. "Let's eat outside."

Despite their imminent departure, he sounded cheerful. Were his pupils dilated?

Ariel went with Tia and Stan to wash up, returning to see Max on the far side of the big oak, spreading a blanket. She was aghast. Though opposite from where the vortex had appeared, it was too close for comfort. As if the tree could shield them from radiation, or the myriad other threats a singularity might pose. And to her chagrin, Tia and Stan didn't hesitate to join him.

She bit her lip and took the corner of the blanket farthest from harm's way, hoping against hope the vortex *would* reappear to give them all a fright and show Max up. Though her friends slighted her concerns, Ariel was certain what she'd seen was no mirage. If not an actual black hole, could it be a *nascent* black hole? A *pre*-black hole? In which case, might today's power boost push it past tipping point into a *full-blown* black hole? Or make it unstable or explosive? No telling what might happen should it appear again. Nor even *where* it might pop up.

Ariel fretted as the clock ticked and the others sat comfortable in their physics, nibbling coffee cake, chatting as if on a picnic. She felt marginalized. At last, when time drew near, she excused herself to chain Newton, then headed for the tree, taking shelter behind. She crouched with her back to her friends, peeking out at the spot where the cloud had formed yesterday.

The others joined her, paying her fears *some* credit, at least. They stacked their heads atop hers like a totem pole, and she told them where to look—toward the house, twenty feet from the tree under its outstretched limbs, five feet in the air.

Stan raised a wristwatch thick with technology, and began a countdown, and Ariel's pulse quickened. When he reached zero, she clenched and held her breath.

Nothing. An occasional brown leaf spiraling earthward.

A minute passed, and everyone raised up. Max paid Ariel an *I told you so* glance, and she exhaled—only to contract again as Newton began to growl. Suddenly she felt woozy, neck and arm hairs bristling.

"Did you feel that?" she asked the others.

"What?" they replied.

Then out of clear skies came rumbling thunder. Newton went wild at the end of his chain, yet soundlessly. The thunder sharpened to a piercing trill, warbled, died off, and an inky swirl materialized midair. Same spot as before, but from the opposite vantage point. Quickly the swirl expanded into an angry, two-foot knot.

Stan and Tia gasped, and Max muttered, *"Holy shit."*

If not a budding black hole, a damn-compelling facsimile. Like staring down the funnel of some cosmic tornado, ominous in its hush. Ariel's sense of vindication gave over to fear, and she glanced at the others to see gawking statues.

To her astonishment, Max straightened and left the protection of the tree, heading for the vortex. The others cried their objections, but he paid no heed, approaching to within feet.

Ariel shot Tia and Stan anxious looks, and Stan raised his watch, punching buttons, fanning its dial at the whirling cloud.

"No radioactivity," he reported with surprise, "*At all*. Not even normal background count."

They waited. And seeing Max none the worse for whatever else he was exposed to, they crept out to join him. He held his phone to the vortex, taking video.

Tia whispered as if shouting might upset a delicate balance, "For God's sake, *don't touch it.*"

Were it a singularity of some kind, even brushing against it could well prove fatal.

"Interesting," Max said. "My phone's got no signal bars. Zero reception."

The others checked theirs. Same, and yet a signal tower was visible on a nearby foothill.

Stan edged behind Max, poking his watch again. "Heavy electrical disturbances," he said.

Max raised his palm to the vortex and moved it in a circle, as if testing the burner of a stove. "Nothing. No heat or cold, no suction or breeze."

The vortex continued unchanged, gyrating clockwise. Stan took more readings, Tia spoke into her phone recorder, and Ariel switched her phonecam to video. TPC would need all the data possible to confront this worrisome development.

Feeling braver, Ariel began to circle the whirlpool at wide berth, and noticed something odd. It shifted in aspect, from round to oval.

"Are you seeing that?" she asked.

Max looked over. "What?"

"It's starting to flatten, like a disc turning sideways."

"No change here."

Ariel pressed on. From her perspective, the vortex continued waning until the ninety-degree mark, where it shrank to a thin line. One step more, and it vanished altogether, invisible edgewise.

She advanced again, and the line reappeared, waxing as she reached one-eighty-degrees—same spot where she'd stood yesterday when first encountering it—back to a full circle once more. Her friends stayed on the other side, oak tree behind them, TPC tower looming in the distance.

Max dropped to a knee, inspecting the vortex from beneath.

"You're right," he said, "it's *two*-dimensional, I can—"

The shrill whine returned to drown him, and Ariel's heart raced again as she realized, *power boost.* The final test of TPC's capacities before the inaugural smashing tomorrow.

At this moment, massive volts of energy were driving the accelerator to its limits, propelling beams around the vast tunnel in opposing directions, ever faster toward the speed of light. No telling what the added power would do to the vortex, and with Max, Stan and Tia in arm's reach of it on the opposite side.

Ariel's warning cry was lost in the din. Before she could snatch another lungful of air, the whine ceased, and deathly silence prevailed once more. As if eternity had paused to observe.

And then Ariel felt the bottom drop out of her stomach. Opening like an iris dead-center in the swirl was an aperture, empty as space itself, compressing the vortex outward.

A black hole.

She fell to her knees shrieking, girding for the cold vacuum about to engulf them. But the others appeared clueless, calling out to her and rushing over.

"What happened?" Tia cried.

Hadn't they seen? Voice failing, Ariel pointed to the vortex.

The hole had swollen to the size of a beach ball. The others turned, and gaped.

Max sputtered, "I-I know what it looks like, but it *can't* be."

Peeling Ariel's fingers from his arm, he headed for the hole, the others begging him to stop. He pulled up scant feet away to call back,

"An event horizon of some sort, I'm guessing. It's a bottomless pit in there." He began to circle, only to brake and cry, *"There's no opening on the other side."* He completed his circuit to report, "I'll be damned, the hole doesn't penetrate!"

Stan and Tia helped Ariel to her feet, and they edged beside Max, gazing into the void. Ariel felt dumbstruck. It was like staring out a porthole-in-the-air into deep space. The blackest black. Absolute nothingness wrapped in a coil of cloud, roiling and pulsing with power. What secret of the universe had they stumbled upon? Surely the boost phase had reached maximum velocity by now. Yet despite the appearance of the aperture, the vortex seemed no more a threat.

Ariel leaned in for a closer view, and abruptly the hole snapped shut, everyone jumping back. Then the vortex dissolved, the whine arose and changed to thunder, fading away, and it was over.

They stared into empty air as normal sounds returned. Birds, a car out on the road, Newton.

Tia gasped, "What the hell was it?"

"That hole wasn't there yesterday," Ariel said. "At least, not the side I was on. Tell me it isn't a black hole?"

For once, Max was speechless.

Stan removed his glasses and mopped his face. "Some form of singularity, possibly, but no black hole. Or white hole, for that matter. Either would be lethal, especially at this proximity. Perhaps something in-between."

Tia rolled the idea around. "A *less-risky* type of singularity…"

Ariel wasn't as knowledgeable about this realm of astrophysics, but understood it in general. Singularities were contact points in the boundaries, known as "membranes," that separated this universe from others. Perhaps infinite others. A connection to different dimensions. Some singularities were lethal, the most dangerous being black holes and white holes—full-blown breaches in the membranes. Each represented opposite ends of the singularity spectrum. Black holes sucked material out of a universe, white holes, in.

And bubbling within the cosmic soup between lay a range of singularities thought more stable. These "in-between" singularities included such things as wormholes—safe passageways connecting one universe to another. There were also singularities known as "inter-dimensional aneurisms." Weak spots in the membranes, more dangerous than wormholes. Ariel knew next to nothing about aneurisms, but had heard banter about them in the TPC lunchroom: *Disruptive Singularities, Catastrophic Point Singularities, Symmetry-breaking Singularities,* and on.

Max found his voice. "Whatever we've got here, we've seen it full power now and it hasn't harmed so much as a blade of grass. No reason TPC should halt the tests."

"Keller has to make that call," Tia said. "He needs to see our videos—assuming the vortex didn't distort our recordings."

They grouped around their phones, relieved to see the videos intact, in chilling high-def. Even on a small screen, the images were astounding.

Stan said, "I can't wait to see Keller's face when he sees these."

Tia replied, "I'm not running that gauntlet at the gate. I say we email them to him."

She got no argument, and Stan added, "Then we should put together a proper presentation, at least. This could be a historic footnote."

It wouldn't hurt their résumés.

Stan and Tia went to fetch laptops, and Ariel and Max returned to the blanket. Max sat with bunched brow, fixated on the spot where the vortex had appeared.

Ariel asked, "What are you thinking?"

No answer. Preoccupied or ignoring her, she couldn't tell. She was used to his fugues, he was often in his own world, a world apart from her, Tia, and Stan. Max had an affliction that he kept in check with meds. But it wasn't just his disorder separating them, he had loftier aspirations.

Tia and Stan returned, and Ariel helped them transfer the videos to their laptops. Together they composed an account of what they'd witnessed: The strange sounds that prefaced the encounter, GPS coordinates where the anomaly materialized, and other detailed descriptions and observations to assist Keller in their absence. All without benefit of Max, who remained distant.

Stan was ready to send things off. "If I know Keller," he said, "he'll have a full crew out here next run. A shame we're going to miss out."

"Keller will come himself," Tia said. "He won't know what to make of this."

As if she'd struck some tripwire, Max came bursting out of his stupor, startling the others.

"*Exactly*," he cried. "For all we know, this is the find of a lifetime." He stabbed a forefinger at the empty spot under the tree. "What if it *is* a singularity? We're going to just hand it over to Keller like a fare-well gift? After he canned us?"

Their last hours together, and Max was going to ruin it with one of his tantrums.

"*We* should be the ones investigating this," he insisted. "It's *our* discovery."

"*No*," Tia came back hard. "It's *Ariel's* discovery."

Max blinked and took a breath. "Okay, yes. It's Ariel's discovery. And she's leaving here empty-handed, going nowhere, just like you and Stan." He exhaled. "I don't know what that thing is, but I know this. *Minimum*, it means white papers. Publication in all the journals. What would that do for your job prospects?"

No one said anything, his words resonating. None of them had published a thing since coming here, counting on TPC's experiments for material.

He continued, intense. "If Ariel's right, if this *is* some kind of singularity..."

He regarded them each in turn:

Stan. "No more groveling for a TA, you're looking at a full professorship."

Tia. "You'll have your pick of grants."

Ariel. "And to hell with that crap in Ohio, you'll launch a whole new branch of research. You can write your own ticket."

Ariel loved doing research in her field of computational science, developing models to better understand the forces of quantum physics. No hope for that now as the Dark Age descended.

Max knew each of their hearts, and how to touch them.

She searched his face. "And you? You'd throw Hadron away on a long shot?"

"Two weeks till I start," he said. "Time enough to consider what we've got here."

Ever one to hedge his bet. Ariel knew *his* heart, too. In it, he was the next public face of science. The new-generation Neil DeGrasse Tyson. All he lacked, in his mind anyway, was cachet. Something to propel him into prominence. Like a major scientific discovery.

But also in his mind, as Ariel and the others were all too aware, lay the true obstacle to his dream—the bipolar disorder he fought to control.

Stan brought everyone back to Earth. "There's no guarantee the anomaly will repeat. Any adjustments TPC makes could kill it. Tomorrow's smash could kill it."

"Only one way to find out," Max said. "And I'll spring for the extra day on your u-hauls."

It was decided, then. They'd invest one more night, hold off contacting Keller to see what tomorrow's epic collision might bring.

CHAPTER 33

Ariel washed up in the bath that adjoined her and Tia's rooms. Popping out her contacts, she changed into a nightshirt and crawled into bed with her laptop. Since her days in high school, she'd kept a daily journal, a way to empty her head so she could sleep. And after today, a day like no other she'd known, she'd much to record.

It was no benefit tonight. Her mind was still racing when she finished, and she went online to search out the latest abstracts on particle accelerators and singularities. No help there, either. Nothing to shed light on the extraordinary events of this morning. Nor did she feel sleepy.

One by one her housemates bedded down, and at last when all was quiet, Ariel threw on a robe and tiptoed barefoot into the hall. Dark but for light under Max's door. She crept close to make out his muffled voice, a one-sided conversation. He was on his phone. At least, she *hoped* so. Was he having second thoughts about tomorrow, hashing things over with a former TPC colleague?

She raised a fist to knock, thought better of it, and withdrew to the kitchen, grabbed leftovers from the fridge, and slipped out the back door.

Balmy. Grass warm underfoot, skies cloudless and salted with stars. A near-full moon peeked over the big oak as she rounded the house, breeze ruffling the leaves, carrying a musty scent. She heard something on the front porch, and turned to see Tia leaning against the clapboard, sobbing softly.

Stunned, Ariel rushed over, and Tia looked up, cheeks glistening in the pale light.

"What's wrong?" Ariel whispered with concern.

Tia brushed off Ariel's arms and ducked into the house without a word. Ariel sighed. No point following, Tia was inconsolable when these moods struck. Two years since her mom died, and there were still moments as if no time had passed. Tia's mom had put Tia and her sisters through college on a nurse's income, and when the last graduated, took her own life.

No one had seen it coming. Only later did Tia learn that depression was a side effect of a medication her mom had been taking. But there was more driving Tia's guilt, Ariel knew, and it reminded her of her own mom, whom Ariel had lost in a different way.

Exhaling, she resumed course for the doghouse. As she neared the spot where the vortex had appeared, her senses sharpened, and she paid it wide berth. A sermon from her childhood sprang to mind. A terrifying exhortation about the opening of Hell's Gate on the Last Day. Ariel shivered. All her years of science hadn't entirely exorcised the old demons. And out here in the autumn quiet under the moon's omniscient eye, she felt their grip again.

Newton was in his house. If asleep, surely Ariel's thumping heart woke him. He emerged with tail wagging so hard his whole frame shook. She knelt to squeeze him as he licked her face, and unhooking him, she led him around to the back door.

Tia was nowhere to be seen or heard, but Max's light was still on. Shushing Newton, Ariel picked him up with a grunt and sneaked to her room, depositing him on her bed.

And snuggling in beside him, she finally slept.

CHAPTER 34

Ariel woke to a dull headache and the muted voices of Max, Tia and Stan in the living room, TV on in the background. She sat up, Newton licked her face, and she hugged him tight.

By her clock, it was an hour until the collider's baptism of fire. Would TPC's gates hold out the mob again so the test could go forward? Would the singularity reappear? And assuming so, would it remain stable through the ferocity of today's matter/antimatter mash-up?

Much hung in the balance today, perhaps the course of her life.

Inhaling deep, Ariel slid from bed, shooed Newton out the window, dressed, and hurried through her morning regimen to join the others.

Sunlight streamed through the bay window of the living room as she entered, striking the stone fireplace on the opposite wall. Mounted above the mantelpiece was an old shepherd's staff; seven feet of stout wood ending in a crook. And hanging from the crook was Newton's leash, its shiny metal fastener catching the sun's rays, and Ariel's attention. She went to get it. If things didn't turn out today, she'd need the leash at rest stops on the long drive to Toledo.

Her friends sat on the floor in front of the TV, sharing a pot of coffee and plate of fruit. Max patted a spot beside him, and Ariel took it, exchanging greetings, grabbing coffee and a canoe of cantaloupe.

On TV was live coverage of the protest at TPC, volume low. The crowd was even larger and surlier as the countdown to the inaugural smashing loomed, and Ariel asked, "Anything new?"

"They tried storming the gates last night," Max said. "Finally, the governor called in the National Guard to keep the bastards at bay."

Ariel saw dozens of soldiers in riot gear stationed outside the fence. Federal forces would hopefully show more initiative than state troopers, who tended to share the protesters' sentiments. All the same, the soldiers were badly outnumbered. Ariel estimated upwards of five-thousand demonstrators now.

Stan added, "Dark Agers are pushing for an emergency bill in Congress to halt the test. A 'stay of execution' for the planet." Few things riled Stan, but Dark Agers were one. "Luckily, they don't have a quorum for a vote, most of Washington is off campaigning."

It was a fierce election year, not only for the presidency.

The TV cut to the portable stage where a rally was underway. At the podium stood a well-dressed man with silver hair and commanding mien, and Ariel froze in the middle of a bite.

Max grinned at her to say, "Well look who showed up for the Rapture, your old guru."

The crowd certainly appeared raptured. Max upped the volume, and a baritone long familiar to Ariel resounded off the walls of the bare living room. Echoes of Sunday mornings at church.

"...Those who ignore the lessons of life," the reverend Penbrook Thornton railed, "are doomed to repeat their mistakes. Those who ignore the lessons of scripture are doomed to everlasting fire." He gestured toward the TPC complex. "What does the bible teach about the grandiose ambitions of man? Genesis tells us God once sent a Deluge to punish the world for its sins. And how did man respond? Rather than mend his ways, man, in his arrogance, began to erect a giant tower, thinking to escape God's Wrath.

"Then as now, you see, we underestimate our Maker. God foiled the scheme with a wave of His mighty Hand, confounding the language of the builders such that none understood the other. And unable to finish the tower, man fled babbling across the lands."

The crowd rumbled approval, and Thornton's eyes flashed. He brought a damning forefinger to bear on the monolith behind. *"Now, man has raised another Tower. More abhorrent than Babel—an insult to God's Intelligence."* His finger swept downward. *"And hidden beneath is a tunnel—a* Tunnel *of Babel. Monstrous in size and extravagance and hubris, intended to expose God's Secrets hidden from us since the very moment of Creation."*

Met by howls of outrage, he turned to the complex, crying out, *"Are you so blinded by your science? The knowledge you seek is fleeting. It leads only to more questions, more technology, more expense. There is but one true and lasting knowledge, and that knowledge is free."*

He faced his audience again, expression and tone softening.

"Brethren, we already have answers to the most profound questions of the universe. Wisdom to surpass all wisdom. And it's readily accessible to everyone. All you need is to open a bible, enter a church, drop humbly to your knees and pray. Ask and you shall receive. Knock and it shall be opened unto you."

"Yeah," Max said. "Screw research, get your science from Bronze-Age goat-herders."

The camera zoomed into Thornton, his eyes brimming with emotion. *"Men and women of TPC, I beg you, heed the lessons of scripture. Continue on this reckless path, and sure as God is Lord, you will suffer His Judgment."*

The crowd wailed and Ariel was a girl again, trembling in a pew at the Voice of God.

Max snapped, "I've sure as hell suffered enough of you, asshole." And tossing the remote to Ariel as if she bore some complicity, he grabbed his coffee, rose, and exited the front door.

Ariel sighed. Max had no tolerance for religion. He failed to see its edifying aspects, equating faith with ignorance, clergy with hucksters. In fact, he had less understanding of spirituality than Thornton had of science. Max attributed Ariel's drawn-out withdrawal from her faith to meekness and superstition, no empathy for the vice-grip of doctrine or the control of a Svengali. Their first Christmas here, he'd given her a flashdrive made to resemble a rabbit's foot.

Tia switched off the TV, and stood, and Ariel and Stan rose, too. With the Big Smash nearing, it was time to join Max on the blanket under the tree...

As they settled in, Ariel felt relieved to see Max had calmed, and the conversation turned to the topic on which so much was now riding. The others had opinions about what the mysterious vortex might be, drawing from some of the latest theories about singularities. Concepts Ariel had never heard of and didn't understand.

Stan liked something called a "negative-mass macroscopic loop." Max advocated for an "extended Schwarzschild negative V." Tia, a "non-baryonic dark matter halo." And not to be left out, Ariel mentioned the one theory in this arena she knew something about, having come across an article on it in a physics journal: a Niles-Begley omniscient wormhole.

Also known as a "window on the universe," a Niles-Begley singularity could presumably link to any location in existence, providing a direct glimpse into whatever was out there. A compelling notion. A window to *anywhere*. Ariel concluded by asking the others, "So what impact do you think today's smashing will have on the vortex?"

Tia replied, "I wouldn't worry about a cataclysmic event, if that's what you mean. Assuming the vortex is created by the streams alone, as seems likely, my fear is the smashing will disrupt the process, the vortex will fizzle, and we'll be left empty-handed."

Max disagreed. "The collision occurs in a separate chamber *outside* the big loop. The streams are diverted for but trillionths of a second. I don't see it affecting anything."

Ariel wasn't so sure. After all, no collider had ever attempted anything of this magnitude, crashing matter into antimatter at such extremes of energy, speed and temperature.

The closer the moment of impact, the more anxious she grew. With five minutes to spare, they all took positions behind the big oak again, crouching, peering in the direction of the house.

Ariel noted Newton safely chained to his doghouse, tail wagging. But soon, he stopped and began to whimper and pace as if reacting to something beyond human perception. Ariel tensed, raising her phone with the others to record, feeling the telltale gooseflesh, a queer tilt to her equilibrium that none of her friends seemed to feel. Thunder erupted, soon giving way to whine, whine faded to ominous quiet, and Newton's mouth moved without sound.

Once again, Ariel watched enthralled as the vortex materialized. Same spot as before, midair. She had difficulty detecting it, at first— a slight distortion of the visual field, circular, heatwave-like ripples. Then the waves grew smoky and started to spiral, expanding into a silent, seething whirlpool two feet across, and the whine returned like the screech of some harbinger banshee.

"Boost to full throttle," Max declared.

At this moment, scant miles away, twin streams of Hadron particles were roaring past each other in vast subterranean loops, propelled toward light speed by a staggering 10,000 megawatts of power, energy enough to run a major city.

Suddenly in front of them, a hole within the vortex opened and expanded to a foot and a half across—a black void wrapped inside a maelstrom. Ariel stole a glance at Max to see him transfixed. The whine trailed off, and Ariel assumed the streams had reached peak speed, quantum impact looming. She closed her eyes.

Dead silence but for her timpani heart. Seconds ticked. Surely, the collision had taken place. Ariel dared a squint to see no change, whirlpool still wreathing around the hole. If, in fact, the smashing had occurred, they and the aperture had survived it.

She exhaled, and Stan mopped his brow. Seems he'd harbored some qualms, after all.

He announced in a wheezy voice, "Ladies and gentleman, I think we're in business."

They all raised to full height, a team now. Collaborators in a quest to identify what might amount to only a scientific curiosity, but could also prove an important contribution to science.

If they could determine what they were dealing with.

Max grinned, gave a thumbs-up, and headed for the vortex. The others followed, and this time Ariel faced the hole not with fear, but pride of ownership. While Max inspected and the women videoed, Stan pulled out a tape measure.

"Not too close," Tia cautioned.

He stretched the tape the width of the event horizon. "Tad under forty centimeters." And the distance from ground to vortex. "One and a half meters."

Ariel watched his eyes go distant behind his glasses, and he turned to her to say, "I'm starting to favor your Niles-Begley window on the universe."

Also known as an "omniscient" wormhole—a telescope to *everywhere.*

Tia nudged her, and Ariel felt flushed, peering closer into the abyss. But strain as she could, she saw nothing in its depths. No stars. No light whatsoever.

All too soon, the hole closed, and the vortex dissolved, signing off with customary whine and thunder. And hardly had the last rumble ebbed, than everyone's phones lit up with jubilant texts and tweets from comrades at TPC. The smashing had gone off without a hitch.

"That settles it," Stan said. "The anomaly is a byproduct of the streaming alone, unaffected by the smashing."

They broke into cheers, Newton chiming in. Ariel stiffened to feel arms envelop her from behind, hugging the breath out of her. Max. He passed her to the others for more hugs and a chorus of cheers.

Her head was still reeling when abruptly Max clapped his hands to say, "Okay, gang, we've got a ton of work before the afternoon run. Ready to make a little history?"

More cheers. Now that the collider's maiden test was behind it, TPC would proceed with twice-daily runs, 10:00 AM and 2:00 PM, seven days a week. Hopefully unimpeded by protesters now, Ariel trusted, given they'd just put their black-hole fears to rest.

"We'll need equipment," Stan said. "*Lots* of it. Sensors, gauges, 'ometers."

Max nodded. "Food and supplies. And, *damn*, we gotta contact the landlord before he rents the farm out from under us."

Tia waved her hands in the air. "Back to Earth, guys. You forget, we've got no income. We can't make rent, much less afford a bunch of equipment."

Unfazed, Max snapped, *"Think outside the box."*

Ariel gritted her teeth. She hated that banality. More, she hated the condescending way Max tended to spout it, as if he were some paragon of resourcefulness. Though he came from money, he was hardly better off than the others, too proud to accept family help.

He gestured to the driveway. "We'll sell our cars. We can get by with just one. Take jobs in town if necessary, night shifts, waiters. Whatever it takes."

Ariel sighed. Max was indeed resourceful. And he was right. This could be the opportunity of a lifetime. They couldn't let it pass.

It appeared settled until Tia said, "I'm in, but on two conditions."

She had everyone's attention.

"...Any papers we publish, we publish *jointly*. We're a team, we *stay* a team."

Instant consensus.

"And," she turned to Ariel, "*Ariel* gets top billing."

Ariel felt herself flush again. She'd never experienced such an honor, ever the outsider. To be given prominence on this power team was most kind and generous.

Stan readily approved, but Max's lips tightened to a thin line. No doubt he'd anticipated the limelight, given his career aspirations. And in fairness, he *was* the best technical writer, likely to shoulder most of that heavy lifting. But Tia wasn't backing down. And for once, Ariel wasn't either, relishing her rare moment.

Tia put a finer edge on it. "If not for Ariel's tenacity, we wouldn't be discussing this."

Three and a half years ago when Ariel joined the household, they'd made a pact. All decisions affecting the group would be decided by majority vote, and in case of ties, no action would be taken. The terms had served them well.

Ignoring Max, Tia extended her little fist to the group. Ariel and Stan latched on like spokes of a wheel, and finally Max, grumbling, made it unanimous.

Wherever this speculative venture led, they were in it together.

Stan let out a whoop, Newton started barking again, and Max told Ariel, "If you're gonna headline this show, one more condition: *keep a lid on that dog.*"

Gritting her teeth, Ariel went to comfort Newton, and the others returned to the house to discuss equipment, leaving the unpacking of their trailers for later.

CHAPTER 35

While the men were off seeking equipment, the women hauled items out to the front lawn in preparation for the afternoon run.

Tia was excited about their plans. As she and Ariel set up a folding table, she heard Ariel muse, "So, the radiation a singularity gives off is like a fingerprint?"

"According to Stephen Hawking, yes," Tia said. "Each type of singularity has a signature radiation. Even massive black holes with their huge gravitational pull emit radiation. If we can identify the kind of radiation ours releases, we'll have a good idea what we're dealing with. Assuming, that is, TPC lets us borrow their equipment."

They would need sophisticated wave detectors and sensors—infrared to ultraviolet, and beyond.

Newton interrupted them, barking. He must have felt left out, seeing all the activity. Ariel excused herself to tend to him.

Tia watched her go with a sigh. The dog had always been a source of friction between Ariel and Max. Watching Ariel laugh and play with him now, Tia thought back to the day they found Newton, and the turmoil that came with him...

165

It was early summer three years ago, a few weeks after Ariel had joined the team. A Saturday morning, Tia recalled clearly. Max and Stan were off to town, she and Ariel alone in the house, when Ariel heard something on the front porch. Investigating, she discovered a stray pup, its fur so matted and caked with mud, it was impossible to know its coloring, much less breed, if any.

Distraught, Ariel brought it in, and they took it to the kitchen, fed it, then out to the backyard for a messy shampoo. Stan arrived in his pickup as they scrubbed, and assessing the situation, he told them, "Hold on, I've got just the thing."

He trotted off to the barn, returning with an old sheep-carding brush. And along with a scissors, a mountain of towels, and Ariel's hairdryer, the three eventually produced a small, black and white border collie, or mix thereof.

Ariel cradled and caressed the dog as it licked her face.

"What will you call him?" Stan asked.

She reflected. "How about 'Newton?' After Sir Isaac."

First time Tia had ever seen Ariel smile. A sweet, endearing smile. And then Max arrived.

Parking his car, he strolled over to ask, "What's this?"

"It appears Ariel's been adopted," Stan told him.

Max folded his arms on his chest, regarding the girl and dog. "Un-uh. No pets, I'm allergic."

"Not a problem," Stan assured. "He can stay outside. We'll build him a doghouse."

"Dander gets on everything, how you gonna keep that out?" He angled his head at Ariel. "Keep her in the doghouse, too?"

Watching the light go out of Ariel's eyes, Tia called for a vote. Seldom did Stan go against Max, but Tia was so proud of him this time, and Max stalked off swearing. Of course, Max held it against Ariel. He had a brusque criteria for evaluating women. Looks, charisma, intelligence—in that order. He'd already judged Ariel deficient across the board, and now it was personal.

Ariel was far more easily intimidated in those days. Seldom would she speak unless addressed, and then in a voice as pale as her complexion. Irritating to Max, who equated timidity with weakness. Even Tia had to wonder how a girl so maladjusted could have made it so far. Ariel had no family, friends or acquaintances with whom she kept in touch, that Tia could tell.

Prior to Newton, Tia's efforts to open Ariel up had fallen flat. The girl was an introvert. She'd drive to TPC separately, avoid the water cooler, eat a sack lunch alone at her desk running cyclotron 3D computer simulations. At home, she wouldn't participate in dinner conversations and declined to join the others for TV, or anything else. She never went anywhere, even on weekends, holed up in her room or out for long walks alone in the back fields.

On the other hand, the girl took it upon herself to do the lion's share of chores around the house, including dishes and grocery shopping, for which Tia and Stan were appreciative. Max benefited as well, yet somehow Ariel's hard work served only to lower her stature in his eyes. He made sport of her, keeping score by the depths of her blush, announcing the results on a scale of one to ten. But mostly, he ignored her, and the household finally settled into a sort of stasis.

The Newton incident, however, threw a switch that sent Max's passive aggression to active. Where before he'd simply held Ariel in contempt, now he came to loathe her. His taunts intensified, more caustic. Cruel. He seemed hellbent on driving her away, rent be damned. Tia's fits, pleas and threats failed to deter him, Stan kept out of it, and fragile Ariel withered, retreating even further into herself, if possible.

Tia was despondent. She saw no hope short of Ariel giving up the dog, which Ariel refused to do, and it seemed Ariel's only option was to find another place to live, or quit and go home. If she had one. She'd never said.

Then very early one morning as the end appeared imminent, Tia awoke to sounds in the adjoining bath. She suspected Ariel was preparing to slip away.

Rising, she crept to the door. It was Ariel's nature to keep it locked when inside, but in her rattled state, not today. Tia opened to see a packed toiletry bag on the vanity, Ariel stepping into the shower. They both froze with embarrassment. Tia had never seen Ariel in less than a robe, nor even with her hair down, and felt her jaw drop—

Tia was wrested from her thoughts by the sound of a vehicle pulling into the drive. She looked up to see Stan's truck loaded with equipment.

CHAPTER 36

Ariel pushed open the screen door with her shoulder, four laptops in her arms, heading down the porch steps. Before her under the oak tree stood a twenty-by-twenty-foot beige canvas tent, meant to conceal their activities from passersby—TPC workers, protesters, state troopers. The men had bought it in town along with other supplies. Its door faced the house, which prevented Newton from seeing inside, and he wasn't happy about it, whining, pulling at his chain.

"Goddammit, Newton," Max boomed from inside the tent, *"shut the hell up."*

Ariel approached the tent to see Max seated alone at a rectangular table, back to the door. On each side of him were empty chairs for the others. Opposite the table was an open area set aside for the vortex when it appeared.

Max was hunkered over one of many electronic instruments arranged around him like a console. Oscilloscopes, wave gauges, energy sensors, and other specialized devices. In front of Ariel's chair were an HD tripod camera, binoculars, and a small telescope. More equipment cluttered the floor, electrical cords snaking out the entrance and across the yard to the house.

Their preparations left much to be desired, the best they could muster for now. Most of the equipment they'd borrowed from colleagues at TPC, who were too busy to ask many questions. Max and Stan had braved the picket lines to fetch things, counting on the National Guard for protection, hoping the collider's successful tests would diminish the crowd.

It hadn't. Max's car had suffered more dents. Worse, he'd gotten another speeding ticket on the way home, nearly arrested for mouthing off. He was still fuming.

Ariel shushed Newton and stepped over electrical cords into the tent, parking the laptops on the table with a puff. Max paid no heed, calibrating a gauge. Catching her breath, Ariel began distributing the computers, noticing how little space Max was allowing for the vortex. Between the table and tent wall, a span of about six feet. *His* estimation, the phenomenon left no footprint.

She offered him his laptop, asking, "You think we're allowing enough room? What if all this circuitry affects the vortex?"

He looked up, stiffening. *"10,000 megawatts of power,* Ariel." Same tone he'd taken with Newton. "Tactical nuclear-blast range, and you're worried about *house current?"*

He snatched the laptop, plonked it aside, and bent back to work.

Ariel blinked. The last thing they needed in the tent this afternoon was a *second* unpredictable force. She recalled with a shiver his previous, disastrous attempt to wean himself from his medication. Not that Valpro prevented his foul moods, it simply gave him a measure of control. A critical measure. There was no sure way to tell if he'd quit his meds, short of him actually going nuts. Or asking him outright—and she wasn't about to touch *that* launch button.

Taking a long breath, she told herself not to overreact. He was under court orders to stick to his prescription, surely he wouldn't defy that. And in fairness, he'd just weathered run-ins with protesters and the highway patrol. Tests of fire that he'd passed. Sort of.

Still, he would bear watching. One more worry for her.

A crunch of gravel in the drive called up another concern. Ariel looked out the tent, relieved to see Tia, who'd gone to fetch last-minute supplies. Ariel was nervous whenever Tia ventured into town on her own. A few weeks ago while out shopping, Tia had an unfortunate encounter with TPC protesters. Either they'd recognized her, having seen her cross their picket lines, or assumed by her ethnicity that she worked at TPC—the town was notably lacking in diversity. In any event, things got ugly. If not for the grocer standing up for her, it could have been serious. Tia wasn't one to back down.

Carrying a paper sack into the tent, Tia deposited it on the table.

"Any problems?" Ariel asked, seeing no sign in Tia's face.

"Not a nut-job in sight. Hopefully, they're slinking home to their own black holes."

She turned to Max, "More good news. A townie asked about my car. He took your number."

Earlier, Max had stuck for-sale signs with his phone number in their car windows, believing himself best negotiator. They needed a sale. Today's purchases had maxed-out their credit cards.

But Max seemed indifferent, ignoring Tia to focus on his gauge.

Stan arrived from the house with odds and ends, and they all took seats with Max at the table. Someone had duct-taped a digital clock to one of the tent poles. It ticked off the seconds until 2:00, and Newton began to howl, soon drowned out by thunder. The table shook, the instruments rattled, then the whine took over, trilling off into stillness.

And suddenly, the gauges went haywire.

Ariel turned anxious eyes to the open space in front of them. The vortex was easier to spot now, translucent little eddies arising eerily against the canvas backdrop. In seconds, the distortion resolved into cloud, swirling and swelling. Darker, more menacing than before— an effect of being shaded from the sun, Ariel told herself. When it reached the same width as previous, it stabilized, and the aperture opened like a camera lens, squeezing the vortex outward, compressing it into six inches of turbulent rim.

Everyone sat mesmerized until Max cried out, *"Goddammit."* Glaring at the gauges, he rapped one with his knuckles. Only moments before, the screens were convulsing like crazy, needles buried off their dials as the collider ramped to top speed. Now, not a flicker.

Tia said, "The power surge toasted them. It fried the circuitry."

"No, the screens are still lit," Max said, smacking another gauge.

Stan said, "Can't be a power failure." He began rooting through items on the floor. "Check the lines for a short, I'll try degaussing."

Degauss. A procedure using a special device to purge magnetic buildup from electronics.

Ariel swiveled the camera to document events while Tia assisted Stan, and Max backtracked the electric cords to the house. When Max returned reporting no problem, Stan said, "Nothing wrong with the instruments, either. They're simply not registering. No input."

Max frowned, sat, and snatched up a Geiger counter, shaking it. "Impossible. There's *always* background radiation."

Stan manipulated his watch, holding it in the air. "Not a trace."

No one had an answer.

While the others puzzled, Ariel grabbed the telescope and scanned inside the aperture for signs of light. A star, a galaxy, anything. Only blackness. Deep, foreboding blackness. If the phenomenon *were* a Niles-Begley omniscient wormhole—a window to anywhere—it appeared to open onto the edge of the universe where nothing existed but empty space.

Time up. The aperture snapped closed, the vortex vanished, replaced by whine and thunder, and abruptly the gauges went wild again. Moments later, the noise lapsed, Newton's barking returned, and the instruments resumed normal function. Bewildering.

Ariel had been reading up on cyclotron anomalies, and pointed out, "This can't be a radiation cone. Radiation cones focus beams of energy on a specific point in space. But maybe the collider's spinning off some sort of containment field."

She had the others' attention, continuing, "Remember the first time it happened? Only I heard the noises, loud as they are. You were all in the house, and yet you could hear Newton. Like I was in a bubble. Inside a-a-a force field."

They reflected, and Max said, "Not a force field, in the conventional sense. I was able to make it to the house to check the power cords. Maybe some sort of wave-interference field. That might explain the effect on the gauges."

Tia asked Ariel, "The HD camera was working?"

"Yes. And my laptop and phone cam. But my phone had no bars."

"*Very* peculiar," Stan said. "Selective wave interference."

"Whatever the barrier is," Max said, "we're screwed." He swept a hand over the instruments. "We can't fight 10,000 megawatts of power with this crap."

No argument there. The collider was the most powerful generator ever.

Ariel felt the air go out of her. If the collider was projecting some kind of force field, it would leave them no means to study the vortex inside it. They and their project were finished.

At length Tia said, "We've no choice but to turn this over to TPC. Maybe we can trade with Keller to get our jobs back. Tell him what we've got, he hires us to investigate."

"Keller's got no budget to hire us," Max said. "Besides, what leverage do we have? We've no claim on this thing. We don't own it. Or the farm. It's *over.*"

Ariel fought her despair. "We may not be able to analyze it, but Keller can. He'll show the world it's no black hole. At least we'll leave knowing we saved TPC."

"Put your brain on!" Max snapped. "If people get a load of that vortex, they'll freak. The Nuclear Regulatory Commission will yank TPC's license faster than you can say 'black hole.'"

Tia rose livid, leaning over Ariel to snap back at him, "Put *your* brain on. TPC's got a hole in its system. *That's* our leverage. We don't tell Keller *where* unless he agrees to keep a lid on it."

Max glowered down at Tia. "And Keller has to report all anomalies to the NRC. Federal law. Stick *that* in your leverage."

They locked inches apart, Ariel frozen beneath, pressure getting to them all.

Stan rushed to grab Tia by the shoulders. "He's right, Tia. The NRC reports to Congress, Congress will spill it to the media. There's no hushing it."

Tia broke free and paced, flapping her arms like a flightless bird. "So what the hell do we do? Drive off and leave the damned thing twisting in the wind?"

She braked and fronted Max. "We've *got* to report it. Sooner or later, someone will stumble across that hole. New tenants, a farm kid, a stray cow. Anything comes in contact—" she made a ball of her fingers and exploded them in his face.

He looked like he'd explode, and Ariel sprang to her feet between them.

"*Please,*" she cried. "There's too much at stake to get this wrong. Let's take a break and think things through."

Stan hurried to agree. "We still have time."

The afternoon sun lit up the wall of the tent, adding more heat. Yet somehow, Max and Tia cooled, and everyone grabbed their laptops and adjourned to the house.

Perhaps online lay a clue to solve their quandary.

And dare Ariel hope, another godsend to keep their project alive.

CHAPTER 37

The team spent the afternoon sifting through astrophysics white papers, searching for clues to understanding and overcoming the mysterious force field. No closer to an answer, they broke to fetch their mattresses from the trailers. Tia and Ariel untied one, handing it down for the men to carry off. Tia felt Ariel's cool hand on her arm, surprised to see anxiety in the girl's eyes.

Ariel asked her in a low voice, "What's your take on Max?"

"He's a dick. As ever."

"I mean, his *meds.* He's acting wired."

"When isn't he?"

"I'm worried."

Tia sighed and stared at the ground. "How can you tell? I mean, what's to distinguish normal-jerk Max from Mad Max until he goes *completely* whacko?"

"Next time he's out, we should check his prescription bottle."

"Can't. He doesn't keep it in his room anymore, he locks it in the glove box of his car." Getting a surprised look, Tia admitted, "He caught me snooping."

175

Tia felt no guilt. She'd every reason to keep tabs on him after what happened. Last winter, the four of them were at a pub off U.S. 86 having a beer when two locals got fresh with Ariel. Though she'd long ago broken up with Max, instead of him blowing it off like the others begged, he tore into the men, maniacal, fists pummeling like a propeller. Tia had never seen such ferocity. Poor Ariel was frantic.

Then one man pulled a gun, and Tia was sure someone would die. But faster than a bullet, Max snatched the weapon and used it to beat both men bloody. He might well have killed them if not for the bartender tasering him. Only after a night in jail, in front of a judge the next day, did Max reveal he'd gone off his prescription semisodium valproate the week before. He'd hidden his condition from the others, albeit Tia had always thought him bipolar, with a dash of OCD. Before that incident, however, she'd never seen him out of control.

He told the court he'd quit his meds when his car needed parts he couldn't afford. It took an affidavit from his psychiatrist in Boston to get him released into TPC's custody, on probation, with the proviso he not skip his prescription again. All the same, Tia didn't trust him. The drug was expensive and irritated his bowels. More, it was an affront to his ego. Max liked to think nothing was beyond him when he put his mind to it. Including his mind.

"If he *is* off his meds," Tia said, "I'm ready." She pulled a small canister of chemical mace from her shorts. "Got it after my run-in with the protesters."

Watching Ariel's eyes grow large, Tia tucked it away. "Don't worry, it won't come to that. I'm afraid we're done here. We're not gonna beat that force field."

She saw the despair in Ariel's face.

The men came for another mattress, and Tia waited until they were out of earshot to say, "But I'm not leaving till we report our findings to Keller. I'm not having this on my conscience, even if it means closing TPC, Max be damned."

Ariel looked off to the sunset, last rays catching a glint in her eyes.

"Promise me," she said, "if our time here *is* over, can we at least leave as friends? *All* of us? It would mean a lot to me."

Tia sighed and gave Ariel a hug, and her word.

The men returned, and Stan announced, "TPC held a press conference today. If we hurry, we can catch the highlights."

And grabbing another mattress, he and Max hustled off.

• • •

Ariel settled with the others on the floor in front of the TV. No point unpacking chairs in light of their bottleneck. Despite all their brain-wringing, they'd come up with no ideas to beat the force field. Though Max may have found a clue to what they were dealing with.

It was accepted theory in astrophysics that all singularities gave off some form of radiation. And in the case of black and white holes, *lethal*, ionized radiation. But Max had come across work by Stephen Hawking showing that the least dangerous singularities, including wormholes, produced no more than a magnetic field. A powerful, if harmless radiation that wrapped the vicinity in a protective bubble called an *Outer Trapping Horizon*.

That seemed to describe the energy field they'd experienced. And importantly, *harmless*. Frustrating to think they could be in the middle of a protective force field—an Outer Trapping Horizon—with no way to analyze the vortex, blocked by the massive power of the collider. They seemed at a loss, but Ariel clung to the hope they'd find a way to salvage their plan and futures.

On TV, the TPC press conference headlined the nightly news. A banner read:

THE BIG SMASH
Talawanda 1, Black Hole, 0

Cameras showed TPC director Winston Keller seated at a table inside TPC's cafeteria, facing an array of microphones and reporters.

Alongside him were senior colleagues looking exhausted, but beaming. Ariel had always admired Keller, especially so after working for him. A brilliant physicist, if hardly an ideal spokesperson. Thin and gray in clunky glasses, rumpled light suit and bow tie, eyes squinching under the lights.

Asked a question, Keller crinkled his nose. The nose thing was a tic. Habit or affliction, Ariel didn't know. He replied, *"We're very encouraged with the quantity and quality of data. Months of work lie ahead, but we hope to make some exciting breakthroughs."* Tic.

A reporter asked, *"What exactly are you looking for?"*

"Our objective is to get closer to the moment of Big Bang. Within trillionths of a second. We're not quite sure what we'll find. New quanta particles, we expect. Insights into the nature of gravity, dark matter, dark energy, we hope." Tic.

Another reporter: *"And no chance of stumbling across a black hole in there?"*

"Absolutely none. We've proven that now. I don't understand why the demonstrators aren't satisfied, why they won't leave us to our work. We need an armed escort just to come and go."

Tic, tic, tic.

Ariel looked to see Max scowling. He was no doubt thinking he'd make a better press liaison.

Tia screwed her face in a tic, too. "The protesters haven't left?"

As if in answer, the picture cut to a live shot of TPC's front gate, the crowd bigger and rowdier than ever. The coverage then shifted to an interview with Reverend Penbrook Thornton.

Max snorted, "And now for an epic display of backpedaling."

A newswoman asked Thornton, *"Seeing how TPC conducted two tests today at full power without a hitch, doesn't that put to rest your concerns about a black hole?"*

Thornton had the demeanor of a man shouldering great moral responsibility. *"We were blessed today,"* he said. *"Tomorrow, God may not be so forgiving."*

Asked for clarification, he replied, *"The odds of a black hole occurring have to do with the random nature of particle stream collisions."* He turned to the camera. *"Unlike some would have you believe, I understand what's going on here. I've studied cosmology."*

Max hooted, "Cosmology according to the *Book of Genesis*." He snatched up the remote and aimed it at the TV.

But Ariel grabbed his hand, reminding, "Know thine enemy."

Thornton continued, *"Ignore for a moment the complex technology and its great cost. A collider, in essence, is a giant roulette wheel. A huge, high-stakes gamble. The higher the energy, the higher the stakes. TPC admits it can't predict how the streams will interact during any given smashing. The results are subject to something called* The Uncertainty Principle. *It's impossible to know if a collision will even produce useful data. That's why they conduct so many runs."*

"And the black hole?" the newswoman asked.

"Same Uncertainty. With such extreme energies in play, a black hole could erupt during any run. Chances are slim each time, yes." He turned earnest eyes on the camera again. *"But it doesn't take a rocket scientist to know, keep spinning the roulette wheel, sooner or later you land on double-zero."*

He spoke in a manner so seemingly learned, rational and heartfelt, Ariel knew many wouldn't question. Just as she'd blindly trusted his pronouncements once. His mangling of the astrophysics enabled him and the protesters to double down.

"I have it on good authority," Thornton finished, *"the Republican National Committee will release an important statement on this matter soon."*

Max fumed, "The bastards are making it a campaign issue. No chance it'll blow over now."

And he switched the channel to football.

Tia snatched the remote from his hand and turned to the History channel—a documentary on John F. Kennedy. Swearing, Max sprang up and made for the hall. But halfway, he halted.

"Far as I'm concerned," he said, turning, "you can send your email to Keller now. If that force field doesn't stop us, the Dark Agers sure as hell will. TPC's finished, and so are we."

It crushed Ariel to see him give up on them. Meds or no, she let him have it.

"Go ahead, walk out on us, you've got somewhere to go."

Inhaling, he calmed. "Look," he said, "if I thought there was any hope, I'd stay. But even if we had more time, I've no clue how to fight 10,000 megawatts of power."

Stan agreed. "We'd need *another* 10,000 megs to neutralize it. We'd need a *second* TPC. And we can't even turn to TPC for help."

No one spoke. Not a sound but the TV—a speech by John Kennedy at Rice University, 1962. Ariel had studied this period of history in high school, and she escaped into it. Into the charisma of the man. His passion, his optimism. It dawned on her what this speech was. A policy address delivered at a pivotal point in the young president's term. And suddenly, she was struck with an epiphany. As quickly as her hopes had crumbled, they snapped back into place.

"We're *not* giving up," she declared louder than intended, jolting everyone. "If that vortex *is* a wormhole, it's our answer. It gives us a way to stop the Dark Agers. We can save TPC *and* end the war on science, once and for all."

The others stared, and Max shook his head. "Don't make this harder than it is."

"I'm dead serious."

He crossed his arms on his chest. "You're dead wrong. The war's lost, Ariel. Doesn't matter what that thing in the yard is, the country's too nearsighted, brainwashed, and broke to care. You don't change that overnight."

Ariel crossed her arms back at him. *"Moon landing."*

His face screwed up, and she pointed to the TV. "When John Kennedy took office," she said, "the country was in a recession, like now. People out of work, future bleak. What did he do? *He promised them the moon.* And what happened? It turned everything around. Overnight. Suddenly space was a national obsession, every child wanted to be an astronaut. Science was king."

She looked them each in the eye. "These are desperate times. Give people another star to reach for, they'll grab it. This is the chance of a lifetime. If we're right about a wormhole, we've got our moon landing. We can save TPC, we can beat the Dark Agers, we can turn it all around. We *can't* quit now."

It had them thinking.

Stan conceded, "If it *is* a Niles-Begley, it offers more than the moon and stars. *A universe.*"

Tia added, "If not multiverses."

But Max shook his head again. "Reality check, gang. We've got a 10,000-meg gorilla in the room. We're boxed in and running out of time." He angled his head at Ariel. "If you've got a suggestion, let's hear it."

She angled her head back. *"Think outside the box.* If I can prove we're dealing with a safer form of singularity, is everyone still on board?"

Tia placed a hand on Ariel's arm. *"Mi corazón,* this is a damned big gorilla."

Ariel grinned. "Leave him to me."

CHAPTER 38

Ariel stood outside the tent door, shifting her feet as the collider's morning run drew near. She and her team were preparing to test the idea she'd proposed last night, trying to determine if the singularity they were dealing with was a less-dangerous form. Ideally, a wormhole.

Now in the bright light of day, however, Ariel wasn't feeling quite so optimistic.

Her approach to their problem was in sharp contrast to how her friends had attacked it. Ariel was applying science at its most basic level. As Max put it, "grade-school tech." She was inspired by something Stephen Hawking once said: All singularities emitted radiation, but less-dangerous types, such as wormholes, produced harmless, magnetic radiation. The team's efforts to study their singularity was blocked by a Trapping Horizon force field that could be masking a dangerous type of singularity. With their sophisticated gauges rendered useless, however, the team had given up. Until last night, when Ariel had an inspiration.

"Maybe the way to deal with our gorilla," she'd offered, "is from *outside* the room."

Since the force field prevented them from analyzing the singularity, Ariel had proposed focusing on the force field, instead. She'd suggested a simple experiment, and though her friends held out little hope, they'd no objection. If Ariel failed, their moon shot was over, regardless.

From her vantage point at the tent door, Ariel had full view of the others. Tia to the east by the doghouse, Stan to the west by the drive, and Max to the north near the porch—well outside the influence of the force field, like Newton. Assuming, that is, the field was a uniform sphere. Ariel could also see into the tent to spot the vortex when it arrived, then signal its phases to the others to begin the experiment.

The seconds ticked away, and suddenly Newton began to yelp. Ariel raised an arm. Once the force field came between her and her friends, she'd be reduced to visual communication only. The others stood holding a small object in their hands. A cheap, directional compass picked up at the dollar store this morning.

At last Newton fell mute, the vortex appeared, the hole opened, and Ariel waved the others on. They inched toward her, eyes on their compasses. But as they drew to within ten feet, they all came to a stop, each inside the force field now. Ariel could hear them cheering.

Tia cried, "My needle clearly pointed straight to the vortex before going haywire."

"Mine, too," Stan said with a grin. "Exactly as you predicted."

Max conceded, "Likewise. No question, the singularity emits magnetic radiation. Congrats."

Ariel felt herself blush. Her idea was so simple, she couldn't believe the others hadn't thought of it. They smothered her in hugs until she begged, *"Enough,"* and beckoned everyone into the tent.

They gathered at the table, still celebrating as the vortex whirled and pulsed before them.

"So," Ariel said, "our singularity is one of the safer types? We're good to proceed?"

She got three, enthusiastic thumbs-up.

Tia asked, "So what's our next step?"

Everyone looked to Ariel as if she had the answer. Taken aback, she regarded the swirling aperture. "I, I'm not sure. But it occurred to me, if we can't use gauges to study it, maybe we could approach it the way Edison did the light bulb. You know, old-fashioned trial-and-error."

Back in the 1880s, Edison had tested more than 1,600 random materials before discovering a filament to invent the electric light.

Stan said, "You mean, toss stuff inside it?"

"More or less."

He blinked. "This light bulb has the wattage to light up a city. We may be in the safer range of the singularity spectrum, but an error could still prove lethal."

"I don't mean be reckless. We can take precautions."

Tia said, "If that thing is some sort of aneurism, chucking stuff inside could rupture it." By "aneurism," Tia meant a weak spot in the membrane separating their universe from another. "Just breaching the event horizon could burst it. We won't get a mulligan."

Max sat back in his chair. "I'm with Ariel. My gut says this singularity is stable. Think about it. It already comes in contact with matter. Atmospheric dust, pollen. Air itself is foreign matter to it. What if a leaf from the tree had drifted into it? All we're talking about is upping the ante. Either we're willing to take some calculated risks, or we fold our tent and go."

The sun broke through the canopy of the tree, bathing the tent in golden light. Ariel inhaled deep, savoring the moment. Never had she felt more filled with hope and expectation.

She also felt Max's eyes, turning to see him agog.

"My God," he cried *"Look at you."*

The others regarded Ariel with astonishment, too.

"Your skin," Tia said. "It's *glowing.*"

Ariel saw her bare arms irradiant. The sun, diffusing through the fabric of the tent, lent her complexion a surreal burnish. An effect she'd experienced before, her skin playing blank canvas to odd lighting. Another quirk of her freakish nature. Another source of unwanted attention and ridicule growing up. She felt her face grow hot, adding tint to the strange optics, no doubt.

CHAPTER 39

Ariel was preparing items in the tent for the new experiment she and the team had devised. In truth, more gamble than experiment. She tried not to think of Thornton's roulette wheel.

The team had approved her idea to emulate the Edison method. Of course, the challenge they faced was vastly more complicated, stakes exponentially higher. But they would proceed with extreme caution, taking incremental steps. To Ariel's relief, Max offered to conduct the tests. He had more guts than she, and there was one experiment she literally could not stomach.

She parked a bag on the table and began removing the contents. Tia was in the house, gathering more items and arranging to have their emptied trailers picked up. The men were returning their borrowed equipment to TPC. But they should have been back by now, and Ariel was getting concerned.

Just as she grabbed her phone to call them, she heard a vehicle in the drive, and peeked out the tent to see Max's car. She relaxed—until she spied a gaping hole in its rear window.

Max screeched to a halt and got out, slamming the door, beads of glass tinkling down the trunk. Stan was at his heels clutching two items Ariel couldn't identify.

"*Goddamned bastards,*" Max railed, face red as a crimson maple.

Tia exited the house to join them, and Stan told her, "The picketers smashed Max's window."

Presumably with the items in Stan's hands, which Ariel could now make out as a dark, stone figurine, and what looked to be a bible.

"Either of you hurt?" Tia asked.

Stan said, "Thanks to the National Guard, no. But the state troopers never lifted a finger."

Max lifted a finger—a middle finger—in the direction of TPC. He stormed into the tent, and the others followed, Ariel and Tia exchanging nervous glances. But when Max saw things set out for the experiments, his attention turned to his preparations, and his swearing subsided.

As the clock neared 2:00, the team stopped what they were doing to assemble in the center of the tent. They faced a tripod camera on the table, Max and Ariel on one side of where the vortex would appear, Stan and Tia, the other. An official portrait to memorialize their work here. As Max put it, "Documenting for the Ages."

The noises arose and cycled through, the vortex materialized, and when the hole opened, Max produced a cigar and stuck it in his teeth. Everyone smiled for the camera. Then, while Max remained by the vortex, the others took their places behind the table.

"Ready?" he asked.

"Ready," they replied.

Max struck a match on the seat of his pants, lit the cigar, turned to the hole, and with the barest breath, he released a donut of smoke. Everyone drew back, and Ariel tensed as the ring floated with agonizing lethargy toward the center of the void. To disappear.

They waited. Max circled the vortex, stating for the camera, "No detectable response to tobacco particulates. The smoke entered inertly, no sign the aperture either attracts or repels."

Stan said, "The event horizon isn't a barrier, it's an *access point.*"

Ariel wasn't breathing easy yet.

Max took a longer drag, and sent a more substantial plume into the blackness.

Again, nothing.

The scent reached Ariel, and she grimaced. It called to mind revival meetings Mom and Phil used to drag her to on hot afternoons like this, under much larger tents. Ariel wondered what Mom would think of this diabolical apparition and the sorcery they were performing on it. Ariel couldn't care less what Phil would think.

Stan switched on a flashlight and joined Max. In the shade of the tent, the beam revealed contrails of smoke. But directed into the hole, beam and smoke were visible only to the point of the event horizon, nothing but clear darkness beyond.

Stan moved opposite Max to angle the light across the width of the hole, saying, "Again."

Max launched more smoke, and it sailed through the beam to vanish, showing that external sources of light didn't illuminate the void. Stan stated that for the record, and Tia took notes.

For the next experiment, Max extended his hand to Ariel, wiggling his fingers. She felt like a magician's assistant. Pouring a tiny amount of talcum powder into a spoon, she handed it to him, and he blew the contents into the hole. To no effect. He turned back to her for the next substance. Powdered zinc. Again, no reaction.

They progressed through denser powders without apparent consequence, finally arriving at the last item. Rock salt. Larger than any material yet tested. Ariel poured from a box into a bowl, dispensing more than she intended. The crystals ranged in mass from dust to pea-sized.

"I'll try a single grain, first" Max assured the others. "A *small* one."

Using tweezers, he picked out a granule, displayed it to the camera, turned, and flicked it in the hole. It vanished without a sound. He graduated to larger specimens, flinging them in one-by-one, to no effect. Then using the spoon, he scooped up a small amount and tossed it in. Nothing.

He shrugged, and playing to the camera, grinned and chucked in the entire bowlful.

The others gasped, there was a brief pause, and suddenly the vortex erupted in bright blue flashes and loud bursts. Everyone shrieked and ducked for cover, tent filling with smoke.

Fast as it occurred, it was over.

Max coughed, "Everybody okay?"

The others reported in, voices rattled. Ariel was stunned.

Literally, her heart hummed as if defibrillated, nerves tingling, arm and neck hairs prickled. She saw Tia's chopped hair bristled like a hedgehog.

From somewhere in the fog, Stan cried, "What happened?"

"I-I don't know," Max said, bravado knocked back.

The men picked themselves up, grabbed the women and camera, and hustled out to the "safe" side of the Trapping Horizon.

Looking back, they saw the vortex restored to its former state, regarding it with newfound respect as it completed its phases and dissolved.

Chapter 40

They regrouped in the living room, still shaking. How close they'd come to losing their lives was anyone's guess.

"That was a stupid-ass thing you did," Tia snapped at Max.

He shrugged. "I *was* a bit hasty. I'll stick to protocol next time."

As contrite as Ariel had ever seen him.

Tia was not appeased. "There'll be no next time till we know what the hell happened and how to avoid a recurrence."

"There could be a simple explanation," Stan said. "Maybe the hole can only absorb so much at one time, and we supersaturated it." He held up the video camera from the tent. "This may tell us. *If* the recording survived the blast."

He switched on the TV to connect the camera to it, and Ariel saw breaking news. The headline invoked groans from all:

NY governor calls to suspend TPC collider tests

Max snorted, "The sonofabitch was all smiles when TPC brought in construction jobs."

With the recession, even some progressive politicians had gone knee-jerk reactionary. And now it appeared another domino in the collider game was toppling. Ariel worried how much longer they had before their window on the universe closed for good.

Stan plugged their camera into the TV, and fortunately the video seemed unaffected by the explosions. Appearing on screen was a high-def recording of the last run, crystal-sharp, vortex dark and sinister against the canvas backdrop. Stan fast-forwarded until just before the mishap, then continued at normal speed as everyone leaned in.

Once again, Max hurled the rock salt into the hole. There was a brief pause, then the image bloomed white, and the audio blared *bang-bang-bang-bang-bang-bang-bang-bang.*

Ariel saw no obvious explanation for the eruptions.

Max said, "Run it again, slower. And move in tighter on the rim."

Stan re-cued and zoomed in on the inner right edge of the vortex where most of the explosions occurred. He repeated in slomo without audio, and Ariel watched a giant bowl swing into view discharging its contents. At this reduced speed, and with no sound, the blasts were no longer startling, if no more revealing.

"Again," Max directed. "Tighter and slower, still."

Stan took them in as close as resolution allowed, inner edge of the vortex forming a border on the right of the screen, the remainder of the picture black. Ariel was enthralled to see a few coarse rocks of salt magnified into little asteroids, tumbling lazily into view from the lower left foreground. They diminished in size as they approached the hole, disappearing into the void, trailed by a residue of powder that also vanished. But as was now apparent, a wisp of residue reached the rim, causing blue-white microbursts to flare. More and more, coalescing in a chain reaction that blinded the camera.

"Aha!" Stan cried. *"Salt dust.* The rim is sensitive to matter."

Ariel shuddered to think what might have happened had Max brushed against it.

Tia said, "I don't get it. The tent was thick with tobacco smoke, that didn't have any affect."

"Smoke particulates are much smaller than dust," Stan said. "The rim must have a tolerance level for size. Or quantity. Or substance. But the hole itself isn't a problem."

"Correct," Max said. "It's time we got a look from inside it."

Tia folded her arms across her chest. "Oh no, we don't."

"We've shown the hole is permeable. What more do you want?"

"Tossing stuff in isn't the same as sticking a camera through. Jump in the air and touch a high voltage wire, nothing happens. Do it from the ground, you're toast. Till we know better what we're dealing with, *no direct contact.*"

Seeing the others in agreement, Max folded his arms, too.

Ariel thought she'd noticed something else in the video, asking Stan, "Can we see it again? And this time, can you concentrate on the hole alone? And slow the speed to a crawl."

Stan focused on the center of the aperture, ignoring the rim. Once more Ariel watched the fusillade of salt rocks enter screen left, disappearing into the void as the camera was blinded periodically by mini flashes.

"Play it again, Stan," she asked. "Even slower."

Stan obliged, and just prior to the point of the explosions, Ariel cried, "Stop!"

The image froze on blackness, and she approached the TV pointing to the lower center of the screen, away from where the bursts were about to occur.

"Once more," she asked. "Everybody, watch this area."

The video repeated, and Ariel saw a crystal of salt appear in the darkness. As it tumbled, its facets picked up flashes of explosion. But it was moving *away* from the hole, growing in size slightly before exiting bottom screen.

Max screwed up his face. "It's heading the wrong way. Did the blast repel it?"

"No," Ariel said. "Watch close, it happens *between* the blasts." She told Stan, "Rewind a half second, zoom in far as you can, and advance frame-by-frame."

Stan did so, and the evidence was indisputable. The granule, larger and clearer now, could be seen departing the hole, moving toward the camera and off screen. And it wasn't the only one. With the tighter focus, Ariel saw more granules careening away in various directions.

Tia said, "I'll be damned. Some rocks struck the event horizon and bounced off."

"Not the event horizon," Ariel said. "The rocks disappear briefly before rebounding, and ricochet in different directions. Whatever they struck, it's *inside* the hole."

Max looked stunned. "But only a few rocks. Why not all?"

As the others continued to study the video, Tia excused herself to head back to the tent and look for rejected crystals. She returned shortly with tweezers and a baggie.

Shaking the bag, she said, "Eleven, if Max didn't spill any."

"Positive," he said. "Same number we counted in the video."

Stan fetched a microscope, and they gathered at the coffee table to examine specimens. No signs of scorching or other adverse effects, rocks none the worse for their roundtrip to wherever.

A stillness settled over them, and Stan said, "I can think of only one explanation. Our singularity has an obstruction inside. Something with an irregular shape that repels the rocks at odd angles. What we've got here is either an inter-dimensional aneurism, or a wormhole."

Inter-dimensional aneurism: a point in the membrane separating this universe from another where the membrane balloons, threatening to burst. Like the bulging of a weakened wall in a human artery. If so, the prospects for the team could not be more extreme. Should the singularity be an aneurism, to continue their tests risked rupturing it. And possible annihilation.

On the other hand, if it proved a wormhole, the prospects were staggering. A wormhole was a portal to another place, universe or dimension. A door enabling objects to pass through. And in this case, apparently in both directions. But as Ariel could imagine, such a trip would likely be lethal for living beings. The journey could wreak havoc on a body's cells and functions, not forgetting the dangers of whatever lay on the other side: heat, cold, radiation, the vacuum of space. Nor was human passage even possible in this instance. The hole was too small, the edge too volatile for so much as a child to safely squeeze through.

Regardless, if they could prove the singularity a wormhole, their finding would be on the order of Columbus discovering the New World. New *Worlds,* perhaps.

"It's a wormhole," Max said. "We've observed it from day one, nothing's entered it but what we've thrown in. Whatever's repelling the rock salt, it's preexisting, it didn't come from here."

Stan nodded, but Tia said, "The risks are too great to assume anything. We need more tests."

Ariel felt giddy. They were explorers on the threshold of a new frontier, and for someone so devoted to research, it was the most appealing dream imaginable.

Max asked her, "What was it you said about giving people a star to reach for? Promising the moon?" He smiled at her with a warmth she hadn't felt in ages. "Budget be damned, I say we go out tonight and celebrate."

CHAPTER 41

Tia and her friends were in high spirits after a wonderful evening. Max had driven everyone to Ithaca for dinner, a real city for a change, leaving pressures and protesters behind. They'd stayed out too late, drank more and spent more than they should have, entirely worth it. It reminded Tia of how cohesive their little team could be when Max's moods were stable. Precisely what they needed if they hoped to achieve their ambitious goals.

Over supper, everyone had agreed to Tia's stipulations that they continue their cautious, low-tech approach to prying secrets out of the vortex. And Max promised to rein in his impulses.

Stan took the wheel heading home, despite Max's slurred insistence he could drive. Tia sat in the back with Ariel, wind whistling through the taped-up rear window. A full moon gleamed above, and Tia dared hope they'd touch its surface yet.

But she had a more grounded concern now. She'd seen the way Ariel and Max had been looking at each other tonight. Ever since Ariel dumped him, he'd been angling for an "in," awaiting a chance to restore his wounded pride. Only a matter of time before he made his move, and given how it ended last time, it added a volatility neither Ariel nor the team could afford.

The surest means to avoid catastrophe was to remove Ariel from Max's clutches. But that wasn't going to happen so long as they were held here by the enigma in the front yard. The answer was to get to the bottom of that hole fast, and move on before Ariel's resistance wore out.

Tia sighed, swearing under her breath. After all, *she* was responsible for Ariel and Max's doomed affair. Eyes on the moon, she drifted back to the moment everything changed. To their first summer here, the day she woke before dawn and walked in on Ariel preparing to flee...

The form Tia encountered in the shower that morning wasn't human, but a white marble statue. Elegant, slim, limbs perfectly turned as if by a lathe. Champagne locks spilling over square shoulders, cascading to a slender waist. Aphrodite startled at her bath, frozen in embarrassment.

Ariel hastened to cover herself, insufficient to hide the flush spreading across her like sunrise. The poor thing's dazzling eyes were red and swollen—a singularly disturbing effect.

Tia said softly, "You're leaving. You found another place to live."

Ariel grabbed a robe off a hook, and slipped into it, blotting tears on a sleeve.

"Another job," she said. "A nuclear plant in Connecticut."

She dropped to the edge of the tub, head in hands, sobbing. Tia switched off the shower and sat beside her, arm around her heaving shoulders, snarling, "That bastard, Max."

Ariel shook her platinum hair. "Not just him. I get no respect at TPC, either. *Nobody* puts any stock in me or what I have to say. It's pointless."

Tia took a long pause, then said, "If you don't mind my saying, *mi corazón*, it's not your ideas they're reacting to. I've seen your work. It's smart, well-reasoned. You're a damned good analyst."

Ariel wiped her eyes, paying Tia a confused frown.

With nothing to lose now, Tia forged on. "But the way you present yourself... You have to realize, Ariel, people, as a rule, are superficial about things like style and clothes."

Ariel's frown deepened. "Wh-what do you mean?"

Tia sighed. "Have you ever given any thought to changing how you dress?"

The girl appeared taken aback. Tia gave her a squeeze, and said, "I don't mean to be critical, but those long-sleeved blouses and full-length skirts. It's *summer,* for chrissakes."

"But this is how I've always dressed."

"Were you born in the 1880s? I'm sorry, you look like you stepped off a Conestoga wagon."

Ariel blinked. Tia expected tears again, but the girl seemed more confused than hurt.

"...And your hair. You have *gorgeous* hair, and to wad it up on top your head? Who around here wears their hair like that?"

Now came the tears again. Ariel blubbered, "It's not my clothes or hair, it's *me.* It's how I look. I'm a *freak.*"

Tia felt a pang in her heart. "Who the hell put that in your head?"

Ariel snorted and tried to rise. But Tia held her back, and Ariel sobbed, "You have eyes, you can see. My whole life people have made fun of my appearance." Face fire red, she turned to Tia snapping, *"Look at me."*

Tia did. "To tell you the truth Ariel, I've never seen a woman more beautiful." She meant it.

Ariel scoffed bitterly. "The skin of a vampire! Eyes of Medusa!"

"You have *amazing* features. All you need is a little fine-tuning. If I told you we can change how people react to you, that you *can* fit in, would you be willing to give things another shot?"

"Change *Max?*"

Tia wasn't so sure, there. But knowing the guy's shallowness, she offered, "I wouldn't be surprised. If so, do you think you could be happy here at the farmhouse?"

Ariel moaned, "You've no idea how happy I've been here. It would mean *everything* to me!"

Tia had no idea because the girl had never before expressed those sentiments. And if, in fact, she'd been happy here despite Max, she had a pitifully low threshold. Just how miserable could her previous life have been?

"Postpone leaving one more day," Tia said. "Put yourself in my hands, and I'll prove it to you."

"Wh-what will I have to do?"

"Just trust me. I'll take care of the rest."

The girl searched Tia's face with those disorienting beacons, and Tia thought she saw a ray of hope. At length, Ariel inhaled and nodded, and Tia told her, "Good. But if we're going to pull this off, I'll need your *full* cooperation. And before we start, I want your solemn word on it."

Ariel reflected a moment, then gave another somber nod.

Tia handed her a shower cap. "Now finish up, get dressed, and meet me in the kitchen."

A half hour later, Ariel appeared in the kitchen doorway looking nervous, hair piled atop her head again, wearing her customary long-sleeved blouse and ankle-length skirt. Tia was at the table surfing the web. Ariel angled for a look, but Tia averted the screen, telling her, "Wait till the guys leave for work."

"We're not going in?"

"Vacation day."

Ariel made oatmeal for all, she and Tia ate, and when sounds of the men stirring drifted to the kitchen, Ariel put down her spoon with trembling fingers.

Tia placed her hand atop and told her, "Go back and lie down till they're gone. Keep your thoughts on how much better things will be tomorrow." She trusted she could deliver on that.

Ariel went to her room and shut the door, and the men rolled in.

"Ariel and I are staying home today," Tia announced, closing her laptop. "Not feeling well."

Max gave Stan a knowing look. "Synchronized menses."

Stan choked on his coffee.

The men bulldozed through breakfast, dumped their dishes in the sink, and left. Tia turned to Ariel and gave her the all-clear, ordering, "Grab your purse, we're going to town."

Ariel poked her head out her door. "What for?"

"To get you ready for the festival tonight."

It was the weekend of the Talawanda Township annual Summerfest, first chance the four had to check out the local social scene. Max was especially keen on it, TPC short on women who met his criteria.

Ariel started to object, but Tia reminded her of her oath. Biting her lip, Ariel grabbed her purse and followed Tia to the car.

"What's the festival have to do with this?" Ariel asked as they drove off.

"You'll see. We've got a busy day ahead."

A makeover was daunting for any woman, much less one who appeared to have just awakened from the 19th Century. But success tonight hinged on Tia's Pygmalion project...

Five hours later, Tia and Ariel were on their way home, backseat filled with boxes, Ariel's metamorphosis well underway. The girl kept gaping at her reflection in the visor mirror as if she'd never seen herself before. Certainly, she'd never seen herself like this. Her white-gold hair, likely uncut for a decade or better, was now shoulder length and smartly styled by Tia's favorite hairdresser. Parted on the right, it swept across her brow in a peek-a-boo, dropping in soft curls.

Ariel had resisted at first, but bound by her pledge, and perhaps secretly longing for a change, she'd relented. She looked stunning. And that was her reaction. Stunned.

She looked at the world differently, too. Tia had taken her to an optometrist to be fitted for contacts. The poor thing was obviously near-sighted, the way she squinted at distant objects and held books close. Also, astigmatic. But correcting her vision wasn't Tia's main objective. Those piercing silver lasers were now a soothing blue—the most transformative change Ariel would undergo. She stared wide-eyed out the window as if seeing everything for the first time.

Tia told her, "Now everyone else will see you in a new light, too. Townspeople. Coworkers."

"Max?"

Tia grunted, "One mountain at a time. How do you feel so far?"

Ariel blinked at her reflection. "Lightheaded."

"About a pound lighter, I'd say. You don't like it?"

"I-I, I don't look like *me* anymore." Dropping her gaze, Ariel scrunched her mouth. "You're *sure* this will work?"

Even in unfinished form, she was a compelling package.

"More than ever."

Ariel turned to regard the stack of boxes in the backseat. "And what are those?"

While Ariel was having her hair done, Tia had made the rounds to boutiques in town, picking out dresses, accessories, and other considerations for tonight. She grinned. "You'll see."

"But-but I can't afford all this."

"I told you, today is on me, *no argument.*" Tia could not deny she was enjoying herself, the most fun she'd had in years. And if it worked, worth every cent.

They arrived home on schedule, well ahead of the men, ferrying the boxes to Tia's room, piling them on the bed. Tia had Ariel change into a robe, and locking the door, she sat her at her dresser faced away from the mirror. Then grabbing a makeup brush like a maestro addressing her orchestra, she declared, "Now to complete the transformation."

Tia was no cosmetologist, but she had skills. She'd been doing her own makeup since twelve. Yet, she'd never faced anything this challenging. While Ariel possessed wonderful features—large eyes, high cheekbones, straight nose, full lips, clean-cut jaw and chin—each lacked definition, lost in a whiteout of pale skin, brows, and lashes.

A blank canvas. It would take an artist's hand to bring out the girl's natural beauty.

"Are you allergic to cosmetics?"

"Don't know, I never used any."

Tia began with foundation, and quickly Ariel's attributes took form. Like a photograph developing. Tia applied foundation to Ariel's entire neck as well, needing to cloak all telltale evidence of her identity. A touch of blush to the cheeks, and on to mascara.

Astonishing. Lashes all but invisible bloomed long and thick, petals of a morning glory unfolding, stark against the brightness of her now-sapphire eyes. A touch of eyeliner.

Ariel reacted to Tia's smile, begging, "Let me see!"

"Not till I'm done. Hold still."

Strokes of an eyebrow pencil brought out graceful arcs tapering to fine points. Crimson gloss ripened full, luscious lips. Tia stepped back to admire her work, keeping eager Ariel at bay. An incredible transfiguration. The woman bore *no* resemblance to the girl.

From outside the house, footsteps clumped on the porch, screen door banging. Ariel tensed, and Stan's voice called softly in the hall, "Hey, how you guys feeling?"

"Better," Tia called back.

"Want to join us for dinner at the festival?"

"No thanks, we'll eat here. Maybe we'll catch up with you later."

"Righto. Hope to see you there."

The men fuddled around their rooms for a time as Tia fine-tuned. Then the front door slammed, and silence again.

"Please let me look," Ariel pleaded.

Tia wanted to add accents of jewelry first. But relenting, she turned Ariel to the mirror and asked proudly, "Who's the fairest of them all?"

Ariel's enormous eyes grew larger still. *"Oh my God."*

Tia beamed. "What do you think?"

"I, I, I don't know what to think. It's not *me. I don't know this person.*"

"It's another facet of you. And importantly, no one else will recognize you, either. Tonight, you'll greet the world as a new woman."

Ariel's eyes glistened, and Tia grabbed her shoulders warning, "Don't cry, you'll streak."

To see this sweet, repressed girl enter the Twenty-First Century was immensely rewarding—

The sound of tires crunching gravel stirred Tia from her thoughts. They'd arrived home, their night of celebration over.

.

CHAPTER 42

The team skipped both runs today. Instead, they spent their time in the living room on their laptops, researching inter-dimensional singularities. While Ariel's experiment with the force field yesterday had ruled out the threat of black or white holes, their path forward still wasn't without risks. If, in fact, the vortex opened into an aneurism rather than the wormhole they were hoping for, their plan to launch test items into the hole could have grave consequences.

So far, however, Ariel's research had turned up nothing useful, and she feared they'd hit another roadblock. One she might not have an answer for this time.

But as they worked, Max helped take some edge off her frustration. She was pleased to see his euphoria from last night continued. He kept things lighthearted, laughing, joking. It reminded her of when they first dated, how fun he could be. She felt like the four of them were true collaborators now, relationships refreshed, rinsed clean of grudges and games. The family Ariel had always longed for. She would have welcomed another of his "looks," but it didn't come.

Not that she would have responded to it.

203

At length, having exhausted the research sources she'd been assigned, she told the others, "I hope you were more successful than me, I came up empty."

Her friends reported faring no better.

Everyone mulled the quandary for a time, then Max said, "Well, we can't just sit around sucking our teeth. What's our next move?"

Tia offered, "How about we go public with what we've got? It's still a great story."

"It's no moon landing," Max replied.

"It's a singularity with something inside it," Tia said. "*That* will get attention."

Max sighed. "You've got no head for publicity. What we have is a moon landing in the dark. It won't last one news cycle. We need visuals. The answer is to mount a camera on a pole, stick it in the hole, and record whatever the hell's in there. Plant a damned boot on the lunar surface."

Tia looked like she wanted to plant a boot somewhere else. "*That's* the scientific method they teach at Harvard?" she snapped, referring to Max's alma mater. "Give in to your impulses?"

Whether or not it was a crack at Max's bipolarity, he surely took it that way. He went fire red, stood, and stamped out of the room.

It seemed the team's interlude of camaraderie was over.

• • •

Uncertainty hung heavy in the air at dinner. Tia and Max sat tight as coiled springs, the silence between them fierce. Ariel had no appetite. As team leader, she felt feckless. There was one positive note, however. From Max's perspective, at least. He announced he'd been successful in selling Tia's Honda, and at asking price. It put them back in the black for the time being.

Tia rose and excused herself to watch the news, taking her plate to the sink untouched, and one by one, the others followed. Max entered the living room last, switching on the overhead. It flickered.

A common issue with the old house. He toggled the switch to no avail, swore, went to the fireplace and grabbed the shepherd's staff off the mantle. Giving the fixture a thump, he got it working and carried the staff to his chair just in case, using it to pry off his shoes and scratch his toes. Ariel watched Tia grind her teeth.

On the news, Republican Roger Filby was at a whistle stop in Ohio, on the steps of the Cuyahoga Falls Library bloviating to a crowd. A caption read: *Filby Smashes Smasher.* The man pointed a forefinger at the horizon, and Max upped the volume.

"*...You know what else they're hiding from you up there, folks, deep underground, all across that valley?*" His voice was smooth and folksy. "*I'm not talkin' 'bout the miles of tunnels an' fancy machinery they got buried there. I'm talkin' 'bout things you can't see 'cause they'll never be. I'm talkin' 'bout hospitals, schools, highways an' bridges left on planning boards, an' the jobs lost with 'em. That's what that white elephant's costin' you, friends. An' ever' time they run their collider, it's smashin' a new school bus, ambulance, fire truck. That's the trade-off. Just so a bunch a lab coats can poke around inside atoms.*"

"If it weren't for us *lab coats,*" Max snarled, "there'd be no TV to broadcast your bullshit."

Filby continued, "*Stand by me in November, give me a majority in Congress, and I pledge I'll end all the techno-pork. I'll stop the waste. I'll take that money an' put it back where it belongs—rebuildin' our country and armed forces.*"

The crowd loved it. Filby quieted them with a hand.

"*One more thing 'bout that collider, folks—and this can't wait till election.*" Dramatic pause. "*You've heard talk 'bout black holes an' radiation leaks an' explosions. TPC says it's all bunk. Well, I asked the U.S. House Committee on Science to look into it...*"

"Science Committee, my ass," Tia growled. "Run by fools who think the world's six-thousand-years old."

"*Turns out the threat is real.*" An anxious murmur swept the crowd. "*In the interests of national security, I'm callin' on Congress to get their butts back to Washington an' halt TPC's tests. An' I'm callin' on you, my friends, to contact your representatives and make sure they get the message."*

With TPC now a pawn of presidential politics, its future was indeed in jeopardy.

A grimness settled over the room. The news moved on, and Ariel said, "I don't understand. The election's just weeks away, why the urgency to close TPC now?"

Stan said, "Filby saw the InstaPolls turn against TPC, and he hopped the bandwagon."

Max added, "He and Thornton *created* the bandwagon. They spent years gunning for the collider, now the prize is in sight."

Tia agreed. "Kill TPC, they drive a stake through the heart of Big Science."

Max and Tia on the same side. If anything could bring this group together, it was their loathing of the anti-science movement. No doubt Thornton and Filby were colluding against TPC. Thornton had a murky history of political shenanigans.

"But why the rush?" Ariel asked. "Why risk the political capital?"

"Because even if Filby wins," Tia said, "the GOP fears they'll lose the Senate. The Dark Agers want TPC dealt with now while they still have control."

Max said, "Long as the polls favored TPC, Filby held off. No sooner do they turn, he's all in. No doubt he and Thornton planned the black-hole scare from the get-go."

Thornton, as head of a tax-exempt church, was prohibited from officially contributing money to politicians. Or collaborating with them politically, in any way. Or even supporting them publicly. Meaning that if he and Filby cooked up the black hole controversy so Filby could take the reins now, it was illegal.

Everyone fell silent. Then Max banged the butt of the shepherd's crook on the floor, startling the others.

"While we dither," he cried, "the noose tightens. For godsake, let's stick a camera in the hole and get on with it!"

Tia whipped around at him. "We've still no idea whether it's wormhole or aneurism."

"*Something* repelled those salt crystals," Max countered, "and it's no damned aneurism. I'm not asking you to risk your necks. Stay outside the Horizon, I'll do it alone."

As if the Trapping Horizon would protect them if Max ruptured the membrane.

Tia was livid. "Let's put it to a vote." She looked to Stan and Ariel. "You willing to stake everything on his hunch?"

Ariel wasn't. And Stan seemed uncertain.

Max pulled himself up with the staff and thumped down the hall to his room.

CHAPTER 43

Last night, Max had emailed everyone an obscure article he'd uncovered on the theoretical stability of cosmic membranes. He managed to gain some traction with Stan, but Tia and Ariel held the swing vote, and they weren't budging. This morning, Max had skipped breakfast to pout while the others sat over coffee discussing "safe" ideas for wresting new data from the hole. All they'd come up with so far were more items to toss inside.

"We haven't tried organics," Stan suggested. "How about fruits and veggies?" He laughed. "Maybe they'll come back cooked, we've yet to test for temperature."

Tia said, "I like the idea of things with soft or absorbent surfaces. If they rebound, the skins could bear impressions and traces of what they struck, giving us clues."

They devised a list of small-to-progressively larger test items, working with things at hand. Finished, Tia asked Ariel, "Can I borrow your car? I want to hit the bank when it opens, make sure this clears." She held up the check Max had gotten for her car last night.

"I'll drive you," Ariel said.

Not that she minded lending her car, she was concerned about Tia in town alone.

Leaving Stan to prepare the experiments, Max to brood, she and Tia grabbed Newton and departed in Ariel's old, rusted Buick.

The car was a high school graduation gift from Ariel's late Nana. Nana was Ariel's only family to stand by her after she revealed her college plans, Mom and Phil averse to secular schools. Big car, small engine, bad mileage. But preferable to Stan's truck, a stick-shift no one else could drive. And Max wouldn't let a dog in his Mercedes.

Tia shared the passenger seat with Newton, his head out the window, black and white fur swept back, tongue trailing like a scarf as they headed down the road.

Talawanda was fifteen minutes north of the farmhouse, a town of about 3,500 on an upper stretch of the valley where plains bumped into foothills. Modest but well-kept homes, steepled churches, town square in the colonial style. A nice place to raise a family, Ariel always thought. Locals were welcoming to TPC employees, even now with the controversy. The collider brought prosperity to the community, and the community brought common sense to its conservative principles. Ariel had never seen a townie among the protesters.

She drove down Main Street headed for First Federal of Talawanda, a brick building also in the colonial style. Two drive-thru lanes, both open, and busy.

Ariel pulled into the left behind two cars, and suddenly Tia hissed, "*Shit,*" and ducked behind Newton. "Don't look—those guys in the orange truck, *they're from the picket line.*"

Ariel couldn't help it. In the right lane a car ahead were two men in a hulking, safari-rigged Dodge Ram. Gun rack with rifles in the rear window, Georgia license plate reading *Born2.* The man at the wheel was huge, red beard, bare arm stuck out the window and covered in Celtic symbols. Ariel gasped to recognize the protester she and Max faced that last day at TPC's gate.

She threw her car into reverse, but a car had pulled in behind, blocking her. Then of all the luck, the car ahead moved up, vacating a space directly beside the truck.

Ariel felt paralyzed.

"Do it," Tia said. "Quick, before someone honks. Keep your head down."

Shrinking till she could barely see over the wheel, Ariel crept forward, stealing sideways glances. The men hadn't noticed, engaged in conversation.

Luckily, the car ahead wasn't long, and Ariel scooted up to the window into the shade of the overhang, feeling less conspicuous.

Tia thrust her check at her. "Make it fast."

Ariel slapped it into the outstretched drawer, but the teller recognized her, chirping into the speaker, *"Morning, Ms. Silva."*

Ariel winced. "We're in a hurry, please."

The woman obliged, dropping a receipt in the drawer along with a doggie treat. Ariel had forgotten about the treat. Not Newton. He jumped into her lap barking, leaving Tia exposed.

Ariel knew before she looked. The truck was at the station next to her now, men staring.

Tia muttered in a panic, "Get us the hell outta here!"

Tossing the receipt and treat to Tia, Ariel floored it, Buick limping away. She saw the truck's hood ornament in the passenger-side mirror, a chrome bighorn sheep, head lowered in a charge.

"If they follow," Tia croaked, "head for the police station."

The station was close, and unlike state troopers, local cops were friendly.

Last Ariel could see as she left the lot, the truck hadn't moved.

Tia peeked around to keep watch. "So far, so good."

They neared the town square. A right turn to the police station, left to the farmhouse. Ariel's mirrors showed all clear, and she began to breathe again.

"What do you think?" she asked.

"I just want to be home."

That sounded *so* good. Ariel turned left, proceeding without incident to the next junction. One more left, and it was on to the farm down the winding, two-lane highway...

Tia groaned, and Ariel felt her stomach clench. A shiny orange vehicle rolled into her mirrors with a flash of snarling, silver grill.

"What now?" she cried. To double back meant confronting the monster truck head-on, but she knew no other route to the station.

Tia's answer came out in a shiver. "Home. Maybe they didn't recognize us."

Ariel debated, then inhaling, she slammed the pedal and veered right, instead. The engine hadn't torque enough to squeal the tires, but Tia made up for it, shrieking.

"You're going the wrong way."

"I'm *not* leading them to the house."

Tia moaned, keeping vigil as Newton whimpered and the Buick's valves clattered like a maraca. Then Ariel heard the bottom drop out of Tia's voice.

"They're coming."

"Call 9-1-1!"

Tia emptied her purse in her lap, snatching her cell, dialing.

"Talawanda PD," Ariel could hear above the whining pistons.

"Help," Tia panted. "A truck's chasing us."

"Where are you?"

"State Route 21, ten miles south of Wayland, heading north."

The road narrowed, winding between fields of withered cornstalks. Ariel had never been this way, the orange in her mirror growing, silver sneer glowering. It occurred to her why they called these trucks *Rams.*

The voice said, *"Not our jurisdiction, I'll patch you to state police."*

"No!" Tia begged. A pause, then, "Hello-hello? *Christ.* No bars!"

"Keep trying. Does Wayland have a police station?"

"No idea."

At the rate the truck was closing, they'd never make it. Ariel fought her nerves as they hurtled along at twice the speed limit. And each time she hit the brakes to round a curve, losing sight of the truck, it would reappear a little larger in the dust she kicked up. Newton howled with fright. Or from Tia's grip.

They barreled into another turn, and Ariel saw a yellow road sign dead ahead, black arrow pointing ninety degrees left, *15 MPH.* Next to it, a raised billboard, *Wayland Life & Casualty.*

She approached too fast and swung wide, attempting to hedge the turn, stomping the brakes with both feet. Too late. Tia screamed, and they fishtailed, skidding, careening backward into the field in an explosion of dirt and corn shucks.

They ground to a halt in blinding dust, stunned but unhurt. Then came the roar of the truck, and a moment of eerie quiet followed by a wallop that rocked the earth. Ariel and Tia cowered, and as the cloud dissipated, they could see the billboard with a gaping hole in it, and behind that, a tunnel of sheared cornstalks. No sign of the truck, lost in the maize.

Newton whimpered, and Tia shushed him as they trembled and listened. Nothing but the tick-tick-tick of their car's stalled engine. The driver of the truck had apparently missed the road sign in the dust of Ariel's spinout, hitting the bank of the curve full speed, launching and soaring through the billboard headlong into the field.

Tia shook her head clear, sputtering, "What are we waiting for, *go-go-go.*"

"What if they're hurt?"

"*Hurt?* I hope they're *dead.*" Meeting Ariel's eyes, she snorted, "I'll call it in when I get a signal. Go—before they come to."

Ariel cranked the engine, it coughed and wheezed back to life, she threw it into drive, and they rattled back onto the road.

• • •

"Still no answer," Stan said, entering the tent with phone to ear, minutes till the first run. He'd been trying to reach the women, each time dumped into voicemail.

Max was bent over the table using the shepherd's staff like a cue stick. He popped one of the test items, a prune, straightening to suggest, "Maybe the check didn't clear."

"Wouldn't they have called us?"

"Coverage is spotty between here and town."

Stan shook his head. "Something's wrong. Come on, I'll drive."

Max pursed his lips. "We can't go off and leave the vortex unguarded."

It wasn't often they got visitors. Passersby asking directions, neighbor kids selling raffle tickets, the occasional Mormon. Still, if someone wandered into the tent and found the vortex...

Max added, "I can handle this myself, and I'll video everything."

Stan paused. He respected Max. All the same. "Swear you won't go sticking a camera in the hole."

Max looked insulted, but Stan wouldn't let him off. *"Swear."*

"I swear."

• • •

The dash clock read *10:00* as Ariel and Tia struggled homeward. They were missing the run, but the car shook so badly, Ariel was afraid to push it.

At last, they had cell service, and Tia reported, "Stan's been calling." She dialed him back. "Voicemail. I'll try Max... *Same.* Damned Trapping Horizon."

"Call in the accident," Ariel reminded.

Tia did, giving the police the location but refusing to leave her name, hanging up when pressed. She kept trying the guys, and to Ariel's relief, Tia finally cried, *"Stan.* Thank God! Yes-yes, we're fine, I'll explain later. How are you getting signal through the Horizon?"

Tia's face darkened and she said, "You left him *alone?* Jesus! Go back, we'll meet you there." She hung up swearing. "The idiot's in town looking for us. Max is by himself."

Ariel had a bad feeling. Checking the clock, however, she calmed. "The run's over, and the world's still in one piece."

"Yeah. But is *Max?*"

CHAPTER 44

Ariel turned the creaking car into the drive, her pulse outpacing her clunker.

"At least the tent's still standing," she noted to Tia.

Pulling in until she could see inside it, Ariel was grateful to spy Max bent over the table puttering, seemingly fine, if oblivious to them. No sign of the vortex.

Stan's truck barreled in behind them, and Tia got out with Newton, telling Ariel, "Park around back where the car can't be seen." And she headed for Stan.

When Ariel returned, Newton was on his chain at the doghouse. Tia and Stan were in the tent with Max, Tia flapping her arms like a bird defending its nest. Ariel could hear her shrill voice pipe across the lawn, unable to tell if Tia was railing at Max or recounting their narrow escape from the protesters. But as Ariel neared, she made out the words "red-bearded bastard."

Max spotted Ariel and beckoned with a cigar, a ribbon of smoke zigzagging in the air. Ariel ducked inside the tent into his crushing embrace, and he rumbled in her ear, "Last time you go anywhere by yourselves. I hope you broke their goddamn necks."

She felt safe in his arms, no longer able to hold back tears. When he released her, Stan grabbed on, and Ariel dried her eyes. Nothing in the tent appeared awry. Apparently, Max had followed through with the experiments, table bare of test items, nothing but the camera and a balled-up hankie. Yet, there was an odd flush to his cheeks. Maybe from Tia's harrowing tale.

Tia asked him, with edge, "So, how'd the run go?"

He paused a beat too long. "Good. *Great.*"

Met with suspicious stares, he added, "I followed the plan, I tossed in all your samples." He pointed to the camera. "See for yourself. Zero results. As I predicted."

There was more, and they stood waiting. He exhaled. "I finished early, and rather than waste the rest of the run..." he directed their attention to the table again. "You're not gonna believe what I found."

Stan wailed like a wounded animal. *"You gave me your word."*

"I said I wouldn't stick a camera in the hole, and I didn't." Carefully he picked up the hankie.

Ariel saw his hand shaking. She'd never seen him like this.

He turned to them. "Allow me to present the evidence we've been searching for." He opened the cloth like a magician unveiling a rabbit. *"Proof of a traversable wormhole."*

In the handkerchief rested a small, ragged scrap of what looked to be green foliage, no bigger than a postage stamp. Ariel leaned in as Max manipulated it with a toothpick, one side waxy, the other matte. He gripped his cigar in the same hand as the toothpick, smoke trailing into Ariel's face.

She pulled back. Like no cigar she'd ever smelled. And then she noticed, *not* a cigar, a smoldering stub of wood.

Tia squinted at the cloth. *"That* came from the hole?" Her tone sharpened. *"How?"*

"Like I said, I finished the tests no wiser, plenty time on the clock. So, I started tossing in anything expendable I could find. I got a little careless, and my fingers broke the plane."

The others gasped, but Max held up a hand to show, "Not a blister. Didn't feel a thing. A fortunate accident." Not that Ariel believed it an accident. "At that point, I figured no harm in a little probing, and the shepherd's staff was handy."

Tia swore, and Max hastened to add, "I was cautious. A blind man with a cane. I used the butt end, and instantly I hit obstacles. Some flexible, some rigid. No idea what. And when I pulled the staff out, that green matter was snagged on a splinter."

Ariel and Stan were upset, but Tia was fuming. As Stan examined the material in the handkerchief, however his frown dissolved. "If it's cellulose," he said, peering at it intently, "we should be able to identify its phylum—assuming it's not alien to our world."

Tia snarled at Max, "What about contamination?"

"It's a clean handkerchief," Max said.

"*No*, you idiot, that green stuff contaminating *us*."

Everyone edged back from the hanky. Stan found some plastic baggies, Max deposited the foreign matter into one, hanky in another, and Stan sealed them.

"And the shepherd's staff?" Tia demanded.

Max shifted his weight. "Already disposed of."

Facing stares again, he explained, "After I found that specimen, I was hoping for a bigger sample, so I flipped the staff to the hook end. But it hung up in the hole, and trying to free it, uh, it brushed against the rim."

He held up his "cigar"—the burnt brunt end of the staff.

Ariel felt her eyes bug. "That could've been your hand!"

"Better for us it were," Tia said, incensed. "That stump he's holding was *inside* the vortex. He's contaminated himself, us, everything he's touched."

Recalling Max's hug, Ariel cringed. He'd also exposed the other side to infection from them, his cowboy bluster elbowing aside his science sense.

All eyes were on the charred remnant in his hand.

Stan produced another baggy to ask, "What now?"

CHAPTER 45

After lunch, anger still smoldering, Ariel and Tia left the house for the tent. The men were already there, prepping for the next run, and what promised to be their most exciting experiment yet. If all went to plan, they'd soon know what lay on the other side of the vortex.

Max, by hook and crook, had proven that contact with the event horizon was harmless, and that there was, indeed, something of substance on the other side. No doubt the vortex was a window to *somewhere*, the evidence for a traversable wormhole, now overwhelming.

In advance of the run, the men had created a device to peer across the divide. An HD video camera mounted to one end of a sawed-off rake handle. While bulkier than a cell phone, the HD camera avoided the problem of recording blindly. By running a coaxial cable down the shaft and into a laptop on the table, the team could view what was happening live, on screen, using remote controls to adjust the picture and help avoid obstacles on the other side.

If, that is, the signal could bypass interference from the vortex.

Ariel crossed her fingers. Hopefully, they were about to verify something the world had never seen. *Physical teleportation.* The makings for a historic press conference to salvage their careers, rescue TPC, and halt the anti-science tide sweeping the country.

She entered the tent with Tia to see Stan at the table, glasses off, squinting into a microscope.

He looked up, beaming. "As we suspected, that green spec from inside the hole is *cellulose*. Plant material. Now to determine if it's a flora known to science." And he resumed his work.

Max sat opposite testing laptop controls for the polecam, and the women donned surgeon's gloves, their job to disinfect the polecam with antiseptics and a sterilizing lamp. Though the contamination barrier had already been breached, they hoped not to make it worse.

They'd hardly begun when Ariel heard the crunching of gravel and Newton's "intruder" bark. Out the tent window, a car was pulling into the drive.

State troopers.

"Shit," Max spit.

Ariel tensed, and Tia asked, "Unpaid traffic tickets?"

None anyone was aware of.

The car parked behind Stan's truck, and two block-shouldered officers in brown uniforms and flat-brimmed hats got out. One headed for the house, the other took down Stan's license plate number, calling to his partner, "TPC parking permit," and he continued to the backyard.

"They can't come in here without a warrant," Stan said. "Zip the tent till the run's over."

"That won't keep them out of the Trapping Horizon," Max said. "If they hear the noises, they'll have probable cause to enter."

The clock read 1:49, and Tia urged, "Get rid of them. *Fast.*"

Max rose, but she stepped in front of him. "No, *I'll* handle it."

Good move, knowing Max's history with state troopers.

Tia rushed out of the tent, and the others crept to the door to peek. One cop headed for the porch, and spotting Tia, changed direction. She broke into a trot and reached him before he crossed the horizon line, trying to usher him to the house. But he held his ground, eyeing the tent.

"Someone reported an accident this morning," he told Tia. "State Route 21 south of Wayland. We traced the call to a cell phone here, registered to Tia Diego."

"That would be me," Tia said. "I called it in."

"You witnessed the accident?"

"Yes."

The second cop rounded the house to join them, reporting to his partner, "Car in back fits the description of the second vehicle. Cornstalks in the bumpers." He referred to his cell phone, adding, "Ohio plates—owner is a 'Ariel Silva.'"

Ariel swallowed.

"My, my roommate," Tia said.

"Silva was driving?" the first cop asked. "You were with her? Anyone else?"

"Uh, yes. Uh, no. I mean, just us."

"We want to speak to her, too," the second cop said. "She here?"

Tia turned for the house, but the first cop grabbed her arm, and Ariel clenched to see his partner pat Tia down. Tia was furious.

"What's this?" the partner asked, holding up a canister of mace.

"Protection from groping men," Tia snarled.

The man pocketed the mace and took Tia's arm again, turning her toward the tent to say, "You girls wouldn't be up to something funny out here, now would you?"

Ariel watched in horror as the cops undid the thumb snaps of their sidearms.

Max growled, "They think we're cooking meth."

He motioned Stan and Ariel to their chairs, and scrambled to join them, their backs to the door. Stan bent over his laptop, Ariel hoisted the polecam in quaking hands, and Max aimed a sterilizing lamp at it. The clock read *1:53*.

Outside the tent, footsteps came to a stop, and Ariel heard the cop say, "Far enough." Then louder, into the door. "You in there, *freeze*— hands on your heads."

Ariel's hands flew to her head, heart threatening to pound through her chest.

Max snapped, "Which is it? 'Freeze,' or 'hands on our heads?'"

"Hands on your head, wise ass," the cop barked, entering with Tia and his partner.

Max complied, but added, "If we were up to something illegal, you think we'd be dumb enough to do it in a tent *in the front yard?*"

The man thrust Tia into the empty chair and began patting down Max and Stan. The second cop sorted through the equipment on the floor, then came around the table to inspect the laptops, the first cop joining him. Ariel noticed little gold crosses on the lapels of their uniforms. They found nothing on the computers but images of plants, and moved on to the polecam.

Max snapped, *"Don't*—it's sterile."

They hesitated, frowning at it. Then the second cop picked it up.

"What the hell's this?" he asked.

"A glutes detector," Max said. "Careful, you'll set it off."

The man handled it gingerly, returned it to the table, and told his partner, "I don't know what they're up to, but it ain't drugs."

"Drop your hands," the cop told everyone. "Keep 'em on the table where we can see."

He backed toward the center of the tent—exactly where the vortex was about to materialize. His partner went to stand beside him, and they faced the team. The clock read *1:57.* Ariel traded anxious glances with the others.

The first cop said, "No more bullshit. Tell us what you're doing out here."

Max replied earnestly, "Waiting for the Rapture." He'd seen the crosses, too.

The cop went livid. Stepping forward, he bent down and stuck a thick finger in Max's face.

"I've had my fill a you, asshole," he snarled. *"Not another word."*

He turned the finger on Ariel. "You got a smart answer for me, too, doll?"

221

Her pulse rocketed and she stammered, "R-r-research."

"Yeah, I can see. What *kind* a research?"

The clock ticked to *1:58*, and the cop walked around behind her, pressing close.

Her head swirled, and she blurted something that popped to mind out of nowhere.

"The effects of gamma rays on man-in-the-moon marigolds."

She stiffened to feel rough hands on her back. And when the hands slid down to her waistband and hips, she gasped, panicking. A long-buried trauma welled up in her like lava, the room spun, grew dark, and she slid from her chair.

• • •

The next she knew, Ariel was lying on the couch in the living room, a pillow under her head, Tia, Stan, and Max hovering. She bolted upright, and Tia grabbed her shoulders to assure, "It's okay, *mi corazón*, the cops are gone. You passed out."

Stan offered water, and Ariel pushed it away. *"The wormhole."*

Max grinned. "We carried you out of the tent just in time."

Stan added, "The second we crossed the Horizon, Newton started howling. Couldn't have cut it any closer."

She sank back, dizzy. "What did they want?"

Tia said, "The truck that chased us this morning? The assholes filed a complaint. Said we ran *them* off the road and left the scene. Lucky we weren't arrested, but there'll be a court hearing."

The thought of facing those brutes in court made Ariel feel faint again. She said in disbelief, "The police took *their* side?"

"If they didn't before," Tia said, "they do now. They know we're former TPC. They think we're out here on a research grant, wasting taxpayer money."

Stan laughed. "Studying marigolds."

Max wasn't laughing. "The bastards made us miss the run."

CHAPTER 46

The team picked up where they'd left off yesterday before the disruption. As the morning run approached, Max stood next to the space in the tent reserved for the vortex, a sawed-off rake handle in his grip like a golf club. Affixed to the other end was a video camera, wire trailing up through his hands and over to a laptop on the table, a live image of the tent floor on its screen.

The plan was for Max to introduce the camera into the hole via the pole, and let the wire carry a signal back to reveal what was inside. If the transmission failed, hopefully the camera's memory card would record details for replay upon removal.

There was concern, however, about Max wielding the cumbersome polecam. His last brush with the vortex had cost him the shepherd's staff, if not some fingers. And to ensure he kept his focus, they positioned the laptop so he couldn't see its screen. Stan would be his eyes, presuming the camera furnished a picture. But there was no doubt among them any longer, they were dealing with a wormhole. The burning question now, a wormhole to *where*?

Tia asked, "What are the odds the plant material Max snagged isn't terrestrial? Has to be."

Stan replied, "Not necessarily. If the other side *is* extraterrestrial, and its physics and environment closely reflect ours, it's possible plant life there evolved along a similar path."

To Ariel's surprise, Max said, "I'm with Tia. I say the wormhole is a portal to somewhere here on Earth. I cite Occam's Razor."

Occam's Razor. A principle of problem-solving also known as The Law of Parsimony. In effect, it said, *Answers must be drawn from known data—and the simpler, the better.* Applying the Razor to the wormhole, Earth was the only place known to have plant life, therefore the most logical outlet for the portal. Ariel had great esteem for The Razor. She'd first come across it as a freshman in high school. Over time, its keen edge had helped sever her fetters to her Faith. And once again, she found Occam persuasive.

Max could hardly contain himself. "A traversable wormhole is a Star Trek beam-me-up-Scotty," he said. "Imagine teleporting to the moon, the planets, and beyond—assuming wormholes can be enlarged enough for human passage."

"Even if we could fit inside it," Tia said, "we've no idea what effect traveling through a wormhole would have on us."

Ariel noted, "It didn't seem to harm that plant material."

"Cellulose isn't flesh," Tia replied. "We've seen the damage the rim can do. No telling what effect the hole would have on human tissue and brains that pass through it."

Max shrugged. "Even if the hole limits us to inanimate objects, the applications are mind-blowing. Only a matter of time before science brings down operational costs, then, *boom,* a revolution in commercial transport. A whole new global industry. UPS will be all over this. The post office. The military. It'll be *huge.* And *we're* at the forefront."

Ariel hadn't considered those aspects. In the next few minutes, they could be exploring a strange new world, boldly going where none had before. Or, visiting some distant, Earthly locale in a new and transformational means of travel. The prospects were indeed mind-blowing.

Newton's barks refocused them, and in moments the vortex formed and opened its dark eye once more. Max adjusted his grip and raised the polecam like Ahab confronting his whale.

"Ready?" he asked.

They were, and he turned and slowly advanced the camera toward the hole. The others huddled around the laptop, Ariel girding for an alien world as the camera crept into jet-black void.

Not Ahab, she thought with a shudder. *Dante.*

The lens broke the event horizon, the image went haywire, and she jumped. But the camera quickly crossed the plane, and the picture settled to black again. Still, Ariel could detect nothing in the darkness, and feared they'd lost signal.

"A-OK so far," Stan said, monitoring the transmission.

Ariel leaned in tighter to him and Tia, feeling their tension.

"Talk to me," Max begged, flying blind.

"Nothing yet," Stan said. "We should've added a spotlight. If we don't see something soon, I'll switch to night vision."

Max had plenty of pole left, pressing ahead. Suddenly Ariel could make out patches of lighter shadow and hints of bizarre shapes all around, unrecognizable.

Stan told Max, "We're starting to get something."

Tia's voice went hoarse. "What's *that?*"

Ariel saw, too. Looming straight ahead, a slim, tapering, forking structure extending up toward the camera from lower left to upper right. Gray, eerie. The camera headed straight for it, and just as Stan gave warning, the image jarred and went out of focus.

"What'd I hit?" Max cried.

"Don't know," Stan said. "Shift right, I'll switch to night vision."

Max did, and the image changed over to ghostly green. He pushed on, and the path cleared. More forking shapes floated into view here and there in the murk. Ariel gasped to see them give rise to what looked to be an unearthly forest of little, pale palm trees.

"My God," Stan said. "An alien world, all right."

"What? *What?*" Max pleaded.

Tia replied, "A network of branches bearing tiny parasols."

Max hooted with glee.

The camera brushed past the last of the thicket out into open space, and stopped. Ariel tore away from the screen to see Max straining at the limits of the pole, but she couldn't resist the surreal landscape, sucked back in. Appearing now was a panorama of gloom pierced by a dozen narrow, parallel shafts of bright green light. The shafts cascaded steeply downward, right-to-left. Beyond were mere suggestions of shapes. Gauzy, indiscernible.

Tia described the scene to Max, asking, "Give us some angles."

He obliged, image arcing upward into black, only to jar again.

"Another obstacle," he grunted, tacking right, directly into the light. The lens flared and bloomed, and Ariel blinked. Stan corrected the iris remotely, and Ariel winced at swaths of brilliance.

"Talk to me," Max said.

"Rays of light," Tia told him. "Keep angling."

The camera tilted down, and Ariel saw the light bathe what looked to be farmland viewed from a distance. A cultivated field of concentric, oblong rows, radiating out.

And it struck her. *That's not what this is...*

Max grunted again, struggling to hold position. "Running outta steam," he admitted, brow glistening. "One last look."

He leveled the pole and swung the camera around like stirring a sideways pot of cosmic soup, hands scant inches from the rim.

"Careful," Ariel told him.

The camera swiveled left and the screen went dark once more. Stan searched for focus, finally centering on distant objects. Ariel could pick out faint outlines and shapes, edges too straight and uniform to be natural. And at last, she put it together.

So did Stan and Tia, all three inhaling as one.

Ariel whispered, *"We're inside a room somewhere."*

"What?" Max gasped, withdrawing the pole, setting it aside on a sterile receiving cloth. With the vortex still churning, he rushed to join the others, shaking cramps from his fingers.

Ariel's fingers ached, too, having clenched the seat of her chair the entire time.

"Rewind, let me see," Max cried, leaning over them.

Ariel felt a warm hand on her shoulder, brawny musk filling her head. Stan cued the video, and once again they traveled through the rabbit hole into the strange, gray-green jungle. In light of what she now knew, Ariel viewed it differently.

Max's hand tightened on her, and he muttered, *"Holy crap."*

The more he saw, the tighter his grip. As the video neared the end and the geometric shapes appeared in the gloom again, Stan froze the image, enhanced the resolution, and zoomed in.

Max's fingers became a vise, and he breathed, "You're right, a room. With a long table. And what's that at the back? A computer monitor and chair?"

No question the wormhole linked to a place of human habitation. Terrestrial, surely, though as Stan noted, "We can't rule out a parallel universe."

Stan rewound and replayed, slowing the video to a crawl, manipulating the controls for added clarity. The eerie forest of parasols materialized once more as the camera drifted through, and when the image shook from a collision, Stan stated the now-obvious. "Our obstruction is a houseplant, and the hole opens directly behind it. We're in someone's home."

Tia and Ariel agreed.

They continued the odyssey, and Tia added, "Past the plant on the right, a window with blinds. And from the angle of the sun's rays through it, this is in our time zone."

The camera tilted down, and Ariel noted, "A hardwood floor with a braided-rag throw rug, like my Nana used to make."

As the view leveled, Stan enhanced the brightness and resolution, and Max said, "A TV. And to its left, a bookshelf."

The view shifted further left, and Stan froze the image, calling everyone's attention to a dark shadow at the bottom of the screen.

"A couch."

It seemed so. The video rolled on, view elevating to take in the rest of the room. A long room. Stan worked the controls to focus on the far end of the table, more items apparent now.

"Next to the computer monitor," Max said, "a printer. Papers, books, odds and ends. Got to be something there with a name or address or phone number."

Tia said, "By the looks of the clutter, the occupant's a man, and lucky for us he's not home. Probably at work at 10:00 AM on a Wednesday."

"Unless the vortex scared him off," Stan suggested.

"I doubt he can even see it, that plant's a thick screen."

Max nodded. "He's still around. All that stuff we threw in there, somebody cleaned it up." He grinned. "In any event, we've got our moon landing. All we need now is to figure out where Tranquility Base is, and it's ticker-tape time."

Tranquility Base—the site on the moon where Apollo 11 landed.

"How do we contact him?" Ariel asked. "Leave him a note with our phone number?"

Max shook his head. "We do that, he'll turn us in for unlawful entry. He may not see the vortex, but he damned-well saw the stuff we dumped on his floor. We're gonna need his cooperation for our press conference."

He stared at the frozen image on the laptop. "Any clues to where this is?"

Blank looks. But Tia thought to ask, "Does the video have a soundtrack?"

Stan replayed, upping the volume, and Ariel heard muffled horn honks, the bustle of traffic, a siren. Wherever it was, it was urban.

"Nice work, Tia," Max said. "Now, *what* city?"

CHAPTER 47

"Tell us about this press conference of yours," Tia asked Max as the team caucused in the living room. He grinned and set his sandwich on the coffee table, tilting back in his chair.

"You're gonna love it," he told her. "Assuming this guy exists in our world, which I'm certain he does, and assuming we get his support, which I'm certain we will, we'll send notices to the major news media—especially TV. We'll promise them the biggest story since Apollo 11. And with our connections to TPC, we'll have no trouble getting their attention.

"On the day of our conference, each media sends us two news teams. Ariel and I meet the first set of teams here at the farm, you and Stan meet the second set at the guy's home, wherever that turns out to be. Then just before the run begins, we do live simulcasts from both locations."

His eyes went distant. "Picture it. All over the world, TV's showing split screens. Screen left, a simple country yard—no tent, just the tree and TPC tower in the background. Screen right, the living room of a home in some far-away place. Then eerie noises, and suddenly a vortex materializes on both screens out of thin air. Black holes open, and just when everyone fears the worst, Stan and I play pitch-and-catch through the vortex with a baseball, miles apart."

Ariel smiled. A stunning, P. T. Barnum-style demonstration of a traversable wormhole, Max as master of ceremonies, of course. No doubt it would rock the world.

Or, as he put it, "Straight from the Dark Ages to the moon."

Assuming, that is, the team could identify where in the world the home was located. If, indeed, it was located in *their* world.

• • •

For the two o'clock run, Max added a small spotlight to the polecam. He hoped to target the room's bookcase and desk to shed light on a mailing label or other means of identification. Again, for safety's sake, he couldn't see the screen, Stan to be his eyes.

Soon Newton began to bark, Max switched on the spotlight and hefted the pole, and when at last the hole opened, he worked the camera through the plant far as the event horizon allowed.

Instantly Ariel saw on screen the bookcase illuminated against the wall near the TV. Much clearer than previous, though most contents were obscured by the arm of the couch. In the bluish glow of the spotlight, she saw DVDs, books, magazines. Stan zoomed the camera in, magnifying items on the top shelf. Ariel was excited to make out the cover of a *Popular Science.*

Stan said, "Videos, books, magazines with English titles. If Tia's right about the time zone, it appears we're in the U.S. or Canada. No address visible yet."

Tia told Max, "Get to the desk before your arms tire."

Max grunted, "It would be a damn sight easier if I just broke the plane with my hands. We know it's terrestrial over there."

"What if it's a different dimension, and you contaminate it?" Tia said. "Stick to protocol."

Max grumbled and swung the pole to the left, fighting branches of the plant. Finally, the desk lurched into view, light exposing items on its surface. Stan zoomed-in tight as possible, calling out to Max, "Back of a flat-screen monitor, a keyboard. Digital clock. Books, papers, pens. Coffee mug, tape dispenser, stapler, stack of mail. Bag of Cheetos, candy wrappers..."

They examined every visible inch of surface without shedding further clues on their mystery. Time up, Max withdrew the pole, panting, "Those magazines on the shelf? The mail on the desk? One's bound to show an address. How do we get to them?"

• • •

That night after dinner, they sat with sketchpads, mulling ideas for a better bead on the room. Not as simple as Ariel had expected. Even the most powerful zoom lens couldn't compensate for obtuse angles, see around corners, or read things lying flat and backwards. Nor was adding an extension to the pole the answer. Strong as he was, Max had struggled the last run.

They considered a smaller camera and lighter pole, but that presented a different problem. *Cantilever sag:* the natural give in a pole when extended horizontally. The greater the distance, the greater the sag. Given the vortex opened less than seventeen inches, even the best graphite composite pole—plus camera, light, and cable—would need to arc so high to reach its targets, trying to compensate for the sag risked contact with both top and bottom of the rim. Like a fly fisherman trying to land a trout through a porthole. A *lethal* porthole.

Exploring alternatives, they sketched out contraptions supported by shoulder harnesses, wires, and counterweights. They looked at adding landing gear on the pole tip to bear the load once it reached a surface. All too unwieldy and impractical.

At length, they took a break, and Ariel ferried table scraps to Newton. When she returned, she saw the team reassembled with arms folded, faces grim.

"What's wrong?" she asked.

Stan said, "We've got good news and bad."

She sat slowly, asking for the good first.

"I got a match on the plant cellulose Max snagged," Stan said. "Earthly origins all right. *Schefflera actinophylla.* A common umbrella tree."

"And the bad?"

"TPC had a glitch during the last run. A quench in the e-mags at the thirty-seven-mile marker. Operations are on hold for repairs."

Quench. Not an uncommon occurrence in cyclotron colliders, caused by a section of electromagnets failing for some reason. Loss of cryogenic coolant, for example. If severe, it could result in an explosion. But with the fail-safes TPC had in place, Ariel trusted that wasn't the case, and they'd be looking at only a minor setback.

Max, however, added, "When operations do resume, both the damage and repairs could alter the quantum mechanics in unpredictable ways. The vortex could well materialize elsewhere. No telling where. Or disappear altogether."

In fact, they'd no idea how the processes within the collider combined to spin off the vortex, or why the hole formed where it did, under their tree, connected to some home, somewhere.

Ariel stared out the window at the harvest moon, orange and huge. So close, so distant.

CHAPTER 48

Last to rise, Ariel wandered into the kitchen, greeted by the others with an update on the collider. Damage was limited to circuitry, she was relieved to hear. The emags had survived unscathed. A minor setback unlikely to affect the wormhole. Repairs were underway, and TPC was planning a test tomorrow at noon, no smashing, a dry run. If it went well, full operations would resume Saturday at 10:00.

"And *more* good news," Stan said. "Max came up with a way to ID the home."

It seemed Max had a gift for working out problems in his sleep.

Tia was quick to add, "But hold the confetti, he won't tell us what the plan is."

"I've got some work to do first," Max said, cagily. "Let's see how it goes."

Sandbagger. Ariel knew that smile. He had an answer, and he wanted to roll it out with pizzazz.

Leaving in his car after breakfast for parts unknown, he returned by lunchtime, a large package under his arm, same smirk on his lips. Grabbing sandwiches, he went to his room and shut the door. Everyone knew not to disturb him.

He came out for supper, only to take his plate back with him. The others dined in his absence, and Tia snipped, "I don't like the secrecy. We can't put all our faith in Mr. Wonderful, we need a backup plan."

"Darned if I've got one," Stan said.

They poked at their food for a time. Then Tia sat up and snapped her fingers. "Wait a minute. Our phones have GPS locaters. We stick one through the hole, and *bingo*, the home address!"

Stan shook his head. "There's a Trapping Horizon on the other side, too. A satellite signal can't penetrate it, the GPS won't work."

Tia pushed back her plate. "I give up. All the money's on Max."

As if she'd summoned him, he popped around the hall doorway and proclaimed with a grin, "That would be *smart* money."

He entered with the panache of a ringmaster, carrying a large object. Setting it on the table, he held it in place with a single finger to say, "Aerial reconnaissance."

A blimp. A gas-filled, radio-controlled model airship with electric propellers. Bright yellow and blue with white letters on the sides reading: *Charles Fort.*

"I considered a drone," he explained, "except the rotors would scatter papers on the desk. This is harder to fly, but creates little turbulence." He pointed to the gondola undercarriage. "Had to make a few adaptations: LED spotlight, micro camera, microphone."

"Brilliant," Stan said, examining it with delight. "And beautiful. But how will you control it? It's wireless, the vortex will block the signals."

Having Stan moor the blimp, Max ducked back to his room, returning with a laptop connected by cable to a three-foot antenna.

"We've proven signals transmit through the vortex by wire," he explained. "We'll launch the blimp through the hole, then insert this antenna. I'll steer from the image the camera sends back to the laptop, safely removed from the rim."

"Impressive," Tia had to give him. "But what's a *Charles Fort?*"

"Who," Max corrected. "Charles Hoy Fort, 1874-1932. A writer

who coined the term 'teleportation' a century ago. My homage."

Everyone smiled, and Stan gave the ship a measured look. "Gonna be a tight fit."

"Less than two inches clearance," Max said. "And before we can launch it, we've got to move that plant out of the way."

Stan said, "I'll bet I can tip it with a rake. I'll give it a try tomorrow during TPC's test run."

But Tia raised another obstacle not so easily overcome. "Even if we do ID this guy, how do we gain his cooperation? We've been trespassing, after all."

"We'll cross that event horizon when we come to it," Max said. And beaming, he took his creation into the living room to hone his flying skills.

Two days to prepare before TPC resumed smashing atoms.

CHAPTER 49

Ariel had never been to the ocean, she couldn't take the exposure. Yet here she was, lying on a beach under a tropical sun, soothed by a soft breeze on her cheek and the burble of waves…

Only to realize as she opened her eyes, the burbling was giggles, and the breeze from whirring fan blades. A bulbous shape hovered scant inches from her nose, and she shrieked.

There was an explosion of laughter, and she turned to see Tia at the bedroom door holding a laptop as Max worked its keys and Stan peeked over their shoulders with an antenna, all howling hysterically. Ariel's fright dissolved and she felt herself flush, laughing, too.

"Come on, you lazy thing," Max told her. "An hour till liftoff."

Ariel felt lucky she hadn't been caught with Newton, too tired to fetch him last night.

• • •

Max led the procession across the lawn to the tent, clutching his airship in front of him with both hands. As usual, the weather was calm and cloudless. Perfect conditions to float their trial balloon.

Ariel took her place at the table, handling the tripod camera today. For the first time since this bizarre adventure had consumed their lives a week ago, she felt they were about to gain control. If only they could identify the owner of the home where the vortex led them, they might present the world with proof of a traversable wormhole. *Teleportation.* The stuff of fiction. A vision to fire imaginations everywhere, rekindling the nation's love affair with science.

So much rode on the flight of the *Charles Fort,* and if anyone could pull it off, it was Max. For once, his overweening attitude was an asset.

Ariel studied him as he stood checking his aircraft. Clean shaven. Black hair neatly combed. In an open-collar shirt, sleeves rolled a turn. The rangy swagger of a cowboy, every inch a bold hero of legends, ready for his moment in the spotlight. Not hard to imagine him a media star. Witty, and when he chose, charming. Offset by his ever-ticking downside…

Everyone had a vital role this morning. Once the wormhole opened, Stan would use a rake to shove the plant out of the way, if necessary. He'd toppled it yesterday during TPC's test run, but surely the occupant set it back. Then Max would launch the blimp through the hole, Tia would insert the antenna, and if all went to plan, video would transmit to the laptop, enabling Max to steer the ship with a joystick. Ariel's job was to record the historic event on camera and track the time, keeping Max posted so he could sail the blimp out before the hole snapped shut.

Eyes on the clock, Ariel gave a ten-second countdown and hit "record," Newton began to howl, cut off by rumble and whine, and at last, the vortex appeared.

Ariel started the stopwatch, the hole opened, and Stan plunged the rake inside. Meeting resistance, he cleared the way and stepped back to give Max a thumbs-up. Max took his place at the vortex, smiling, presenting *The Charles Fort* to the camera. But when he turned to the hole and prepared to launch his ship, a noise came from outside the tent. Newton, howling again.

Except, that wasn't possible. No sound could penetrate the Horizon's bubble. Max turned to look, and his eyes went wide as a shape brushed past Ariel onto the table. It bounded off straight into Max, off Max into the hole, and vanished inside the void.

A puff of fur-scented smoke filled the air.

Max stormed at Ariel, *"You didn't chain him?"*

Rising on shaky legs, Ariel staggered to the hole and gaped inside. No trace but pungent odor.

"Oh my God," she cried, horror-stricken. She *had* chained him.

She burst into tears, and Tia dropped her antenna and ran to her.

Stan whispered, "Holy smokes—*it vaporized him.*"

Tia shot him a glare. "We don't know that. He could have made it through." She called into the void, "Here, Newton. *Here, boy.*"

Nothing.

CHAPTER 50

Hours passed, and Tia sat with Ariel on the living room couch, still trying to comfort her. The poor thing was heart-broken, having refused lunch to hole up in her room sobbing. Finally, Tia was able to coax her out with a cup of tea, if unable to stop the tears.

The only other time Tia had seen her like this was back when Ariel and Max were an item, and Ariel had learned he cheated on her. Tia blamed herself for that mess. In helping Ariel transform herself, Tia had also changed Max's mind about Ariel. But never in a million years had Tia imagined the girl could fall for a man who'd so abused her and her dog.

Tia thought back to the night of the town festival. To that strange, magical evening three years ago when Ariel emerged at last from her cocoon...

It was the event of the year. The annual Talawanda SummerFest. Max and Stan had already left for town to have dinner, Tia keeping Ariel under wraps in her room. Once the coast was clear, she and Ariel ate in the kitchen, in robes. Tomato soup and grilled cheese, Tia recalled only too well. She remembered gawking between bites

239

at Ariel's utter metamorphosis, as Ariel flashed smiles of embarrassment and smudged lipstick. Tia nagged to keep her from scratching her makeup, wondering how anyone could grow up so repressed in this day and age. But after tonight, Ariel would become more open about her past.

"So, what's the plan?" Ariel asked, blue eyes anxious.

"The plan," Tia said, "is to conduct a little experiment. Get you in front of people you've never met, let them see you for the first time, see how they react."

"I'll tell you how they react," Ariel sighed. "They stare, they gape, and they point."

Tia smiled. "For different reasons tonight, I'll bet. And if that goes well, we'll test out some TPC colleagues. There should be plenty at the festival. Now, go change into your new dress."

A short time later, they rendezvoused in the kitchen, and Tia marveled to behold the finished product. Ariel had been unable to pick from the several outfits they'd brought home, so Tia chose for her. A simple, elegant, sleeveless black dress. Very flattering to her figure, and Ariel was uncomfortable with it, face flushed. Yet, she looked absolutely breathtaking. Red-carpet-ready in matching black pumps and purse, a far cry from her old, puritanical wardrobe.

But the color of her face, changed by foundation cream, was in sharp contrast with her opalescent arms and legs. Tia corrected with more foundation and pantyhose. Then adding final touches of zirconium post earrings, a gold-heart pendant, and dab of perfume, Tia sprang a last-minute surprise. She opened a box to reveal a jet-black, pageboy wig.

"I don't understand," Ariel said. "We redo my hair only to cover it up?"

"If we run into people we know from work, your hair color is a dead giveaway. I don't want to spoil our experiment." And pinning back Ariel's tresses, Tia fitted her with the wig to achieve the classic Berlin-cabaret look she was going for.

Finished, Tia took Ariel by the hands to gaze deep into her altered eyes. "Remember," she said, "no one will recognize you. Not even *you* recognize you. Tonight, you're Wonder Woman. Now, let's go unleash you on the world."

But as she herded Ariel toward the door, Ariel held back, moaning, "I'm *sooo* nervous."

Tia grinned. "I've got that covered, too."

And stopping at the fridge, she stuck something in her purse.

"What did you get?" Ariel asked, radiant in the sunset as they walked to the car. She was indeed unrecognizable, looking like a *Cosmo* cover. Perhaps Tia had overdone the makeup.

"A little Dutch courage for when we get there," Tia said, giving her a peek.

"But I don't drink. I've never even tasted alcohol."

"One beer never hurt anyone. It'll take the edge off."

Twenty minutes later, they arrived at the Talawanda fairgrounds, and Tia squeezed into a nearly full parking lot, killing the engine. The sounds of merriment and music filled the air.

"Wait here while I scope things out," she said, popping open the beer, handing it to Ariel. "Start on this, I'll be back in five minutes."

Ariel sat staring unhappily at the bottle, and Tia left in the glow of mercury vapor lamps, scent of cotton candy and popcorn in the air. Past the lot was a midway with carnival booths and rides, including a small Ferris wheel and roller coaster. Beyond that was a bandshell with a concert underway, people lounging on blankets and cavorting on an open-air dance floor.

Perfect. Tia returned to the car to see Ariel slouched in her seat, sipping the beer. Maybe it was the lamplight, but her skin looked less rosy, and she appeared calmer. As Tia approached, Ariel held up the bottle, grimacing to say, "I don't get this stuff. Bitter. And I don't feel a thing."

"Never mind, bottoms up."

Waving Ariel out, Tia stashed their purses under the seats and locked the door. Taking the empty bottle, she tossed it in a garbage can and raised her palm to Ariel for a high-five. Ariel puzzled, then grabbed Tia's hand instead, giving it a shake. Tia laughed, and they headed off.

On their way, Tia kept close watch on Ariel and passersby. People were indeed noticing. Men *and* women. Stopping, turning with gazes of appreciation. And in the cases of some women, perhaps envy. While Tia was no slouch—she'd worked hard on her own look, too—she caught far less attention than her shy friend, feeling like a proud big sister.

Ariel was unaware, eyes downcast, as was her custom. But she couldn't miss the man at the ticket counter. When he saw her and Tia, his eyes widened, and he broke into a big grin.

"Well hellooo, ladies," he beamed, though he focused on Ariel.

Tia gave Ariel an elbow, getting only a grunt in return. It would take more convincing.

They continued to the gate, and Tia ordered, "Head up, girl."

This time Ariel couldn't miss the effect she was having, especially on young men they passed. Then again, Tia realized, it likely felt no different to Ariel than the stares she always got. There was a short queue at the gate, and at the back of the line were two male technicians Tia recognized from TPC. Forties, married. Ariel saw too, slowing, and Tia pulled her aside.

"Excellent," she said. "Our first real test. You know Pete and Juan from Operations?"

Ariel made a face. "I tried to get their help with my computer once. I never heard back."

"Well, let's see how they treat you now. I'm gonna hang back, I want you to mosey up and take your place behind them. Let's see if they recognize you."

Ariel's face showed dismay, as if she were being deserted, sent alone into the line of fire.

"No worries," Tia said, "they won't bite, and I'm right here."

"If they don't recognize me, should I tell them?"

"No, let's not spoil the experiment. Don't look at them, just stand there minding your own business. When they move on, I'll join you."

Inhaling, exhaling, eyes down again, Ariel bit her lip and sidled toward the men. Tia ducked behind a lamppost to watch.

At first nothing. The two men talked as Ariel busied herself with her phone. Then one man must have cracked a joke, the other laughed hard, and in the middle, happened to take in Ariel. Suddenly, he was serious. His jaw dropped, and he leaned into his buddy to whisper in his ear, eyes never off Ariel. The other man took a sly glance and gaped, too. Had they recognized her?

They kept scoping Ariel, and surely she felt their gazes, shifting her feet, red-faced. At last, the men left through the turnstile, sneaking looks back as Tia hurried to her friend.

"Did they recognize you?" she asked while the ticket lady beckoned them on.

"Not sure. They were doing a lot of whispering back and forth." She gave Tia a fearful look. "Honestly, I can't say I notice *any* difference in how people look at me."

Tia sighed. "All right, time to kick this experiment up a notch. You want definitive proof? Follow me."

Tia led Ariel toward the bandshell, where a country-music group had the crowd up on its feet dancing. There was a throng of young people gathered in front of the stage, and Tia headed for them.

Ariel came abreast, raising her voice above the music to ask, "What now?"

"We'll test some available men and gage *their* reactions."

"And how are we going to do that?"

Tia pointed to the dance floor. "We'll strut our stuff and see what happens."

There were lots of men observing from the sidelines, a bit too countrified for Tia's tastes, but ideal for showing off her creation.

Ariel's eyes turned more anxious. "You mean, *dance*? You and I? *Together?*"

"Sure."

"Oh, no, Tia. I can't dance. I don't know how."

Coming to a stop, Tia faced her. "You mean you've never been to a dance before? *Never?*"

The girl lowered her eyes. "A few. But I never danced. And won't people think us gay?"

Tia was astounded. What repressive community produced this poor child? Taking her hand, she dragged her onto the floor, reminding her of her promise. "There's nothing to it. Just close your eyes and move to the beat. No rules, no special steps, simply let go."

Tia demonstrated, shutting her eyes, swaying and undulating. She sneaked a peek to see Ariel watching her, agog. But when Ariel noticed other eyes on *her,* she blushed, moved closer to Tia, closed her eyes, and followed suit.

Her movements were awkward, self-conscious. No matter. Soon several men converged, insinuating themselves around Tia and Ariel, gyrating and displaying like peacocks. Ariel didn't seem to notice, eyes closed as she followed Tia's advice. More men appeared, and soon Tia found herself edged out. Last glimpse of Ariel, the girl actually appeared to be enjoying herself, swinging to the music, unaware of the activity around her, eyes still closed. Before Tia could re-engage, she felt a tap on her shoulder. Stan.

"*Wow,*" he said, looking Tia up and down. "You're a knockout!"

She thanked him, returning the compliment, albeit he looked stiff in a coat and tie.

Rolling up next to him was Max in an open-collar sport shirt and khakis, sipping a beer. He was accompanied by a man Tia didn't recognize, and Max introduced him as a bouncer he knew from a local nightclub.

Max told her glibly, "You clean up well."

She thought, *You ain't seen nothin' yet.*

The song ended, and the band segued into a slow ballad, when out on the floor appeared Ariel, escaping the circle of men, heading for Tia holding her shoes. And smiling, Tia was elated to see—until Tia realized with alarm, a *tipsy* smile. Ariel wobbled up giggling, and suddenly some guy took her by the arm and wheeled her away, leaving Tia holding Ariel's shoes.

Stan, Max and the bouncer gaped, and Stan cried, "Holy moly! Who was *that?*"

Max decided, "She's sure as hell *not* from TPC."

The bouncer replied, "Well she's not from around here. No forgetting that face and figure."

Max turned to Tia, frowning. "How the hell do *you* know her?"

"She had a wardrobe problem, and I helped her out."

Soon Ariel and partner danced back into view, and Max was all but drooling. He fancied himself a man with moves, and was no doubt looking for a chance to impress the lady in black. But to meet her, he'd have to take a ticket. More than a score of men was clustered ahead of him, angling for their own shot. Likely more prospective partners than the band had songs.

Max crossed his arms on his chest, staring at Ariel. Tia gave him a moment more to simmer, then offered, "I can get you a dance."

He paid her a withering look, and Tia explained, "She owes me."

He scoffed. "And why, exactly, would you do that for *me?*"

"Not out of the goodness of my heart," she said, tugging Stan's coat to bring him in as witness. "I'll hook you up, but I want something in return."

Max unfolded his arms, and Tia dropped her voice a full octave. *"I want you to end your war on Ariel and let her keep her dog in peace."*

That caught him off guard. He studied Tia warily, and she returned his gaze. Finally, he realized she was serious. Looking to see Mystery Lady glide across the floor in the arms of another suitor, Max snorted, "Fine. You got yourself a deal. Now, *deliver.*"

Tia stuck out her hand and they shook. She couldn't restrain a grin. Telling Max to wait for her signal, she headed for Ariel, pulling her from her partner's arms, ignoring his protests.

"You won't believe what just happened," she shouted with glee into Ariel's ear. "Max just agreed to let you keep Newton."

"*Oh my God,*" Ariel gasped, tears welling in her glassy eyes. "Are you serious? *For real?*"

"For real," Tia replied. "One dance, and it's done."

The elation in Ariel's eyes turned to fear. "*Dance?* You never said anything about a dance! I've never even been *close* to Max."

The song ended, replaced by a country version of the old standard, *Get Lucky.* Squeezing Ariel's hands, Tia assured, "One little dance, that's all. Hang in there just three minutes, and Newton's safe. *You can do it.*"

Max stood poised like a runner at a starting line. Tia waved him in before Ariel could object, and he bolted ahead of his competitors. Ariel looked to Tia with panic, but too late, Max swooped in and spun her away, men crying foul from the sidelines. Ariel gaped back over Max's shoulder, terrified as they vanished into the crowd.

Tia rejoined Stan, who asked, "What the heck did you tell her?"

"I said, if she wants to keep Newton and get Max off her back, she had to dance with him."

Stan nodded, smiled, and did a double-take. He squinted at Tia, then Ariel, watching as she twirled into view again. "*Can't be,*" he sputtered. "*That's* our Ariel?"

"That's our Ariel."

Max waltzed her by, flashing his teeth. Next trip around, however, Ariel looked wilted, eyes glazed. Max was oblivious as he put on a show, swiveling nearer to Tia and Stan, setting up a dance move. Then planting his feet, he took Ariel's hand and flung her toward them to the extent of his outstretched arm.

She snapped to a halt, and for an instant, Tia got a closeup, alarmed to see Ariel's complexion a very different shade. *Green.* And when Max reeled her back to catch her, she exploded on him in a purge of tomato soup, grilled cheese, and beer.

The shock on the floor was palpable, as if the barometer had just plummeted. Dancers stopped, the band trailed off. Stunned silence. Max let go of Ariel, gaping down at his sodden self. Ariel faltered, and Tia and Stan rushed to shore her up.

"She needs to sit," Tia told Stan.

They ushered her off the floor, the crowd parting like a curtain. Spotting an empty bench under a streetlamp, they made for it, gently depositing her. Stan fanned her face with a handkerchief, and Tia snatched it to tidy her up, surprised at how unsullied she was. Max had borne the brunt.

A volley of expletives drifted over on the night air, and Tia looked to see Max shaking himself off in the grass, bending to empty his shirt pocket. His bouncer friend brought him napkins to clean up, and Stan fetched Ariel water. She recovered quickly, green hue fading.

Tia squeezed Ariel's hands. "Bad idea giving you that beer."

Ariel blinked, her eyes clear now, and Max approached smelling ripe. Tia braced for battle, but when Max beheld Ariel again, he softened.

"How you feeling?" he asked Ariel.

She looked up, eyes gleaming blue and huge in the lamplight. "I'm *so* sorry."

"My fault," he exhaled. "Spinning you around like a cyclotron."

"I never danced before," she tried to explain. "Never had a beer. I was so nervous." Tears welled, and her voice broke, pitiful. "You're not mad at me again, are you? You'll still let me keep Newton, won't you?"

Max went rigid, eyes bugging. He examined her close under the light. *"No way,"* he gasped. And turning on Tia, he snarled, "I don't know what your game is, but I'm not falling for it."

Tia stood, hands on hips, telling Ariel, "Show him, *mi corazón.*"

Ariel bent forward and shed the wig, undoing pins in her hair, giving her head a shake. Her platinum locks unfurled to her shoulders, and she raised up again looking even more gorgeous than before. Tears etched her makeup, and she blubbered, "We went to town today.

I got contacts, my hair cut, new clothes." She trailed off adding, *"I just want to keep my dog."*

Her voice and hair color were indisputable. Max went crimson.

Unable to contain herself, Tia burst into laughter. "Men are *sooooo* superficial," she said with a smirk. "Same woman you've seen every day for weeks. Give or take a little primping."

Max fumed, "You punked me!"

"A deal's a deal," Tia declared. "And we're damn-well holding you to it."

CHAPTER 51

Tia brought another cup of tea to the living room, and Ariel accepted it numbly, still in shock over the loss of Newton. Taking a sip, she felt its warmth radiate, and quickly fade.

Stan was in the tent, Max in his room, and Ariel heard footsteps in the hall. She turned to see Max with a new blimp in hand, rolling his fingers on its gasbag. The *Charles Fort II*, product of another trip to town. During his breakout, Newton had damaged the original beyond repair.

"Come," Max snapped, still brooding, "let's do this."

The men would need help to pull off the delicate maneuver. Tia gave Ariel a squeeze, telling her, "Stay here and drink your tea, we've got this covered."

Ariel set down her cup. "There's still a chance," she sniveled.

Poor Newton. Not much of a life she'd given him here. Barred from the house, tethered most of the time for fear he'd run off or get run over. Neglected, deprived of the companionship he craved.

She'd had a dog before. Well, it was Nana's—Dad's mom. Nana took in Ariel and Mom after they lost Dad (special ops, Middle East). Ariel was three at the time and didn't remember him. Mom and she left Dayton for Nana's old house outside Toledo, and spent the next four years in an idyllic little town where no one seemed to think twice about Ariel's rare condition. Nana was kind and doting, and her little mutt, Otto, followed Ariel everywhere.

Then Mom found Phil, and God, and within a month, Ariel had a new father, a new home, a new city, and no dog. Phil, like Max, didn't like pets.

Ariel dried her eyes and followed Max and Tia to the tent. But stepping inside, she was met by the acrid scent of burnt fur, and the horrors of this morning flooded back, bringing tears again.

The clock neared 2:00, and Max took his place in front of the table with the blimp, Stan close by with a rake. Hopefully, *something* good would finally come of all their work and sacrifices.

No sound of barking to herald the thunder this time, and when the vortex appeared and the hole unfurled, Stan inserted the rake to report, "All clear."

Max replaced him at the hole, raising the blimp, and as he did, a black and white blur came leaping out of the hole straight into him, bouncing off, past Ariel, out the door. Ariel shrieked and chased after, and Newton reversed direction and bounded back to her. She collapsed to her knees on the grass, wrapping him up, bawling as he licked and wriggled.

He was a mess. The fur atop his head was singed, as were the tips of his ears and along his back and tail where he'd brushed the vortex rim. No burns to his skin that she could see. Miraculously, other than looking ridiculous and smelling awful, he appeared fine.

Stan and Tia raced up smiling, and Stan panted, "That's one small leap for dog, one quantum leap for mankind!"

Ariel laughed through her tears, and Max stamped from the tent looking as crushed as the blimp in his hands.

CHAPTER 52

For the third time in as many runs, Max stood poised to breach the vortex with a remote-controlled blimp. He stood near the center of the tent grumbling, holding the *Charles Fort III*, the product of another trip to town.

Though the previous launch attempts had failed, they were by no means a total loss. Thanks to Newton, the team now knew that living creatures could safely navigate the wormhole. And while the aperture was too small for a human, it nevertheless opened vast new possibilities for science and industry.

On the other hand, Newton's reappearance was also cause for concern. No one on the other side had either returned the plant to its upright position or dealt with a surprise, four-hour visit from a strange dog, enabling Newton to leap back out the hole into Max. Yesterday was a Saturday, not a workday, and Max feared Newton's intrusion caused the occupant to pack up and flee, perhaps leaving nothing behind to identify himself or his location. If so, the voyage of the *Charles Fort III* would be a short and dry run, spoiling Max's plan for a press conference.

Ariel watched him sulking in a corner of the tent, drumming his fingers on the blimp's gasbag. Gone was the bombast, and she worried about these mood swings. How would he react today if his blimp encountered an empty room?

Before her on the table sat a laptop wired to an antenna in Tia's hands. Its screen showed live video of the tent floor—the blimpcam's current perspective. If things went as planned, everyone would have a bird's-eye view of the ship's maiden voyage as Max guided it remotely.

The top of the hour arrived, and Newton began to bark, now safely tethered to his house by a new chain. Then came the familiar sequence: thunder, whine, silence, vortex, wormhole.

Ariel gave a countdown and started her stopwatch, and Stan raised his rake and attacked the hole with the cry, *"Once more unto the breach, dear friends."* He quickly added, "The plant's back!"

Max blinked, and like a switch flipping, he was his old showman self again. Stan removed the rake and stepped aside, and Max took his place, blimp's little propellers whirring soft, searchlight on. Smiling for the camera, Max presented the blimp to the hole, aimed, and let go. The ship set off without incident, disappearing into the narrowness of the black abyss.

Tia replaced Max at the hole, inserting the antenna, and he hustled to the laptop keyboard, all eyes jumping to its screen. Snow at first, then darkness as Max adjusted the lens. Quickly there materialized the dim suggestion of a room.

"All systems 'go,'" Stan hooted.

The room appeared gloomier than before. Perhaps due to the blimpcam's tiny spotlight. Apart from that, the only illumination came from the window, in diffused shafts.

Stan observed, "Wherever this is, it must be cloudy."

It was perfectly bright and clear outside their tent.

Ariel observed no movement. The blimp tilted down, and a white halo appeared at the bottom of the screen. Ariel watched enthralled as the spotlight wafted over foliage of a fallen plant, large and bushy, green leaves popping vividly out of ghost-gray ambiance. Surreal.

Like being in a deep-water bathysphere exploring the ocean floor.

Suddenly the light exposed a large black ring seared onto the back of the plant, and Stan noted, "The vortex singed the leaves!"

The halo advanced past the plant to reveal hardwood and a braided rug. Max had equipped the blimp with a microphone, and Ariel heard muffled horn honks and what sounded like a loose manhole cover clunking now and again under passing wheels.

Max sailed on, entering the aura of light from the window. He stopped to rotate toward it, asking, "How about a glimpse outside?"

The image momentarily bloomed as the lens confronted the light. It adjusted, and blinds materialized, closed, blocking the view. Max completed the turn for a look back at the wormhole from the opposite side. Almost invisible in the dark corner.

"Got to be impossible to see it behind the plant," he said.

Making an about face, he flew past the window toward the TV in the corner. To its left against the wall stood a small bookcase, a prime target. As Max drew close, Ariel saw DVDs, books, magazines. Most looked tattered. *Chewed*, she realized with dismay.

Stan asked, "Any of those magazines have mailing labels?"

Max sailed in tighter and hovered, his mastery of the blimp impressive. The only magazine facing out was a *Popular Science*, four years old, and no label.

Ariel also saw DVD sets of the *Rocky* series, *Terminator, Star Wars, Battlestar Galactica,* and a host of sci-fi books and videogames. The blimp came about, and the better part of the room swung into dim view. In the foreground facing the window was a sofa with jagged rips across the backrest and arms. Only one cushion, ragged.

"*Newton,*" Max spit. "When we *do* contact this guy, he's gonna sue us."

Throttling up the blimp, he soared over the couch to the long wooden table behind. Shadowy forms resolved into the familiar. A flat-screen monitor, facing away. A computer keyboard and various other items they'd seen before. Max made for the monitor and circled to face it. As the screen became visible, Ariel saw animated fish swimming across its display.

"Holy smokes," Stan said. "He left his computer on! If we could get a look at its desktop."

Max replied, "I think I can manage that."

He reversed engines and tilted down to reveal a computer mouse next to the keyboard. Speeding forward again, he dove at it, struck it, and the blimp jarred and rebounded. The screen awoke, brightening the room as Max regained control and leveled off, squaring the ship to the monitor. Ariel thrilled to see the screen had changed from fish to an image of the Crab Nebula. In the toolbar, a clock icon displayed: *Tues Oct 14 10:06 AM*. The correct date and time, but the day was off—today was Sunday. Regardless, wherever this was, it appeared to be in their Eastern time zone.

On the right of the screen were eight file icons. Max homed in on: *Sent Emails; Browser Cache; Acct Recs; Ivy Fund; PL; R/U/God; Infinitiman;* and *Blue Angels.* The files might hold clues to the owner's identity. But skilled pilot though Max was, he couldn't possibly work the keyboard to open them with such a blunt instrument.

"We're recording all this," he said, "we'll study it later."

He moved on, shifted right, and panned across the desk to reveal ugly scratches.

Ariel had been so absorbed, she'd almost forgotten her timekeeping. They couldn't risk stranding the blimp and frightening the poor occupant more than they already had.

"Four minutes to go," she alerted Max.

He started to bring the ship about, but suddenly Tia cried, *"Wait. Stop. On the corner of the desk. What's that?"*

Max swung back to throw light on a stack of unopened mail. *Jackpot.*

Unfortunately, the top envelope faced down, blank. But no problem for Max. Circling away to approach from a different angle, he hit the throttle, lowered the nose, and crashed the pile kamikaze-style.

The blimp staggered, corrected, and turned to troll the scattered pieces. Ariel was excited to see some envelopes right-side up, if askew and hard to read. She recognized a Con Ed logo, everyone calling it out. Then one envelope slanted their way. Its return address appeared first. Some charity from Eastpointe, Michigan: *The American Autoimmune Association.*

The spotlight brought the mailing address into view, and Ariel held her breath:

Scott Butterfield
Apt. 2-A
252 S. 34th Ave
Queens, NY, 11369

The tent erupted, Max howling like a coyote. It seemed the collider generated a wormhole reaching some two-hundred-fifty miles to an apartment in New York City. Not Hong Kong, exactly, but a momentous feat of technology, nonetheless. All that remained was to contact Scott Butterfield, gain his support, and it was onward to the press conference.

"*Hello Nobel,*" Max cried.

Indeed. Their discovery meant vast new fields of R&D. The teleportation prospects alone, if refined and made cost-effective, offered untold commercial applications. A giant leap into the 22nd Century. Worldwide acclaim, booster rockets to their careers.

Ariel wondered what Mom and Phil would think of her now.

Then suddenly she realized, "Max, *thirty seconds.*"

Whatever they'd done so far to hurt their chances with Scott Butterfield, leaving a spy drone in his apartment could prove fatal. Max was in the middle of a victory dance with Stan, blimp idling above the desk, when Ariel gasped to see the image go haywire, lurching, spiraling.

Max saw too. "What the hell?" He dashed back to the controls, quickly righting things, searching for the cause.

Ariel leaned into the screen—only to come eyeball-to-glowing-eyeball with an image of something *alive*. She jumped back, it hissed, let go a swat, and the image reeled again. This time the blow did damage, airship dropping, listing.

"Get out of there," Stan cried. *"Hurry."*

Max veered the nose around cockeyed and poured on the speed, gondola bumping along the desk, plowing over indiscernible hazards. Ahead, the shadowy hump of the couch loomed like a mountain. Ariel cringed, but somehow Max cleared it and swooped for home in a drunken loop.

"Go-go-go," Tia hollered.

The ship's bladder was leaking, buckling. Max aimed for the vortex, ship off-kilter and approaching too low. Ariel clenched to see him gun the rotors and tilt for the ceiling. But at the last second, he brought the nose down and told Tia, *"Now."*

Tia plucked the antenna from the hole and dove for cover as the blimp careened through lopsided, hole snapping shut behind, catching the ship's rudder.

CHAPTER 53

A half hour later, the team sat around the table in the tent, still vibrating. They'd reviewed the blimpcam video to confirm it was indeed a housecat that attacked the *Charles Fort III*. Now Ariel and Tia were on their laptops searching online for information on Scott Butterfield, while Max and Stan hunkered over a large map of New York State, mulling theories about what caused the phenomenon they were dealing with.

At length, Ariel heard Stan declare, "Makes sense, yes." And he turned to the women to say, "Hey, check this out."

Ariel looked to see Stan had scribed a circle on an area of the map with a magic marker. He pointed to it with a yardstick, explaining, "Here's where the collider lies along the valley."

A one-hundred-mile, circular tunnel of electromagnets buried two-hundred feet down.

Moving the yardstick slightly northwest of the circle, he said, "This is our farm." Then sweeping the stick to the far end of the map, he said, "And here, two-hundred-fifty miles to the southeast, is Butterfield's apartment in Queens, New York. Now, if we draw a line from farm to Butterfield…" he placed the yardstick on the map accordingly, "we have a straight line passing directly through the center of the collider's tower."

"I see the correlation," Ariel said, "but what's it mean?"

Max replied, "It could take us years to nail down the math, but we can hazard a guess." He nodded to Tia. "Remember your comment about a moiré effect?" Moiré effect: waves of energy crossing paths to create a mutant reaction. "Like you said, the collider generates the most powerful magnetic field in the world, second only to the Earth's itself. What if the fields interact somehow to spin off two Trapping Horizons, connected by a wormhole?"

Stan clarified, "I wouldn't call it a moiré effect, per se. But that's a good metaphor."

"All well and good," Tia said, "but let's get back to Scott Butterfield. Ariel and I aren't finding any info on him, he seems to fly under the radar. Closest we've come is a Joseph Butterfield, except he lives in the Bronx and has for over twenty years. And he won't take our calls."

"Keep looking," Max said, "nobody exists in a vacuum."

The women went back to their laptops, and Stan and Max put away the map to stretch out the crumpled blimp for a postmortem.

"Here," Stan said, pointing to punctures in the airbag. "And here—a crack in the gondola."

Ariel speculated that the housecat responsible for damaging the blimp might also explain the damage to Butterfield's apartment. Newton wasn't destructive by nature, but after years of confinement, starved for activity, he went nuts over other critters. Perhaps his acute senses had somehow alerted him to the presence of the cat, and drawn him into the wormhole.

The men completed their examination of the blimp, and Stan clapped Max on the back to chirp, "Stellar display of aeronautics, my man, the way you piloted this cripple home. I say we mount *Charlie* in the living room above the mantle to replace the shepherd's crook."

Max sniffed, "Hell no. *Charlie's* going in the Smithsonian next to *Apollo 11.*"

"Not so fast," Tia told him, "we may need *Charlie* again. Ariel and I are still nowhere on Butterfield. No phone number, email, social media. Like he's off the grid."

Max angled his laptop to display a frozen image from the blimp-cam—the return address on the envelope sent to Scott Butterfield. He asked Tia, "Have you tried this Autoimmune place?"

"Yes, they won't release donor data. We need *Charlie* to drop Butterfield an airmail letter."

"And risk spooking him? Let's just overnight him a letter through regular mail."

"That's a problem, too," Ariel said. "We can't locate his apartment building. When we *Street View* his address, here's what we get." On her screen appeared a three-hundred-sixty-degree sweep of a run-down neighborhood. "Butterfield's address is 252 South 34th Avenue, Queens. But see, there's no building there." She stopped on a rubbish-strewn patch of land between two old brownstones at 250 and 254 South 34th. "Nothing but an empty lot."

Max sat back, reflecting. "No Butterfield, no building. Are you thinking what I'm thinking?"

The others paid him blank looks.

"...The reason we can't find him is, *he doesn't exist.*"

No one seemed any better enlightened, and he explained, "We're looking in the wrong place. Butterfield doesn't exist in *our* world. The wormhole is taking us to a *different* world, a *different* dimension. *A parallel universe.*"

The blank looks turned skeptical, and he added, "How's a parallel universe any less plausible than a wormhole?"

Stan's eyes went wide. "If you're right, and we can prove it, it's evidence of *multiverses.* It will prove Superstring Theory. And you know what *that* means!"

Max nodded. "We solve The Grand Equation. *The Theory of Everything.*"

Awed silence filled the room. The Grand Equation. A yet-to-be-discovered mathematical formula to unite all fundamental forces and particles of nature into one, elegant reconciliation. As Max put it, "Answer to the most profound question of all: *Why do we exist?*"

Ariel felt her skin grow taut. For more than a century, physicists had been working on The Grand Equation, considered the Holy Grail of science. To date, no theory to support it held up. The quest had frustrated even Einstein and Hawking.

One theory that had shown great promise, known as *Superstring,* stated that all objects in the universe were composed of vibrating atomic strings of energy. The theory had strong support in the science community for a time. But *Superstring* hinged on the existence of multiple universes. *Multiverses.* Perhaps an infinite number of multiverses. No one could come up with a way to verify such a thing, and the theory fell out of favor.

If, however, the team could prove the wormhole led to a parallel universe, they could tie Superstring back together to help reveal the true nature of the cosmos, including life itself. A discovery even more profound than wormholes.

Max's Nobel Prize quip rang in Ariel's head.

But Tia had a sobering thought. "If we *are* looking at a parallel universe, we'll not only have to prove Butterfield exists over there, we'll have to prove he *doesn't* exist here. How in the hell do we prove a negative?"

Like trying to prove Bigfoot didn't exist. Or ghosts. Or God.

"Tough, but not impossible," Stan said. "First, we have to document Butterfield's existence in the parallel universe. Get his birth certificate, driver's license, school records, photos and such from over there. Then we contrast that with the absence of those items over here."

The excitement in the tent was palpable. Ariel's hands trembled.

Max said, "The only way to get anything from the other side is with Butterfield's help. Time to contact him through the wormhole."

Getting enthusiastic support, he added, "Let's send him that airmail. I'll repair *Charlie*, you guys keep searching for Butterfield on our side. Before we go announcing a parallel universe, let's make damn sure he's got no doppelgänger."

And gathering up the blimp carcass, he left for the house, the others rushing after him.

. . .

An hour later, Max strolled back into the living room whistling. Ariel looked to see the blimp under his arm, inflated and like new but for patches on its airbag and tail. His timing was spot on, they'd just finished scouring the web for signs of Butterfield. With unsettling results.

"We've got good news and bad," Tia greeted him.

Taking a chair, Max tethered his blimp to the armrest. "Give me the bad first."

"We found Butterfield in our world after all. And his apartment in Queens."

Max soured and stared at the floor. "So much for The Grand Equation," he said. "But we've still got the wormhole. Let's contact Butterfield, and on to the press conference."

"Can't."

He squinted at her. "Why not?"

"Because Butterfield doesn't live in our world."

As if he'd misheard, Max shook his head. "You say you found him in *our* world, but he lives in *another?*"

"Exactly."

He clenched, Tia enjoying it, and Stan said, "Enough, Tia, just show him."

She turned her laptop so Max could see. "It seems the Scott Butterfield we visit through the wormhole does, in fact, live in a parallel world. Because according to this article, the Scott Butterfield in our world is *dead.*"

Stunned, Max leaned into the screen. It showed a *New York Times* article and photo of smoldering ruins. His lips moved silently as Tia said, "The Butterfield in our world *used* to live at 252 South 34th Avenue, Queens. The building burned four years ago, and all tenants perished, including Butterfield and a sister who was visiting. The rubble was cleared, the lot left empty."

"I'll be damned," Max said. "Our job just got a lot easier."

Stan pointed out, "Convincing people our Butterfield is dead will take more than a news article and an empty lot. We'll need a death certificate, coroner report, autopsy. Photos of his tombstone would be nice."

The gears behind Max's eyes raced. "Exactly. Perfect way to differentiate the two worlds. Show the man dead in one, alive in another. Imagine the press conference: Butterfield's surviving relatives on camera watching him resurrected live through the wormhole."

Ariel was appalled. "We're talking about a *life*," she cried. Exploiting the poor man's death and family to further the team's cause would taint their discovery. Tia agreed, surely thinking of her mom.

As the others talked, Ariel's attention wandered to the TV. Frozen on its screen was a closeup of the Autoimmune Association envelope, and Ariel noticed something odd. Something they'd overlooked in their excitement over Butterfield's address.

She grabbed the remote and went for a closer look. Still confused, she rewound the video to examine the other envelopes splayed across Butterfield's desk. Each bore the same peculiarity.

"This makes no sense," she said, and the others stopped talking. Rolling back to the Association envelope again, she zoomed in on its postage cancellation mark—a circle showing time, day and month at the top, city and state in the middle, year at the bottom.

"...Check the date."

Tia read, *"1:07 PM, Fri, Oct 3.* Yes, the day's wrong. The 3rd was a Wednesday, not a Friday. Same inconsistency we saw on Butterfield's computer."

"Not just that," Ariel said, pointing to the mark's bottom line. "The year. This letter's four years old." She fast-forwarded to the other scattered envelopes, everyone tilting to and fro to read them. All were four-years old to the month, all unopened.

Stan said what Ariel was thinking. "Why would Butterfield leave mail on his desk unopened for four years? Especially bills?"

An answer popped into Ariel's head, and bracing for ridicule, she let it spill. "What if this isn't a different world after all, but our world at a different *time*? Our world, two-hundred-fifty miles away, *four years in the past?*"

Quiet. Then the others shook their heads in unison, and Max said, "Quantum mechanics only allows for forward progress in time. Virtually all physicists agree, regression is impossible. It creates absurd, self-negating paradoxes."

Ariel recalled the classic brainteaser of a man traveling back in time before his birth to kill his father, thereby canceling his own birth, consequently saving his father, thereby enabling his own birth, on and on in an irreconcilable loop.

Regardless, Stan and Tia seemed to give her idea consideration. Tia told Ariel, "Rewind to that shot of Butterfield's computer screen. Let's see its time/date display again."

Ariel did so: *Tues Oct 14 10:06 AM.* No year given.

Stan said, "The date and time match ours, but the day is off."

Today was *Sunday,* October 14.

Pulling his laptop in front of him, Stan checked a perpetual calendar to confirm, "Wow. Four years ago, October 14 fell on a *Tuesday.*"

They all exchanged looks, and Tia reminded, "That magazine on Butterfield's bookshelf is four years old, too."

Stan added, "And his computer and operating system are at least ten years old. Who uses technology that obsolete?"

Max shook his head. "Did you see his TV? Tube-style, with an HD converter box. And a VHS player. How old is *that*? All it proves is he's behind the times. What you suggest is nuts."

"Most physicists would say traversable wormholes are nuts," Tia pointed out.

Max exhaled. "Before we go all H. G. Wells, show me hard evidence."

"We'll need Butterfield's help for that," Tia said. "Except now, considering the risks, we can't ask him."

The others puzzled, and she explained, *"Butterfly Effect."*

Dead quiet again.

Also known as *Chaos Theory,* the Butterfly Effect explained how a seemingly insignificant change to a system can wreak havoc over time. Its name derived from a famous analogy: the beat of a butterfly's wing over Africa ruffling into a breeze, growing as it travels across the Atlantic, becoming a hurricane by the time it reaches the Caribbean. Applied to the fourth dimension of Time, the Effect warns that even the tiniest intrusion on the past can change history in surprising ways, cascading forward in time to impact the present with disastrous consequences.

At length, Max said, "No. If we were dealing with a time warp— and we're *not*—butterflies would have already flown. All the crap we've chucked into that hole, a dog, for chrissakes. Nothing's come of it. The world's no different."

"That we *know of,*" Tia said. "If butterflies changed our memories, too, how would we even be aware? The danger's too great, we're on hold till we settle this."

Max went red, but Stan intervened to say, "I may have the answer, and it doesn't involve Butterfield *or* butterflies."

CHAPTER 54

The afternoon run arrived, and Max stood near the center of the tent, awaiting the vortex. He held in his hands the antenna he'd used to control the blimp, wired into Stan's laptop on the table where Stan sat flanked by Tia and Ariel.

Stan had indeed come up with an apparently safe, discreet means to determine the time period on the other side, *if* he could pull it off. He was inspired by something he'd spotted on Butterfield's computer toolbar. Among dozens of icons was one reading "wifi-enabled."

For a former IT specialist at the National Security Agency, wifi was an open door to a computer. Stan's idea was to send a wifi signal through the wormhole to Butterfield's router, hack past his firewall and security systems into his computer, and upload a hosting program. If successful, he could control Butterfield's computer remotely from a laptop in the tent and call up a browser on Butterfield's side. Then on to a news site or other source of current date, determine the year, and exit, undoing the hosting program on the way out. All without releasing any butterflies, Butterfield none the wiser—presuming he wasn't present to catch Stan in the act.

While Max and Tia were fully capable of attempting this hack, Stan was literally a pro at it. Even so, it would be a tricky maneuver to pull off during the ten-minute wormhole window, depending on the sophistication of Butterfield's software security.

The thought of hijacking the man's computer made Ariel uneasy, yet she saw no choice. If the team hoped to save TPC and their moon shot, they had to settle the issue of when Butterfield existed, and in what universe. Ariel had no clue about either. Occam's Razor was no help, both scenarios equally incredible.

But if somehow it turned out the team was, in fact, trespassing on their own past, their endeavor would be over, the risk of fracturing spacetime, too great. Ariel took heart in Max's conviction that traveling back in time was impossible. His instincts seemed prescient so far.

The final minutes peeled off the clock, and Ariel felt her anxieties crowd once more. Tia added to her fears with an ominous warning:

"For the record. If we confirm we're dealing with a time warp, we'll be forced to shut TPC down. And we *won't* be able to reveal why. If word ever got out that TPC is a time machine, every country in the world would be racing for the technology. And God forbid it fell into the hands of terrorists, you think nukes are a nightmare!"

The threat of sabotaging history made Ariel's head reel. If such a thing were to happen, the future might never unfold. The present could be trapped in whipsaws of revision, looped back on itself, stretched and twisted until, ultimately, spacetime imploded into nothingness. She couldn't dwell on these thoughts. Butterfield simply *had* to exist in a different dimension, and Stan had to prove it, and rescue their dreams.

Once more, the vortex appeared, the hole opened, and Max inserted the antenna, all eyes on Stan's laptop.

Stan's fingers flew across the keys, turning the screen into a sea of code. Quickly he announced, "Butterfield's router is as outdated as his computer, first hurdle cleared. Same with his firewall..." Then smiling, he added, *"I'm in."*

Ariel was encouraged to see the image of Butterfield's desktop suddenly replace the code on Stan's screen. The Crab Nebula, with two rows of file icons on the right. Stan examined the date/clock display to show it was consistent with what they'd seen before: the day of the week was off, the date and time the same as theirs. And again, no year.

Tia reminded Stan, "Make sure the coast is clear."

Stan commandeered Butterfield's webcam, and the screen changed to a live shot of an empty chair bathed in the ashen light of the monitor. Behind it on a wall hung a framed photo of a pretty blonde woman in a dated dress and hairstyle.

Switching back to Butterfield's desktop, Stan said, "Now, let's see if we can determine what year, and hopefully, what universe." He called up a browser and tried to jump online to *The New York Times*.

"Good thinking," Max said from where he stood by the hole, holding the antenna.

But nothing came up on screen.

Puzzled, Stan tried a few other tricks, and when those failed, he opened "network preferences" to find no Internet connection.

"Of course," he groaned. "There's a Trapping Horizon force field on Butterfield's side, too. No signal can penetrate it, in or out."

"Now what?" Ariel asked.

Max told Stan, "Check his browser archives."

Stan did, exposing a lengthy list. And scrolling down to one week ago, by Butterfield's calendar, he came upon a saved *Times* article, clicking it open.

It popped up too small for Ariel to make out the date, but the headline read:

Unemployment Claims Mount

Nothing telling about that. Stan located the date, and zoomed in, and a moan filled the tent. Ariel felt the air go out of her, and Max hissed, "I'll be damned."

There in black and white—Monday, October 6—*four years ago.*

"Christ," Tia cried. "Get out, *quick,* before we set off more butterflies!"

"Wait," Stan said, "gotta cover my tracks."

He closed the browser and returned to Butterfield's desktop, and Tia reminded, "Now the hosting program."

But before he could act, his screen abruptly reverted to lines of code. He turned to Max, who stood in front of the vortex waving the antenna. He'd pulled it from the hole.

"What are you doing?" Tia snapped. "He's not done."

Max leveled frustrated eyes. "Look, every time we think we've got this thing figured out, it throws us a curve. We *assume* we're hooked into our own past, but we're in unchartered waters. For all we know, Butterfield exists in a parallel world, on a four-year delay. According to Superstring, he could be in any number of *infinite* worlds, why not one in a time warp?"

In fact, they'd already upended several accepted wisdoms of quantum physics.

Ariel asked, "But how do we determine something like that? How can we tell our past from a mirror past?"

Looking at the clock, Max replied, "I don't know yet, but we haven't come this far to walk away empty-handed. Four minutes left, think outside the box."

Against Tia's grumbles, he re-inserted the antenna, and Butterfield's desktop appeared on Stan's screen again.

They refocused, and everyone drew blanks until finally, Stan offered, "Maybe Butterfield's files hold clues to the nature of his universe. Something to prove it different from ours."

Tia asked, "Like what?"

"I'm not sure, I'm fishing. Inconsistencies, maybe. Things that happened over there that didn't here, or vice versa. A long shot, but what have we got to lose?"

Max asked, "Anyone have a problem with us copying his files? There's no risk of butterflies, he'll never know."

Ariel had reservations. It felt wrong stealing the records of this unsuspecting man they'd never even seen and knew so little about. Albeit, they knew the terrible fate awaiting him if, in fact, he occupied their universe. A fire that they could reach back in time to prevent, but for fear of altering history. She and Tia exchanged searching looks, and Tia said, "If we're gonna do it, *hurry.*"

Stan rushed to download the eight files on the desktop, and no sooner had he sucked out the last cache and uncoupled the hosting program than Ariel sounded closing bell. Max withdrew the antenna, the vortex snapped shut, and Tia switched off the camera, perhaps ending for good their acquaintance with the mysterious Scott Butterfield.

CHAPTER 55

The team reconvened in the living room at the coffee table, gathered around Stan's laptop, eyeing Butterfield's stolen files as if waiting for them to speak.

Ariel clung to the hope that hidden somewhere in these documents lay evidence the wormhole led to a different dimension—one running four years behind theirs. Prove that, and she and her friends could not only proceed with their press conference, but they could also warn Butterfield about the coming fire without releasing "butterflies" into their world.

She sighed. "If only he were still alive on our side of the hole, he could settle this right now."

No doubt if Butterfield still existed in their world, he'd recall the bizarre ordeal he'd gone through. Especially the damage Newton did to his apartment. But if Butterfield *couldn't* recall, it would be compelling evidence there was another Butterfield in another dimension who did. Unfortunately, the man's tragic death ended that prospect.

Max wasn't deterred. "Somewhere in these files are clues," he said. "Surely Butterfield filed a police report about our 'break-ins.' Or made an insurance claim, or notified his landlord."

Ariel asked, "What good would knowing that do us?"

"It gives us a basis for comparison. Say we learn Butterfield made an insurance claim. We can hack the insurance company's files in our world to see if there's record of it. If so, we're screwed. But if there's *no* record, it's evidence Butterfield exists in a different world."

Stan added, "Also, Butterfield may have contacted friends about his problem. If we can find out who he told, we can track those people down in our world, assuming they're still alive, and see if they recall anything."

He pulled his laptop closer, and the others crowded in, viewing the icons of the eight folders copied from Butterfield's desktop. Stan selected *Sent Emails,* opening on numerous messages. He scrolled back to a few days before the vortex's emergence and began skimming while the others read along.

Their first glimpse into the person of Scott Butterfield.

Ariel saw appeals to creditors asking for extensions. Job-feelers to bookkeeping firms. Inquiries about student loans. But when Stan caught up to the time period where the vortex first appeared, the emails dropped off. Only one after that, a week later, a response from Butterfield to someone named "Zing," with a cc to a "Reggie." In his reply, Butterfield stated simply that all was fine now, thanking them for their help.

Max said, "The message *could* refer to the problems in his apartment, let's come back to it."

Stan moved on to the next file, *Browser Cache.* "This should tell us if he uses social media," he said, "and if so, he may have gone there to confide in someone."

He opened and sorted through multiple links: science and math sites; online videogames; a self-improvement site. And more recently, spiritualist and occult sites. No social media accounts.

"Christ," Max said. "Of all people that hole could connect us to, we get a superstitious recluse. What else we got?"

The remaining folders were, *Acct. Recs; Ivy Fund; PL; R U God; Infinitiman; and Blue Angels.* Ariel assumed the first file was accounting records, the next an investment fund, but she'd no clue about the rest. She asked, "What's *PL?*"

"Profit/loss statements?" Stan guessed, clicking it.

He was wrong. Ariel saw a journal, and Max corrected Stan, "Make that *Personal Log.*"

Everyone pressed tighter as Stan went to the most recent entry, last night, four years ago:

> *how much more can i take? came home to find the apartment a wreck, homer terrified, my belongings ripped up as if by demons. feel i'm losing my mind. archdiocese refuses exorcism, at end of my rope.*

Tia said, "Homer's the cat, I bet. Here's a guy desperate to confide in someone."

Max sat back with a strange gleam in his eyes. "Demons, archdiocese," he said. "Butterfield believes his apartment's possessed. *Interesting.* Keep going."

Stan picked through earlier entries, which also chronicled Butterfield's growing nightmare. He stopped on one.

> *zing thinks the cause is microwaves, and reggie thinks the apartment's haunted. i'm scared i'm going nuts. if reggie's right, i'll have to move out.*

"Bingo," Stan said. "Zing and Reggie are friends he told. Bet they haven't forgotten. And now we've got their email addresses."

If so, and if the team could reach them in the present, Zing and Reggie might finally settle what dimension lay on the other side, helping to justify this invasion of Butterfield's privacy.

Max seemed not to be listening. *"Haunted,"* he murmured with intrigue.

Stan continued backward through more accounts of the strange goings-on. Events familiar to the team, if terrifying to Butterfield. As the poor man made clear, he was fearful for his and his cat's safety, fearful of ridicule, of losing his privacy, his job, his home, his sanity.

At length, Stan arrived at log entries corresponding to the first collider runs. Ariel was excited to see Butterfield had spoken to neighbors about "loud noises."

"One of the neighbors has to remember," she said.

Max reminded, "All tenants died in the fire with Butterfield. Also, his sister."

Ariel felt sad and confused. In the warped time of the wormhole, these people still lived.

Stan saw nothing more of value, closing out the file, and Max said, "Enough groupthink. Let's divvy up the rest of these and do some solo digging."

Ariel picked two items. The entirety of Butterfield's personal log that they'd previously touched on, and a large Word file called *Infinitiman*.

As the others settled in with their choices, she started with the log, working backward through a glut of entries. It was disorienting to trace the man's life in reverse, watching it rewind from a state of terror and desperation into de-escalating fear, ultimately furling up in a tiny, forlorn little existence not unlike her own, once. She felt an odd affinity.

Eye out for more mentions of Reggie, Zing, and others who Butterfield may have disclosed his problems to, Ariel pushed to the end, coming up empty. The log proved less an account of the man's day-to-day than his thoughts and dreams. Seemed he'd no close friends, and no girlfriend. In fact, from what Ariel gathered, he'd never been in a serious relationship.

Again, not unlike *her* life at one time. She'd have new introspections to record in her own journal tonight.

Moving on to the file, *Infinitiman*, Ariel saw the draft of a novel. She'd hardly begun reading when Tia, announced, "Anyone care for a look at this guy?

Popping into Ariel's in-basket was an email with attachments. A dozen color images. First, a copy of a yellowed photo presumably of

Butterfield as a babe in the arms of his mom—a pretty, sweet-faced blonde doting on her cherubic child.

Max noted, "That's the woman in the photo on the wall behind Butterfield's desk."

More shots of child and mom as he grew into boyhood. He and the woman seemed to share a close bond. Also, facial shape and mouths. But his teeth came in crooked, and he was dark while she was fair.

Next, a snapshot of a man who had to be Butterfield's dad, the resemblance so strong. Dark hair, clean features. The man stood alone in the tiny front yard of a small, shingle-sided house, hand resting on a "sold" sign, expression somber. As if, *I'm in over my head.*

Then a dozen pictures of a fair-haired girl advancing from infancy to teens. Cute, impish. The last photo showed her in what appeared to be a high school uniform. White blouse, pleated plaid skirt. Pretty girl. The very image of her mom, who was absent in the girl's shots.

Only one photo of Scott Butterfield as an adult. Twenty, perhaps. Identifiable by his resemblance to his father. Especially the troubled eyes. A young man of average build and bad haircut, slouching in the same front yard. Every inch the introvert Ariel had imagined.

As night fell, Tia ordered pizza while they worked. Max turned on the TV, keeping it low in the background. But soon he upped the volume for a news bulletin. The headline read:

U.S. to End Funding for Hadron Collider

The collider where Max's new job awaited. Or not. He went livid. *"The bastards."*

The doorbell rang, and Max leaped up swearing, hurling the remote in his chair. He stalked to the door and threw it open, causing the pizza boy to drop his pies.

CHAPTER 56

SUNDAY, OCTOBER 14, 6:00 PM, TALAWANDA

They continued sifting through Butterfield's files as they ate, and at length, Max grumbled, "How about a status report?"

The others turned to him, and he led off. "All I learned new is that Butterfield took some community college courses online, but never graduated. No contact with classmates or profs. That file, *Blue Angels,* is a porn video. Not porn, actually—lame-o, R-rated stuff."

"Yeah," Tia sniffed. "*Real* men watch hardcore."

Stan went next, eyes sparkling. Ariel knew he'd found something.

"I looked into the accounting info," he said. "Butterfield kept the books for a small grocery chain." He broke into a smile. "And in the payroll records, I came across the full names of his friends in his log. Zing Li Po, and Reggie Watson. Married. Families. Shouldn't be hard to track them down if they still live in New York."

He got a round of applause and Ariel felt the tension in the room abate. Finally, they were getting somewhere.

Stan continued, "Regarding that file, *Ivy Fund,* it's a college savings account. Not much savings, a few hundred bucks. And last, the file *R U God,* an online simulation game. I've played it before, a real mind-bender. I didn't last a month, but Butterfield was a phenom, still going strong after more than a decade."

Tia's turn. "I looked into his other online accounts. Two of note. A matchmaker service called 'DateMe,' and a transcendental site, 'selfhelpguru.' Here's his profile from the dating site:"

She tapped keys, and Ariel received another attachment. A headshot of the young man she'd seen before, a bit older. Dark hair, long and draping into his face. A sallow face, redeemed by the strong nose and jaw he got from his dad. Tight-lipped smile at odds with melancholy eyes. Ariel scrolled down to view his personal stats. If honest, he was 26—Ariel's age—5'9", 160. His interests were videogames, science/math, sci-fi novels and movies.

Stan offered, "The age syncs with what's on his tax returns."

Tia added, "Doesn't appear anything came of the dating service. A few fleeting matches. Regarding the guru site, he did some online seminars and chats about self-esteem issues, but all before the problems in his apartment. He went quiet afterward, and that's about it."

Ariel's turn. "I went a year deep into his personal log, and like Tia, I found him a loner." She paused. The man had also appeared lonely and lost in life, and all but resigned to it. But that smacked too much of Ariel's own past, and she omitted it. "He writes mostly about himself. Hopes, dreams, worries. He's smart, and well-read.

"He talks about his family, too. There's his father, Joseph Sr., and little sister, Ivy, who lived together in the Bronx. Ivy's the beneficiary of that college fund Stan mentioned. As to whether Scott confided in either, the way he spoke of them, I doubt it. He wouldn't burden his sister, and he wasn't on good terms with his dad. His mother, Rose, was deceased. Of course, Scott and his sister died in the fire four years ago, leaving his dad sole survivor."

The others took down the names. Ariel continued, "Reggie and Zing come up on occasion, coworkers of Butterfield. He also speaks of a neighbor downstairs, Mrs. Steiner, another victim of the fire. And he mentions his boss from work, Margo, but not favorably, not someone he'd unburden to, I suspect. He lived in fear of losing his job.

"And finally, the file *Infinitiman.* A novel he was writing. I'm just a few chapters in, but I don't see it helping us, either. Still, there appears to be more to this man than I think we've credited him."

Stan asked, "What's the novel about?"

"A dystopian future. America under the rule of technophobes and luddites."

"Not fiction," Tia said.

"Seems Butterfield had a crystal ball," Max said. "Four years ago, the Dark Agers weren't in power, the economy was recovering, and Shackleton looked like a lock to beat Filby."

Ariel winced to recall the eleventh-hour meltdown of the woman's presidential campaign.

Max said, "Makes you wonder if someone in the future isn't looking back at us right now examining *our* lives the way we are Butterfield's."

The others shifted in their seats.

CHAPTER 57

The living room fell quiet as Ariel resumed reading Butterfield's novel, and the others moved on to investigate theories on parallel universes and Butterfly Effects.

After a time, Max broke the silence to declare, *"That does it."*

The others looked at him, and he said, "I've been reading white papers on time regression. Some of the greatest minds, including Stephen Hawking, *all* agree. It's *impossible.*"

Getting uncertain looks, he explained, "If you recall, back in '09, Hawking held a 'party' at Cambridge University inviting visitors from the future as his guests of honor. None attended. His point, exactly. A stunt to support his theory that traveling into the past defies physics. He called it his *Chronology Protection Conjecture.*"

Max closed his laptop as if he'd settled the issue. "There's only one rational explanation for what lies beyond that hole. A separate, parallel dimension. A mirror universe, running four years behind ours. There *are* no butterflies. It's safe to contact Butterfield."

Tia went red. "Our lives and futures hang on our decision, and we base it on a *Conjecture?*"

"A Conjecture supported by our experiments," Max argued. "We've been mucking around in that hole for weeks, and no blowback. Not so much as a temporal burp."

After discovering a four-year gap between Butterfield's world and theirs, the team had been searching for ripples in the timeline, checking the news for signs history had been tampered with. So far, nothing seemed to suggest it—not that they'd any idea what such a disturbance might look like. And to Tia's point earlier, if butterflies altered both history *and* living memory, how would they even know?

Stan offered, "Maybe the reason we haven't noticed any rifts is, none of the butterflies we caused escaped Butterfield's apartment. Or, any that did were too inconspicuous to make their presence felt. Tia's right. Until we know for certain we're dealing with a separate universe, we can't risk further exposure. Too much at stake."

Max sat back sullen. Then he straightened and snapped his fingers. "Talk about exposure. What's the date of that fire in Butterfield's apartment?" Opening his laptop again, he checked. "Thursday, November 6, three weeks away, four years ago." He arched his brow at the others. "For argument's sake, say you're right, and we *are* in the same world. Do you realize what's going to happen?"

Blank looks.

"When that apartment building burns down, the vortex is gonna be hung out for the whole world to see, whirling in the air above the ashes like a sinkhole in the sky. Imagine kids playing cosmic hoops, tossing stuff in the hole, cheering when it disappears inside, or explodes on the rim. How's *that* for a conspicuous butterfly?"

An astrophysical garbage disposal, appearing twice daily in the heart of Queens.

Stan's face went pale. "Objects entering the hole *there*, will instantly pop up *here*. But in effect, they'll be out of existence for *four years*. That would create a massive break in the spacetime continuum. We could be looking at a full-blown, chronologic collapse!"

The end of Time.

Ariel shuddered. She pictured a wormhole swirling in the air, virtual butterflies fluttering out in a deadly stream, razor wings shearing the fabric of Time. Until, ultimately, there emerged a monster butterfly of cosmic-rupturing proportions.

"We've got to warn Butterfield," she cried. "Stop the fire before it's too late."

Tia shook her head. "That will change the past, too. And regardless, it'll only protect us in the short run. Sooner or later, Butterfield or someone else is bound to discover the wormhole in his apartment, leak it to the world, and we'll face the same disaster."

"You're missing my point," Max said. "If we *were* in the same universe as Butterfield, there'd *already* be a vortex appearing above that parking lot. We'd know about it *now*."

That gave everyone pause.

Stan considered, "Maybe it's less conspicuous than we think. Concealed somehow."

"Easy to find out," Max said. "We'll drive down to Queens tomorrow and see for ourselves."

"There may be an easier way," Stan offered. He began clicking on his laptop. "New York City has security cameras in most high-crime areas." He was drawing on his background at the NSA. "The videos feed into the metropolitan police grid. No sweat hacking them."

Moments later, he rotated his screen to display a live nighttime shot of dilapidated brownstones and an empty lot, seen from a utility pole across the street. Date and time were burned in at the bottom. Tapping more keys, Stan rewound the image, time racing backward into daylight. He stopped when the clock read *1:59 PM*.

"Here's Butterfield's address this afternoon," he said. "We know there was a vortex at 2:00."

Punching more keys, he magnified the image, and Ariel saw the upper front corner of the building to the left of the empty parking lot, approximately where the vortex should appear. A bit fuzzy, but clear enough against sunlit bricks. Stan hit "play," and they waited.

The timestamp ticked past 2:00, a few pigeons flew by, nothing more. Stan sped back through the rest of the day, stopping to check at 10:00 AM. Nothing. He jumped back another day, still nothing.

Max sat back smirking as if he'd just hit a walk-off home run. "I'm telling you, *we're not in the same universe.* Let's contact Butterfield, and I'll prove it."

Tia turned to him. "And what if you're wrong? We're in totally uncharted territory, and given what's at stake, we've got to make *damned* certain." At stake was not only their fate, but perhaps the world's as they knew it. "If Butterfield's friends from work are still alive, we can try reaching out to them. They knew what was going on in his apartment. If they're in our universe and recall what he told them, we're done, the butterflies win. But if they *can't* recall, you've got my vote to contact Butterfield."

Stan gave Max a conciliatory look. "Shouldn't be hard to track them down."

Ariel agreed, and Max shrugged. It took Stan no time to determine the two men still resided in New York City, at the same jobs, and he came up with their addresses and phone numbers.

"Okay," Max said, "let's make some calls."

CHAPTER 58

The clock on the mantelpiece chimed eight bells, and Tia flexed her neck and shoulders like a boxer before a bout. She sat at the coffee table, her phone cued to *FaceTime*, preparing to call Scott Butterfield's work friend, Zing Li Po. The others sat opposite, out of camera range.

Using *FaceTime* and having one of the women place the call was Max's idea. He reasoned that Li Po would be more receptive to a call from a female. Tia certainly didn't trust ham-handed Max to manage the delicate conversation—a total stranger asking another about a long-departed friend. Ariel was uncomfortable with the deception, so the task fell to Tia.

Calling for quiet, Tia typed into her laptop a number Stan gave her, the computer emitted a ringing, then a man's falsetto voice.

"Yeah?"

Tia smiled into the face of a fortyish man in *Mensa* T-shirt. Slight build, wary eyes.

"Mr. Li Po?" she greeted him. "Forgive the intrusion, I'm Tia Diego, calling about an old friend of yours."

"How'd you get my number?"

282

"Google."

"What friend?"

"Scott Butterfield."

Li Po blinked and frowned. *"Scott? Scott died years ago. Why you asking?"*

"I was an acquaintance of his. I'm trying to learn what happened. I understand he was having problems in his apartment shortly before his death. Strange occurrences. Do you recall him mentioning anything about it to you?"

Zing's eyes grew warier. *"You an arson investigator? Let's see some ID."*

"No, nothing like that, I'm simply a friend. I just have a few questions."

"Maybe shit was going on, maybe it wasn't. Unless you got credentials, lady, buzz off."

The screen went blank, dial tone.

Jesus, New Yorkers were rude. Tia sat dumbfounded, turning frustrated eyes to Ariel. "You need to do this, *mi corazón,*" she said. "Who could say no to you?"

Max turned to Ariel, too. "We've one, last shot. Just bat your eyes and stick to the script."

Stan nodded, and Ariel, looking miserable, traded places with Tia.

· · ·

Chest tight, Ariel inhaled and entered Reggie Watson's number into her laptop. There came a ringtone, and moments later appeared the glowering face of a middle-aged black man. The glower deepened as he took her in.

"H-hello, Mr. Watson," Ariel said. "Sorry to disturb you. You don't know me, my name's Ariel Silva. I was, uh, uh, acquainted with Scott Butterfield."

She'd gone off-script to avoid an overt lie.

The man's eyes searched. He smiled, but his glower remained—a permanent fixture, it seemed.

"Nice to meet you, Ariel. Not sure I recall the name."

"You, too, sir. I understand you used to work with Scott."

"None of that 'sir' stuff. I'm Reggie. What can I do for you?"

"Well, Reggie, I'm trying to learn more about what happened to Scott."

"You know about the fire, of course?"

"Yes. But I've been looking into the last weeks of his life, and it seems there were some strange things going on in his apartment. Things that upset him. It's been on my mind. I'm hoping he talked to you about it, and you might recall."

Someone offscreen interrupted the man. He turned away, then back. "Afraid you caught me at a bad time, Ariel, I'm about to put my daughter to bed."

"If you can spare me just a minute, please." She batted her eyes.

Reggie sat back folding big arms across a big chest. He looked down, nodding. "Yeah, Scott told me and a friend about it. He was hearing weird noises, seeing weird stuff."

Ariel deflated, hearing groans from across the table, stifling hers.

"We thought it was microwave beams, or maybe his place was haunted."

Ariel sank further in her chair. The man had just connected Butterfield's past to their present. It appeared they did indeed inhabit the same universe, butterflies and all.

The worry must have shown in her face. Reggie said, "But it was something else caused the fire. A lamp in an apartment down the hall. Nobody's fault, one a those terrible things."

He paused, exhaled, and when Ariel failed to respond, added, "Let me give you some peace of mind, Ariel. You should know, at the end, Scott got himself right with the Lord. Before all that stuff happened, he had no faith. We argued about it all the time. But those last days he got to reading his bible. He finally saw the Light. You can take some comfort knowing that."

A voice offscreen called, "Dad," and Reggie paid Ariel a rueful look. "Sorry, gotta go. But if ever you feel like talking more, or praying, you call again, you hear?"

She thanked him and signed off, and Tia snapped at Max, "So much for Stephen Hawking. Anyone care to Conjecture how we shut down TPC without spilling our guts?"

Max swore. "It makes no sense. If we *are* in the same damned universe, what the hell happened to the vortex after Butterfield's fire? Why is it gone?"

No one could answer that, and Stan said, "Tia's right, we don't dare come clean to TPC. There's no containing something this big, every military on the planet will rush to build their own time machines before an enemy beats them to it. It'll make the race for the Bomb look like a soapbox derby. We need a plan to shut TPC down that *doesn't* let the genie out of the bottle."

Tia said, "No way I can think of—short of sabotage."

The idea of destroying the magnificent technology they'd labored so long and hard to create revolted Ariel. She couldn't imagine the others having the heart or courage, either.

Still swearing, Max seemed to have accepted the situation. "The race for the Bomb is a good analogy," he said," but you're looking at it wrong. What did we learn from all that? How many decades have we had nukes? How many decades have pundits predicted apocalypse?" He gave them each a searching look. "We've proven we can live with the Bomb, the world's learned restraint. Why any different with a Timebomb? Besides, it's not like you can build a supercollider overnight, much less undetected. I say, set that genie free, the world can handle it."

Stan sighed and shook his head. "Yes, the machinery to create a wormhole is massive. But technology never stands still. Initially, the Bomb took a Manhattan project to build, and weighed tons. Now weapons-grade fuel is plentiful, and a nuke can fit in a suitcase. How long before science finds a shortcut, and some terrorists build a Time machine in a basement?"

Max turned to Ariel for support, didn't get it, snatched his laptop, and headed to his room, leaving the others to wrestle the dilemma.

• • •

An hour later, Max's door opened, and he called out, "Hey Stan, got a sec?"

Tia called back, "Dammit, Max, we could use your input out here. What the hell you working on, anyway?"

He responded matter-of-factly, "A Grand Plan to solve *all* our problems."

Ariel had little faith in that, Max's shield of invincibility gone. Only an hour ago, he was certain Butterfield existed in a parallel universe.

Tia, however, seemed willing to cut him slack. "So long as it doesn't involve butterflies."

And she waved Stan on.

CHAPTER 59

Ariel woke to find the house quiet. She assumed the others were still asleep, everyone having stayed up late struggling for ideas to shut down TPC without betraying the existence of the wormhole. As of her bedtime last night, however, no one had anything, Max and Stan still working alone in Max's room.

She rolled out of bed yawning, slipped into a robe, let Newton out the window, popped in her contacts, and headed for the kitchen, surprised to hear voices. Soft.

Max was saying, "…not till we know for certain. Only way to get the girls aboard."

"Aboard what?" she asked, entering, and Max and Stan broke off.

They looked exhausted, hunched over laptops and coffees, bleary-eyed and stubbly. She wondered if they'd slept at all.

Stan closed his laptop, and Max angled his away, telling her, "In due time."

"Am I intruding?"

Max slid out a chair with his foot. "Not at all."

Ariel heard Tia in the bathroom, and poured two coffees, taking the seat.

Neither man would make eye contact, and Stan seemed down-right sheepish. Tia shuffled in and flopped, looking as haggard as the men. Worse. Pensive, upset. Ariel knew that look, and a glance at the calendar on the fridge confirmed why. Two years ago today, Tia lost her mom.

This weary group needed a boost, and Ariel rose to fix waffles for all. Tia wiped her eyes to ask, "Any fresh thoughts how to end this mess without setting off a Timewar?"

"I've got one," Ariel offered, pouring flour in a bowl. "But you're not going to like it." She had the floor, and continued, "We could try to co-opt the black-hole scare."

"What do you mean?" Stan asked.

"I mean, go ahead and expose the vortex to the world, but not as a time warp, as a black hole. The Dark Agers will go nuts and force the Nuclear Regulatory Commission to shut TPC down."

The others groaned, and Max said, "Stoke the false hysteria and kill science? *Great idea.*"

Tia said, "TPC will know it's no black hole. They'll investigate it and peg it a wormhole before the NRC can get its pants on. No stopping the genie. We need faster-acting poison."

"Then I've got nothing."

Tia asked Max, "Any progress on your secret project?"

He was slow to respond. "I hit a snag, but thanks to Stan, I think I'm back on track."

"You let Stan in on it, not Ariel and me?" Tia's skin was extra-thin today.

"Too many chefs."

"And what do you call Stan?"

"Sous-chef."

Tia scowled, and Stan said, "We just need more time to iron out some wrinkles. If we tried to explain now, you'd think us crazy."

Without warning, Tia grabbed Max's laptop, turning its screen. Ariel was surprised to see a seating chart of Yankee stadium.

Tia cried, "What the hell? Your fix involves going to a ballgame?"

Max shut the lid, and Tia swore and went to help Ariel.

After breakfast, the men dumped their plates in the sink, excused themselves, and retreated to Max's room again, leaving the women to brood.

Tia glared after them. "What do you make of those two?"

Ariel wagged her head. "I *never* know what to make of Max. How can you live with someone for so long, and really not know them?"

Tia slammed down her mug, spilled her coffee, and stared at it with tears in her eyes.

It took a moment before Ariel made the connection. *Tia's mom.* Shortly before her death, the poor woman had slipped into a depression no one detected. Not even Tia, who was closest to her. Her mom had called Tia asking her to come home, and Tia had sensed something was wrong. But at the time, she was in the throes of a problem at TPC, her mom insisted she could wait, and Tia made a choice she would always regret.

"Oh, Tia, I didn't mean…"

Tia stood. "Mind if I leave you the dishes?"

"Of course not."

And taking the leash, Tia went outside, departing with Newton for the back pastures.

• • •

Tia was still out, and Ariel was alone in the living room with her laptop when Stan entered from the hall heading for the front door. She heard the shower running in the men's bathroom.

"Nearly ten o'clock," Stan told her.

He and Max had been alternating guard-duty in the tent, watching for passersby. Stan's turn, apparently. Ariel paid him a smile as he left, and soon Max strolled in, dressed, hair still wet.

"Where's Stan?" he asked, laptop in hand. "I need something."

"Guarding the tent. And speaking of duties, I need to make a grocery run. Mind if I borrow your car?" Hers was way past trustworthy.

"I won't be a moment," he said, "I'll drive you. You shouldn't go by yourself."

Was he being protective, or simply didn't want her driving his Mercedes?

Shortly, he returned, Ariel grabbed the grocery list, and they left.

She was seldom in Max's company alone these days, by choice. But he was the right choice for a bodyguard. Strong, fearless—albeit, his temper was a worry. An odd blend of brute and brilliance. And despite all their time together, Ariel felt no closer to unraveling him.

As they headed for town, he switched on the radio. A national, live talk show hosted by a pompous blowhard they both despised.

"Please," Ariel said. But he ignored her. She never understood why he subjected himself to such aggravation. The host was in a heated exchange with a caller, interrupting him:

"No-no-no. Federal research grants are nothing but glorified welfare. Most of these so-called 'researchers' never worked for a real, for-profit company. They spend more time raising funds than doing science. It's a racket, like everything else government gets its tentacles into."

The caller fired back, *"That 'racket' is responsible for tremendous breakthroughs. The computer. The Internet. Lasers. Nanotechnology. Mapping the human genome and brain. On and on. All a direct result of federal funding."*

"You neglect to mention the huge number of projects that fail."

"Even counting failures, return on investment for the country is enormous, a thousandfold. Research creates new industries, jobs, medical advances—"

Dial tone, and the host snorted, *"Folks, the real issue here isn't R&D. It's who's doing it, and who's funding it. Bureaucrats think they know better than the private sector. They blow our tax dollars on projects no corporation in its right mind would ever touch."*

Max yelled at the radio, "Because private industry doesn't do pure research, you asshole. All it cares about are profits. *Short-term* profits."

"Millions of tax dollars these scammers flush down the hole," the host continued. *"Including the biggest buck-sucker of them all—that massive*

black hole up in Talawanda. Nuclear colliders aren't just a waste of billions, folks, they risk our lives. The entire planet!

"Fortunately, there's new legislation to yank TPC's funding. But to succeed, the white hats on Capitol Hill need your support. So I'm asking you, for the sake of your kids, grandkids, God and country, drop what you're doing, get on the horn, call your senator and representative, and demand they pull the plug—*"*

Ariel switched the radio off to say, "And to think we're siding with that jerk against TPC!"

Max said nothing.

They rode in silence past endless waves of brown cornstalks, arriving in town to find it quiet on a Monday morning, grocery nearly deserted. As Max steered their cart down an aisle, Ariel asked the question uppermost in her mind. "Are you making any progress on your Grand Plan?"

"In fact," he said, "we are. A little more refinement and we'll roll it out for review."

Against all odds, Ariel felt heartened. She smiled a hopeful smile. "If anyone can figure this out," she said, "it's you."

Max halted. Ariel, too. And before she realized, he grabbed her, pressed her against a dairy case, and kissed her hard on the lips. She was stunned. But she didn't stop him, emotions flooding. Finally, she regained her senses and pushed him off, sputtering and reeling.

He stood there in that cocksure way of his, and she felt herself flush head to foot. For an instant, she'd fallen under his spell once more, allowing him a moment she'd sworn would never repeat. *And now he knew...*

Turning, cursing herself, she fled.

And rode home pressed silently against the passenger door.

• • •

That night, Ariel sat up late in her room reading, trying to wash Max from her mind. She finished Scott Butterfield's novel, *Infinitiman*—far as he'd gotten, anyway. A cliffhanger about America in peril, on the precipice of doom, and no ending.

Uncanny how the story foresaw the country's current state of affairs. Unscrupulous rulers sacrificing the well-being of the many for the special interests of the wealthy and powerful few. A government that promoted reactionary ideologies over reason and science; manipulating, dividing, breeding fear and distrust. A depressing read.

For all Butterfield's oddity, Ariel found him intriguing. A would-be revolutionary tilting at impossible odds. In his fantasy life, anyway. In reality, he appeared cynical and disengaged. A sad, frustrated, troubled soul who'd turned his back on the world to fight fictional foes.

Ariel switched to her journal to record her thoughts, but she'd not gotten far when she stopped, recalling the creepy idea Max had stuck in her head earlier.

The sensation of someone watching over her shoulder.

CHAPTER 60

For the first time since encountering the enigmatic vortex weeks ago, Ariel was able to catch her breath. Peace and calm had returned to the farmhouse. The past few days, the men were so preoccupied with Max's secretive research, Ariel had hardly seen them. They'd been holed up in each other's rooms mumbling together, coming out only when necessary for meals or to take watch over the vortex, refusing to discuss their work. Meanwhile, Tia mostly kept to herself.

Ariel had used the time to read, tidy up the house, and play with Newton. But her respite was coming to an unpleasant end. Later this morning, she and Tia were due in court for a hearing in their "hit-and-run" accident. They would have to face their nemesis protesters once more, and depending on the judge's decision, they could be looking at a trial, lawyers, fines, who knew?

There came a tap at her door and Tia's tiny voice.

"Am I disturbing you?"

"No-no, come in."

Ariel sat up, and Tia joined her on the bed.

"I changed my mind," Tia said. "I think Stan should take us to the courthouse."

Ariel puzzled. "But Max is better protection if there's trouble."

"He's *also* trouble. Not just his temper. What if our judge is the one who heard his assault case last winter? You want Max for a character reference?"

"Have you told him?"

"It was his idea."

That didn't sound like Max, he was always spoiling for a fight.

Tia clarified, "He's too busy with his 'Grand Plan.'"

In fact, Ariel had never seen the men so absorbed. Constantly on their laptops. Up early, up late. The few times she'd glimpsed their screens, they were reading *The New York Times* archives.

"Fishy," Tia said. "Steady drumbeat of quiet from those two."

"Maybe Stan will open up on the drive today."

"Either he talks, or we all have a come-to-Jesus over lunch. Two weeks till Butterfield's fire. I want to know if Max is on to something."

• • •

Stan gave up little on the way to the courthouse. All he'd say was that Max was "a genius," and they'd soon see why. But as Tia made clear, "soon" meant when they got back home.

Things could not have gone better with the judge. A black lady who'd seen and heard it all, siding with Ariel and Tia, warning the two men that to press their case was a huge mistake.

On their way home, Tia growled, "We should've counter-sued. At the least we could've forced the bastards to pay your car repairs."

Ariel's hand flew to her heart. "Make them madder than they already are? I'll gladly pay never to see those two again."

Stan agreed. "The way they were glaring at you. *Scary.*"

Indeed. The smaller man had paid Ariel discreet gestures, running a finger across his throat. And when the hearing concluded, the big man with the red beard and Celtic tattoos made a pistol of his hand and fired it at her. The bailiff had wisely detained the men until Ariel and her friends were safely on their way.

It was 11:30 when they got back, Max there to greet them out in the front yard, pacing, hands cupped behind his back. Ariel knew that look. He was wrestling something. Something *serious.*

"Well, you're not in jail," he said as they piled out of the truck. "How'd it go?"

"Our way," Tia said. "Over."

He looked pleased. "Excellent. I need you in a good mood. I need your help."

"Another snag?" Stan asked.

"A *big* one."

They filed into the house to gather in the living room, and Max resumed pacing as the others took seats. He looked wrung out.

"I didn't want to go into this yet," he began, "but something unexpected came up. The Plan Stan and I are working on? It *will* work. If I can get over this hurdle."

Ariel could see the conviction in his eyes. He stopped and turned to Tia. "What would you give to toss the Dark Agers out of power and send Filby and Thornton packing?"

She scoffed.

"There *is* a way," he insisted. "But it'll mean opening your mind to a compromise."

Tia raised a brow. "You mean, opening the wormhole to more butterflies?"

"*Exactly.* Butterflies be damned, let's do what has to be done."

Ariel was afraid to ask. "Which is?"

"Reverse the last presidential election."

Confused, Ariel looked to Tia, who replied coldly, "He's saying, we should tamper with the election four years ago. Steal it from Filby and throw it to Shackleton."

Ariel gaped at Max. "But-but what will that do to *us?* Our pasts? Our *futures?* All that's happened to us between then and now. *Everything* would change."

"Yes. *For the better.* We'll be able to keep our jobs here. TPC won't have a mob at its gates. We'll have a government that values science and wormholes—presuming we rediscover ours."

Aghast, Ariel cried, "We can't be sure of *any* of that. *Anything* could happen. We could all be dead. The world could end!"

"Highly unlikely in just four years. *Think.* Shackleton's flaws aside, she supported science. If she'd beaten Filby, we'd surely be the better for it. She was ahead in the polls, she'd be president today if it weren't for that video. Thornton hijacked the election, Filby turned the country into a theocracy, and now we've stumbled onto a way to undo it. Yes, there's risk. And well worth it."

Tia buried her face in her hands. "You are certifiably *nuts.*"

"Please," Stan told her, "hear him out."

Tia calmed, and Max resumed pacing.

"It's pretty straightforward, he said. To change the election, we stop the Shackleton video from going public."

As a Congressional investigation later disclosed, the video that damned Shackleton's presidential bid was released the Sunday before the election by Reverend Penbrook Thornton. Thornton had kept it secret from the public beforehand, and within hours, the video was a viral rage, all over the news. Shackleton went into hiding, the race over before the polls even opened Tuesday morning.

Prior to the video, Shackleton had been an astute legislator. A reformist with a pro-science agenda that would have served the country well. Afterward, she faded into obscurity, and Thornton was never called to account. The Dark Agers had maneuvered to quash the investigation.

Tia snapped, "How do you propose we stop Thornton from releasing the tape? Bribe him?"

"Money isn't Thornton's hot button. And from what Stan's NSA contacts say, Thornton has no skeletons. Blackmail is out."

Stan confirmed, "Squeaky clean."

Max paid Ariel a long look. "The way we reach Thornton is through his faith. Through *you.*"

As if altering the past weren't bad enough, the idea of Ariel confronting the towering figure of her youth sent her heart reeling.

"No way," she said. "I can't argue theology, I'm not qualified."

Even if she found the courage, her knowledge of scripture was paltry. She stood no chance debating the scruples of that horrid video with the likes of Penbrook Thornton.

"Relax," Max said, "that's not what I need from you, I'll get to that. Like I said, Thornton's hot button is his faith, and for our purposes, his Achilles heel. It plays right into our hands."

He stopped pacing to face Tia. "Thornton's a Fundamentalist, yes? He believes God knows all, including the future. We *also* know the future. Four years of it, anyway. Ergo, from Thornton's perspective in the past, *we're* God."

Stan said, "The Law of Transitive Property. If A equals B, and B equals C, A equals C."

Max said, "And we use it to our advantage."

Tia snorted. "Your Grand Plan is to play God to Thornton?"

"Not directly. We'll have a go-between carry our message. Scott Butterfield."

Tia threw up her hands. "Even if it isn't suicide for us to contact Butterfield, do you honestly think he could get Thornton to meet with him? Much less finagle that video away? A bowl of noodles has more charisma than Butterfield."

"Butterfield's sharper than you think."

Tia eyed Max closely. "You know something about him I don't?"

Max didn't respond, and Tia's face darkened.

"I'll be damned," she hissed. "You *already* contacted him."

She spun on Stan. "And you knew! You're helping him!" On fire, she cried, *"Traitors.* Both of you. *You broke our pact."*

Ariel had never seen her so incensed. Stan turned bright red, shrinking to the end of the couch, as far removed as possible.

"How *could* you?" Tia howled at him, waving a blind hand at Max. "I expect it from Machiavelli, here. But *you?* I trusted you!"

Stan replied in a pitiful voice, "Now, Tia, keep an open mind."

She appeared about to explode, and Ariel jumped to calm her with a hug.

Max and Stan exchanged uneasy looks, and Max said, "In fairness, this was all my idea. When I told Stan, he was upset, too. But I convinced him it'll work."

Tia broke out of Ariel's grasp and paced the room, arms crossed.

Max allowed her a moment, then continued, "I got the idea the day we learned Butterfield shared our universe. Like you, I thought we were finished. But on my own, I searched the news archives, hoping for something to spark an idea. And finally, I came across a *Times* article. A bus accident in Queens, still a few days off, Butterfield time.

"I recalled from Butterfield's journal he took a bus to work. The accident was on his route, at the right time, and the article said passengers were taken to Queens General. I hacked the hospital files to find Butterfield's name among them. He was only slightly injured, and released."

Ariel said, "What possible help was that?"

"I wasn't sure at first. The accident hadn't happened to Butterfield yet. I figured there had to be a way to leverage it. So, I went back to the archives looking for something bigger to grab his attention. And I found it. An explosion the day before in Brooklyn. Not terrorism, a bona fide accident. News Butterfield was bound to hear about. While you three were in the house and I was out guarding the tent, I sent him an email predicting the blast."

Tia's jaw tensed.

"...I recalled from Butterfield's personal log, he feared his apartment was haunted by an evil spirit. All I had to do was make him believe the spirit was godsent. And what better way than with a prophecy? I worded it so he wouldn't know where the explosion would be, and couldn't prevent it—" Max nodded to Tia, "keeping butterflies to a minimum."

It didn't appear to lessen her anger.

Ariel asked, "Did he reply to your email?"

"No. He was at work and probably thought it spam. In any event, the day of the explosion, I sent a second email warning him not to take the bus the next morning. Given my first prediction bore out, I figured he'd listen. I kept watch on the hospital admissions, curious to see how Time would handle the change. Would Butterfield's name vanish in a flash, or what?

"But nothing changed. Turns out, Butterfield blew off my warning and took the bus, anyway." Max smiled. "The *last* time he ignored me. After the accident, I sent a third email, and he was home to receive it, recuperating."

"What did it say?" Ariel asked.

"I predicted another disaster. I'd found an article about high winds toppling a crane in the Bronx that night. Again, I kept the wording vague so he wouldn't know enough to interfere. But this time, he emailed me right back. Upset, confused, demanding an explanation."

"And?"

"Time to set the hook. I told him I was a herald of the Lord, and that the Lord had chosen him for His messenger."

Tia covered her eyes, and Max countered, "I gave this a lot of thought. How does a nobody like Butterfield connect with a bigwig like Thornton? Especially with Thornton in the throes of the election back then. Email? Phone? Drop by his house? For my Plan to work, we've got to make Butterfield into someone Thornton will respect. And we do that by giving him 'God-cred.' We make him a *prophet*."

Stan emerged from detention, cheeks still rosy from Tia's tongue-lashing. He said, "We've got all the tools at hand. Full digital archives of the *New York Times*."

Max explained, "The idea is to feed Butterfield a few sensational stories, have him take them public, and *bingo*. His predictions come true, the media picks up on it, and overnight he's a sensation. A modern-day Elias. Thornton can't help but notice, and *then* he'll accept a meeting." He paced again. "It worked like a charm. At first. The crane collapse got Butterfield aboard, and I built on it. I sent him on other tasks to see if he could handle the pressure. He proved he could."

Tia was winding up again, and Max hastened to add, "I took precautions *not* to disturb the timeline. I picked events that would play out the same, irrespective of Butterfield. I sent him to a Yankee's game to help a fan struck by a baseball—*prior* to it happening. The fan would have survived, regardless."

Tia groaned, and Ariel asked, "Assuming Butterfield could set up a meeting with Thornton, how does he get the video?"

Max said, "We could always threaten Thornton with the Wrath of God, but I doubt it'll be necessary. If you recall, four years ago, the world didn't know the video existed. There was only one copy, apparently, and as the Congressional investigation revealed before it was shut down, Thornton had shown the tape to no one. The very fact Butterfield has knowledge of the tape will blow Thornton's mind. Add to that Butterfield's prophecies, it should erase any doubts about his legitimacy, and set Thornton up for an offer he can't refuse: in exchange for turning over the tape, God promises the election to Filby."

"I don't get it," Ariel said. "Without the video, Filby will *lose.*"

Max grinned. "Yes. God will break His Word. By then, it won't matter."

"It won't matter," Tia snapped, "because the life we live now will be swept away in a torrent of butterflies."

Max countered, "And what is it about this life of ours you care to preserve? We've no jobs, TPC is closing, science is dead, and the nation's run by Creationists. We've *everything* to gain, little to lose."

"We could lose our damned lives!"

"And if we do nothing, we lose the country. You wouldn't risk your life to stop that?"

Stan added, "We're only talking four years. A mere blip in Time."

Blinking, fuming, Tia said, "Too many loose ends. Your Plan hinges on controlling Butterfield. How can you guarantee that? Bribe him?"

"No. Butterfield isn't stupid, but he doesn't have the acting chops to fool Thornton. In order to convince a shrewd man like that, Butterfield has to believe to his core he's obeying God. I about had him persuaded, too, till he threw me a curve."

He stopped pacing. "When I contacted Butterfield this morning, he was frantic. The ballpark thing happened on a Saturday. I'd made the mistake of assuming he'd be off work. He wasn't, he called in sick, his stunt was caught on Jumbotron, and it made the news. His boss saw it and fired him, and suddenly he was without a job, and broke. He wanted no more to do with me."

Tia formed a butterfly out of her hands and flapped its wings.

Max continued. "I had to get him some money, get him back on track. But I drew a blank." He placed a hand on Stan's shoulder. "Stan came up with the answer. The lottery."

Tia's butterfly turned to fists. "Are you out of your goddamned minds? Altering the results of a lottery will do *major* damage to the timeline—*before* the election."

Stan said, "The interesting thing is, Tia, we've seen no serious disruptions. Not that we're entirely sure what to look for, but Time appears more resilient than anyone would've thought."

Tia cried, "Oh my God, you already did it, you rigged the lottery."

She collapsed in her chair, and Ariel confronted Max. "You've no way to know whether the Timeline changed. If altering the past alters your memory, too, you wouldn't be aware. You wouldn't remember what's different, or missing."

"This much we know," Stan said. "We're all still here. Our meddling doesn't seem to have made our lives any the worse. In the course of Time, after all, four years is but an instant."

Max added, "There *is* a way to check for changes to the past. A litmus test, of sorts. Before contacting Butterfield the first time, I downloaded the entire *Times* archives for the last four years. Stored it on my hard drive. Each time I email him, I compare my stored files against the live files online, looking for inconsistencies."

Ariel said, "But how do you know butterflies don't change the archives in your stored files?"

"Because I spotted some differences. The ballpark thing. My stored archives show nothing, but the live archives mention it. There *are* changes to history, but nothing big, so far. Nothing that's rippled down for us to notice."

Stan said, "If we encountered a Time rift, we would have aborted. We both want to be damned sure before we take the big step."

The big step of altering the election. A step off the ledge, Ariel feared. She no longer trusted Stan, either. She asked, "What about the lottery? That's where you hit the snag?"

"Stan found a winning number with dual ticket holders," Max said, "and I passed it on to Butterfield for a three-way split. Not *too much* money, enough to keep him going. We didn't want him bailing for the Bahamas. But seems it wasn't sufficient, he got cold feet again today. He refuses to cooperate further unless I prove I'm who I say I am. He wants a face-to-face this afternoon, online."

Tia crowed, "He's got you now, smart ass. *Game over.*"

Max did not look beaten. He replied, "You leave us two choices. Come clean to TPC and start a Timewar, or destroy the collider and face prison. Well, I'm giving us a third option. I say we go back in time and correct a mistake that should never have happened to begin with. Turn the country around, turn our lives around—"

Stan interjected, "And save science."

"—But I can't do it without your help."

"Enough," Tia declared, standing. "I call a vote." Turning to Max, she raised a finger in his face. "And mark my words, if you lose, you so much as go *near* that tent again, *I'll brain you.*"

The room fell silent, and Tia asked Stan, "You?"

He said without hesitation, "I'm with Max."

Everyone looked to Ariel, and she felt herself flush. She was pulled both ways, yearning to change the course of deplorable events, fearful of annihilation.

She swallowed and said, "I-I'm sorry Max, it's too much to ask."

Tia's triumphant eyes met Max's.

But he held up a hand.

"Before you vote, Tia," he said, "one last thing. If you *do* side with me and we flip the election, we've no reason not to make other changes, too. We can warn Butterfield about the fire." He raised a brow. *"And we can warn your family about your mom."*

PART THREE

CHAPTER 61

Ariel marched from the tent to the house, into her room, collapsing on her bed in a funk.

Minutes ago, against her better judgment, she'd given in to Tia and the men. She'd presented herself falsely to Scott Butterfield as a Paraclete of the Lord. Live, online, in "angel mode," as Max now called it. No makeup or contacts, the pale ghost that he used to make fun of, in a white, strapless tunic, hair up in elaborate curls, thanks to Tia. Stan had set up klieg lights in the tent to recreate the sun's burnishing effects on her skin, and voila, *Angel Ariel.*

But no more. Fearing they'd made a dreadful mistake, this angel was hanging up her wings. Her premiere was her finale.

A soft rap came at her door, and Ariel opened on a tentative-looking Tia.

"Still upset?" Tia asked.

"*Uncomfortable* is the word," Ariel replied, waving her in.

Ariel bent toward her, and Tia began undoing her hair.

Tia said, "I wanted to thank you again for what you did. I know Max's Plan is a longshot, but if there's any chance to save my…"

306

She broke into tears, and Ariel raised up, shook out her hair, and hugged her.

"Assuming Butterfield's back on board," Ariel said, "it was worth it. But after meeting him, I'm convinced it was a mistake."

The man all but screamed eccentric introvert. Still, he appeared rational and reasonable.

Tia wiped her eyes. "I don't like the deception any better than you. Max should have been straight with Butterfield to begin with, maybe we could have earned his help outright. But if we come clean now, we'll lose all credibility. Just another Internet scam."

Ariel sighed. "If he bought my act, hopefully you won't need me anymore. You can get the job done with epistles."

"We'll know soon enough."

CHAPTER 62

Hawk News reporter Kyle Heath was on assignment with his crew, inside a posh apartment on the Upper East Side to document a purported "demonic possession." But so far, all they'd managed to record were the screams of a ten-year-old girl behind her locked bedroom door.

With Heath were several of the girl's relatives, a "spirit guide" to lead the girl into the light, and her mother, an overly coifed and Botoxed woman. The mother jiggled the doorknob and pleaded, "Now, Kimberly. We're all waiting. You want to be on TV, don't you?"

Heath hated these time-filler projects. The child wasn't possessed, she was spoiled.

His phone buzzed, and he checked it, startled and excited to recognize the name. Stepping away, he answered, "Ms. Butterfield, what a pleasant surprise."

"We need your help," the anxious voice replied. "Scotty just got a new prophecy."

Heath couldn't believe his luck. "Of course, whatever you need. What's the prophecy?"

"A tornado's coming. It's gonna strike a town in Georgia, tonight. You gotta warn them."

He nearly dropped his phone. "Where are you now?"

"Scotty's apartment in Queens."

"Scotty's with you?"

"Yes."

"Have you told anyone else about this?"

"Not yet."

"Good. Speak to no one, I know your address, I'm on my way."

"No need for that, just get your station to issue an alert. The town is Jasper, Georgia, not far from Atlanta. The tornado will strike tonight at eight-thirty."

"It's not that simple. Hawk won't air an unsubstantiated claim. We've got to meet."

"Then hurry. The angel said to get it on the air for the six o'clock news."

Angel?

"Stay put and wait for me, I'll take care of everything."

He hung up doing a fist pump. This could be the break of his career, *if* he handled it right. Turning to his crew he ordered, "Pack up gang, we're done here."

The mother gasped, *"What?* What about my daughter? We have to save her!"

Heath looked to the relatives, and gesturing toward the mother and spirit guide, he said, "If you really want to save that kid, *get her away from these wackos."*

And he and his crew headed out the door.

• • •

An hour later, the *Hawk News Eye* van entered the alley behind Butterfield's apartment building. Few groupies back here, as Ivy promised when Heath called to report they were close.

The driver parked, and Heath told his crew, "Sit tight till you hear from me."

He was hoping to get some footage of Butterfield at home, then talk him into coming down to the studio. Having him live at Hawk would not only allow for a more dramatic reveal of the new prophecy, it would also give Heath time to get to know the man, having yet to meet him. A familiarity that could pay dividends if the Prophet phenomenon proved to have legs.

Slipping out of the van, he ran to the door of the building and rapped out the secret knock Ivy had given him. She was there inside to admit him, needing help with the rusty hinges.

"What took you so long?" she cried, leading him up a dark, narrow stairway into a dingy hall.

"Traffic. No worries, we've plenty time."

The last door on the right was ajar, and Ivy led him inside. A large living room, sparsely furnished, and what there was of it was old and bedraggled. Butterfield stood near a shabby sofa at the front of the room, arms folded on his chest, eyes chary. Even less impressive in person than on Jumbotron. Average height and build. Bad hair, scruffy beard.

Heath approached to extend a hand. "Kyle Heath, Hawk News."

Butterfield took it. Soft grip. The man offered Heath a seat on the sofa next to a big, orange cat. The cat had the only cushion, and Heath sat gingerly on hard frame, looking around to see what appeared to be a shepherd's crook hanging on a rack by the door. Butterfield sat on the other side of the cat, and Ivy took a seat on the floor at their feet.

"Thrilled to get your call," Heath said, petting the cat. "I'm a big fan." He pulled out his phone. "If you don't mind, I'd like to bring my video crew up for some shots."

Butterfield shook his head. "This isn't an interview, it's a warning. Tonight, at exactly eight-thirty-three, a tornado will level the town of Jasper, Georgia. Hawk needs to broadcast an alert."

Heath turned his phone into a notepad. "How'd you come by this information?"

Butterfield seemed hesitant, and Ivy replied, "From God. He talks to God through an angel."

Wincing, Butterfield blurted, "The message speaks for itself. It has to be on the air by six."

Heath stopped thumbing. "As I told Ivy, Hawk won't air an unsubstantiated claim like this."

"That's never stopped it before."

"We can't go telling people a disaster's about to strike with nothing to back it up. The station won't be held liable for that."

"You have to believe me, *lives are at stake.*"

"It's irrelevant what I believe, Hawk isn't going to run a second-hand story. You have to take responsibility and deliver the prophecy in person."

Seeing panic in the man's eyes, Heath added, "We'll make it fast and easy. I've got a van downstairs, I can get you to the studio, have you on air by six, home by seven."

Ivy said, "But you've got a camera crew here."

"This is way bigger than a taped statement."

He turned to Butterfield. "I was at Yankee Stadium that day. I've been following you ever since. If you're sure about a tornado, you need to come with me."

"I'm coming, too," Ivy insisted, standing.

Butterfield grumbled, rose, and trudged to the coat rack like a man condemned to the gallows. Ivy followed and he helped her into a jacket, grabbing a black hoody for himself.

Heath pointed to the shepherd's staff.

"It's TV," he said. "You want people to believe your prophecy, look the part."

CHAPTER 63

It appeared Scott Butterfield had bought Ariel's angelic performance. About an hour ago, as the team Googled old TV and print news, Stan spotted a historic change. Hawk News was suddenly plugging a special announcement scheduled for 6:00 tonight, four years in the past. "A Frightening New Revelation from the Prophet of Queens."

The update in the media archives was further proof Butterfield existed in their universe.

Ariel's friends cheered and congratulated her, and she was relieved. The tornado was one of several disasters they'd considered for this latest prophecy, chosen for its seeming low risk of butterflies. The fewer butterflies in advance of the election, the less likely one might disrupt their Plan to reverse it. The storm had claimed no lives in flattening the little town, and a prediction would in no way prevent the tragedy, or alter its outcome to any appreciable degree. Also, Jasper, Georgia was in Reverend Thornton's backyard. Better to attract his notice.

As the top of the hour approached, Tia and Ariel joined the men on the couch. They were watching archival Hawk News footage from a laptop they'd plugged into the TV.

Ariel asked them, "When we cause a major change to the past like this, will we feel it as it ripples down?"

"'Ripple' is a good word for it," Stan said. "Physicists who theorize about such things refer to temporal shifts as 'Timequakes,' and their effects on subsequent events as 'Timewaves.'"

Max said, "Changing the past creates a quake in the Timeline that releases a wave of energy. The wave flows forward in Time to the present, altering history in its path."

"To answer your question," Stan said, "I suspect the only way we'll feel anything is if a change impacts us *personally*. Say Butterfield found out who I am, looked me up four years ago, and knocked my teeth out. Flash-forward, the Timewave hits, and suddenly I've got dentures."

Max nodded. "We felt no effects from my messing with the Yankees game, or my other tampering. So long as Butterfield's actions don't accrue to us directly, the only way we're apt to spot butterflies is by combing the archives."

Tia replied, "Maybe the tampering you did before wasn't substantial enough, historically. Reverse a presidential election, we're damn-well gonna feel *that*."

Though the men had softened her fears about their Plan, Tia still had reservations.

Stan said, "Each step we take from here on gets more problematic. At any point, a butterfly could derail us. Or alter our memories so we forget our Plan altogether. Yes, there are risks. But if we've any hope to fix this country, we have to take them."

Six o'clock arrived, and an old-but-updated Hawk News Special played on TV, fed through the laptop. Ariel watched in awe as history changed right before their eyes. On screen appeared a man at a news desk in Hawk's New York studios. Splashed across the picture, a banner read: *Hawk Exclusive: Breaking News/Special Announcement.*

The view widened to show Scott Butterfield seated at the desk across from the host. He wore a loose-fitting black hoody, floppy cowl raised, head bowed, face shaded to reveal little more than bearded chin. In one hand he held a shepherd's crook—the one Max had lost to the vortex.

"I'll be damned," Max said.

The hood and staff gave Butterfield a monkish air. Like he'd just emerged from some mountaintop cave. In the background, a digital date and time displayed four years ago to the day, hour and minute. The picture zoomed in tighter, and Butterfield appeared edgy, fidgeting. Stan upped the volume as the host addressed the camera.

"Tonight, we welcome to Hawk News, Mr. Scott Butterfield of Queens, New York. Viewers will remember Mr. Butterfield for the stir he caused last weekend with his uncanny psychic abilities. He foresaw not only a freak accident at Yankee Stadium, but an attack on Mayor Andy Beard, helping to avert both potential tragedies."

While the man spoke, the screen split into side-by-side videos of the Yankee Stadium incident and shaky phonecam footage of the attempted assault on the mayor.

"Mr. Butterfield joins us this evening to warn of an even-bigger disaster." The host turned to him. *"Mr. Butterfield, would you care to share with viewers what you see in your crystal ball?"*

Butterfield looked miserable, shoulders drooping, fingers drumming the staff. He raised up to mutter, *"Tonight at 8:33, Eastern Standard Time, a tornado will flatten the town of Jasper, Georgia."* He shrank again, adding without looking up, *"People need to listen, this is no joke."*

A color map popped up on a screen behind, highlighting a red dot in north-western Georgia, labeled "Jasper." The host noted it to viewers, asking Butterfield, *"Can you please tell us how you come to know these things?"*

Butterfield shook his head. The man pressed, *"I'm told you speak to God through an angel."*

Getting no reply, the host groped for a moment, and gave up.

"Well, there you have it," he told the camera. *"Prophet Scott Butterfield—two-for-two in his predictions so far—now claims a tornado*

will strike the town of Jasper, Georgia in two-and-a-half hours. Stay tuned. And for those of you in the Jasper area, you may want to take cover."

Butterfield stood, and the video cut to a close-up, freezing on his wretched face.

The team congratulated Ariel again, but she took no pride in it.

Tia wasn't happy either, pointing to the image of Butterfield frozen on the TV. *"This* is our Prophet? This wimp's gonna persuade Thornton to give up that videotape? Great Plan, Max!"

Max seemed unconcerned. "So far, so good. By the way, how's everyone's memory?"

Ariel thought hers intact. The others did, too.

Before Ariel could relax, Stan added, "We expect to notice it the instant we revise history, but it may not work like that. Some theories say only major changes to the past have an immediate impact. That small changes simply build up behind the temporal membrane until they reach critical mass, and erupt in a Timequake/Timewave. If so, a memory-altering event could occur at any time."

Anxious, Ariel asked, "Aren't there precautions we can take to protect our memories? What if we left reminders on our phones, memos to our future selves?"

Tia said, "What's to say a Timewave won't wipe away the reminders?"

"Or wipe out the *New York Times* archives in Max's files," Stan said. "We need to shield them, too."

"How?" Ariel asked. "The hands of the clock touch everything."

Max had downloaded the last four years of the *New York Times* as a baseline to compare with 'live' *Times* archives. Any differences they detected between the two would alert the team to changes in history. But in the event a Timewave updated both new *and* old archives, their means to spot the changes would vanish.

They mulled that, and then Max said, "Shield the files, *that's it.* We can't block a Timewave, but we can damn-well dodge it."

No one followed him.

"The answer is to back up the old news archives I saved and put them on a memory stick. When the hole opens tomorrow, we hide the stick in the plant on the other side. That'll protect the files from changes this side. Each time the hole opens, we retrieve the stick, copy its data for comparison, and put it back."

"*A time capsule,*" Stan said. "Brilliant."

"Only one catch," Max said. "Will we remember to retrieve it?"

Not if tonight's tornado caused a Timewave to wipe the thought from their minds. Regardless, they decided to record memos to themselves and proceed with the time capsule.

Stan asked, "Anyone got a flashdrive they can spare?"

Paying Max a sideways look, Ariel stood and went to her room, returning with a furry, faux rabbit's-foot keychain/memory drive. A gift Max had given her their first Christmas here—a jab at her "superstitious" upbringing. She tossed it to him, still in its wrapper, and he set about transferring the *Times* archives from his laptop.

Tia said, "The archives may help us identify changes in world history, but we need to detect changes in our *personal* lives, too. The more we interact with Butterfield, the more likely we are to alter our own pasts. How will we know?"

Stan said, "We all use daily planners. If we add them to the memory stick, we can compare them against our planners in real time."

Tia shook her head. "We need more than a schedule of past events, we need to know what went on *during* those events. The more details we have to compare, the better our chance to spot changes before they snowball."

Max finished transferring the archives to suggest, "How about Ariel's diary? She's detailed every day of our lives since we got here."

"*Hey,*" Ariel cried. "It's *not* a diary, it's a journal. And it's not for public consumption."

More than an account of her experiences here, her journal chronicled her life in high school and college. Her most intimate thoughts and dreams, including the highs and lows of her tumultuous affair with Max. She'd *die* if that got out.

Max assured, "No one else has to see. Each time we retrieve the stick, you get the only copy, and the stick goes right back in the hole. You check the copy against your journal and the archives, and alert us to changes. You're in full control."

Everyone looked at her as if there were no alternative. She could think of none. Begrudgingly she gave in, and Max tossed back the rabbit's foot.

Stan said, "After the tornado, what's our next move?"

Max said, "If Butterfield's prophecy grabs Thornton's attention the way I expect, it shouldn't be hard to reel him in. One more prediction ought to do it. Something aimed directly at Thornton this time. A personal crisis. Something Butterfield can warn him about in time to prevent. Make the stakes high enough, Thornton will be so god-smacked he'll walk on coals if Butterfield asks."

Tia said, "Coming up with something personal will take digging."

"Already on it," Max told her, turning his laptop toward them.

Ariel saw links to websites from the City of God. Its daily newspaper, local TV and radio stations, church bulletins and newsletters, police and medical centers, municipal court, and more.

"For instance," Max said. "Obits. Given the City's population, people die every day. Say we find someone close to Thornton who'll suffer a fatal heart attack. Butterfield warns Thornton, Thornton intervenes, and Butterfield submits God's bill: one videotape."

Ariel's stomach soured. Playing with people's lives. Playing God.

Stan said, "Reversing a death could toss a *big* wrench in the Timeline and put our Plan at risk. I suggest saving that till after the election, for Tia's mom."

Tia agreed. "A *non*-fatal heart attack serves the same purpose. I'll take the medical websites, it shouldn't be hard to hack the files."

"That's super illegal, by the way," Stan reminded.

"No way we'll get caught before the election," Max replied. "And after that, the Timewave will wipe away any evidence."

Stan said, "Then I'll take the police and court records."

Max obliged, and turned to Ariel. "How about you do the newspaper and church bulletins, I'll take radio and TV."

Assignments divvied up, they ordered deli delivery and settled in to await the Jasper tornado, and perhaps, a Timewave.

CHAPTER 64

Reverend Penbrook Thornton sat alone in the softly lit cabin of his Learjet, reading the bible on his iPad. He was headed to Atlanta for a visit tomorrow morning with protégé and presidential candidate, Republican Roger Filby.

Joining him in Atlanta would be Reverend Tobias Melcher of Dallas. Melcher was a friend and fellow Council member of the Coalition of Christian Conservatives, the covert political action committee Thornton founded and chaired. Afterward, the two would fly to New York for a meeting Wednesday with the full Council. A meeting Thornton had long been dreading.

But Thornton hoped to bring some good news with him. Filby hadn't fared well in the first debate and was busy prepping for the second, scheduled for this Wednesday night. Filby couldn't afford another stumble, and was hard at work with the finest forensics coaches in the country. Thornton wanted to see for himself the man's progress, with Melcher to bear witness.

Thornton needed some positive news to present the Council. Ellen Shackleton's lead in the polls was holding, and the Council

319

was pressing hard for Thornton to drop his bombshell tape. They'd demanded he bring it to the meeting, and against his better judgment, he'd agreed. He'd no intentions of surrendering it, but having the tape on hand was a gamble that could well blow up in his face.

Turning to the briefcase on the seat beside him, he stared through it to its troubling contents. He'd seen the video only once, right after he was presented with it. Shocking. Disgusting. No question it would destroy Shackleton. Yet, to release it would be the height of hypocrisy. How in good conscience could Thornton ruin this woman's reputation when God had spared *his*? And for a far-worse sin? The tape was neither godsend nor curse. It was a test of faith.

"Oh Lord," Thornton prayed, "let this cup pass. Not my will, but Thine be done—"

Hardly had he spoken than the plane took a nasty jolt, and he cried out.

The pilot buzzed back on the intercom. *"You okay, Reverend?"*

"Y-yes."

"Sorry, we're skirting a nasty storm. Stay buckled."

Lightning flashed outside the window, and Thornton mopped his brow and replied, "The Lord's restless tonight."

"Yes. You catch that announcement on the early news?"

"No."

"That guy up in New York who sees the future? Says a tornado's gonna hit a town not far from here."

"He's a weather forecaster?"

"No, a prophet. Or so they say. Check it out before we lose wifi. Hawk News."

Puzzled, the reverend closed out his bible and called up the news site. There it was, leading the day's top stories. *Psychic Predicts Tornado Tonight in Georgia.*

He clicked a video to behold a quirky, timid young man delivering an ominous message.

CHAPTER 65

I vy went to the window, parting the blinds to peer out. There came an instant roar.

"Don't encourage them!" Scotty said, on the couch with Homer.

"Double the size it was this morning," Ivy reported.

The situation was out of control. Returning from Hawk Studios an hour ago, Scotty and Ivy found the alley as crowded as the front street. They narrowly escaped inside the rear door, desperate souls pleading for predictions and miracles. Despite Scotty's insistence otherwise, people attributed the prophecies to him. His own neighbors, stopping by to beg favors. It upset him to turn them away.

Ivy joined him on the couch. "The crowd's on their phones, watching the broadcast."

Same live broadcast they were watching on TV. Hawk had been heavily hyping Scotty's prophecy. Rather than simply warning the residents of Jasper to take cover, the network turned the emergency into a spectacle. It sent storm-chasers from Atlanta to set up on a hill overlooking the town, and now as the appointed time arrived, the team was braving wind and lightning.

Ivy curled close to Scotty as the TV went split-screen. Left, a live shot of the deserted town with a gust-whipped reporter in the foreground, nasty clouds roiling above. Right, Doppler radar showing a signature "hook" cloud. Suddenly the reporter ducked for cover, and the picture went full-screen on the town to show a corkscrew of thunderhead swirling to earth.

"*OMG,*" Ivy cried. "It's really happening!"

The funnel bore down on Jasper like the wrath-of-God, and outside Scotty's window, the crowd erupted.

CHAPTER 66

Awakening on the couch, Scotty heard Ivy in the shower. He sat up with a groan, Homer regarding him closely from the backrest. Scotty looked at the clock. "Ivy hasn't gotten you breakfast yet?" *Half a can. She thinks I'm getting fat. You gotta get a handle on that girl.* There was no handling Ivy.

"Hang on a minute, and I'll feed you the rest." Yawning, Scotty located his phone, surprised to see how late it was. He'd slept poorly out here, the throngs in the street restless all night.

A scroll through the morning headlines showed last night's tornado and Scotty's prophetic warning among the top stories. He moved on to text and voice messages. Lots of them. His phone had rung nonstop after the broadcast till finally he'd shut it off. Calls from Kyle Heath and tons more media. Reggie, Zing, other former coworkers. Even Margo. And Samood—upset the crowd was blocking the building. And lots of other numbers Scotty didn't recognize, no idea how they'd gotten his.

Ivy had also been besieged by calls she ignored. Pop, friends, Kyle Heath. She'd switched her phone off, too, informing Scotty she was ducking school till the commotion blew over. Scotty was upset about that. Truancy wouldn't look good on her transcripts. But Ivy was stubborn, and after the gauntlet they'd run returning from Hawk, Scotty understood. A big mistake letting her be seen with him in public.

Homer batted Scotty's head with a paw. *Food.*

Laughing, Scotty rose and got them both breakfast, taking his back to the couch as Ivy exited the bathroom in jeans and a T-shirt. "Hey, sleepyhead," she said, wrapping a towel around her hair, joining Scotty atop the blanket and pillows of his makeshift bed. He'd given her the bedroom. "I can't wait to meet the angel! And to think, I never even believed in God, and here we are doing His work!"

Scotty didn't respond, and she elbowed him, nearly spilling his Cocoa Puffs. "Come on," she cried, "don't be such a grump. You're saving lives."

"You don't find it a bit odd, this 'Lord' stuff?"

"That's why they call it 'supernatural.'"

"Talking over the Internet? On videochat, for heaven's sake?"

"Beats the heck outta stone tablets."

Scotty sighed. "And did you see the news? An earthquake in Chile last night. *Thousands* died. More than the entire population of Jasper. Why didn't we get *that* prophecy?"

Ivy frowned and shrugged. "You can't second-guess the Lord. You gotta have faith."

Faith. *Mom* had faith. It's what killed her. Scotty put *his* faith in science. Science could have saved Mom. And yet, given all he'd witnessed recently, what explanation did he have *but* faith?

A knock at the door startled him. He set down his bowl and went to the peephole expecting more neighbors seeking miracles. Instead, he saw a stone-faced cop. Come to arrest them again?

Setting the chain, he opened a crack.

"Yes?"

"Sorry to disturb you, sir. We got a Joe Butterfield downstairs, claims to be your dad. Seems upset, should we send him away?"

Frantic, Scotty looked to Ivy. She gave him a panicked head wag. But reflecting, Scotty told the cop, "No. No, it's okay."

The cop left, and Ivy cried, "Are you *nuts?* Don't let him in! Don't tell him I'm here!"

Scotty had to face this sooner or later, and wanted to get it over with. Stepping out into the hall, he closed the door. Moments later, he heard a creak below, then plodding, swearing, and snorting in the stairwell. Pop's tall form lumbered into view and rounded the corner with a huff, eyes scowling to see Scotty.

Not yet fifty, Pop had aged since Scotty last saw him. Gaunter, more grizzled. Unshaven, pants and jacket wrinkled. Ivy would never have let him out like this.

He snarled, "First ya get her arrested, now she ditches school. *Where is she?*"

Scotty folded his arms tight on his chest to hide his trembling.

Pop loomed large. "You can fool them TV people, you don't fool *me.* I warned you 'bout that damned videogame. You *ain't* God, boy. And a shepherd's cane don't make you a prophet."

Scotty felt himself flush. "Ivy's fine. She's staying with me. Just till things die down."

"*Hell she is.* Whatever crap you're up to, you ain't draggin' her into it. Not while I got a breath in my lungs."

Shoving Scotty aside, he tried the door. Locked.

"*Open it.*"

"She's old enough to make her own decisions."

Pop wheeled on him. "She's a minor, goddammit! *My* minor."

Trembling, Scotty held his ground, and Pop banged on the door, shouting for Ivy. Other doors on the floor opened, and closed, and from downstairs, the cop called out, "Everything okay up there?"

Scotty replied, "Yes, he's leaving now."

Pop stuck a long finger in Scotty's chest. It hurt.

"I'm comin' back with a court order," he barked. "An' a sheriff."

And retreating, swearing, he stormed back down the stairs.

Scotty waited in the hall till the front door screeched, then a soft voice called up from below.

"Scott, Sweetie, you okay?"

"Fine, Mrs. Steiner. Sorry to disturb you."

"I'm sorry for *you*. All these strange goings-on. Can I help?"

"No-no. It'll be over soon, and I'll tell you all about it."

A pause. "Well, I'm here if you need me. Don't ever hesitate."

He thanked her, her door closed, and he called for Ivy to let him in. She opened with nervous eyes, clutching Homer to her chest, her yellow hair towel-dried and wild like a troll doll's.

Scotty warned, "He'll be back. He's got legal custody, you know."

Ivy moaned. "How long do I have?"

"However long it takes for a court order."

"Well then, whatever the Lord has in store, let's get to it."

Indeed. Scotty was long past ready to end this madness.

Ivy disappeared into the bedroom, and there came another knock at the door. Scotty stole back to the peephole, surprised to see the same cop. He opened, and the cop removed his cap.

"Sorry to bother you again, sir," the man said. "Could I have a moment, please?"

Scotty invited him in, and Ivy entered from the bedroom brushing her hair. The man nodded to her, cleared his throat, and said to them both, "I, uh, I have a favor to ask. It's my nephew, Teddy. Smart, wonderful boy. Six years old. He's very sick, and no one knows why. We've taken him to specialists, and *nothing*. He's getting worse, we're losing him." His eyes teared. "Please, *you gotta help us.*"

Taken off guard, Scotty looked to Ivy, saw her tearing, and swallowed to say, "I don't know what I can do. Everyone thinks I'm some sort of miracle worker. I'm just a messenger."

"But you speak to God." Pulling a paper from his pocket, the man thrust it into Scotty's hand. The nephew's name, address, and medical particulars.

Ivy said, "Scotty speaks to God through an angel. A *lady* angel."

Scotty flashed Ivy a frown, and the cop said, "Please, I beg you, ask her for us. Your angel is our *last* hope." And blinking back tears, he thanked them, turned, and left.

Scotty stared at the paper, and Ivy snatched it from his hand, reading, eyes glistening.

"We gotta ask, at least," she said.

"You realize what will happen if we do? You think that mob's crazy now?"

She went to finish dressing while Scotty paced. As the clock neared 10:00, Ivy returned to join him at his computer, face flushed. Or was that rouge? Soon came the noises, and when all was finally quiet, the computer screen went black and the icon of God from the Sistine Chapel appeared.

"*Noooo,*" Ivy cried, "not an epistle. I want to see the angel!"

Scotty was disappointed, too. He opened the email to read:

> wait for further instructions

Scotty typed back:

> what do I call you? herald? paraclete?

A long pause, and the angel responded,

> my name is ariel

The Angel Ariel.
Scotty typed:

> we're trapped in my apartment by a mob, cops holding
> them off. you said the lord has a plan, please tell us
> what it is.

Another long pause, and:

what do you mean we

Scotty:

my sister ivy and me.

Ivy said, "Wouldn't she know that already?"
Scotty shrugged. Angels weren't omnipotent, only the Lord.
Ariel replied:

you were told not to involve anyone else

Scotty:

ivy was visiting when the cops busted me. they got her
too, she's living here now.

Another long pause, then:

do nothing till you hear back from me

Scotty:

face to face from now on.

He felt a punch to the shoulder, and Ivy stuck the slip of paper in
his hand. He typed,

one more thing…

Copying the details about the cop, little Teddy and his condition, Scotty finished and hit "send."

No response.

Ivy asked, "Did she get it?"

"I don't know, but the link's still live."

Not for long. The bizarre noises returned, and the link died.

"So," Ivy said, "we wait here till the mob breaks down our door?"

Scotty shook his head, forlorn. His eyes wandered to another icon on the screen, the *R U God* disembodied eye inside a triangle. He sat up and clicked on it to tell Ivy, "How about you fix us lunch while I do a little cyber maintenance?"

She threw up her hands and went to the kitchen muttering, "You and your stupid videogame!"

He was already off, Homer joining him in his lap as he dropped in on Times Square to check out the news ticker.

Homer shook his head. *Dude, you've been away too long.*

Scotty moaned to read:

Anti-immigrant riots spread...PanEuro
parliament in turmoil...Rhomboids force
early elections...Threat of civil war...

The cat frowned up at him. *We're in deep shit, aren't we?*

On Scottworld, virtual time moved at a faster clip than real time, and situations could rapidly spin out of control. But never had Scotty let things get *this* bad. To fix so many problems would take more show of godly force than he'd ever used before, if a fix were even possible now.

He rushed to stamp out the riots, uncertain how to quash the other fires.

CHAPTER 67

Having done her angelic part to restore Butterfield's belief in "the Lord," Ariel had skipped the collider's first run today. She'd instead spent most of the morning in her room on her laptop, combing the City of God newspaper for articles on Penbrook Thornton. The team's hope to flip the election hinged on the reverend believing Butterfield was a messenger of God, and to that end, they were searching for a crisis event in Thornton's past that Butterfield might thwart with a prophecy. They'd found nothing helpful so far, but had good news on another front.

Last night at 8:30, the team again watched history rewritten—a "new" four-year-old TV special showing an F3 tornado sucking apart the town of Jasper, Georgia. And like the original tornado, not a single life lost. The broadcast attracted a huge audience, which hopefully included the reverend Thornton.

Also important, the team seemed to have escaped their latest time-tampering unscathed. After the tornado, they'd spent anxious moments awaiting a Timequake/Timewave. Yet, they saw no evidence of it. Their biggest intrusion on the past to date, and no apparent consequences, physical or mental. It prompted Max to declare the Butterfly Effect overblown.

Ariel had slept poorly last night regardless, fearing she and her friends would awake different persons. At breakfast, however, no one had been able to detect any changes in themselves, or each other. All the same, they intended to proceed with planting a time capsule in the wormhole, a precaution to catch butterflies that might otherwise fly in their faces. Ariel had returned to her room afterward to continue her search of City archives.

She sat on her bed hunched over her laptop, clicking open another newspaper article. Seven years since she'd left the City of God, and reacquainting herself now brought back a flood of memories, mostly painful. Little seemed to have changed in the town other than the population. Same old fare of church propaganda, civic puffery, and local minutia.

Until her eyes happened across a book review and a headline that caused her to tense.

The Science of Theology, by Dr. Philip K. Neuhoffer, PhD

Her stepfather. This was the first she'd heard of her family since leaving home. The article featured a photo, Phil in a plaid blazer and bowtie, sporting a gray goatee. A different look for him. Face fuller, combover thinner, chin uptilted in a wise and confident pose.

Dr. Neuhoffer, indeed. He was a product of Liberty University, his PhD in fundamentalist theology with a concentration in fire and brimstone. His science was of the Creationist ilk. Ariel felt her stomach knot as the years peeled away...

She was twelve the first time Phil laid hands on her. The memory played clear as a video. Mom fixing supper, Ariel at the kitchen table in an ankle-length skirt, hair braided and wound atop her head, writing a chemistry report on refractories. Phil on the phone, arguing with an underling at his Institute.

Abruptly, he covered the mouthpiece to bark, "Ariel, stop and set the table."

He resumed his dispute, and Ariel hurried to get an important point down before she forgot. No defiance to it, she was a dutiful child—though she despised Phil. If he wasn't lecturing or nagging or puffing himself up, he was invading her privacy. Entering her bedroom unannounced, intruding on her morning shower to shave at her sink. Complaints to Mom went nowhere.

And then that night in the kitchen, things took a nasty turn.

"Now," Phil snapped.

Apparently, Ariel was a beat too slow. Phil banged the phone in the cradle and stormed over, sweeping her from her chair like the wisp she was. He sat and threw her across his lap, dress up, drawers down, paddling her bare buttocks till they burned.

Never had she experienced corporal punishment before. Stunned, horrified, mortified, she jumped up and covered herself, gaping at Mom. Mom simply gaped back, lips quivering. Ariel burst into tears and bounded upstairs to her room, slammed the door and leaped in bed, bawling.

She listened for footsteps outside. For her door to open. For the soft, halting voice mom used when talking unpleasantries. Drugs and periods and such. But nothing. Muffled voices drifted up. Still shaking and smarting, Ariel wiped her eyes and crept to the door, cracking it.

"...no spoiled brat in my house," Phil snapped. "You coddle her, you tolerate her. Proverbs, 29:15: *The rod and reproof giveth wisdom; but a child left to itself bringeth the mother shame.*"

"She means no disrespect, dear. Imagine having no friends, never invited anywhere. The poor thing lives in a world of her own."

Phil didn't soften, Mom resumed her subservience, and no one spoke of that evening again, or of the incidents that followed—

Ariel was startled by a knock at her door.

Tia called out, "Got a minute?"

Hastily Ariel composed herself. Inviting Tia in, she patted the bed, and Tia joined her.

"I don't know how to tell you this," Tia began. "While searching the City's medical records, I stumbled across something, uh... *disturbing.*" Ariel puzzled, and Tia continued, "Your stepfather runs a psychiatric clinic down there, yes? Dr. Philip Neuhoffer?"

There he was again. Ariel clenched again. "Yes."

"He's an associate of Thornton's, so I fished his files, too. Encrypted, and I hacked them to find nothing on Thornton, but are you aware of the problems the City has with its teens?"

Ariel had heard things, rumors.

Tia said, "Suicides, self-mutilations, and the like."

"No more than most cities that size, I suspect."

"Waaaay more. *Four times* higher, and then some."

Upset, Ariel asked, "What's that got to do with my stepfather?"

"According to his files, Thornton brought him in to fix the problems. Treat disturbed kids." Her eyes flashed. "And *oh* how he treated them. The number of suicides *increased.*"

Ariel couldn't believe Reverend Thornton would stand idly by, and said so.

Tia shrugged. "He and Neuhoffer met regularly, but Neuhoffer knew how to manipulate him. Thornton bought into his psycho-babble. Fundamentalists excel at rationalizing, don't they?"

Ariel felt nauseous. Phil had never much talked about his work, but his Institute had a murky reputation, at least in her school. She'd heard tales of teens plucked from the community to vanish forever behind the Institute's doors. Urban legends, she'd assumed. Though she was aware of one girl who'd disappeared without explanation or trace. Another outcast. Goth. Gay. Ariel had only a passing acquaintance with her, but recalled her name.

Nicole LeClair.

The discomfort must have shown in Ariel's face. Tia drew back to say, "Maybe you should see for yourself. I'll send you the files, we'll discuss them later."

Ariel wasn't sure she wanted the files. Or to discuss them.

"Anyway," Tia said, "I found zilch to help us with Thornton. You?"

"Nothing so far."

Clapping hands to knees, Tia stood. "Okay then, let's go see what the guys came up with."

Ariel joined her, grabbing her rabbit's foot flashdrive, now containing both the *Times* archives and her journal.

They found the men in the tent experimenting with a hand-operated pole claw Stan had improvised. A mechanism for hanging the memory stick on the plant inside the hole. Mounted on the pole above the claw was a small camera and transmitter/receiver. A cable trailed from it down the pole and to a laptop on the table.

As the women entered, Max asked, "Were either of you in the tent after the morning run?"

"No," they answered.

"Strange," Stan said. "When we got here, stuff was scattered across the floor like someone was rooting around. Wasn't a squirrel or mice, the door was zipped tight, no holes or openings."

Max said, "From here on, let's keep a closer eye on things. We can't risk anyone snooping."

The others agreed, and Tia asked, "What's our plan for Butterfield today?"

"Unless you and Ariel fared better than us," Max said, "we're still on hold."

Stan said, "Twelve days till Thornton releases the tape. Still time to pick the right bait. Surely *somewhere* four years ago is an event we can use to draw Thornton to Butterfield."

Max held out a palm to Ariel. In it was a short length of hooked wire. He wiggled his fingers and said, "Rabbit's foot, please."

She surrendered it, he attached the wire, and she snatched it back to await the vortex.

CHAPTER 68

Penbrook Thornton was only half-listening as Roger Filby and a Shackleton stand-in sparred from lecterns in the front of a conference room. Thornton sat at a table in the back with fellow Council member, Tobias Melcher, and the chairperson of the Republican National Committee. All here to mark Filby's progress before the second presidential debate tomorrow night.

The importance of this rehearsal aside, Thornton's mind kept returning to last night's tornado, and more specifically, to the odd young man who'd forecast it.

How was such divination possible? Yet Thornton had witnessed the very storm from his berth in the skies, a God's-Eye view. It had shaken him, disturbed his dreams. Then on this morning's news, he'd learned that the prediction wasn't the first miraculous prophecy the boy had made. Exactly who was this Scott Butterfield?

Thornton forced his attention back to more pressing matters. Filby stood before a panel of debate coaches as he fielded an accusation from his mock opponent. He declared forcefully, "I favor open-carry anywhere folks are at risk, but the floor of Congress isn't one of 'em.

Hard 'nough gettin' bills passed in the heat of an argument without people floutin' firearms."

His opponent pounced. "So you admit the presence of guns is intimidating and inappropriate? You agree with gun-control advocates who say—"

One of the coaches broke in, "Roger, if I may... As we were saying, watch getting drawn into a defensive posture. Stay on *offense*. Remember, *you* hold the moral high ground. Don't fall into the trap, turn it around, put your adversary on the dime. Attack her record. She's soft on the Second Amendment, soft on crime."

Another coach said, "And that's *'flaunt'* firearms, not *'flout.'* Also, *your hands.*"

Filby looked sheepish. Nodding, he pulled his hands from his pockets. His opponent raised a question about the budget deficit, and again Thornton's thoughts drifted to last night's newscast.

The Prophet of Queens, the media called the boy. A *true* Prophet? Thornton had his doubts. Hardly a commanding figure. Not the stuff of Biblical lore. Meek, soft-spoken, awkward.

And yet, how to explain his astounding predictions? Thornton knew better than to second-guess the Lord. Was David not a humble young shepherd when he slew Goliath? Transformed by God into a mighty warrior king? Could it be that after an absence of two-thousand years, God had chosen this pivotal election to re-enter the human fray? A staggering thought. Thornton could almost feel Almighty Fingers flitting.

"No, Roger," one of the coaches interrupted Filby again. *"Fiscal* responsibility, not *physical.* Common mistake. Please continue."

Thornton's throat tightened. The topic tomorrow night was domestic policy, ostensibly Filby's forte. But even well-armed with pat answers, the man still struggled. And God-forbid the final debate, a townhall/ open-question format where Filby would have to survive off-the-cuff.

The RNC chair leaned into Thornton and murmured, "We need a miracle."

The man had no idea that just such a miracle sat in Thornton's briefcase between them. A miracle that Thornton felt morally resolved to keep forever under wraps.

Nevertheless, at tomorrow's meeting, the Council would demand to know how this rehearsal went.

CHAPTER 69

Ivy sat at Scotty's computer, in makeup and her favorite blouse, picking at her nails.

"Come on," she called to him in the bathroom, "it's nearly 2:00." Then softer to herself, *"Assuming* she graces us with her presence this time."

Ivy was still upset from this morning when Scotty got one of those stupid epistles. She so wanted to meet Ariel in person. Gaze into those incredible, mesmerizing, supernatural eyes.

Scotty slipped into the chair beside her as the noises began, and Ivy saw he'd attempted to comb his hair. Apparently, he'd been captivated by the angel, too.

The whine finally faded into silence, and Ivy's heart raced to see materializing on screen, not the God icon of the Sistine Chapel, but the angel, herself.

Again, Ariel was visible from the torso up, ghostly gorgeous in a white tunic, shoulders bare, skin glowing. So radiant, it was difficult to distinguish her pale features, save for those eyes, like twin lighthouses. Her silver-gold hair was woven into ornate braids atop her head as before, ringlets spiraling past her ears. And again, she looked uncomfortable in the presence of mere mortals.

"Hello, Ivy," she said in her silky voice.

"H-hello," Ivy gasped, awed to hear her name spoken by celestial lips. "An honor to meet you, your, your Godliness."

"Please, I'm simply 'Ariel'." She turned to Scotty. *"I'm sorry to tell you, Scott, but the Lord is not happy you've brought another into His confidence. From here on, no one else."* She refocused on Ivy. *"And Ivy, you must pledge your fealty to the Lord and reveal* nothing *of what you see and hear. Do I have your word?"*

Ivy wasn't sure what "fealty" meant. She replied, "Yes."

"Your brother is being entrusted with an important role in a Great Mission. You must do all you can to assist him, do you understand?"

"Of course I will."

Scotty asked, "What *is* my role? The crowd outside is getting bigger and crazier by the day."

"The Lord asks your patience. I'll return soon with details when the time is right."

She moved as if to go, but Ivy waved her hands at the screen.

"Wait," she cried. "The boy we wrote you about this morning? Teddy? Will you help him?"

Ariel appeared unsettled. *"I'm sorry, the Lord must decline all such requests."*

Ivy felt her jaw drop. "The Lord saved the man at the ballpark, he won't help a little boy?"

Ariel lowered her eyes, and Ivy pleaded, "Will you at least tell us what's wrong with him?"

"I, I don't know, I-I…"

Scotty added, "I have a request, too."

The angel directed her troubled beacons back at him.

"I've done all the Lord's asked of me to the best of my ability. I ask one thing in return."

Ariel appeared anxious.

"Years ago," Scotty said, "I lost my mother. If I could just see her again. Speak to her one last time. It would mean *everything* to me."

Ivy's heart leapt. What an incredible wish! She had no memory of Mom. There were tears in Scotty's eyes—Ivy had never seen her brother cry—and tearing too, she held her breath.

Ariel blinked and looked around. *"I, uh, that's not possible. I mean, the Lord won't allow it. Right now, He requires you to prepare for the Great Mission that awaits you, nothing more."*

And the screen went blank.

Scotty closed his eyes, a tear escaped, and he whispered, "So much for a merciful God."

Ivy sighed. Her brother blamed God for Mom's death. But Ivy knew there was more to it than that. And whatever it was stuck in his craw all these years, he refused to let it out.

CHAPTER 70

"Well *that* went well," Max snapped, withdrawing his antenna, the vortex still whorling. "We had things under control till the sister entered the picture."

Tia was upset, too. "How long till she posts Ariel's videochats on YouTube, and they go viral? The media will see through our charade like an x-ray!"

Ariel pointed out, "Ivy gave me her word."

Max said, "She's a teen in an all-girl's school. You trust her?"

Ariel felt terrible. Mostly for the Butterfields. She loathed her deceptive role in all this, still not sold on the team's risk-fraught decision to reverse the election. But with Tia desperate to save her mother, and Butterfield refusing to cooperate unless Ariel met face to face, she'd given in and played the angel once more.

Stan switched off the klieg lights, and Ariel stared at her reflection in her screen.

So, who was this Ivy? First blush, she was smart, like her brother. Spunky. And she wore an Ellen Shackleton T-shirt. But Max and Tia were right, the girl's presence added untold complications to an already delicate and mind-boggling challenge. The team needed no more obstacles. And now that the girl had moved in with Scott, it seemed they were stuck with her.

There were also the matters of the child with the life-threatening illness, and Scott's plea to see his departed mother. Ariel certainly sympathized with Scott's longing for his mother, as did Tia. Put on the spot, Ariel had handled it badly, never a good liar. Yet, while they could do nothing about Scott's mom…

She asked the group, "Can't we do *something* for little Teddy?"

"We've been over that," Max said. "A tragic situation, but we're physicists, not physicians. And even assuming we *could* cure him, would it be wise?"

Stan reminded, "Butterflies."

Tia said, "Slim risk of that." She showed her laptop screen to the others. A photo from a newspaper—an obit of a cherub-faced little boy. "I checked on Teddy. He doesn't die till *after* the election."

Max exhaled. "Saving the boy may not pose a big risk, but turning Butterfield into a miracle worker *does*. A prophet's one thing, let him start curing the sick, there won't be enough cops in New York to keep the crowds away."

"But helping the boy will buy us time, and help build Butterfield's God-cred. Besides, getting Butterfield in good with the cops may come in handy."

Ariel and Stan thought that made sense, and Tia added, "I could hack Teddy's medical files and see if his doctors ever came up with a diagnosis."

"All right," Max relented, "give it a shot if you want. Meanwhile, the rest of us stay focused on Thornton, the clock's ticking."

Issue settled, they headed for the house, and Ariel went to her room and closed the door. During the last run while she was hedging with the Butterfields, Stan had been busy extracting her rabbit's-foot memory stick from the wormhole. He'd copied its files to her laptop, following procedure, and returned the stick to the plant. Now Ariel took a moment to check the files against the live *Times* archives and her journal, using an app designed to flag disparities. She was relieved to find no changes of significance, and moved on to the more-pressing Thornton project.

The City of God newspaper was a trove of information on the reverend. All the same, despite searching every issue in the weeks leading up to the election four years ago, Ariel could turn up nothing helpful to their cause. She turned next to Church bulletins and newsletters, only to run across a notice that froze her:

Joan Neuhoffer Elected Secretary of Outreach Program

It was the first news of Mom since Ariel left home seven years ago. Ariel had tried many times to contact her. Emails, texts, phone calls, letters. All went begging. And now once more, Ariel felt intense emotions of affection and betrayal clash inside her...

She was thirteen when Phil laid hands on her again. Nearly a year after the first incident. Given the time that had passed, Ariel came to think Mom had intervened to prevent a recurrence. Still, she'd often felt her stepfather's eyes, which kept her in an anxious state and on her best behavior when around him.

He also continued to intrude on her privacy, forcing Ariel to find workarounds. She'd learned to dress in her closet in the dark, mastering the art of the quick-change. And she shifted her showers to after school, fortunate that Phil worked late most nights and weekends. Her strategy was successful for the most part. Until one day, she made a mistake.

Phil's position as director of the Research Institute required long hours away from home. At the same time, Mom's roll at the church grew. Bible study, choir, social services, charity causes. To avoid being home alone should Phil pop in, Ariel took to spending her in-between hours at the library. She soon consumed every science publication available, (all church-approved fare, of course), and thirsting for more, did something very out of character.

One afternoon when she was in the stacks reading a biology text, she came across a chapter arguing the case for Creationism over evolutionary theory. Penciled in the margin was a note: *Bullshit! Open your mind!* And scribbled next to the note was a URL.

Ariel resisted for days before entering the link in her tablet browser. And suddenly, like magic, she found herself transported past the City's Internet filters. And from that point on, a forbidden new world lay open to her.

She'd long heard terrifying tales of the worldwide web, sermonized into her since childhood. A spider's web of perversion and perdition. Yet, she was also aware of its promise. And having finally overcome her fear and guilt, she discovered to what an enormous degree the Internet surpassed her expectations. The horizons seemed limitless, filled with exciting, challenging—and heretical—ideas.

The dark side was unavoidable, of course, intrusive as it was. The appalling porn she stumbled into. Flagrant, shocking. She'd taken sex ed in school, she understood a wife's duty in the interest of propagating a good Christian family. And to see intimacy so exploited and cheapened online, she fled at every instance. Not until Max, did she at last come to see sex as more than chore and submission, rather, a profound means to fulfill a relationship.

Or in the alternative, destroy it.

Ariel had reveled in her new, forbidden intellectual freedom. She'd entered the last year of middle school her most content since coming to the City. Each day online brought new revelations, helping her escape her shallow, theocentric orbit, charging her with such radical notions she felt she'd burst.

She began to look differently at the world. Before the web, she'd come in contact with only a handful of other beliefs and races, the City almost entirely White, Right, and Evangelical. But the more she saw Outside, the more she questioned the tenets Reverend Thornton boomed from the pulpit each week. She came to realize, the message of her Church was but one of countless, often hotly opposing interpretations of the Christian bible. And there were thousands more *non*-Christian religions that populated the planet.

Ariel felt confused and ungrounded. She'd no one to share her thoughts with. Her teachers and Church deacons would have been outraged, and surely tell her parents. She'd no friends, no confidante, no one she could trust with seditious secrets. And lacking the courage and confidence to venture into chat rooms or online discussions, she'd kept everything to herself, downloading articles into a locked file on her tablet to peruse on the sly.

Not sly enough, to her regret.

One Sunday evening, Ariel vividly recalled, Mom and Phil were watching TV in the living room while she sat apart in a chair—a token show of sociability. They thought she was reading a school assignment, but it was an article in *The Smithsonian* on climate change.

It never occurred to her she'd get caught. Phil was by no stretch an attentive parent. Aside from ogling her on occasion, he was indifferent. No interest in her schooling, he'd never even attended a PTA meeting. And that night Ariel was so absorbed, she'd failed to notice him behind her until catching a whiff of nasty cigar.

A chill swept over her, and too late, she tried to switch off her device. He snatched it away, eyes smoldering as he took in the article, and she sat terrified.

"*Where* did you get this?" he demanded.

She flapped her lips wordlessly, and he wheeled on Mom as if she were responsible. "Look at this claptrap, Joan," he bellowed, fanning the tablet in the air, turning back to Ariel in a rage. "Where did you get this? *Answer me.*"

She'd prepared an emergency answer. "F-f-from a flashcard someone left in the cafeteria."

"*Who?*"

She shook her head.

"Give it to me."

"I-I-I threw it away."

Roaring, he seized her out of her chair, took her place, spun her onto his lap and delivered The Humiliation. Longer, fiercer than before. Ariel wailed helplessly in pain and shame, and through her tears and embarrassment, she watched Mom leave the room.

CHAPTER 71

Kassandra Kraft slipped out her apartment door and downstairs to the foyer, only to pull up. The throng outside was larger than ever, the two cops on the stoop, woefully outmanned.

Her dark mood worsened. Whatever that dork in 2A did at Yankee Stadium to get hauled off to jail, the public should have moved on to a new du jour by now. Kassandra didn't need this disruption, things were *not* going well at work, she *had* to get in early.

She pushed out the door, sending a wave of excitement through the crowd before it lapsed into disappointment.

"How much longer?" Kassandra snapped at the cops.

"They got the right to free assembly," one said.

"Assemble for *what?*"

He gestured to a second-floor window. "The Prophet. His prediction on the news about the tornado. He nailed it."

Kassandra hadn't seen the news in days, working every waking moment. She hit the steps swearing, and the crowd surged to meet her. Many were on crutches, in wheelchairs, all ages and ethnicities, pressing, babbling, thrusting notes at her, begging her to intercede to "the Prophet." An alarming uptick in emotion from what she'd encountered previously. She was terrified.

At the fringe were media crews wedging in to get to her, shoving mikes and cameras in her face, shouting questions. She cried to the cops for help, but they held fast to their posts. Shielding her face with crossed arms and her purse, she lowered her head and pushed on until the resistance faded, and breaking free, she fled for the subway.

Kassandra was still swearing when she exited the elevator on the 25th floor of Endicott, Percy & Moore. She made her way to her little workstation, one of forty such cubicles packed into the wing like a honeycomb, and as she shed her purse and jacket to her desk, a folded piece of paper fell to the floor.

A note—foisted on her earlier by one of those freaks outside her building, no doubt. She retrieved it. Handwritten in pencil.

Mr. Butterfeild,
Our daugther has spina bifida and is cripled. We have no money.
We are good prayerful God fearing Christians. Please, please help
us. God bless you.

Signed illegibly by someone with a Flatbush address and phone number. Kassandra wadded the note, tossed it in the trash, and fired up her computer. On the other side of the half-wall in front of her, a chair squeaked, and the smiling face of fellow intern, Bobby Driscoll, popped up.

The schmuck. Kassandra hadn't let on she knew he'd sabotaged her. Her eyes went back to her screen.

"Lookin' a bit tousled today, Kassie," he chirped.

"A minor commotion outside my building this morning," she said, dismissing him with a roll of her fingers.

He persisted. "You hear about Brian? Shonda canned him last night. Just you and me now. Maybe she'll make an exception this year and hire us both."

"Wouldn't that be something."

Even before Bobby's double-dealing, Kassandra knew it would be tough dispatching him. He had a leg up on her from the get-go. One of EP&M's principles was a Dartmouth alum from the same fraternity—how Bobby got his internship, surely. Nor was she going to sleep her way in. According to the vox pop, all *that* would net her at this jaded place was a spent condom.

She'd only one path. Beat the bastard straight up. Nepotism aside, EP&M was about results. Devise a better strategy than Bobby for winning the swing-states, and Kassandra could overcome the politics. Not that an intern's concept stood a chance of being implemented, all she needed was to demonstrate superior potential. But with the election just two weeks off, the hill was getting steeper by the hour.

Tomorrow, a galaxy of directors from the Shackleton camp and the Democratic National Committee were convening here for a confab. They were expecting a solution, having paid EP&M heavy retainers. Yet, all the firm had for them to date was a dry heave. The stress was unbearable, desperation palpable. Kassandra had always thrived on pressure, yet Thornton and his Crusaders left her stumped. She had no head for religion, an atheist by way of Unitarianism.

She continued to fret, unable to work, and as lunchtime arrived, Bobby interrupted her again, calling from behind his divider, "Hey Kassie, check it out. Isn't this your apartment building on the news?"

Panic shot through her, and she jumped up. *Had those damned fanatics set fire to it?* She gaped over the partition to see the news playing on Bobby's computer. A TV station was broadcasting live from the street in front of her apartment. Thousands more people than this morning. The image cut to the building's stoop and a close-up of the cop Kassandra had spoken to earlier. He was flanked by a dozen more cops now, beset by a swarm of mikes and cameras.

"...*An angel*," he was saying, tearfully. "*A lady angel, according to the Prophet's sister.*"

A reporter asked, *"Your nephew's gravely ill, and the Prophet asked the angel to cure him?"*

The cop wiped his eyes. *"Yes. The angel told the Prophet that Teddy has a rare condition."* He read from a scrap of paper, *"'Childhood Pulmonary Hypertension.' There's a treatment. We're very hopeful. Very grateful to the Prophet and his angel. And God."*

The camera jostled as people began chanting, *"Miracle! Miracle! Miracle!"* and the picture shifted entirely to the reporter.

"You heard it," he said. *"For the Prophet's growing legions of disciples, another miracle."*

And suddenly, like a miracle, Kassandra had an answer to *her* problem.

"By the way," Bobby said, "did you see the memo? No one's leaving today, Shonda's called an all-nighter." He laughed. "At least you won't have to fight that crowd tonight."

Kassandra hadn't checked her email, but no matter. Grabbing her jacket and purse, she turned to say, "Tell Shonda I'll have to pass. I have other plans."

And leaving him with his mouth ajar, she left.

CHAPTER 72

"Oh my God, *I've got it,*" Ariel cried softly, lying on her bed staring at her laptop. Unless she missed her guess, she'd just found the answer she and the team had been searching for. A means to forge a bond of trust between Butterfield and Thornton.

She was still in angel mode after an uneventful morning session with the Butterfields. Ivy had been in attendance again, Scott still pushing to "end this thing." Ariel had placated him with a diagnosis for little Teddy, and assuming she now had a solution to the Thornton impasse, she was indeed hopeful to end this thing. For which she had Tia to thank.

Ariel's answer had been inspired by the tactic Tia used to identify Teddy's illness. Tia had simply fast-forwarded in time through the child's medical files to come across a postmortem, which Ariel passed on to the Butterfields this morning in the form of a diagnosis. It must have been accurate. By lunchtime, the team was excited to see Teddy's obit vanish from the *Times* archives, indicating the boy's life had indeed been saved. And no threat to the election timeline, given his death would have occurred afterward, regardless.

Ariel used the same approach for Thornton. Rather than focusing on events leading up to the election four years ago, she jumped forward in time several months, and hit pay dirt.

Excited, she rushed from her room to share her discovery with the others.

She found them gathered around the coffee table, and Max was *not* happy. He glared up at her from the couch, rotating his laptop so she could see the screen. It showed a news clip of a cop standing on the stoop of Butterfield's building, surrounded by fellow cops, a bevy of reporters, and a teeming crowd.

"So much for trusting Butterfield's sister!" Max snapped. "She blabbed about you, now the world knows of Angel Ariel. You better rain hell on that girl next session!"

Ariel sighed, "On a happier note, I found our answer to bring Reverend Thornton around."

. . .

2:00 PM, and like clockwork, the vortex materialized. Ariel sat at her laptop in angel mode, videochat up and running, her friends at their stations. They were as enthused as she about her solution. While they still had critical details to work out, everyone felt confident enough to present Butterfield with initial marching orders.

But first, Ariel had an issue to address.

Once more Scott and Ivy appeared on screen, and by the looks of him, this next step was coming none too soon. He sat slouched with arms crossed. Ivy, nevertheless, appeared upbeat.

They exchanged "hello's" and Ariel began, "I'm afraid we have a problem." She trained her eyes on the sister. "I'm disappointed in you, Ivy. And the Lord is *very* upset."

The girl's face fell. *"Wh-what? What'd I do?"*

Ariel exhaled. "You betrayed our confidence. You spoke of me to Teddy's uncle."

Ivy looked bewildered, then horrified. *"Oh my God, I did! I'm realllly sorry. I was so excited for him, it just slipped out. It'll never happen again, trust me, I swear!"*

The girl looked sincerely contrite and embarrassed, and Ariel told her, "The Lord will forgive you this once. But you must never let Him down again."

"I won't, I promise. You can count on me." She crossed her heart.

Ariel heard Max grunt and swear under his breath, and Ariel turned to Ivy's brother. "Now, Scott, if you're ready for your final Mission, the Lord is ready, too."

That seemed to perk his interest, and Ariel continued, "First, you must arrange a meeting with someone. Do you know of the religious leader, Reverend Penbrook Thornton?"

"Yes," Scott replied, looking puzzled.

"The Lord wants you to deliver a personal prophecy to him. A forewarning. Someone he is close to has a serious illness."

"Who?" he asked.

"The Reverend's secretary, Alice Willoughby. Breast cancer."

Ariel caught Max wagging his head. He'd cautioned against divulging too much, too soon. She hastened to amend, "But you're to say nothing to him about it yet. This prophecy must be presented in person."

The Butterfields traded confused looks, and Ivy asked, *"Is it curable?"*

Ariel didn't know, the poor woman died the following spring. "Hopefully. But time is of the essence, the disease is aggressive."

"So how do I get ahold of Thornton?" Scott asked. *"Do you have a number for me?"*

The team had discussed the issue of how Butterfield, a virtual unknown, might get through to a celebrity of Thornton's stature. Odds of Thornton accepting a direct call or text were vanishingly slim. Butterfield would need a go-between.

"Contact the news network you've been working with," she said. "Have them arrange a meeting right away in the City of God."

Assuming Thornton kept the tape in the City, the team wanted Butterfield in striking range. Of course, placing the two men in public together could imply that the Prophet favored the Dark Agers, and Filby. But as Max pointed out, circumstances left them little choice. And they could always correct the record later, if necessary, by having Butterfield publicly renounce Filby.

"Set up the meeting," Ariel said. "But do nothing further till we talk tomorrow."

CHAPTER 73

Penbrook Thornton and his associate, Tobias Melcher, sat in the back of a cab, somber. They were headed to a meeting with fellow Council members of the CCC, the Coalition of Christian Conservatives. The two had spent the night at an airport hotel under pseudonyms, taking their meals in their rooms in advance of their unlawful gathering. Instead of their customary clergy attire, they wore dark suits.

It was impossible to anticipate what would come of today's summit. Twelve powerful, prideful, anxious men, convening under such pressure. Should the looming election go badly, Thornton and colleagues stood to lose everything. Yet, with two weeks to go, there was no cause for panic or rash decisions. Thornton had to settle the Council down, make them see reason.

Melcher was a thin-faced man with pale eyes and a shock of wild, white hair. He was Thornton's staunchest supporter on the Council, and offered his encouragement. "I've got to hand it to you, Brooks," he said, "your plan for the swing states is brilliant. Shackleton won't know what hit her."

He was being kind. With tens of thousands of Christian volunteers preparing for battle, Ellen Shackleton was surely aware. And God-forbid their plan should fail. A *President* Shackleton would no doubt bring the full force of the IRS down on Thornton and the CCC.

Thornton sighed, and Melcher changed the subject.

"So what do you make of this 'Prophet' fellow all over the news?"

A fascinating subject, indeed. Thornton replied, "Two millennia since John of Patmos and the Book of Revelation. I'd say we're long due another prophet."

"All the same," Melcher said, "St. Paul tells us, 1 Corinthians 13:8: *'But where there are prophecies, they will cease; where there are tongues, they will be stilled.'*"

Thornton smiled. "Perhaps Paul can explain how the Prophet predicted the storm I flew through, and the exact time and place the tornado would hit, hours before. Now I see he diagnosed a dying boy when doctors couldn't. How do you explain either without God?"

Melcher seemed transfixed. "Wouldn't *that* be wonderful? After all these centuries, *divine intervention again.*"

The thought lifted Thornton's spirits.

Their cab continued through Manhattan, arriving at the corner of Madison and East 50th in front of a magnificent, 19th Century, neo-Gothic stone mansion. Fifteen-thousand square feet, Thornton had heard. Behind it loomed a far-larger structure, St. Patrick's Cathedral.

The Cathedral was known as "America's St. Peters;" the mansion as "the Powerhouse." Especially to the elite who dropped by in homage to its resident, "America's pope," Cardinal Bartholomew Rand, Archbishop of New York. Neither Thornton nor Melcher had ever set foot in the mansion. Rand hadn't extended invitations to Council members before, fearing the media would detect the collaboration. But now, with so much on the line, it seemed he was willing to risk it as a show of pomp and power to influence members.

Thornton and Melcher donned hats, pulled the brims low, grabbed briefcases, and exited onto the busy sidewalk, weaving toward the mansion. Ascending a short flight of steps, they reached a recessed stone archway and double doors of wrought iron and leaded glass. Melcher rang the bell, a squinty eye took their measure, the door opened, and an elderly priest in black cassock gestured them inside. They exchanged greetings, and the priest escorted them through a foyer into a spacious hall with tall windows, a grand staircase, and walls draped with oil paintings.

"Have a seat," the priest told them, showing them chairs, taking their hats and coats. "Please turn off all electronic devices. His Eminence will receive you soon. Would you care for coffee?"

They declined, switched off their phones, and he left.

Melcher wondered, "Are we first here?"

Though only a few minutes early, they were alone in the room. Thornton tried to take his mind off matters, noting the paintings in the gallery. A larger-than-life portrait of Archbishop Rand in slimmer days. Paintings of other Catholic dignitaries stretching back to the founding of the diocese, two centuries ago. Photos of Rand conferring with popes, presidents, and other heads of state.

Voices drifted in, and Thornton saw the priest return with Council member Phineas Gage, President of the Church of the Latter-Day Saints. They exchanged greetings, and Gage took a chair, turned off his phone, and the priest left again.

Gage was a serious chap. Stiff, staid. Wispy gray hair. Mormons were the outliers of the CCC, regarded by most of the Council as more cult than Christian. But no denying the Church's power and wealth. Its membership had been added to the CCC begrudgingly, last of the Twelve. And fortunate for Thornton, as Gage tended to support him. Assuming the man's support held today, it left Thornton just two votes shy of the five he would need to block a revolt.

They made small talk, and at length the priest reentered to say, "His Excellency will see you now. This way, please."

He led them up the staircase to the third floor, down a hall to an anteroom ending in large, carved mahogany doors. The priest rapped softly and opened onto a conference room. The balance of the Council was gathered on the opposite side.

An impressive space. Walls paneled in mahogany and bearing a Constantine cross and portraits of saints. In the middle was a mahogany conference table beneath a crystal chandelier. On the far end were Cathedral windows. And in a corner, a large video screen and media center.

Thornton placed his briefcase at the head of the table next to a gavel and bible, his accustomed place as Chairman of these gatherings. In a corner sipping wine with other Council members was Archbishop Rand. An imposing figure in black cassock, crimson sash and cummerbund. He turned to greet Thornton, raising his glass along with his associates, and Thornton nodded back. Rand disengaged and went to a refreshment bar, scooped up a decanter and glasses in a big hand, and approached.

"Brooks, Toby, Phineas," he said warmly, pumping their arms one-by-one. Powerful grip. He poured for Melcher, Thornton and himself, Gage didn't imbibe. Clinking glasses, he toasted them all, smiling, cheeks ruddy and dimpled.

Thornton saw past the smile and wire spectacles to blue eyes hard as the mansion's stone. Rand had been working fellow Council members for weeks, lining up votes, Thornton was well aware. No doubt the man had brought in the other Council members today ahead of Thornton to firm up softening spines. Thornton wondered if Rand had left him any allies beyond Melcher and Gage. He couldn't count on his fellow Evangelicals. What should have been his strongest bloc had been undermined by his old nemesis, Henry Durban, who stood aloof across the room.

The Baptist representative, whose Church had no president or hierarchy, as such, was the most guarded member on the Council, and not weathering the pressures well. Chewing his nails, eyes flitting.

Thornton saw little hope for support there. He also questioned the Presbyterian and Episcopalian, who tended to side with Rand. That left only the Methodist and Lutheran. Good, open-minded men, but not risk-takers, and what Thornton had to ask today was a great leap of faith. All he could do was speak from the heart and pray he reached two others.

Rand struck his glass with his Cardinal's ring, bringing the room to attention, and everyone gravitated to the table. But as Thornton moved toward his chair, Rand slipped in ahead, moving Thornton's briefcase aside. It was Rand's house, after all. And now, it seemed, his show.

Thornton quietly accepted another seat. Once they settled in, Rand bowed his head with the others to intone, "Oh heavenly Father, we thank you for the faith that gathers Your humble servants here today, and we ask Your blessings on our proceedings to Your honor and glory."

"*Amen.*"

Raising up, he struck the gavel to ask, "And now if no one objects, I suggest we forego the minutes and reports. We've more pressing matters, yes?"

No one objected, and he added, "God willing, we'll get through this quickly, and you'll be back in your hotel rooms in time for dinner and the debate."

The second presidential debate was tonight—another knot in Thornton's gut.

Rand turned to Melcher. "Speaking of the debate, Toby, I understand you and Brooks dropped by the rehearsal yesterday. Can you apprise us how Filby's doing?"

Thornton had intended to put his own spin on developments, but once again, Rand outmaneuvered him. All eyes went to Melcher, who cleared his throat to reply, "I, I must say, I feel Roger's giving an admirable effort." He looked to Thornton as if seeking approval. "I believe he'll do better tonight. In fact, I'm confident he will."

Any attempt to un-damn the faint praise would have fallen flat. Thornton let it go, and Rand said dryly, "We're looking forward to an improved performance." He turned to Thornton, an edge creeping into his voice. "Now, to the matters at hand. Brooks, will you please confirm you brought the video, as promised."

The room grew still as Thornton opened his case. Atop books and papers sat an old, black-plastic VHS cassette, unlabeled. Everyone gawked as if it were a live snake.

Rand gestured to the audio/visual center behind him. "We've the equipment to play it, if anyone wishes. I, for one, prefer not to burn that incident into my skull."

They all knew the gist, and Thornton sighed, "I can assure you, it *is* indelible."

There was no appetite, and Rand pushed on. "As everyone will recall, when Brooks came in possession of the tape and brought it to our attention, he committed to us that in the event of a close race, he'd release it. Well the polls couldn't be tighter. The time has come."

Thornton regarded the uneasy expressions around him. Though he'd prepared his response long ago, a succinct one, he'd no sense how the Council would receive it. He began, "I welcome the opportunity to discuss this issue face-to-face. As you're all aware, I've had to make many a difficult decision over the years in the pursuit of our goals. But I will tell you, none harder."

The tape gleamed under the chandelier.

"I ask you to consider that the video is decades old. Ellen Shackleton was in college at the time. A foolish girl caught in a sordid stunt." His eyes turned inward. "Who among us hasn't made mistakes in our youth? Decisions we regret, choices that shame us to this day? Who among us is sinless that he'll cast the first stone?"

Looking around the table, he was encouraged that no one would meet his eyes. Until he arrived at Rand, who leveled a defiant glare. Thornton was surprised. If his line of reasoning resonated with anyone here, it should have been Rand. Years ago, as a bishop, Rand had endured allegations of a cover-up in the pedophilia scandal, avoiding prosecution only through legal maneuvers. No one knew better the tar of public humiliation, yet his gaze never wavered.

Thornton finished, "After much soul-searching, I've no choice. I believe that to destroy another soul for a mistake harmful to no one but herself would be a grave moral injustice." The room hummed like a tightening guitar string. "It puts me in great conflict. Never before have I felt my duties on the Council required me to offend God."

He sat back, and the Baptist leaned forward to blurt, "What of the position you've put *us* in, Brooks? The laws you've had us break to sit where we do today?"

"Man's laws, yes. *Never God's.*"

An Evangelical countered, "Due respect to God, it's *Man's* laws we must worry about. If Shackleton wins and we're exposed, she'll set the IRS on us with a vengeance. Bankrupt our Churches, crush us."

Another added, "And the Democrats will investigate every election we've ever influenced. Every politician, every judge. *We'll all face federal charges.*"

The air was heating, but then the Lutheran cleared his throat to ask calmly, "What would you have us do, Brooks?"

Thornton took a long breath. "Do any of us truly believe God led us to the promised land only to abandon us at the gate? The decades we've spent working and sacrificing on His behalf can't be for nothing." He pointed to his briefcase. "That tape is a test of faith. I say, put our faith in God and let the cup pass."

Rand went scarlet. *"Have you lost your mind?* In twelve days, *everything* we stand for will be at risk." He appealed to the table. "Gentlemen, there are few absolutes in life, but we've been gifted one here today." He aimed a thick finger at the briefcase. "That tape is a godsend. Release it, and Filby wins in a landslide. Why in God's name would we gamble against a sure bet?"

He reached for a bible in front of him and laid his hand on it. "As God is my witness, if we squander this blessing, *it will be our ruin.*"

Stunned silence but for muffled traffic outside.

At length, the Lutheran sighed and shook his head. "Believe me, Brooks, none of us feel good about this. If there were any other way."

Thornton's eyes drifted to a stained-glass window. A famous scene of the Old Testament. Abraham, raising a knife to sacrifice his only son in obedience to God, hand stayed by an angel. The supreme test of faith. Thornton had one last hope.

"I'd like to make a proposal," he said. He waited till all eyes were on him. "As we anticipated, the polls are tight, and the race hinges on three states. The weekend before the election, we embark on a political crusade in those states the likes of which the country has never seen. If God blesses our efforts, as I believe with all my heart He will, the polls will shift decisively to Filby—in time to decide about the tape. *A test of faith,* gentlemen."

After a pause, someone asked, "What constitutes a decisive shift in the polls?"

Thornton replied, "In all three states, Filby and Shackleton are in a dead heat. If we bump Filby four or five points, we're safely above the margin of error."

Durban countered, "Currently, undecideds make up twelve percent of voters in the swing states. Even if Filby gains five, that still leaves seven for Shackleton."

Rand leaned forward. "Make it *ten.* Ten percent. If your Crusade can raise Filby's numbers in the swing states to fifty-four, you'll earn my faith."

Heads began to bob, and Thornton felt his jaw tighten. In this hotly contested election, Rand's terms were ridiculous, and Rand knew it. Nowhere was Filby leading by ten points, not even in his home state of Oklahoma.

Thornton replied, "Ten points is impossible."

"Where is your faith now?" Rand asked. Seizing the moment, he called for a vote. Durban seconded in his tinny voice, and the "ayes" prevailed, nine to three.

Durban added a final nail. "The last debate is Saturday before the election. I say we make our decision *after* the overnight polls. Either Filby's up ten points in all three states by Sunday morning, or Brooks releases the tape."

Thornton clenched. The last debate was a townhall. *Not* Filby's strong suit.

The Baptist said, "But that leaves us just two days till the election. Too close."

"Actually," Rand said, "It's perfect. Release the tape Sunday at noon, it makes all the evening newscasts and *60 Minutes*. It will dominate Monday's headlines and talk shows, and Shackleton will have no time to recover."

There was overwhelming agreement, and Rand slid his bible down the table to Thornton.

"Your oath," he demanded, knowing Thornton would never break a pledge sworn on the Good Book. "If Filby fails to meet our numbers by Sunday a week, you release the tape."

Putting his trust in God, Thornton placed his hand on the book and swore.

• • •

Thornton and Melcher were quiet in the cab as they headed back to their hotel. Finally Melcher said, "Fifty-four percent. Might as well be the moon. The only thing that can get us those numbers is the Shackleton tape."

Thornton quoted Matthew 19:26: "*With men many things are impossible, but with God, all things are possible.*' Have faith, my friend, God is with us."

"Just for once," Melcher said, "I wish God would give us a sign."

Thornton switched on his phone, surprised to see it light up with alerts. Multiple texts from Ms. Willoughby. It wasn't like her to pester, and Thornton read with concern:

Reverend, Kyle Heath is desperate to reach you. He says
he has very important news he'll share only with you. I
informed him you're in New York, and included his text
and phone below.
Alice

Puzzled, Thornton scrolled down to read:

rev thornton—urgent message from prophet of queens,
2 deliver in person 2nite. can u be at hawk news
studios by 5:45?

Thornton's heart skipped. Alerting Melcher and the driver, he
texted back to Kyle Heath:

Yes!

CHAPTER 74

L eaving their apartment building, Ivy and Scotty stepped out the
door into a frightening scene. The crowd, still pumped from the
"Teddy miracle," erupted at the sight of their Prophet. It took a full
detail of NYPD to convey the two into the waiting limo as people
strained to get a glimpse or touch. Ivy knew Scotty hated the ruckus,
but she also knew he was as gratified as she to have helped the little
boy. And now, as they headed for Hawk News studios, she trusted
they'd soon be helping someone else.

Ivy checked her makeup in the mirror of the minibar, grinning.
What would the kids at school think now? Despite an avalanche of
calls and texts from friends begging her for details, she'd managed
to keep her vow to Ariel, revealing little of what was going on. But
she wasn't sure how much longer she could hold her tongue. This
was just too exciting!

Scotty's phone rang, and he took the call mouthing to Ivy, *"Kyle Heath."*

For once Scotty looked presentable, thanks to Ivy. Hair washed
and combed, though he wouldn't let her cut it, and refused to shave.
He wore his floppy black hoody again, and Heath had insisted he
bring his shepherd's staff.

Earlier, after Scotty spoke to Heath about meeting Thornton in the City of God, Heath had contacted Thornton's Church to learn the reverend was in New York. He'd called Scotty back to suggest they meet at Hawk instead, and given Scotty's desire to be done with the Lord's work, and considering the gravity of the message he carried for Thornton, he'd agreed. And Heath, trusting Thornton would accept the urgent meeting, had sent a car for Scotty and Ivy, calling now to confirm that Thornton was indeed on board.

As Scotty hung up, Ivy reminded him, "You know, Ariel told us to set up a meeting only. We're not supposed to actually meet with Thornton till she gets back to us."

Scotty shrugged. "She also said the lady's illness is serious, and time is of the essence."

In which case, they couldn't have moved any faster. Their limo soon pulled to the curb in front of Hawk studios, and to Ivy's surprise, a crowd was on hand to greet them. Word of the Prophet's coming must have gotten out.

An attendant opened their door, and Scotty raised his hood and exited into a buffer of security guards. He left his shepherd's staff behind, but Ivy snatched it and followed.

At the sight of Scotty, the crowd cheered, and Ivy raised the staff, pumping it like a majorette, sparking applause and laughter. The guards were *not* amused, sweeping her and Scotty inside the building, through the lobby into an elevator, upstairs and down a hall to a green room where they were met by Kyle Heath and a woman in an apron.

"Hello," Heath welcomed them, shaking hands. "The reverend's on his way." He motioned Scotty to a table facing a large mirror rimmed with lights. "We're short on time, if you'll have a seat, we'll get you ready."

Scotty puzzled. "Get me ready?"

"You're on air with Reverend Thornton in fifteen minutes."

Scotty took a step back. *"On air?* But this is a *private* meeting."

Now Heath looked puzzled. "You never said anything about

'private.' You must know we've moved heaven and earth to make these arrangements."

On the wall, a TV monitor aired a promo promising, *Latest Prediction from the Prophet of Queens, Live at Six.*

Scotty frowned. "But this is a *personal* matter. Someone close to the reverend is very ill."

"Yes. I made that clear to him. Sorry for the confusion, but if there's going to be a meeting, it's got to be on air."

Of course, ratings trumped decorum.

Ivy leaned into Scotty. "Postpone, and meet Thornton in the City of God, like Ariel said."

A trip out of town sounded fun to her.

Scotty grumbled to Heath, "Let's get this over with. And *no* makeup."

• • •

The Reverends Thornton and Melcher exited the cab in front of Hawk studios, guards hustling them through a swell of onlookers.

A big screen TV on the marquee juxtaposed stock video of Thornton and the Prophet with a banner reading, *Life or Death Prophecy, Live at Six.* Thornton felt both worry and bewilderment. If indeed this Prophet were genuine, why the theatrics? Was God adapting to the media age?

He and Melcher were rushed inside, met in the lobby by Kyle Heath and a lady in an apron.

"Welcome," Heath greeted them looking relieved, giving their hands a quick shake. He directed them ahead. "Sorry to hurry you, we're on air in eight minutes."

He ushered them into an elevator, and the lady pancaked Thornton's face on the way up. Between powders, Thornton asked Heath, "Any more details?"

"I'm afraid the Prophet is rather tight-lipped."

Thornton had concerns about the broadcast, and not simply for its pending bad news. He did *not* wish to be party to some sideshow. While drawn to publicity, he was careful to manage it. Unlike the Pentecostals and Charismatics, Thornton spurned sensationalism, careful to maintain his dignity as a man of God.

Melcher asked Heath, "You've met the Prophet, is he truly on the up-and-up?"

Heath paid him a sober look. "I've been on this story from the start, and I have to admit, it defies all reason. But if Butterfield isn't the real deal, I don't know how to explain him."

They exited into a hall, a man in headphones urging them into a backstage holding area filled with TV monitors. Thornton knew the drill, a frequent guest on Hawk News. Another handler miked him, then Heath whisked him out a door into the bright lights of a sound-stage. Pointing to a news desk in the center, Heath wished him good luck, and held back with Melcher.

Thornton took his place across a triangle desk from the Hawk host and the uncomfortable-looking cause célèbre. As Thornton had antic-ipated, the boy was hardly the image of a biblical prophet. Downcast, slumped in a black, hooded sweatshirt, hood thrown back, longish dark hair neatly parted, but mussed. On the desk nearby rested a stout shepherd's crook.

The newsman welcomed Thornton and nodded to a crewman who gave a countdown. Then taking a breath, he spoke into a camera through a teleprompter.

"Welcome to a special edition of *Hawk News Live at Six*. Tonight, another Hawk exclusive. We're pleased to have back on our program two well-known guests who need no introduction."

He turned to his left. "Longtime friend of the show, Reverend Penbrook Thornton of the Church of the Divine Message." He ges-tured to his right, "And Mr. Scott Butterfield, better known to viewers as the Prophet of Queens, considered by many to be the world's fore-most oracle since Edgar Cayce. Mr. Butterfield has made quite a splash recently with his prophecies."

Butterfield interjected, "Not *my* prophecies, I'm simply a messenger."

The newsman corrected, "Uh, 'messages,' which Mr. Butterfield says he receives from an angel emissary of God. So far, the predictions have all proven accurate, and the Prophet has a new one for us tonight." He nodded to his guests. "Thanks for joining us on such short notice."

Thornton nodded. The young man simply sat with head bowed.

"Reverend Thornton," the host continued, "I understand this is the first time you and Mr. Butterfield have met."

"Correct," Thornton said, smiling to the Prophet. "An honor to meet you, sir."

Butterfield raised his head and paid a quick "Hello."

Thornton added, "I'm familiar with your pronouncements, Mr. Butterfield. In fact, I weathered one personally Monday night, flying through that storm you forecast. I confess, I'm concerned about the message you bring tonight."

The newsman turned to Butterfield, and the young man compressed his lips to respond, "I don't know why I was picked for this job, Reverend, I hate bearing bad news. What I have to say concerns someone you know, and I hope it's in time."

The studio fell quiet as a church. Thornton's hand went to the gold cross on his lapel, and Butterfield inhaled and stood. Thornton watched in puzzlement as the boy rounded the desk and approached. Thornton shifted to face him, taken aback. Butterfield came close, stopped, and leaned down to whisper, "I'm sorry to tell you, an associate of yours is very ill. Your secretary, Alice Willoughby. Cancer. Breast cancer. An aggressive form."

Thornton felt his heart seize. *"My God,"* he gasped.

The host demanded, "What? What?"

Thornton recovered to ask, "Will she—*will she be okay?"*

Butterfield raised up and replied soberly, "The angel didn't say."

"Are you *certain?"*

"I'm certain what the angel said. I'm sorry. I hope this message is in time."

Stunned, Thornton gaped at him. The host begged Butterfield to enlighten viewers, but the young man grabbed his staff, bid Thornton good luck, and strode off set.

There was an awkward pause, and the host managed, "Well, Hawk viewers, we're all hoping to learn what troubling news the Prophet delivered. Please stay tuned."

The station took a break, and Thornton drooped in his chair.

• • •

Scotty and Ivy were quiet as they left the station in the limo. By the time they arrived at Scotty's building, it was dark. No deterrent to the waiting throngs, however. Scotty despaired to see even greater numbers than before. Fortunately, the police detail was on hand.

He and Ivy dashed from the car into bedlam, cops running interference. People shouted to Scotty, pleading for miracles, and someone seized his sleeve. He turned to see a grubby face he recognized—the homeless man he'd encountered in the alley the first day of this ordeal.

Scotty reached for his wallet, but the man pulled him close to implore, "Prophet, save us! Winter's coming. We got no homes, no food, no hope!"

"I'm no prophet," Scotty insisted. "I have no powers."

Before the cops could peel the man off, he poked a grimy finger in the middle of Scotty's forehead to declare, *"Foresight is power."*

Scotty drew back confused, and the cops removed the man to expose Ivy behind, smiling and waving to the crowd. Scotty extended his crook to haul her in by the waist, whisking her ahead of him to the front steps, hustling her inside the building past a flood of mail.

Once safely upstairs in the apartment, he slammed the door and leaned against it, panting.

"Woohoo," Ivy cheered, heading for the bathroom. "We're like rock stars now!"

He glared after her. "We're damn-near mauled to death, and it's a game to you?"

"Chillax, bro, nothing will happen to us, we're doing God's Will."

In fact, Scotty felt like a tool. He replied, "God's Will is fleeting. Now that Thornton has his message, my Mission's over. It's back into the woodwork for me, but there's still hope for you—*if* we don't let this wreck our plans."

Ivy disappeared into the bath, and Scotty looked down to see Homer frowning at him. Swearing under his breath, he shed his hoody and staff to the coatrack, and headed to the kitchen. Homer followed his every move. Snatching a can of cat food from the pantry, Scotty promised, "No more late meals, Homey, Ariel said I'd get my life back."

The cat paid him a doubtful glance. *You're forgetting what the guru says. Step 39.*

Scotty remembered. *Those who live in the past have no future.*

He could take no more. Collapsing to a chair at the table, he let out a wail.

Ivy responded from the bath, "Have faith. The Lord owes you big time for all He's put you through. I bet He's got another Lotto number in His pocket. Regardless, you're big as Jesus now. Imagine the doors that'll open!"

There came a knock at theirs, and Scotty exhaled. Composing himself, he went to the peephole to see Kassandra in the hallway looking sultry in an off-the-shoulder knit top.

He opened, and her eyes went to the can of cat food in his hand.

She smiled and cooed, "I hope you haven't eaten yet."

CHAPTER 75

"Oh no," Ariel moaned.

She was in the living room with her friends, on her laptop checking current archives against those retrieved from her rabbit's foot last session. No problems, until now. The others looked up from their chairs, and she rotated her computer for them.

"An update from four years ago..."

They gathered around to see a Hawk News special. *Life or Death Prophecy*. As it played, Ariel watched her friend's faces go from curious to horrified. Max broke the silence, his eyes flashing at Ariel.

"*Goddammit,* Thornton was *in* New York when you spoke with Butterfield today. You spilled too much, we've lost our leverage."

She felt terrible.

"Lay off," Tia told him. "It was your brilliant idea to push for a meeting. Why didn't you check on Thornton's whereabouts, first?"

Stan hastened to say, "Now-now, all's not lost. Assuming they catch the secretary's cancer in time, Thornton may be willing to give up the tape out of gratitude."

That gave Max pause. After a moment's reflection, he decided,

"Better for us, then, if the prognosis is bad. Butterfield can promise Thornton a cure in exchange for the tape."

A cure they couldn't deliver. Ariel was appalled, and she saw the same in Tia.

Tia asked, "How long will a diagnosis take? The tape goes public in ten days."

Historically, the tape was released the Sunday before the election.

Ariel said, "With Thornton's connections, not long, I'm sure. He'll pull every string he's got."

"Meanwhile," Max said, "we're back to stalling Butterfield."

Ariel apologized again, Max stalked off, and she headed for her room, smarting.

Tia caught up with her at the door. "Got a second?"

"If it's about Max, I'm okay."

"No, a different asshole."

She drew Ariel inside and closed the door. "Did you check the files I sent on your stepdad?"

Ariel confessed, "I haven't had the nerve."

"Well I hate to tell you, but there's more. I dug deeper, and it's worse than I thought." Her eyes showed pain. "Let me ask—and don't answer if you don't want—did he ever take photos of you as a kid? You know, *compromising* photos?"

Ariel stiffened. *"Oh my God.* Not to my knowledge."

Phil had never approached her about such a thing, thankfully. Though now that she thought about it, she recalled uncomfortable occasions where he lurked with his phone. Had he sneaked shots of her in the shower?

She grabbed Tia's arm. *"Please* tell me you didn't find pictures."

"Not of you, so far. Other girls. Lots. I quit, I couldn't bear it."

Ariel felt sick.

Tia lowered her voice. "Did he ever...put his *hands* on you?"

The knot in Ariel's stomach rose to her throat. She felt such humiliation, she shook her head "No."

Tia gave her a long, fierce hug before pulling back, eyes watery. "You were lucky," she said. "First off, he's no doctor. No medical or psychiatric doctor, anyway. Theology degrees from a divinity school. No qualifications whatsoever to run a mental institution. All the same, Thornton brought him in to deal with the suicides and other problems. An epidemic back then, and from what I gather, it still is. Most kids he 'treated' he labeled 'sexually dysfunctional.' Meaning, they didn't meet Church standards for 'normal.'"

Ariel was aware. The Church put huge pressure on the community to conform to its values. Those falling short suffered ostracism. And apparently, worse.

Tia said, "It seems many 'sexually dysfunctional' teens were gay. And for Neuhoffer, that was a sin, a choice, and curable."

Ariel knew of gay-conversion therapy, if unaware of its practice at the Institute. Cruel, dangerous, and long-discredited by the American Psychiatric Association and other authorities.

"...He called his method *Sexual Identity Reorientation*. Pure bullshit. A mix of pseudo-psychology, behavior modification, bible study, and prayer. To him, homosexuality was rooted in childhood, the result of abuse by someone of the opposite sex. His remedy was to 'reorient' the afflicted to the pleasures of natural sex 'in the manner God intended.' He treated some girls personally—the pretty ones. And when I say *personally*...'

Ariel felt nauseous.

"A miserable failure," Tia said. "Kids sent to his clinic were already fragile, and he made them worse. Not a single cure. Self-mutilations and suicides spiked. And the more desperate the situation, the more extreme his methods."

"Was Reverend Thornton aware of what was going on?" Ariel couldn't imagine it.

"Hard to say. From what I gathered, Neuhoffer concealed his activities from all but handpicked staff. And not even they knew what he did in his private sessions."

Tia took Ariel's hand. "I'm sorry, but your stepfather is a sick son of a bitch. And we need to do something about it."

It would destroy Mom, yet the truth couldn't come as a complete shock. She *had* to know, somewhere deep down.

Ariel nodded. "What do we do?"

"There's enough in his files to put him away for life, but I need your help. I need you to add those files to your journal so they're transferred to the rabbit's foot for safekeeping. Once all this is over, we'll get them to the authorities."

"Not the photos he took! *Child pornography on my computer?*"

"No-no, I left those out. There *is* one video, an underage girl he abused, but I edited and pixilated it where necessary. That, along with his notes, is *plenty* to convict him."

Ariel shivered. More of a monster than she'd ever imagined. To think she'd lived in the same house, and her mother lived with him *still.* Ariel resolved to try contacting Mom once more, though she knew what the outcome would be.

She asked, "Did you happen to see a patient in his files named Nicole LeClair?"

Tia stared at her, blinking. *"Christ.* That's the girl in the video."

CHAPTER 76

Scotty stood outside Kassandra's door, rolling a bottle of rosé in sweaty palms. Ivy was against him doing this. She didn't like Kassandra.

"You think she'd give a flip about you if it weren't for your fame?" she'd clamored at him.

No, but wasn't that a perk of fame? As the guru said,

Step #43: Embrace the rewards you've earned.

It wasn't like the Lord's tasks had been a cakewalk. And now that Scotty's strange ordeal was ending, he drew some satisfaction from the good he'd accomplished—along with a spot more self-confidence. So his flash in the pan had netted him a date. At least he'd come away from all this with *something*. Once he reported back to Ariel tomorrow, his Mission would be over, and his celebrity would fade. And unlike Ivy, he'd no faith a golden parachute awaited.

When he'd left for his date, Ivy had gone to Mrs. Steiner's for dinner and the debate, bearing Scotty's regrets. Scotty knew Mrs. Steiner would forgive him, she was in his corner on this.

Smoothing back his hair, he inhaled and knocked.

The light in the peephole darkened, and the door opened. On a vision. Kassandra looked stunning. Her bobbed hair was now flipped, chic, her big brown eyes magnified by mascara and eyeliner, brows penciled into perfect arches. Lips crimson to match her blouse, which opened three full buttons to hint at flawless breasts. The prettiest woman he'd ever met—angels aside.

"I love a man who's punctual," she said, smiling, showing him in.

An aroma of oregano filled his head. He loved Italian.

The apartment was laid out the inverse of his. Living room smaller, no window, starkly furnished, architectural salvage stuff. A few minimalist paintings. Cool. A treadmill with one of those attachments for a laptop so you could work while you jogged. How did people do that?

He handed her the wine, something he'd dug out of his cupboard from who-knew-when.

"How sweet," she said, squinting at the label. Thanking him, she set it aside and directed him to a white, faux-leather sectional. It faced a flat-screen TV, switched off. In between stood a glass coffee table with two place settings side by side, a decanter of red wine, and two glasses.

"A drink?" she asked as he took a seat.

"Sure."

She leaned into him to pour from the decanter, and Scotty inhaled the scent of lavender.

"To good neighbors," she said, raising her glass.

Concealing his mouth, he grinned, clinked, and sipped.

Dry. He didn't especially like wine.

• • •

"Care for another tart?" Kassandra asked. Her cheeks were weary from smiling.

"Oh yes, please," Scott said.

His *third.* The man had no regard for nutrition. Rising, she took their plates to the sink and dumped her desert in the garbage along with her pre-conceived notions about this guy. All that clamor on TV today? Those fanatics raving about his wise, prophetic abilities? *Hype.* As she'd learned over dinner, Scott Butterfield was neither sage nor seer. After only one glass of wine, he'd admitted he was simply a messenger boy. Two glasses, he divulged the surprising source of his revelations, an "angel of the Lord." He'd said it with straight face, and swearing Kassandra to secrecy, added, "We meet on the Internet."

She'd nearly choked on her garlic roll.

Returning with another pastry, she asked, "So what's this angel look like?"

His eyes turned inward, dreamy. "You can't imagine how beautiful, Kassandra. The most perfect being imaginable. A goddess. Otherworldly."

It didn't take a PR degree to see what was going on. The fool had fallen victim to a scam. After which, the media stumbled across him and his carnie show, and whipped the public into a frenzy over a few coincidences. News stations had no scruples about pushing bullshit these days, not with 24/7 airtime to fill.

What *did* surprise Kassandra was that Butterfield hadn't figured it out by now. The guy wasn't stupid. Nerdy, shy, trusting, yes. But well-informed, well-spoken. And yet, from all she could gather peppering him with questions, he was as duped as the zealots who followed him. The stooge of some online charlatan.

Which put a kink in her plan tonight. Had he proved the con artist she'd thought, the evening would have been cut and dried. A simple business transaction. She'd have bribed him to go back on TV and make another pronouncement: the Lord's pick in the election, Ellen Shackleton.

Money would have been no object. The DNC would cough up whatever it took. What price an endorsement from God? Swing states be damned, Christians *everywhere* would drop Filby like a graven image and switch sides, turning a tight race into a debacle. Shackleton would sweep into office with a mandate, Butterfield would go quietly away a wealthy man, and Kassandra's coup would establish her as a PR wunderkind, ensuring her career at EP&M.

Win-win-win.

But of all the luck, this nebbish with confectioner's sugar in his beard had turned out the type of man Kassandra had no experience with. *Honest.* Offering him a bribe might well offend him and blow her chances. Her best hope now seemed to hinge on how much control Butterfield's online master had over him, and if Kassandra could somehow pry away his allegiance.

She had one advantage, at least. The guy had a crush on her. He'd been eating out of her hand all night, *Stouffer's* not-withstanding. It seemed he had no girlfriend. That elf in his apartment was his sister. In fact, when Kassandra stopped by earlier to invite him to dinner, the girl was in an *Honest Ellen* T-shirt. With luck, Butterfield was a supporter, too.

The night was growing long, and if the wine, food, and flirtations had done their job, the man was sufficiently softened. She took her seat next to him, closer, touching, handing him his éclair.

"So, Scott," she said sweetly, "who do you like in the election?"

She held her breath, watching him shrug.

"Neither."

Could have been worse. "You favor one party over the other?"

"I don't see the point, they're both owned by lobbyists."

Kassandra couldn't help herself. "Shackleton supports the working class, you know. Education, healthcare, job growth."

"Till elected. Then government goes back to gridlock. Nothing ever changes."

The guy wasn't so much naïve as cynical. Figuring she'd little to lose, she laid it out there.

"I don't know if I told you," she said, "but I work at EP&M."

He frowned, and she clarified, "Biggest PR firm in the world. Ellen Shackleton's a client. It's been an amazing experience. I've gotten to observe her up close. See her when the cameras *aren't* on, see how she treats us 'little people.' I have to tell you, she's not who you think. She's warm, caring, and kind. Someone you'd admire and respect—if ever you met her."

Scooting closer, she placed a hand on his knee, feeling him stiffen.

"Can I ask a favor?" she said, paying him a coy look. He blinked. "Would you consider having coffee with her? Just the two of you, one-on-one. Get to know her, see what she's like?"

If she could just get them together, shaking hands, tête-à-tête-ing, Lady JFK would work her famous charm. A killer photo op. An implied endorsement. Kassandra's heart pounded. Whatever it took, she *had* to get him to agree.

He appeared vulnerable, and she pressed, "I'd be *so* grateful." She squeezed his leg again.

CHAPTER 77

Reverend Thornton landed at the City of God airport shortly before midnight. He remained in his seat well after the plane taxied to the tarmac and parked, eyes closed. He felt the pilot tap him on the shoulder, and Thornton gathered himself to deplane.

His driver stowed his bags in the car and asked, "Home, sir?"

"I know it's late, Mark, but could we stop by the chapel?"

"Of course."

In the wake of this grueling day, Thornton needed a shot of faith. His debacle with the Council; the Prophet's dire diagnosis; the debate—Filby's performance was no better than before. Nevertheless, the reverend's concern at the moment wasn't politics. The thought of losing Alice had rattled him to the soul. Immediately after his appearance with the Prophet, he'd rushed to call her, hoping to reach her before the news. But Hawk had been promoting the event, and apparently the entire City had watched. Unfortunately, during the broadcast, Thornton's lapel mike had picked up the Prophet's whispered words, and the station was quick to make hay of it.

When finally Thornton had gotten through to Alice, he'd found her calm and composed as ever. *"To think God would bless me with a warning,"* she'd told him.

Thornton feared it was no blessing, but kept that to himself. In his heart, he believed her illness was the last installment on an old debt, the reason God had singled him out for the Prophet's message. A final toll for the grievous sin he'd committed long ago. And now, despite his steadfast efforts at atonement, God was foreclosing on the love of his life.

But Thornton was a master at concealing his emotions. He'd assured Alice on the phone that all would be fine, and jumped off to call the hospital that bore his name, arranging to have her seen by the head oncologist first thing tomorrow, promised answers sometime that afternoon.

His car rolled to a stop at the summit of Chapel Hill, and he exited telling Mark, "A half-hour should do." He departed down the path into the trees, paused tearfully over his family's graves, and went inside the church. This time he made certain he was alone, taking a back pew.

"Oh merciful God," he cried, burying his face in his hands, "I beg You. I've worked loyally in Your service all these years, and I pray once more for Your absolution. Please, *spare her life."*

He broke down, and his mind flew back decades to the accursed sin that brought him to this moment of reckoning...

Alice Willoughby had come to Thornton's attention during the period his ministry was undergoing its first growth spurt. He needed administrative assistance, and she'd applied fresh out of college, daughter of a respected elder. A wonderful addition. Bright, enthusiastic. Thornton had come to rely on her, and she assumed the duties of his personal secretary.

At the time, Thornton had been married to Doris for eight years. A solid marriage. Doris was a good woman. Intelligent, devoted, devout.

A bit formal and plain, perhaps. Quiet, shy. But honorable and a loving mother. She'd raised Paul and Sarah to the highest standards. A God-fearing family the community looked up to.

Thornton had no excuse to stray, and no notion to do so. All the same, he couldn't help but notice Alice's admirable qualities. She was quite pretty. Wavy brown hair, large green eyes. And working together, often late, they grew close. Unlike Doris, who shunned complex topics, Alice was someone Thornton could share his thoughts with. He ran sermons past her, bounced ideas off her. She was insightful, she inspired him, challenged him, elevated his game.

He grew increasingly fond of her, yet remained blind to—or perhaps in denial of—his incubating affections. But slowly, he came to realize he'd never known *true* love before. What bound him to Doris was respect, common values, his children. And his sacred wedding vows.

Then one beautiful autumn evening not unlike tonight, Thornton was in his office past hours, working on a script for an important televangelical broadcast. Alice was out at her desk assisting with edits, and Thornton hit an impasse. Needing a break, he lay on his couch for a moment to clear his head. Next he knew, he opened his eyes to someone hovering over him, lights soft. Alice, covering him with a blanket. He looked up into her sweet face, their eyes met, and mindlessly, helplessly, they melded into each other.

Immediately after, they felt frightened and an enormous guilt. They prayed together, begged God's forgiveness, vowed to avoid a recurrence. Even so, they were weak. The late-night liaisons continued, and it seemed their only recourse was for Alice to resign. Yet neither was willing to throw away their successful collaboration. The situation dragged into winter, and finally came an evening that would never end. That dreadful night God's patience wore out.

Once again, Thornton was in Alice's arms on his couch after hours, lights dim. Abruptly the door opened, the lights flashed on, and Thornton turned to see Doris, Paul, and Sarah gaping in horror.

Doris held her fist to her heart, uttering the most anguished sound Thornton ever heard. She grabbed the children's hands and fled, footsteps and sobs echoing down the hallway.

Thornton threw on his clothes and rushed after, out to the parking lot. But they were already in their car, speeding off. It was sleeting, and he raced to his car to give chase, pleading with God to forgive him, to somehow heal this ghastly wound. But as he drew close to her car, she sped up, and fearing to push her on the slick roads, he backed off. Soon he lost sight of her.

He knew before he saw. Deep in his soul, he knew. As he rounded a curve, there on the side of the road lay shapeless metal wrapped smoldering around a tree.

After the funeral, Thornton went into seclusion, too mortified to admit his sin, insisting Alice take over his administrative duties. A full year later he emerged at last, heart still crushed, determined to earn the Lord's forgiveness. And re-consecrating himself, Thornton hefted his burden and resumed his duties, thereafter living in self-imposed chastisement, a hardworking, righteous and celibate man to this day. Yet his love for Alice Willoughby never waned.

CHAPTER 78

K assandra was shaking. For the third time, she approached the door to the conference room, seeing through its glass to the bigwigs inside. Gathered at the table were EP&M's top officers, including Franklin Percy, a dozen DNC heavies, another dozen Shackleton campaign directors, and Shackleton's chairperson. Kassandra could hear them still arguing.

Franklin Percy was saying, "...split-screen comparison TV spots—clips of Shakleton's best moments in the debate contrasted with Filby's fumbling."

A DNC official countered, "Yes, she bitch-slaps him in the debates. But it's not resonating. The swing-state polls barely budged. We need separation. We need to peel off some of those damned bible-thumpers."

The Shackleton chairman piled on. "He's right, Frank. Where's your answer to the Crusade? Now I see Thornton's chummy with that prophet the country's nuts over." He tossed his pen on the table. "We don't need new TV spots for godssakes, we need an endorsement from the pope!"

Seeing the entrée she was looking for, Kassandra opened the door and barged in, moving fast to conceal her trembling. The meeting came to a standstill, and Shonda Gonzalez sputtered, *"Excuse me. This is a closed meeting."*

Kassandra headed to the front of the room, taken off stride to see Bobby Driscoll seated behind an EP&M principle. She faced the table as everyone stared, and in the most confident tone she could muster, declared, "You want Christian support? I can get it for you." She looked the campaign director in the eye. "What would you say to a meeting between Shackleton and the Prophet of Queens?"

The man looked surprised, and Shonda cried, "We've no time for this! We've tried reaching the Prophet. No one gets through, he's property of Hawk News, and they're sure as hell not letting him out to meet a Democrat. Please leave. *Now.*"

Kassandra held her ground. "His name's Scott Butterfield, and we're friends. We had dinner together last night."

She whipped out her phone to display a selfie of herself and Butterfield toasting.

Bobby Driscoll's spa-tanned face went white. Murmurs filled the room, and the campaign chairman raised a hand for silence. He asked Kassandra, "What's your name, young lady?"

Shonda responded, "She's one of our interns, Kassandra Kraft. And she's cleared *none* of this with me."

The chairman said, "Well, I'm glad to see someone around here has initiative." He looked hard at Kassandra. "You honestly believe you can get Ellen a meeting?"

Kassandra wasn't sure. Butterfield had waffled last night when she'd asked. But she'd made it very clear that he'd be *very* happy if he did. He'd almost melted.

"Yes," she snapped. "I'm *certain.*"

"Have a seat."

There wasn't one, and the chairman pointed to Shonda, saying, "Yours will do."

Flushing, Shonda snatched her things and retreated to a corner, and Kassandra took her place.

CHAPTER 79

Ariel and her team's hope to pry the Shackleton tape away from Thornton had taken a big hit.

Last night, watching a four-year-old Hawk News special, they were stunned to see Butterfield give away their bargaining chip. The Prophet had informed Thornton of Alice Willoughby's illness.

The team had been forced to stall Butterfield again, scrambling to handle today's morning session with an epistle, ordering the Prophet to sit tight till further notice. Meanwhile, Tia had detected a change in the City of God Hospital records. Four years ago this morning, Alice Willoughby was admitted for medical tests. Which helped assuage Max's anger.

"If the tests come back positive," he'd decided, calmer, "we get our leverage back."

Ariel didn't appreciate the macabre silver lining. In her room now, she was preparing for the next run, changed into angel mode once more, sitting on her bed staring at her laptop.

Her stepfather's secret files stared back.

Ariel had done as Tia asked. She'd copied Phil's files to the rabbit's foot, the damning evidence now safely stored on the other side of the wormhole, hanging from a limb of the houseplant.

But Ariel still couldn't summon the courage to read the files.

Lying back, she stared out the window, thoughts drifting to a dark place...

She was fourteen the last time Phil laid hands on her. Autumn of her sophomore year in high school. She recalled with a clarity born of trauma. Classes let out at 3:00, and as usual, she'd walked home to an empty house. Mom typically arrived from Church by 4:30, Phil a few hours later, and Ariel went to her room to start her homework. She'd hardly begun when she heard the front door slam—Phil's signature response to a bad day at work.

A chill shot through her. A *very* bad day for him to leave this early.

He called out, "Who's here?"

Ariel went stone still.

Phil cried louder, "I said, *who's here? ARIEL?*"

She cowered in her chair, unable to speak. There came heavy footsteps on the stairs, bursts of Phil swearing, and Ariel trembled beyond control. The swears reached her door, and it burst open to reveal Phil, red-faced and glaring. He bellowed, "When I speak to you, by God, *you answer.*"

Ariel couldn't, frozen with panic, and he made for her. *"I'll teach you respect,"* he snarled.

She recoiled, helpless as he hauled her into his arms and to the bed. Sitting with his legs spread, he threw her facedown over one knee, slung his other leg over the back of hers to curb her kicks, and forced an elbow in her spine to pin her. Pulling up her skirt, he yanked down her drawers, and she felt faint, tensing for the sting of his palm.

It didn't come. Nothing but hot breath on her bare skin...

An eternity, Ariel's heart pounded ever faster, Phil's breaths grew shorter. Then a voice at the doorway cried, "Phil? *Phil? Oh my God.*"

He released Ariel, and she jumped up into Mom's arms, wailing.

Later, Ariel learned there had been multiple suicides at the Institute that day. Three young women in some sort of pact, details never disclosed. Phil had left work distraught, his secretary phoned Mom out of concern, and Mom rushed home in time to save Ariel from God-knew-what. Mom must have finally confronted Phil. Though the leering and uncomfortable atmosphere persisted, never again did he lay hands on her —

The sounds of whooping in the living room jolted Ariel back to the present. There came heavy footsteps in the hall, her door flew open, and Max blew in, grinning.

"*Positive for breast cancer,*" he cried. "Back in business!"

Only Max could celebrate such news. Ariel asked anxiously, "Did they catch it in time?"

"Seems so. They're doing a simple lumpectomy." He grabbed her wrists and pulled her to her feet. "Regardless, *you're on.*"

They joined Tia and Stan in the living room, and everyone hustled out to the tent. But when they unzipped the door and ducked inside, they stopped cold in their tracks.

Once again, the table was askew, things scattered everywhere across the floor.

"It wasn't one of us," Tia said. "No one left the house since the morning run."

Ariel asked, "But if it was a stranger, wouldn't Newton have warned us?"

Trading concerned looks, they picked up, awaiting the next run.

CHAPTER 80

"For Pete's sake," Ivy cried, joining Scotty at his computer. "A chance to meet Ellen Shackleton! Why should it matter to the Lord now? You delivered His message to Thornton, Mission accomplished, you're free!"

Scotty sighed. Apparently not. Ariel had skipped their morning session, sending in her place another annoying epistle, ordering Scotty to do nothing more till further notice. No "thanks" for his efforts to help Thornton's secretary, which appeared to be in time—Kyle Heath had called earlier with an encouraging medical update.

Ivy prodded, "If you won't see Shackleton, let *me*."

Scotty shrugged her off. He'd no desire for either of them to be used as political pawns. Not even for Kassandra.

The thunder arrived on cue, and when the noises ceased, the angel appeared in her customary splendor. Again, Scotty thought he detected a sadness in her. They exchanged greetings and he reported, "Good news. Looks like they caught Ms. Willoughby's illness in time. I trust the Lord's pleased, and we can wrap things up now."

Ariel replied slowly, *"I'm afraid there's more to it than that. The Lord wants you to contact Reverend Thornton again. You're to schedule a private meeting in the City of God, right away."*

Scotty's gut tightened. He'd no intentions of going anywhere. "I don't understand."

"Your role in the Lord's Mission is not complete. All will be revealed soon. Set the meeting first, contact Thornton immediately. I'm sending you an epistle with his private number."

A new message appeared in Scotty's mail, and before he could protest, Ariel added, *"You must meet no later than this weekend, and only in the City of God. Confirm to me tomorrow morning that Thornton has accepted the meeting, and I'll have further instructions for you. Do nothing more. Patience, your Mission will soon be over."*

Ivy blurted, "Wait-wait. Before you go, Ellen Shackleton sent word she wants to meet us. The Lord can't object to that, right?"

Ariel's eyes widened. Glancing offscreen, she turned back to insist, *"Neither you nor Scott must meet with any politician under any circumstances. You must not talk politics with anyone, including the media, or show favoritism to any candidate. Is that clear?"*

Ivy snapped, "How does Scotty hanging out with Thornton not favor Filby?"

Ariel looked confused. *"The, the Lord has His reasons. He forbids you to meet with Ellen Shackleton. Tell me you understand."*

Ivy went red, and Scotty placed a hand on her shoulder to reply, "Understood. One more thing. There are people out here in the streets, hundreds, broke and hurting. Times are tough. The Lord helped Ms. Willoughby and Teddy, can he *please* do something for these people, too?"

Ariel bowed her head. *"I'm sorry. Focus on your Mission, we'll talk again tomorrow."*

And she was gone.

Scotty and Ivy sat silent till the noises returned and dissipated, then Ivy snipped, "Seems the Lord works in oblivious ways!"

"I get the feeling Ariel is as frustrated as we are," Scotty said. "Apparently, it's not all bliss and tranquility on the other side."

THE PROPHET OF QUEENS

He opened the epistle on his screen, took out his phone, and dialed. Thornton's distinct baritone answered, and Scotty put him on speaker for Ivy.

"Hello, Reverend, this is Scott Butterfield. The angel gave me your number."

There came a gasp, then, *"Mr. Butterfield! Oh, praise God, what an unexpected pleasure!"*

"How's Ms. Willoughby doing?"

"They're operating as we speak. A simple procedure at this stage, prospects are excellent." The man's voice was thick with emotion. *"I-I'm sooo grateful to you. You, and the Lord."*

"Great news," Scotty said, seeing Ivy give a fist pump. "And please, call me 'Scott.'"

"Bless you, Scott. If only there were a way I could repay you."

"There is, I think."

"Anything."

"The Lord wants me to meet with you in the City, right away. I don't know the purpose yet, but I know it's important. Would this weekend be possible?"

"Oh my goodness, absolutely! Wonderful! Saturday is Harvest Homecoming. We have a parade, a football game, a banquet. You'll be my guest."

Feeling an elbow in his ribs, Scotty added, "And can I bring my sister, Ivy?"

"Of course. I'm thrilled. I'll send my plane for you both whenever you wish."

Scotty thanked him, promising to get back with specifics. They hung up, and Ivy squealed, "We've never been on a plane. Heck, we've never been *anywhere.*"

True. Scotty might have been excited, too, but for the mysterious purpose of their trip.

There came a knock at their door, and Scotty went to the peephole to see Kassandra in the hall looking gorgeous in a black bodystocking.

CHAPTER 81

Ariel was in her room, catching up on journal entries when she was startled by a loud bang. Something had struck her window. A small branch.

She'd failed to notice a storm brewing, sky murky.

Max was aware, booming in the hallway, "All hands on deck, we're about to lose the tent."

Hurrying out, Ariel joined Stan and Tia in the living room. The door stood open, breeze rushing through, fresh scent of rain. Max was already at the tent, holding onto a tie rope, trying to pound in a loose peg with his shoe.

They raced to his aid, and Max looked to Stan. "Ground's too hard, get a hammer." To Tia, "Plastic sheets." To Ariel, "Grab the corner and don't let go."

Stan hustled for the barn, Tia the house, and Ariel grasped the loose canvas, wind whipping it like a sail. Cold drops began to pelt. A turn in weather was long overdue, and it was turning with a passion. But as Ariel dug in, she felt queasy.

The collider? An unscheduled run? In fact, they were inside the Trapping Horizon, but she'd heard none of the warning noises. Then suddenly, the ground trembled and she lost her grip, tumbling onto Max, ending up in his lap in the grass. He managed to hang onto the loose canvas, saving the tent.

"Earthquake," Ariel cried.

A brief one. Ten seconds or less. As it subsided, Ariel heard a strange, deep rumble all around. Max stared past her to the horizon, alarm in his face, and she followed his eyes to a terrifying sight. A dark, ominous, towering wall of cloud, sweeping toward them from every direction, converging on the tent. He gasped.

"No earthquake, Timequake. *And here comes the wave."*

Ariel grabbed Max with all her might as he hung onto both her and the tent. Her fears turned to Tia and Stan, and she saw Tia scramble down the porch steps with plastic tablecloths, Stan rounding the house, hammer in hand. Both seemed unaware of the looming disaster.

Ariel shouted to them. They didn't hear, and too late regardless. The wave bore down with ferocity, tall as the house, impact imminent. She shut her eyes.

Moments passed, and she felt nothing, only the storm. Then Max cried, *"I'll be damned..."*

Through a squint she saw the wave had passed, vanished seemingly without effect.

"You okay?" Max asked, and Ariel nodded, unable to speak.

Stan and Tia arrived in front of them unscathed, staring down at the spectacle of Ariel and Max in each other's grasp.

Tia said dryly, "Rhapsody in the rain?"

Ariel blinked to see Tia's hair had changed. Formerly chopped and pink, it was now trimmed even and tinted purple as it lashed her face in the wind. Nothing else appeared different.

Ariel and Max unclenched.

Max said, "We were hit by a Timequake/Timewave. You didn't feel it? See it?"

Stan and Tia exchanged blank looks, and Ariel sputtered,

"Th-the ground shook, it knocked us off our feet—"

"Five-point-oh or better," Max estimated. "Over in seconds."

"—then a wave of darkness, coming at us from all sides. Twenty feet high, at least!"

"But when it reached us," Max said, "it just evaporated."

Stan and Tia looked around warily, insisting they'd neither seen nor felt anything.

Stan whispered, "Holy cow, *our first butterfly.*"

A rift in Time, accumulated changes in the past catching up to the present.

The rain broke hard. Max lifted Ariel to her feet, motioning everyone into the tent. Taking the hammer, he went around pounding in the stakes while the others ducked inside, soaked.

Everywhere on the tent floor, items lay strewn and broken. Ariel picked up as Tia and Stan spread plastic sheets over equipment. Soon Max joined them, dripping, frowning at the clutter to note the obvious. "This wasn't our first Timequake."

"Or Timewave either, I'll wager," Stan said.

Tia frowned. "But when the wave hit, it disappeared? You felt the quake, but *not* the wave?"

"Exactly." Max said. "The wave had no effect on either of us, far as we could tell. It died out the instant it hit, without a trace."

"What caused it?" Ariel asked. "Saving Thornton's secretary?"

Max said, "Anyone's guess. But judging by the mess in here, the quakes are getting bigger."

Tia asked, "So why did the quake affect you and Ariel, and not Stan and me?"

Max took a lock of Tia's wet hair in his fingers. "I don't know about the quake, but the *wave* affected you. You had *pink* highlights before it struck."

Ariel added, "Your hair was cut differently, too."

"But I've worn it like this as long as you've known me," Tia said, and Stan backed her up.

Max frowned. "Seems the wave affected more than your hair. Our *memories* are out of sync."

The rain slackened, and he unzipped the door. "Come," he said. "Let's warm up by a fire while we think this through."

· · ·

Toweled off and changed into dry clothes, the team settled in with coffee by the fireplace to discuss this latest twist in the space-time continuum.

"So what the hell happened?" Tia asked.

Ariel offered a theory, although unable to support it.

"The Trapping Horizon/force field," she said. "Max and I were inside it at the time, you and Stan weren't."

Max shook his head. "How could there be a force field, the collider wasn't running?" He checked his phone. "No word from TPC of an unscheduled test."

"Assuming it was a butterfly," Stan said, "*something* enabled you and Ariel to experience it while shielding you from its changes. Vice-versa for Tia and me. Like you and Ariel were in a separate dimension, looking through a two-way mirror, Tia and me on the one-way side."

Ariel asked, "A dimension that formed inside the force field? But if the collider wasn't running, what caused it?"

Stan drew a long breath. "Here's a thought. What if butterflies create their *own* force field, independent of the collider?"

Getting intrigued looks, he continued, "A butterfly, even a tiny one, would release a massive amount of energy. Like an earthquake creating a tidal wave. The energy would travel down the Timeline from past to present, ending here where it all began, creating a Trapping Horizon/force field to complete the circuit." He looked to Ariel. "Because you and Max were inside it, you were spared the wave's updates. You and your memories were unchanged."

Tia exhaled. "We're damned lucky if memories and hair were all it affected."

Ariel shivered to recall the monster swell, imagining it sweeping through history, washing away inconsistencies to reconcile present with past. She told Max, "If we hadn't been inside the Horizon, none of us would be the wiser. Which begs the question, how many rewrites have we been through already that we *can't* recall?"

Things were getting super strange.

There was worry in Tia's eyes, and she said, "No doubt as we push ahead there'll be more quakes and waves, and they'll grow more intense. If today's was a five point, imagine what flipping the election will cause. The Mother of all Big Ones."

"We'll have to take turns in the tent, watching for Timequakes around the clock," Ariel said.

Stan said, "How about we set up a seismograph instead? I know where to borrow one."

Max sat back with a smile. "Imagine the papers we'll be writing when this is over." He turned to Ariel. "From here on, whenever we detect a quake, you'll need to check your rabbit's foot for changes in the archives. And now that we know the Horizon shields against Timewaves, no need to hide the foot in the plant anymore, you can keep it in the tent."

Ariel folded her arms on her chest. *"No thanks,* I like things just as they are."

She wasn't leaving her journal lying around for prying eyes.

CHAPTER 82

Kassandra Kraft sat in her new private office behind a *real* wood desk and a computer screen bigger than her TV at home. A small, windowless office, yet a huge leap in status. For the first time since she'd started here, her male associates appreciated her for other than her looks. And that slime mold, Bobby Driscoll? Sulking in his little cubicle, all but conceding.

Except now, her coup was in jeopardy. Yesterday, she'd left work early, determined to meet with Butterfield and nail down a date and time for a Shackleton/Prophet rendezvous. After forcing her way past the annoying roadblock in front of her apartment building, however, she hit another inside. Butterfield answered her knock to inform her that his "angel" had nixed the Shackleton meeting and ordered him to steer clear of politics and politicians altogether.

Kassandra was devastated. She'd pressed him hard, to no avail, retreating to her apartment, frantic. Only to be stunned minutes later by an announcement on Hawk News from Penbrook Thornton. Butterfield was traveling to the City of God this weekend as his guest.

Thornton. Roger Filby's crony shill. So much for Butterfield steering clear of politics!

Storming back across the hall to confront him again, Kassandra was told his trip was "a spiritual mission only." As if the far-right media and religious zealots would buy that. Butterfield wouldn't give up any specifics, and Kassandra took another swing at a Shackleton meeting, again striking out—

Suddenly Shonda burst into her office, snapping, "Why didn't you take my calls last night?"

Kassandra didn't dare reveal her predicament. "I was with Butterfield," she said. "Negotiations are at a delicate stage."

"Delicate, my ass. He's going off to Tennessee to hobnob with Penbrook Thornton. Percy's breathing down my neck, and the DNC is apoplectic."

"No cause for alarm," Kassandra assured. "It's a spiritual retreat, nothing more."

Shonda's tone went knife sharp. "I'll hand it to you, Kraft, your stunt in the conference room took balls. You're Wonder Woman. For now. But make no mistake. Screw this up, I'll see to it there isn't a PR firm in the country that'll have you."

And she blew back out, slamming the door.

Kassandra's heart pounded. There *had* to be a way to change Butterfield's mind. She didn't need him to commit to a full-on sit-down, a simple meet-and-greet would do. Just enough for a photo op that EP&M could spin. Something, *anything* to bail her out of this looming catastrophe.

CHAPTER 83

Scotty sat with Ivy at his computer, awaiting Ariel's appearance. Ivy seemed to have recovered from her Shackleton disappointment, and Scotty was feeling better about things, too. They'd both warmed to the idea of visiting the City of God. As Ivy had said, they'd never ventured beyond Greater New York, or flown before. And the Homecoming festivities would be a welcomed diversion from all the pressure they'd been under.

Ivy asked, "Who'll watch Homer while we're gone? You ever leave him overnight before?"

"No, but it's just twenty-four hours. I'll put out extra food and water. He'll be fine."

That was the least of Scotty's worries about this trip. He and Ivy were both concerned that the Prophet's fraternizing with Thornton would imply support for Filby, sending voters the wrong signal. Not to mention, the mysterious purpose of this Mission. Scotty had no clue yet what it entailed, but hopefully he was about to find out.

Rumble and whine announced the coming of the Paraclete, and once more, Ariel materialized.

"*Good morning,*" she greeted them with a furrowed brow. "*I trust you have good news.*"

"Yes," Scotty said. "The Reverend's flying us down to the City this weekend."

"*Us?*"

"Ivy and me. There's a festival Saturday, and we're invited to attend and spend the night."

Ariel looked anxious, glancing at Ivy, off screen, back to Scotty. "*The meeting's between you and the Reverend, alone. It requires your undivided attention. Ivy and the rest are a distraction.*"

Ivy leaned forward to say, "We've *both* been trapped in this building forever. The only time we leave is to do the Lord's bidding. We've earned some R&R."

Scotty added, "If the Lord wants my help, those are my terms."

He felt Ivy squeeze his hand.

The angel seemed rattled, glancing away again, and Ivy blurted, "Is someone else there with you? Is it the Lord? Can we meet Him?"

Ariel froze. "*Uh, the Lord is everywhere, but, but He can't be seen by mortals.*"

"He can speak, can't He? Why won't He speak to us?"

Ariel brushed her off. "*I'm sending you instructions for the meeting; what to do, what not to do. We'll discuss it this afternoon, at which time the Lord will decide your requests.*"

An epistle appeared on Scotty's screen, and he acknowledged it.

"*Read it carefully. I'll have more details and answer any questions at our two o'clock.*"

And the screen went black.

Ivy huffed, "Couldn't get rid of us fast enough. Why the big deal about the trip? It's not like they have to pay our expenses!"

Scotty opened the new epistle from Ariel. A long one. They read it together, and Scotty said when finished, "My role in the Lord's Great Mission is to fetch a *videotape?*"

The email didn't say what was on the tape, one of those "details"

Ariel would discuss this afternoon, presumably. It went on to warn against getting chummy with Thornton, or revealing information about Ariel and the Lord, or speaking with the media. It also advised how to avoid complications and handle unexpected situations. And it ended reminding Scotty not to forget his shepherd's staff.

Ivy saw something odd in the text, pointing to it. "What's *this?*"

Scotty had missed it. The word *your,* where the context called for *you're.* Their written instructions were always letter-perfect before.

"...A grammatical error? I thought the Lord was infallible."

CHAPTER 84

"Not good," Max growled as the team retired to the living room to ponder the latest complication. "Who the hell does he think he is, giving the Lord terms?"

Butterfield had insisted his sister accompany him on his trip to the City, and that they both attend a festival, and overnight there.

Stan said, "We're at a critical stage, we can't be out of touch with Butterfield that long. It's setting him loose in a minefield. And if he hits one, we've no way to know, or advise him."

It reminded Ariel of the old Apollo space missions where astronauts would lose contact with Earth as they attempted to round the far side of the moon—tense moments during a do-or-die maneuver, world helplessly awaiting their fate.

Max said, "The sister is trouble. I don't trust her down there."

"Forget it," Tia said. "You heard Butterfield, his mind's made up. Force a confrontation, we could lose everything."

She got no argument. But Max continued to grumble, and Ariel assured him, "If I know the Reverend, he'll be so grateful for his secretary he'll hand the tape over in a heartbeat."

Ariel felt she knew Thornton's heart. He'd expressed it from the pulpit countless Sundays.

Max told her, "I don't trust Thornton, either. The election's too important to him."

"Yes," Stan said. "We need more leverage. An insurance policy."

"A generous donation to his Church?" Tia suggested.

"Money won't move him," Ariel said. "Think theologically."

Max snapped his fingers. "No. Think *politically.* If Thornton proves stubborn, the Prophet will make him a deal he can't refuse." He grinned. "Give up the tape, and the Lord will guarantee Filby the election. Refuse, and Filby loses." He turned to Ariel. "What do you call a pact between God and man?"

"A Covenant."

"Yes. *A Covenant.*"

A Covenant the Lord would ultimately renege on.

Stan said, "His sister's not going to like it."

Everyone had seen Ivy in a Shackleton T-shirt.

"Then we can't let her know," Max said. "Only Butterfield. He can keep the Covenant in his hip pocket, use it only if Thornton needs some persuading."

· · ·

Two o'clock arrived, and the team took their stations. The noises came and went, and the Butterfields appeared on Ariel's screen once more. She greeted them asking, "Is your visit with Thornton proceeding as planned?"

"*Yes,*" Scott replied. "*We leave first thing tomorrow morning.*"

"Very well. The Lord's decided to grant your requests. You may attend the festival and remain overnight, and Ivy may go with you."

They both smiled, and Ariel told Scott, "But there's a private matter about your Mission that you and I must discuss. *Alone.*"

Ivy's smile faded. She turned to Scott, he shrugged, and she stood, looking betrayed. Giving Ariel a pout, she exhaled and exited the screen. Ariel heard stamping and a door open and close.

"Ivy is gone?"

"Yes."

"I'm sorry for that, but what I'm about to tell you is for you and Reverend Thornton only. Do I have your word?"

Scotty shrugged again. *"Yes."*

"Have you read the Lord's instructions I sent?"

He nodded. *"Pick up a secret videotape from the Reverend and bring it back."*

"I trust it will be that simple. Reverend Thornton will know what tape the Lord seeks, he should give it up gladly after his recent blessings. But if not, the Lord is entrusting you with a sacred Covenant to present in exchange. You are aware of the coming presidential election?"

Scott blinked. *"Of course."*

Unable to look him in the eye, Ariel said, "As the election now stands, Shackleton will win. But if Reverend Thornton gives up the tape, the Lord will grant victory to Roger Filby instead."

Scott's jaw dropped. *"That is the Lord's sacred Covenant?"*

"Yes. But you're to present it to Thornton *only* if refuses you the tape. The Covenant is your ace in the hole. Assuming he accepts, he must keep the Covenant to himself, alone, or the deal is off."

Scott clenched. *"You'd steal the election from Shackleton over a tape? That's...ungodly."*

"The Lord has His reasons, you must trust Him. All will be well, *if* you return with the tape."

A pause, and Scott asked, *"You say Thornton will know what tape the Lord wants. What if he doesn't? I should at least know how to describe it to him."*

Glancing offscreen to blank faces, Ariel replied, "You may call it 'the Shackleton tape.' That's all you need to know. You're forbidden to view it, or let the Reverend divulge its contents to you. Make certain you get every copy, if there are more. And keep their existence to yourself."

"But Ivy knows about the tape. She read your instructions, too."

"Uh, Ivy's forbidden tell anyone, either. You must see to that."

Scott screwed up his face. *"Wait a minute. If the Lord knows everything, why doesn't He know if there are more copies?"*

Ariel hesitated. "Well, the Lord knows all, yes. But then, He's given man free will, you see? He has to allow for that variable."

By his expression, Scott didn't see, and Ariel hurried to wrap up.

"If you've no more questions, all that remains is for you to make certain you return home with the tape for our session Sunday morning. That's *very* important. Do you understand?"

"Be home with the tape by 10:00, Sunday."

That last stipulation was Max's idea. In order for Scott to make the morning session in his apartment, he and Ivy would have to leave the City by dawn. Which would hopefully compel them to retire early the night before and limit their time with Thornton.

"We'll talk again Sunday at 10:00," Ariel said, "and that will complete your final Mission for the Lord. Until then, don't forget your instructions. Godspeed, and good luck." And she logged off.

CHAPTER 85

After her session with Scott Butterfield, Ariel retired to her room, exhausted and demoralized. She locked her door and lay on the bed with her laptop, took an anxious breath, and clicked on the file Tia had sent her, marked *Private*. She'd put it off long enough. Time to peek behind the curtain of her stepfather's mysterious Institute—a psychiatric asylum that Ariel feared was at the heart of the grave problems the City faced with its youth. The file opened, and she read:

Therapy Evaluations and Notations
Dr. Philip K. Neuhoffer, PhD
Director of Psychological Services
Christian Family Research Institute

What followed was a document with jpeg and mpeg attachments, labeled:

#F-393
L, Nicole
Patient Evaluation/Therapy Assessment
Feb 5–Mar 23 (case terminated*)

The asterisk gave Ariel concern. But seeing no answer to it, she took another breath and clicked on a jpeg. A mug shot appeared, and Ariel winced to see a face she once knew, the girl's prettiness diminished by a scowl. Dark hair pulled back, dark eyes, ankh neck tattoo. Evidence of piercings in ears and nose. Every inch the rebel Ariel recalled, a poster child of the City's woes.

There were more photos, but Ariel was too skittish. And recalling Tia's warning about the video attachment, she skirted that as well. What followed were notes Neuhoffer had taken during Nicole's course of "treatment" a decade ago.

Ariel scanned, skipping over nondescript sections, slowing periodically for key points.

Feb 8:
Patient F-393, Nicole L. 16-yr old female Caucasian, junior at Tabernacle High, admitted to Institute after repeated incidents of poor comportment and attitude.

Diagnosis: Social maladjustment with associated anxieties, anger issues and suicidal ideation. Substance abuse suspected.

Feb. 13:
Further evaluation confirms homosexual proclivity. Seeking to determine cause, beginning regimen of reorientation therapy.

Feb. 19:
Subject stubbornly resistant to treatment. During morning session, struck attendant with chair, tried to escape. Subdued, sedated, placed in isolation, introduced to recorded devotional sermons. Subject later observed stuffing scraps of clothing in mouth in apparent attempt at self-suffocation. Clothing, bed sheeting removed, 24-hr surveillance.

Ariel had to blot her eyes before continuing.

Feb 28:
Patient F-393 persists in belligerent, defiant attitude. Initiating
program of behavioral modification/corporal discipline.

Mar 5:
No improvement. Patient remains uncooperative, incommuni-
cative, defiant. Refuses food, force-fed, may require intravenous
supplement. Remains under physical restraints, particularly dur-
ing reorientation therapy.

Ariel shoved aside her laptop as if it were contaminated, staggered to the bathroom, and vomited. After a time, she pulled herself
together. Wherever this story ended, she *had* to know. And returning
to her stepfather's notes, she jumped to his final entry.

Mar 8:
Most unfortunate development. Approximately 8:30 last evening,
F-393 escaped solitary and accosted female member of cleaning
staff with shiv, locking her in janitorial closet stripped of uni-
form, bound and gagged. Search of grounds and surrounding areas
to no avail.

*Update. After one year, patient F-393 remains unaccounted for.

Ariel trembled again. With relief.

CHAPTER 86

"Safe travels," Mrs. Steiner wished Scott and Ivy, seeing them off to their cab from her door. It had been storming all morning. She watched them push out the front entrance with a screech, police rushing to hold back the crowd. They looked so nice, Ivy in a pretty yellow dress, Scott in a button-down shirt and tie, hair combed, leaving on their first trip away from the city.

What strange days these were! Over scones and coffee earlier, Ivy and Scott had opened up about some extraordinary developments—as much as their secretive angel would allow them. Mrs. Steiner was still trying to sort it out. She'd never given much credence to the divine, but how else to explain all this? Messages from the Lord? Prophecies? Lifesaving interventions?

Exciting, confusing. And worrisome. Mrs. Steiner recalled childhood lessons of the Talmud where man's encounters with God didn't always end well. Sodom and Gomorrah, for one.

Hardly had she shut her door than she heard another screech, reopening to see three men in the foyer. Two had their backs to her, their hair and shoulders wet. One man was tall and gray in a rumpled jacket, the other short, in a dress coat. They faced a cop

410

in a rain slicker who said, "I told you, you just missed them."

The tall, gray-haired man snarled, "Where'd they go?"

The cop replied, "Don't you watch the news?"

"TV's busted."

"They're out of town till tomorrow. Go home."

The man in the dress coat placed a hand on the other's back, saying, "Come on, Joe, nothing more we can do today."

Joe shook him off. "Not leavin' till the storm breaks."

"Suit yourself," the cop said, and he and the short man exited.

Joe spun and barreled into the hall swearing, and Mrs. Steiner closed her door as footsteps passed. She heard him continue up the stairs, and seconds later there came a pounding and a doorknob jiggling. More pounding and jiggling and swearing. Then the footsteps reversed, down the stairs, only to cease midway.

Mrs. Steiner opened her door, peeking around to see Joe sitting in a ball on the steps, head down, fingers laced behind it, elbows on knees. She asked softly, "You're Scott's dad, aren't you?"

He looked up, miserable, and she said, "You're soaked, you must be freezing. Come, let's dry you off and get you some coffee."

Grumbling, the man finally exhaled, rose, and followed her inside. She took his jacket and hung it on a chair by the radiator, seated him on the couch, and headed to the kitchen.

"I'm Elizabeth Steiner," she called back. "Betsy." Returning with a tray, she set a pot of coffee and some pastries and napkins on the table in front of him, handing him a dishtowel.

"Joe Butterfield," he said, drying his hair, raking his fingers through the tangle. "How'd you know I'm his father?"

She sat beside him. "He has your eyes."

He grunted and took a long drink. "Good java," he muttered. "Much obliged."

"Try a strudel."

She pushed the plate nearer and refilled his cup. He grabbed a slice, took a bite, and his eyes widened. Swallowing, he took a larger bite, and she suggested, "They're made to dunk."

He dipped and gobbled as if he'd had no breakfast. Pausing to wipe his mouth on the towel, he said, "So, Betsy, you know the boy."

"And Ivy. They're delightful. Scott's been very kind to me."

He took another drink, and scowled. "Then maybe you can explain what the hell he's up to with this prophet bullshit."

"I wouldn't call the ability to see the future 'bullshit.'"

"It sure as hell ain't a miracle. I raised that boy, and I'm telling you, he *ain't* no prophet. He's got no religion."

Mrs. Steiner shrugged. "Who knows why God chooses the leaders He does? Moses was a reluctant prophet, too."

"Moses, my ass. Somebody's dupin' him. He's an easy mark, livin' in that fantasy world a his. Damned if I let him drag Ivy into it."

The anger in his eyes burned deep. Mrs. Steiner suspected an old wound that this current rub with Ivy had simply inflamed. Whatever the rift, it was disturbing. The man couldn't even bring himself to use his son's name.

"I told that boy when I threw him out, leave your sister be, and he goes behind my back."

"If you don't mind my asking," Mrs. Steiner said, "what did he do that you threw him out?"

Joe laid a hard stare on her, and she feared she'd overstepped herself. But he replied, "Boy's a shiftless dreamer. His mom made him that. Spoiled him. Before she passed, I swore I'd raise him right. I tried, and I failed."

"Aren't all boys shiftless dreamers?"

"A *man* grows out of it. Livin' at home, he never wanted a job. Just stay in his room like a bum. On the Web, playing games and God-knows-what all hours. Still, I fed him, clothed him, kept a roof over him. Then one day he's out somewheres. I walk by his room, and here's Ivy on his computer watching filth. Filth *he* brought into *my* home. Things no girl should *ever* see."

Not knowing how to respond, Mrs. Steiner said nothing.

"Boy was a burden even 'fore he was born. Ivy's all I got, I *ain't* lettin' him ruin her, too."

Mrs. Steiner blinked. "For heaven's sake, Joe, how can a child be a burden before its born?"

The man's face clouded. Slapping his knees, he stood and retrieved his coat. "The rain's let up," he said. "Nice to meet you, Betsy, thanks for breakfast."

And he left.

CHAPTER 87

Scotty smiled. He'd never seen Ivy so excited. He followed her eyes out the window of their little jet as Lady Liberty raised her torch to them in passing. And no sooner had the seatbelt light switched off than Ivy was up chatting with the flight attendant, inviting herself into the cockpit.

The thrill in her face was well worth whatever Wrath Scotty had risked by bringing her along. He shared her exhilaration. This was a lifestyle neither had ever experienced—and after tomorrow, would likely never experience again.

Far below, the grid of city and suburb gave way to patchworks of forest and broad farmland, and Ivy returned to her seat with drinks and snacks.

"Try the shrimp," she urged. *"Delish."*

Scotty did, and it was.

She cocked her head and squinted at him in that quirky way Mom used to when she had something on her mind. "So, you won't share the Sacred Secret?"

"Believe me, you don't want to know."

414

"I'd like to know why the Lord won't trust me. At least tell me about the Shackleton tape."

Scotty cringed, glancing around, relieved to see the flight attendant occupied. "No one can know about our Mission," he whispered. "I made a mistake telling you who's on that tape."

"I know you're thinking what I'm thinking."

Everyone knew the salacious rumors of Shackleton's past. Drinking, drugs, and wild parties.

"No, I'm thinking, what's Thornton doing with a tape like that? And more to the point, why does the Lord want it?"

Ivy sat back. "I don't know, but I gotta say, there's something wrong about this. Ariel may be an angel and all, but she sure acts *human*. And don't forget, when this business is over and done with, and she and the Lord vanish, *we're* on the hook for any problems they leave behind."

Scotty shifted in his seat. He had to admit there was troubling incongruity to these Missions. The Lord had sent Scotty to save a spectator at a ballpark, the mayor, a town in Georgia, Alice Willoughby. But He'd also allowed people to die in a restaurant explosion, a bus to crash, people injured. In fact, as Scotty recalled from the bible, while God was loving, merciful and caring, He was also angry, spiteful, jealous and vindictive. An almighty Jekyll & Hyde. Divinely bipolar.

Their jet sailed into cloud, the cabin darkened, and Scotty said, "Maybe if I fetch the Lord His tape, He'll pull some strings for us in return. Get you into a good college. Help me find a job. Maybe there's a silver lining in here after all."

• • •

It was smooth cruising to Tennessee, where they swooped over the autumn brilliance of the Smoky Mountains to land at a tiny airport carved out of forest. The hatch opened onto a perfect, balmy day. Too warm for Scotty's hoody, and he left it in the plane, almost forgetting his staff.

Reverend Thornton was on the tarmac waiting, gold cross lapel pin flashing in the sun. Behind him was a car and driver, and further back, cordoned off by chain-link and security, representatives of every news media Scotty knew of, and many he didn't. Next to them were hundreds of neatly dressed, cheering people, if few minorities. Scotty marveled at how different things were here, reminded of the poor wretches huddled in the rain outside his building at home.

Thornton greeted them smiling, handing Ivy a bouquet of flowers. He seated them in the back of the car, the driver stowed their overnight bags and staff in the trunk, and they were off.

"We're so thrilled to be here," Ivy told the reverend, and Scotty seconded.

"My honor," Thornton told them, beaming. "I can't thank you enough for your blessings, praise the Lord. We have a full day planned for you. And if you don't mind, I'd like to begin by taking you to meet someone very special."

They chatted on the short jaunt to town, media following in a caravan. Scotty liked Thornton. He found him warm, jovial, upbeat, easy to talk to. Ivy seemed to like him, too. It would make their Mission here easier, Scotty trusted.

"I've so many questions," Thornton said, eyes dancing. "I want to hear all about your experiences with the angel and the Lord."

Scotty sighed. "Sorry, I'm not allowed. The Lord will only let me discuss the reason He sent me. If we can set aside some time later."

Thornton flashed disappointment, but recovered with a smile. "Of course."

The car rounded a curve to emerge from a timberline onto a spectacular vista. Before them loomed a giant white structure that reminded Scotty of the U.S. Capital building. A church. Drawing closer, he saw a nearby park with a prominent hill at its center. Beyond that, another extraordinary white structure rising into the skyline—an office building. Then the full City came into dazzling view, and Scotty gasped, *"Heavenly."*

Ivy said, "A magic kingdom."

Thornton beamed again.

They turned onto a main boulevard, traveling past a gatehouse into the parking lot of a hospital. A gateman held out the media, and Thornton took Scotty and Ivy inside into a private suite overlooking a garden. There they met a lovely lady, Alice Willoughby, in bed recovering from a successful medical procedure. She and Thornton were effusive in their thanks, Scotty assuring them the credit accrued entirely to the Lord. Scotty couldn't help but note the tenderness the woman and Thornton shared. Ivy saw, too, shooting Scotty a wink.

Back at the car, Thornton asked them, "Do you enjoy parades?"

"I never miss Macy's Thanksgiving parade," Ivy said, adding with a laugh, "Not that I can get close enough for more than a glimpse."

Thornton chuckled. "I promise you a perfect vantage point to enjoy ours."

They arrived at a town square, parking in a reserved spot, and Scotty exited to see helicopters circling—National news networks. The streets were filled with festival-goers, who recognized Scotty when the driver handed him his shepherd's staff.

"Prophet," they cried, rushing for him. But Thornton hustled Scotty and Ivy into a roped-off area in front of City Hall, up steps to a pavilion. There were buffet tables in the back, and bleacher seats facing the street. Also, a podium decorated with red-white-and-blue bunting and American flags. Not the stars and stripes, exactly. In the blue square of the flags' corners where the stars should be was a large, golden cross.

The pavilion was crowded with well-dressed people bearing gold-cross pins like Thornton's. Spying Scotty, they cheered and swarmed. Thornton introduced Scotty and Ivy to the mayor, city officials, Church dignitaries, and on, who showered Scotty with praise and thrust pens and paper at him. He was embarrassed, not least of all by his atrocious-looking signature.

People asked, "What's the latest prophecy?" "What's the angel look like?" "What's God like?" "Can you help my arthritis?"

Scotty demurred.

A woman peered closely at his shepherd's staff, and gasped, "The rod of Moses!" Scotty held it out for people to touch, and they did so cautiously as if it might strike them dead.

Down by the street, a familiar voice called to Scotty and Ivy. Scotty saw Kyle Heath of Hawk News in an area restricted to media. Other reporters shouted questions. Scotty waved.

Thousands of spectators filled the street, some displaying signs with bible passages, others with messages such as, *"Power to the Prophet!"* and *"God Lives!"* Scotty's view of the parade route was blocked by buildings on his right, but he could see left across an intersection to marching bands, floats, and giant balloons queued behind a ribbon that spanned the street.

Soon a man in a tuxedo took the podium, tapping a microphone. It howled, and the proceedings came to order. He announced himself as master of ceremonies, welcoming all. And in particular,

"…Our beloved Reverend Penbrook Thornton and his esteemed guests of honor, Scott and Ivy Butterfield, of Queens, New York."

The crowd roared.

"We have much to be grateful for today," the man said, bowing his head, and everyone followed suit. *"Oh Heavenly Father,"* he intoned, *"we thank You for the bountiful harvest You've bestowed upon us this season. We come together in tribute to Your beneficence, and to celebrate in Your honor and glory. Together we pray for Thy continued blessings upon us, our guests, and our festival."*

A chorus of *Amens* answered, and he raised up to add, *"And now, it's my great privilege and pleasure to present to you this year's Harvest Homecoming Festival Grand Marshal—"* he turned to Scotty, *"Mr. Scott Butterfield."*

The crowd was jubilant, and Thornton urged Scotty to his feet. Scotty felt his face redden, half-standing, terrified he'd be asked to speak, quickly retaking his seat. The noise ebbed, and the man at the podium cried, "*Let the festivities begin.*"

Another roar, and the street began to clear, people packing shoulder-to-shoulder along the sidewalks, crowding into storefronts, every niche and gap. The band struck up a hymn, a woman with giant scissors cut the ribbon, and the band strutted forward, followed by floats and balloons and more bands. As they passed the pavilion, they turned to pay homage.

A large float lumbered by—Noah's ark, with a man in flowing white beard standing alongside pairs of stuffed animals, including dinosaurs. Scotty felt Ivy's elbow in his side.

The parade continued, and Scotty's arms grew weary waving. At last, he spied the end, a driver in a shiny convertible, no passengers. The car stopped in front of the pavilion, and Thornton said to Scotty with a smile, "Your ride, sir."

The mayor offered Ivy his arm, Thornton escorted Scotty, and they made their way down. Scotty was seated in the back of the car, Ivy one side, Thornton the other, mayor in the front. The driver started up again, and the media tracked along behind, some on foot, others in cars and vans as choppers hovered above.

The length of the street was now visible, lined with spectators celebrating Scotty as if he were royalty. He was reminded, oddly, of Palm Sunday and Christ's triumphant entry into Jerusalem. Only to recall with discomfort the Fate that awaited Christ. Scotty felt a fraud. People still clung to the belief he was some holy emissary, despite his insistence otherwise, and it struck him the magnitude of the wave he was caught up in. The Prophet phenomenon had spread far beyond New York, deep into America's heartland. Scotty was now the face of something over which he exerted no control; a strawman in whatever divine game was playing out. More than ever, he was determined to finish this Mission and melt back into the refuge of anonymity.

But he worried about Ivy. Watching her drink in the attention, he feared that having tasted the good life, she might never again be content with how things were.

Then again, maybe that was a good thing.

Their car reached a block of taller business buildings, and suddenly a blizzard of streamers began to fall, so thick Scotty could hardly see. Each streamer contained printed words, he realized, like fortune cookies. Catching one, he read:

Philippians 3:13—*"Forget those things which are behind; reach forth unto those things which are before."*

The crowd thinned, floats and balloons breaking off.

Thornton glanced at his watch. "Okay, Mark," he told his driver, and the car swung onto a side road, media pursuing.

A beautiful white stadium came into view, reminiscent of the Coliseum in Rome. Attendants waved their car through a gate, closing the media off, and it stopped in front of the stadium. The bright sounds of John Phillip Sousa emanated from within. Thornton and the mayor escorted Ivy and Scotty from the car, through an archway and ramp to box seats on the fifty-yard line.

Scotty was thrilled. He'd never seen a football game live.

Once they'd settled, Thornton leaned in to say, "After dinner tonight, if it suits you, I thought we could discuss the Lord's purpose in sending you here."

Scotty nodded, surprised to see the shine in the man's eyes fade.

"I've known this day would come," Thornton said as if to himself, as if resigned to some dreaded fate. "The Lord will have His reckoning."

CHAPTER 88

S tan was out in the tent checking equipment, Ariel, Max, and Tia in the living room on laptops monitoring the Butterfields' four-year-old trip to the City of God. The media had been all over it, updated news appearing constantly in the archives.

Ariel watched the parade through tears, careful to hide them from Max. Every autumn when Ariel was young, Mom would take her to Homecoming, just the two of them. A magical time. Memories flooded back for her to cherish again. The flash of marching brass bands, jubilant in the sun. Bright uniforms, spectacular floats, inflatables, fancy cars, cheering crowds.

She missed her mother so. After coming to grips with Phil's files, Ariel had reached out to her again. No response. Ariel told herself Mom was in no danger, Phil's sickness targeted only young girls...

The camera cut to a panoramic shot of the City, and Ariel wiped the nostalgia from her eyes. Not a City of God, but a gleaming-white internment camp, with impregnable walls of ideology.

Stan popped in the front door, startling her to announce, "Another Timequake last night. Five-point-three magnitude, eleven-second duration."

The new seismograph had hardly been in operation a day.

Ariel asked anxiously, "How big will the Big One be? Like the 1906 San Francisco quake?"

Stan replied, "The San Francisco quake measured eight-point-two. Three points higher than what you and Max experienced. But seismograph scales are a logarithm, meaning the Frisco quake was actually *eight hundred* times bigger than yours. Compared to what's coming, a *hiccup,* I expect."

Ariel grabbed Tia's hand, and Tia squeezed back.

Max rapped his knuckles on the coffee table, turning from his computer to say, "I just read a theoretical article on Time travel, and it may shed some light on the quakes we're experiencing."

He had everyone's attention.

"The article gives an analogy to explain how changes to the past could affect the present. Imagine a sheet of cellophane stretched tight, with a bowstring penetrating it in the middle. The cellophane represents a membrane dividing past from present. The string is a timeline. The article suggests small changes to the past travel down the Timeline and build up against the membrane, creating pressure on one side."

Ariel pictured a flock of butterflies floating down the string, crashing into plastic wrap.

"...Every now and then, a small change leaks through, causing quakes, and waves, and minor alterations to the present. Like what we experienced during the storm the other day—Tia's hair, and her and Stan's memories."

Ariel asked, "What happens to the butterflies that accumulate against the membrane?"

Stan said, "They build up pressure until, eventually..."

Tia said, "When we reverse the election, it's going to send a *monster* butterfly slamming into the membrane, bursting it for sure. *The Big One.* It'll release a *massive* wave. A *Time-tsunami.*"

Ariel felt panic. "The only way we and our memories will be safe from the Tsunami is *inside* the Trapping Horizon. *But being inside it will expose us to the Big One.*"

Damned if they remained in the bubble, damned if they left. Ariel's head was spinning.

Max said, "As the election nears, we'll need to keep to the tent. First sign of the Big One, we step outside the Horizon till it's over, step back in before the Tsunami hits. A two-step dance."

"Assuming," Tia said, "some Timewave doesn't strike between now and then to make us forget the dance. And speaking of memories, there's something we all seem to have forgotten."

Everyone turned to her.

"Do any of you remember hearing about a Prophet in the news four years ago?"

Getting confused looks, she clarified, "The changes we've made to the past should be baked into history by now. Four years ago, we were in school, but we weren't blind to current events. We would have all noticed a national sensation like the Prophet. I've no memories of him, do you? If Timewaves update our memories about things as incidental as my hair, where are our updated memories about the Prophet of Queens?"

That had everyone stewing. Then Stan's face darkened, and he whispered, "I hope there's another explanation, but I can think of only one."

Tia finished for him in a whisper. "In the new reality to come, we'll cease to exist. The Time-tsunami is going to erase us..."

Silence.

Ariel felt a chill unlike anything she'd ever known. She rose as if drawn by some invisible force, approaching the bay window to stare out at the tent. "Assuming that's true," she said softly, "when the Tsunami hits, all that will be left of us and our universe will shrink to the size of the force field bubble, *if* we remember to hide inside it."

More Silence.

At length, Tia said, "Knowing that, do we dare continue?"

"Knowing what the world has become," Stan replied, "do we dare quit? What are our lives to us without science?"

There were tears in his eyes. Ariel had never seen him like that.

Max said, "Regardless, there's no going back. Whatever our fate, it's already rewritten."

CHAPTER 89

The car turned onto the grounds of a country club. A sign boasted an eighteen-hole golf course, an Olympic-size swimming pool, tennis club, and five-star restaurant where tonight's dinner would be held. All beautifully landscaped on the edge of town abutting a mountain whose peak the sun was now dipping below. Scotty had never seen such opulence firsthand.

They circled a packed parking lot to arrive at a fountain round-about in front of the dining hall—a magnificent, four-story glass conservatory. As Scotty, Ivy, Thornton, and the mayor exited the car for the hall, Scotty noticed the media tailing them. But when the media tried to follow them inside, security cut them off. Tonight's event was members only, and despite angry protests, the reporters had to content themselves observing through the glass walls.

Scotty left his shepherd's staff at hat check, proceeding with the others down wide stairs, reaching a magnificent atrium under a glass roof. The room was filled with guests, and when a host met Scotty at the bottom, the guests burst into applause.

"Welcome, Mr. Butterfield, Ms. Butterfield," the host greeted. "An honor to meet you. If you don't mind, some of our patrons would like to meet you, too."

Scotty had had enough socializing for one day, but saw no gracious way out. A receiving line formed, and he and Ivy shook hands and chatted with all who cared to make their acquaintance.

Exhausting.

Finally, the last person was accommodated, and Thornton led Scotty and Ivy to the head table where they joined the mayor, his wife, and other dignitaries. Ivy was seated with the wives, Scotty between Thornton and the mayor.

It was the finest meal Scotty ever had, no slight to Mrs. Steiner. Five courses served without alcohol while VIPs made speeches. Scotty's only complaint were the many interruptions of undeserved accolades paid to him. And just when a killer-looking chocolate torte was being served, a man in a dark suit appeared beside Thornton to buzz in his ear. Thornton nodded, the man left, and Thornton blotted his lips with a napkin, turning to Scotty.

"May I suggest we stretch our legs before dessert?" he asked. "There's one more person I'd like you to meet."

Eyeing the torte, Scotty rose and followed Thornton up the stairs. When they reached the foyer, Scotty saw more men in dark suits wearing sunglasses, despite nightfall. Perhaps because of the media lights. Reporters crowded the windows like kids outside a toy store.

Thornton led on toward a knot of more dark-suited men. As Scotty drew close, the knot unraveled to reveal a tall gentleman in a grey suit. The man turned, grinned wide, and extended a hand. Scotty recognized him, taking the hand before realizing it.

Thornton beamed to say, "Scott, let me introduce the next president of the United States…"

Scotty froze mid-shake, media watching, camera lights glaring.

"…Roger was in Memphis campaigning, and came up to pay his respects."

"Mighty pleased to meet you, Prophet," Filby drawled, "I'm a huge fan."

Scotty recoiled and let go of the hand like it was leprous. The dark suits moved to block the cameras, and Thornton sputtered, "Roger simply wanted to meet you, Scott. He's an admirer."

"The Lord forbids it," Scotty cried.

Thornton turned to Filby, agog. "Best you go, Roger. I'll call..."

Filby appeared fuddled, and as his entourage hustled him off, he gushed over a shoulder, "Well sir, it was a real honor—"

Scotty leaned into Thornton. "We have to talk. If it's not already too late."

Looking stricken, Thornton nodded and ushered him away.

• • •

Reverend Thornton led the Prophet out a rear door of the building, feeling the cool night air sizzle on his cheeks. They passed through a garden toward the serenity of golf greens.

"Forgive me," he told Scott again, "I had no idea—"

He caught himself. That wasn't true. Indeed, he'd considered the risk of springing Filby on his guest, and had forged ahead regardless. Thornton needed a bone to toss the Council after the disastrous debate, and what better way to bolster Filby's poll numbers than to pair him with the celebrated Prophet? Bring the two men together, let the ever-present media imply a relationship.

A dreadful miscalculation. Whatever Judgment the Lord sent the Prophet to pronounce on him, Thornton had surely made it worse.

They walked in silence out onto soft grass, the scent of fallen leaves on the breeze, distant mercury vapor lights throwing long shadows. The Prophet broke the stillness.

"If I can cut to the chase, Reverend, the Lord wants something from you."

Thornton felt a shiver in his soul. Indeed, he owed the Lord. In all this time, he'd never truly reconciled his Great Sin, concealing it from the world these many years, hiding his shame. And now, his day of recompense had come. He sighed. The revelation would humiliate him before his countless supporters. Destroy him. But better to settle his score in this life than the next.

He replied in a whisper, *"I know."*

"The angel said you would."

Thornton hung his head. "How should we do this? Hold a press conference?"

"That won't be necessary. The Lord wants to keep it quiet. Just give it to me."

Thornton puzzled. "You mean, give you my Confession?"

Now Scott looked confused. "No-no. The videotape. I've come for the videotape."

Thornton pulled up short. "The *tape? That's* what the Lord wants?"

Scott halted, too. "The Shackleton tape, yes. Original and all copies, to take back with me."

Even in the low light, Thornton knew the shock on his face was evident. No mention of his Sin. Of course, God in His omniscience knew of the video, and of the Council's plan to release it. And it appeared the Lord was more intent on preventing that wrong than righting another.

"There's only one copy," Thornton said. "Locked in my office." The Prophet seemed relieved. "Except, I can't give it up yet."

"But it's the Lord's Will. He sent me on this Mission."

"Yes, and of course, I respect the Lord's wishes. It's complicated. I chair a powerful Council of churches. Twelve of the country's largest ministries. We're deeply vested in Filby's election, and the tape is our insurance. Its contents can guarantee us victory—"

The boy covered his ears. "I can't know what's on the tape, I just need you to give it to me. You wouldn't deny the Lord, right?"

"Let me explain. I'm sworn on the bible, a sacred oath before my Council. Filby is down in the polls, and unless he takes a substantial lead by Sunday a week, I must release the tape to the public. I've given my solemn word, the Council will hold me to it. *The Lord will understand.*"

Butterfield hesitated. "There's more. In exchange for the tape, The Lord is willing to grant you a Covenant."

A Covenant. The words pierced Thornton's heart, and he held a hand to his chest. God's most sacred bond with man, like the Covenant of the Ark. To Thornton's knowledge, God hadn't made such an accord in two millennia. He stammered, "Wh-what does the Lord propose?"

"It's simple. Hand over the tape, and the Lord will bless Filby with victory. Otherwise..."

Thornton was astonished. "I need more time. Once I present the Covenant to the Council, surely they'll release me from my oath."

Scott shook his head. "The Covenant is between you and the Lord, alone. Reveal its terms, and Filby will lose."

The reverend began to pace. The Prophet joined him. They circled the green in silence for a time, then Thornton stopped. "I have it," he said. *"Raise Filby's poll numbers.* The three swing states are all that matter. An easy feat for the Lord. If He'll grant me that tiny blessing, I won't have to break my vow. I'll be free to give you the tape."

"You want the Lord to raise Filby's poll numbers? To what?"

"To fifty-four percent. By a week from tomorrow."

Chapter 90

Their jet descended into fog, New York's dismal weather lingering on. Scotty had been quiet on the flight home. Ivy watched him slouched in the seat next to her, looking like he hadn't slept. Her attempts to engage him had met little success, and discouraged, she'd given up.

Last night in their hotel after the festivities, he'd told her of the roadblock he'd run into with Thornton and the tape. How he worried about facing Ariel empty-handed, how the Lord would receive the news. Not to mention Scotty's forbidden encounter with Roger Filby.

Ivy felt guilty. Scotty was returning in turmoil while she'd just had the time of her life. Though she had to admit, she'd felt bogus yesterday chumming with all that wealth and privilege, knowing that the poor wretches outside Scotty's building were huddled in the rain, far removed from the sparkling, sunny City of God.

"Well," she told Scotty, "we can feel good about one thing, anyway. Ms. Willoughby."

It got a nod out of him, and she added, "Did you see how close she and the reverend are? So sweet. I wonder why they aren't married, they're both single."

"How do you know they're single?"

"The mayor's wife said. Thornton lost his family years ago. I guess he never got over it."

Scotty shrugged, and she punched his shoulder. "Come on, snap out of it. You did your best."

"You don't know the whole of it," he told her, eyes troubled. "Like you said before, *there's something fishy going on.*"

"I don't know because *you won't tell me.*"

"I'll say this much, the tape deal feels like a deal with the Devil, and I don't mean Thornton."

They landed at JFK airport and deplaned in mist, grabbed their bags, and headed across wet tarmac—to a surprise welcome. Thousands were at the gates to greet them, erupting at the sight of the Prophet and his shepherd's staff, media on hand to record it.

TSA guards worked them through the bedlam, but Ivy feared Scotty would be late for his crucial session with Ariel. And then suddenly, a big, uniformed policeman and short man in a long coat blocked their path. The short man raised a badge and an official-looking document, and the TSA guards stood aside.

Ivy's heart sank. A truant officer. And stepping out from behind the cop, *Pop.*

"You can't do this," Ivy cried. "I'm an adult."

The cop said, "Sorry, Ms. Butterfield, the papers are in order."

She felt a hand on her shoulder. "No use fighting," Scotty said. "We knew this was coming."

Pop came forward and snarled at him. *"No more.* You keep away from her, by God. Or next time, they'll be coming for *you.*"

The cop led Ivy away, and she turned to wish Scotty luck. But he'd vanished. Last she saw, the top of his staff hovered above the melee like a question mark.

The turmoil at the airport cost time, and now Scotty's cab was slowed by fog and traffic, threatening his already-problematic session with Ariel. Then just a block from his apartment, his cab screeched to a halt. Scotty groaned to see the street filled with thousands of milling souls. And as the cab crept forward again, people recognized Scotty, swarming, begging his attention.

The cabbie locked the doors, frowning at Scotty in the rearview mirror. "Hope your angel's on your shoulder today," he said.

"No. I'm supposed to meet her at home by 10:00."

"I'll do my best, but it don't look good."

The cab inched on, crowd pressing. Suddenly a man banged on Scotty's window, panic in his face. "I lost my job, my home," he cried. *"I've got nothing."*

Scotty felt for him. One week ago, he was nearly in the same spot. The man was replaced by new supplicants, and the cabbie yelled over the chaos, "Government don't do nothin' for nobody no more. These people got nowhere to go, now the governor's threatenin' to clear the streets."

"What's the mayor have to say about that?"

"He told the governor to stay out of it, leave people alone—he's changed his tune after what you did for 'im. But he can't help 'em, city's broke. All these people got is you."

Scotty gripped his shepherd's staff in both hands. "No one understands. *I've got no powers.*"

The man's eyes held hope. "Sometimes, you know, the way to get power is to seize it."

Progress was slow to the apartment building, the clock well past 10:00. Fortunately, cops were still on duty, and helped muscle Scotty inside. He trudged upstairs and into his apartment as fast as his weary legs allowed, knowing he was too late.

Homer awaited him inside the door. *You look like crap.*

"I feel like crap."

Dropping his bag and staff, Scotty went to his computer and woke it. As expected, the videochat window was silent, link dead. But an email alert was flashing. Another epistle:

> where are you
> where is the tape

Scotty got Homer food, dragged to the couch and flopped, head in hands. Shortly Homer appeared, licking his chops.

Bad trip?

Scotty sighed. "I failed my Mission, and now I missed my session. I'm in *big* trouble."

And swearing, he lay back on the couch and stared at the ceiling.

• • •

The next thing Scotty knew, it was overcast outside, a bright light in his window. Thunder crashed, and he could hear the throngs in the street crying and wailing. Louder than before, more than misery in their voices. Fear. *Panic.*

He jumped up and peered through the blinds. The crowd was bigger than ever, more agitated than ever. Sirens and horns blared in the distance.

Scotty bolted to the door and down, exiting onto the front stoop to find Mrs. Steiner and his other neighbors drawn out by the clamor, too. Also, the cabbie who'd driven him from the airport. Ivy with Homer in her arms. Reverend Thornton and Ms. Willoughby. Reggie and Zing, and Margo. On the sidewalk stood the homeless man he'd given money to, yelling up at him, "Troopers are comin' for us, we've nowhere to go. *Do something!*"

Someone shouted, "Save us, Prophet! Lead us!"

What could he do? Lead them *where?* He was no more leader than prophet.

Another cried, "To the promised land! To the land of milk and honey!"

Ivy pleaded, "Help them, Scotty, *there's no one else.*"

The sirens grew louder, and Scotty found his shepherd's staff in his hand. As if possessed by a higher power, he stamped it against the steps. The crowd stilled and looked to him, and he called down to them, *"To the mayor's office."*

They opened a pathway for him, and Scotty raced down to the street, turning west into fog. The people fell in behind, sirens and klaxons closing. He picked up the pace, looking for the Queensboro Bridge. He should have reached it by now, but nothing looked familiar in the mist.

Lost, he stumbled down an embankment and came to a halt at a shoreline. The procession stacked up behind him, and abruptly the fog dissipated to reveal the choppy waters of the East River, the island of Manhattan gleaming on the other side through dark, menacing clouds. Scotty froze, he and his exodus trapped.

Homer cried, *They're coming!*

Frantic, Scotty tapped his inner power once more, stretching his staff over the waters, commanding in a loud voice, *"Behold the power of the Lord."*

Instantly the river began to roil and boil, drawing back from itself across the channel like a drape parting. A passage opened, flanked by walls of surging water. The crowd cheered, the sky rumbled, and Scotty felt a great heaviness in his heart.

He opened his eyes to find himself on his couch in the daylight of his window, Homer sitting on his chest.

A last growl of thunder rolled through the apartment, and as Scotty's head cleared and the sound faded, he realized he'd just missed his afternoon session with Ariel, too.

CHAPTER 91

"We were fools letting him overnight down there," Max snapped, glaring out the tent door.

The second run of the day just ended, and still no word from Scott Butterfield. Albeit, the team knew he was back from the City. They'd seen updated archives of his arrival at JFK, including Ivy being apprehended by her father. Discord in the family. Had that drama impacted their Plan?

Ariel was at the table in angel mode, all dressed up, and no Butterfield. A videochat window sat dormant on her screen, and finally she clicked out of it to expose beneath a new/old *Times* article from four years ago. A photo showed Butterfield shaking hands with Roger Filby. Not only had he disobeyed the Lord's command to avoid politicians, he'd sided with the enemy for the whole world to see. And then skipped his last two sessions with Ariel.

"What do we do if he's quit us?" Tia cried. "We're screwed."

"The hell we are," Max said. "There are four PhDs in this room," he paused to glance at Ariel. *"Three.* And we're gonna let a Bronx College dropout beat us? A week till Thornton releases that damned tape. It's time for some fire and brimstone."

Ariel didn't know what he had in mind, but it couldn't be good.

Stan said, "Let's give him one more chance."

Ariel and Tia agreed, and Max snapped, "His *last* chance. 10:00 tomorrow. He shows, or we go Wrath of God on him."

And he stormed out of the tent.

CHAPTER 92

K assandra sat outside the office of Franklin Percy in a knot, star-ing at the brass nameplate on the man's door. She could hear muffled voices inside. Loud at times, if unintelligible.

This was her first visit to what employees here at Endicott, Percy & Moore called *Valhalla*, an opulent penthouse suite of glass, brushed-steel, and fine art. Percy's secretary sat at a desk nearby, fielding constant phone calls. Yesterday, while Kassandra was working at her desk, the secretary had hand-delivered an envelope to her with a cryptic note that kept her up last night:

Franklin Percy's office, tomorrow, 8:00 AM, sharp.

Kassandra had arrived early, only to be informed that a prior meeting was running late. She'd spent the last hour trying to stifle her anxiety.

At last, Percy's door opened and a train of sobersided depart-ment heads filed out, intern supervisor Shonda among them. She paid Kassandra a slicing glare as she passed. Moments later, the secretary's phone buzzed, and she told Kassandra, "Your turn."

Kassandra rose on balky legs, smoothed her second-hand designer dress, inhaled, and slipped through the door into a room with a panoramic view of the city. The walls were filled with oil paintings by modern masters, some of which Kassandra recognized. Percy sat at a glass and steel desk, a dozen empty chairs facing him. He looked every inch a giant of his industry, diminutive stature notwithstanding. Thick hair swept back, gray and distinguished, rimless glasses, finely tailored suit. He was signing papers, and said without looking up, "Close the door, take a chair."

Kassandra did as told, and momentarily Percy straightened, tugged his glasses down his nose, and stared over them to regard Kassandra blankly.

"All right, Ms. Kraft, brass tacks. Your Prophet's trip to Tennessee was a disaster for us. It moved the polls—now Filby *leads* Shackleton in all key states. I want to know what's going on, and I warn you, *the whole story.*"

Kassandra moistened her lips to deliver rehearsed lines. "Like I told Shonda yesterday, the Filby thing was unplanned. Butterfield had no warning, they blindsided him. It was no more than a handshake, I don't care what the Filby campaign says—"

"You met with Butterfield after he returned?"

"Yes sir, last night." Finally, after Butterfield ignored her all day.

"And still he hasn't set a date to meet Shackleton?"

Kassandra had no answer, and Percy sat back in his chair. "On account of *your* assurances," he said, "this firm went out on a limb. I *personally* stuck my neck out. Shackleton agreed to a meeting, and you leave us hanging." His eyes boiled. "You've no idea the damage we face."

She held up a trembling hand. "I give you my word, I'll get the meeting."

"*When?*"

"I have a plan. I'm still working out details, I need more time."

"The election's a week away."

Kassandra lowered her eyes, and after an uncomfortable silence, Percy exhaled and said, "Tell me your plan. Spare me nothing. And make no mistake, young lady, this is your *last* shot."

CHAPTER 93

Scotty slumped in front of his computer, picking at a soggy bowl of cereal. In minutes, he'd face Angel Ariel once more, having failed to acquire the mysterious videotape from Reverend Thornton. Then aggravating the problem by missing his last two sessions with Ariel.

The Lord would *not* be happy.

Homer hopped into Scotty's lap, startling him.

Jeez, dude, you're as jumpy as me on a hot tin roof.

Scotty scratched the cat's head, and sighed. "Day of reckoning. Cross your claws the Lord's feeling merciful this morning."

Just do like the guru says, be positive. You followed the Lord's orders best you could, why should He go Armageddon on you? Make your case to Ariel, she'll run interference for you.

Hopefully. Scotty *did* sense sympathy from the angel.

Ariel. Such a strange, alluring creature. He'd seen misgivings in her from the very beginning. It seemed she didn't want to be a Paraclete any more than Scotty wanted to be a Prophet. As if she were a pawn in all this, too, same as him, caught in the *same* trap. Helpless. Expendable.

Scotty was lost in thought when he felt Homer's eyes.

439

The cat gave him a sly grin. *You're sweet on her, aren't you?*

"What? Who?"

Come on, bro, Ariel. I've seen the way you look at her.

Scotty frowned. "How do I look at her, smart ass?"

Like a puppy dog. You don't look at Kassandra the same way, now do you?

"How do I look at Kassandra?"

Like a wolf.

Scotty blinked. "That's, that's *nuts*. Ariel isn't human. She isn't even *alive*. She might as well be a, a, a *cloud*—"

He broke off, struck by his own analogy. In fact, Ariel *was* a cloud. A vapor, a spirit that would vanish from Scotty's life once his role in the Lord's business was over. *If* he survived. Ariel and her penetrating gaze, lost to the ethers, never to be seen again. In this lifetime.

Suddenly thunder pealed inside the room, and Homer fled. Scotty rubbed his thighs, wiped his eyes, and turned a heavy heart to his monitor as the noises played out.

Once more he experienced that familiar rush as the angel materialized on screen. She said nothing, brow in a scintillating frown.

Worry, or anger?

Scotty began, "Sorry about missing the sessions. Pop grabbed Ivy at the airport when—"

"The tape? Did you get the tape?"

"I, I'm afraid we have a problem."

He watched her clasp her hands, and thought he heard a male voice swear in the background. He pressed on. "I did exactly what you told me. I even used the Covenant, but I hit a hurdle. It's not that Thornton won't hand over the tape, he *can't*."

"For heaven's sake, why not?"

"The election. Thornton says Filby and Shackleton are too close in the swing state polls, and unless Filby pulls into a safe lead, Thornton's sworn to take the tape public."

"Sworn to whom?"

"A Council of religious leaders. They think the tape holds the key to Filby winning."

Ariel looked confused.

"A tiny setback," Scotty assured. "All the Lord has to do is raise Filby's poll numbers in the three swing states, and Thornton will surrender the tape."

"Raise them to what?"

"Fifty-four percent, by this Sunday morning."

"Impossible."

"Not for the Lord."

Scotty thought he heard a male voice again, and Ariel said, *"Why did you meet with Roger Filby? You violated the Lord's trust. You've made matters worse."*

"I had no idea he'd be there, I swear. He ambushed me."

Ariel seemed distraught, glancing around. *"The Lord is* not *pleased. I'll get back to you at 2:00 with his judgment. Do nothing more till you hear from me. Give me your word."*

Scotty promised, and she signed off.

A temporary stay of execution.

He sat silent as the noises returned and left. Then came a knock at his door, and he dragged to the peephole to see Kassandra, an anxious, determined glint in her eyes.

CHAPTER 94

Ariel ended her session with Butterfield, and Max flung his antenna to the floor.

"Is there *nothing* that idiot can't screw up?" he stormed.

Tia said, "There's got to be a way we can boost Filby's poll numbers. How hard can it be? Look at the bump Filby got just shaking Butterfield's hand. We get them to sit down together—"

Max snarled, "Drive Filby's numbers any higher, he'll win again anyway, tape or not."

"Not necessarily," Stan said. "Assuming history repeats, Shackleton will crush Filby in the final debate and retake the lead."

Max threw up his hands. "The debate is *Saturday night*. You heard what Butterfield said, the Council will rule on the tape *Sunday morning*. No way they'll give it up after the drubbing Filby takes in the debate. Either we get it *before* the debate, or it's all over."

Quiet. Then Tia said, "Why not let Butterfield present the Covenant to Thornton's Council?"

"Give them that Covenant," Max snapped, "they'll run to the media faster than you can say *God endorses Filby*. Filby won't just win, he'll coattail both chambers of Congress in a landslide."

Ariel suggested, "Scott can swear the Council to silence. They're men of the cloth, after all."

"Yeah—the same pious men who want to tar Shackleton with that tape. I guarantee you, when Filby tanks in the debate, their cloth will leak like a sieve."

"It won't matter once we've got the tape," Tia countered. "If the Council breaks its word, we'll make Butterfield come out for Shackleton. Who will voters listen to, Thornton and his cronies, or the infallible Prophet of Queens?"

That gave Max pause.

Stan added, "Unless you've got a better idea, it's a chance we've got to take. And whatever we do, we better do it fast. There was another Timequake last night, the biggest yet."

The three looked at Max, and at length, he swore and said, "All right, all right. But the way Butterfield's bungled things, we don't dare trust him with this. Thornton knows best how to deal with his Council, let *him* present the Covenant."

CHAPTER 95

Scotty sat at his computer staring at a blank videochat window, waiting for Ariel to arrive and render a verdict on his failed Mission. He'd no idea what to expect, but surely not to be released from his duties with the job unfinished.

A loud knock at his door rattled him, and he swore. Kassandra again, no doubt. The woman was impossible. Three times today she'd come by pleading to talk, and each time he'd turned her away without opening the door, insisting he was busy. After Ariel's warning to do nothing until further orders, and with the Lord already angry, Scotty was taking no chances.

The knock came again, louder, and a familiar voice piped, *"Let me in, will ya?"*

Scotty hurried over and flung wide the door to see Ivy in her school uniform.

"What are *you* doing here?" he cried.

She popped in, closed the door, and wrapped him up. "I woulda come sooner, but I couldn't shake my truant officer. Had to crawl out a bathroom window."

Scotty could only imagine the hell the old man would unleash on him this time.

Ivy shucked her things, eyeing him with a grin. "Appears the Lord didn't smite you after all."

"Not yet. I missed *both* sessions yesterday—long story, not important. When finally I reported to Ariel this morning, she said the Lord was pissed." Scotty glanced at the clock. "And I'm about to find out how bad."

Another knock at the door gave them both a start.

Ivy stopped Scotty with a hand, whispering, "It could be Pop!" She tiptoed over, leaned into the peephole, and made a sour face. "That vamp from down the hall."

Scotty whispered back, "Ariel will be here soon, get rid of her."

Ivy chained the door and opened it a crack. "Yes?"

Scotty heard Kassandra's lilting voice, "Scott, please."

"He's busy," Ivy replied.

"But I *have* to speak to him, it's *very* important." She tried to push in, chain preventing her.

"Leave a message," Ivy said.

Manicured fingers thrust an envelope through the crack.

"It's *urgent*. Can I trust you to give it to him right away?"

Ivy snatched the envelope and sniffed, "He'll get back to you," and slammed the door.

Just in time. The thunder rolled, and Ivy and Scotty grabbed chairs at his computer.

CHAPTER 96

Again Ariel sat at the table in the tent under the lights, inhaling the scent of warm canvas. The wormhole opened, and Max inserted an antenna, awakening the videochat on Ariel's laptop. Stan stood ready with a grabber pole to retrieve the rabbit's foot, and next to him, Tia smiled her encouragement to Ariel, giving her a thumbs-up.

Ariel returned a sober nod. With Time closing in, her hopes for their moon landing had all but evaporated. It now came down to a long shot—Thornton prying the tape from his Council with the crowbar of the Covenant. To lend Ariel added leverage today, Max was having her apply a desperate, heavy-handed tactic that made her all the more uncomfortable.

Digging deep, she watched Scott Butterfield appear on screen, and froze to see his sister beside him. It seemed the girl had escaped her father again. An unexpected curve. Ivy would *not* welcome a Covenant intended to throw the election to Filby.

Ariel mouthed to her teammates in panic, *"Ivy."*

Max went livid, mouthing back, "Get her the hell out of there!"

Ariel greeted the Butterfields in a fret. "I, I didn't expect to see you here, Ivy."

"And miss the final act?"

"Scott's Mission isn't over, not till he's in possession of the tape. The Lord has new instructions for him, and they're confidential. I must ask you to leave this session."

Ivy stiffened. *"What am I, second class? Why haven't I earned the Lord's trust, too?"*

Scott bent forward. *"Ivy has as much at stake in this as I do. She has a right to know."*

His eyes were adamant, and Ariel looked to the team. Stan and Tia looked to Max, and Max swore, looked at the clock, bared his teeth, and waved Ariel on.

Ariel took a long breath and turned back to the screen. "The Lord has come to a decision," she said. "Given Reverend Thornton's oath to his Council about the tape, the Lord has decided to extend His Covenant to them, also. The terms remain the same: the Council must surrender the tape immediately.

"In return..." the words stuck in Ariel's throat, "the Lord will grant Roger Filby victory in the coming election. After which, Reverend Thornton, his Council and their churches shall prosper in the blessings of the Lord, forevermore."

Ivy's mouth fell open, and Ariel pressed on. "But the Covenant comes with a warning. If for any reason the Council fails to deliver the tape to Scott before 10:00 AM this Saturday, November 1st, not only will Filby lose the election," Ariel faltered again, "the, the Lord will bring down His Wrath upon the entire Council and their churches, and *all* shall fall to ruin."

Now Scott's jaw dropped. He and Ivy exchanged alarmed looks, and he asked, *"What if the Council refuses to see me? The reverend says they rarely meet, and only in private."*

"That's not an issue. The reverend, alone, is to present the terms to his Council. Your only duty now, Scott, is to inform him of the Lord's decision, report his progress to me at our sessions, and await the tape. Beyond that, you're to remain in seclusion and talk to no one. Once you have the tape, I'll deliver final instructions, and your Mission will be over."

The Butterfields gaped at Ariel, and she hastened to add, "The Lord thanks you for your time and services, for which He will soon bestow a great blessing upon you both."

That didn't seem to placate them, and Ariel asked, "Are there any other questions?"

Scott snapped, *"As a matter of fact, yes. Is it asking too much to know the point of all this?"*

Ariel saw Max mouth *No!* But she felt she owed the man a response.

"The point," she replied, "is to save the country from a Dark turn of events. Success of the Lord's final Mission will ensure a far brighter future for all."

The Butterfields seemed to mull that. Then Scott said, *"And what about Ivy and me? What becomes of us once the Lord's finished? You know our future, tell us."*

Flashing into Ariel's mind was the fire in the man's building nine days away, destined to take his life, his sister's, and neighbors'. To forewarn him was the "great blessing" the Lord would bestow. But to tell him now was to risk spooking him at this critical juncture, which Max underscored with frantic shakes of the head.

Ariel replied, "I can't say yet, not till this is over. I'll be in touch."

Scott and Ivy must have read the anxiety in her eyes, Ariel saw it reflected in theirs. Ivy stammered, *"Wh-what is it? Something's wrong. Please tell us what's coming!"*

Before Ariel could respond, her screen began to quiver, table and keyboard trembling. And to her horror, she realized, *Timequake.*

Max slashed a finger across his throat to cut the session, and Ariel made a stab at her keys—a moving target.

Suddenly a more violent tremor upset the table, and she and her computer tumbled to the ground.

CHAPTER 97

Ivy watched Scotty rooting under his desk, checking wires. Moments ago, during their session with the angel, his videochat window abruptly convulsed and went blank.

She bent down to ask, "Anything?"

"Nothing." He crawled out and retook his seat as the rumbles and whines returned and faded. "I think she dumped us."

Ivy felt a chill. She'd seen the look on Ariel's face when Scotty asked her about their fates, just before the transmission dropped. "Something *bad* is gonna happen to us," she whispered. "Ariel knows, and she couldn't deal with it. She cut us off."

Scotty was slow to respond. "Didn't she say the Lord was going to bestow a great blessing on us? She won't let anything happen, not Ariel."

He didn't sound convincing. Ivy felt her heart shrink. "If the Lord chooses to make martyrs of us, what choice does she have?"

"The Lord *owes* us," Scotty snapped. "Not just for these Missions, for what He took from us seventeen years ago." He locked eyes with Ivy. "For whatever reason, the Lord wants that tape, and He wants it to go through *me*. If I do get it, we've got a bargaining chip. I say we create our own Covenant. In return for the tape, the Lord gives *us* a bright future, too. Same deal He made with Thornton and his cronies, and all the countless other chosen people down through the ages."

The idea of imposing a condition on the Lord seemed ill-advised to Ivy. "What if He just smites us and takes the tape?"

"Why didn't He just smite Thornton and take the tape to begin with? Why involve us at all? It makes no sense to me. Not that anything about God ever has."

"Like throwing the election to Filby. How divine is *that?*"

Ivy's awe was wearing thin, too. If, in fact, their futures were bleak, what did they stand to lose by haggling with the Lord?

Scotty gave Ivy's hand a squeeze, only to stop and ask, "What's *this?*"

Ivy had forgotten the envelope Kassandra had given her, now crumpled in her fist. Smoothing it, she passed it over.

He opened what looked like a fancy invitation, trimmed with ghosts, goblins, and demons.

"Well?" Ivy said.

"Seems I'm invited to a party."

"*That's* what Kassandra's so amped about? Lemme see."

He handed it back, and Ivy felt her eyes bug. "Not just *any* party. *Webster Hell*, VIP floor!"

Scotty scrunched his face. "What the hell is *Webster Hell?*"

"You from another planet? It's the biggest, baddest Halloween costume party in the world."

Every kid in her school knew about Webster Hell, aka the Devil's Playground. An outrageous spectacle staged annually at Manhattan's oldest, largest nightclub, Webster Hall. Each October 31st since 1886—with the lone exception of the Covid crisis—the Hall's four stories of bars and dance floors metamorphosed into a massive blowout unlike any other.

"Lots of celebrities go," she said. "Rock stars, movie stars, sports stars. People *kill* for tickets. A VIP pass costs thousands, *if* you can get one. You gotta do this!"

He shook his head. "Ariel has me in solitary."

"Fine, then *I'll* take your place."

Scotty snatched back the invitation. "You're underage. Anyway, I don't have to respond tonight, I'll run it by Ariel."

Turning the card over, he saw a handwritten note, and his brow furrowed. "Kassandra says, *Come as you are.* I thought you said it was a costume party."

CHAPTER 98

Ariel was still shaking as she and her team picked up the tent. A Timequake had sent her laptop crashing to the floor, abruptly ending her session with Scott Butterfield. Strongest quake they'd yet recorded, tipping the seismograph at five-point-eight, followed by a Timewave.

Timequakes were caused by changes to the past impacting the membrane that separates past from present. In turn, Timequakes generated Timewaves—vast pulses of energy sweeping down the Timeline, updating history as it went. This was Tia and Stan's first hands-on experience with the phenomena.

"I've never been so scared in my life," Tia said, holding a hand to her heart. "Those giant swells coming at us from every direction!"

Max noted, *"Twice* the size of the wave Ariel and I faced."

The Timewave appeared to pass harmlessly, but the team had no way to know its effects until they left the protection of the Trapping Horizon. So long as they remained inside, they and their memories were shielded.

"I have a confession," Stan said. "I was trying to grab the rabbit's foot from the wormhole when the quake struck." He paid Ariel a sheepish look. "I dropped it. It's still on the other side."

Ariel's stomach knotted. But she assured him, "No worries, you'll retrieve it next run."

Max wasn't so forgiving. "Make *sure* you do. If Butterfield gets hold of it, *we're screwed.*"

Indeed. The flashdrive contained four years of *New York Times* archives. Also, Ariel's journal detailing the team's activities in the wormhole, and sensitive documents regarding her stepfather.

The tent was back in order at last, and Max brushed off his hands and pointed to the door. "How about it? Ready to step outside the bubble and see what surprises the Timewave left us?"

Ariel wasn't. The team had no clue how leaving the Trapping Horizon would affect them. They might experience minimal changes like before—hairstyles, minor memory adjustments. Or something far more consequential.

"Nothing to be gained putting it off," Max said. "I suggest we pass through one at a time and assess developments as we go."

Not waiting for an answer, he left the tent for the Horizon line.

The others exchanged antsy glances and rushed to follow. Stan caught up to Max and placed a hand on his arm, stopping him.

"Allow me," he offered, and for once, Max let him take point. Stan turned to face the group, paid them a brave smile, shut his eyes, and backed across the threshold, halting on the other side.

He opened his eyes and blinked. *"Nothing,"* he said with relief. "I don't feel any different."

He didn't look any different. And his memory was intact enough to recall what he was doing.

But suddenly his phone buzzed, startling everyone. He pulled it out, read its screen, and his face fell. *"Oh no,"* he moaned. "The collider's down again. *Another* quench. *A big one.*"

The others checked their phones to find no such news. A new wrinkle in Time, it appeared. The timing couldn't be worse. With the collider down, the team would be unable to keep tabs on Thornton as he and his Council wrangled over the vital videotape.

"Of all the dammed luck!" Max spit. He stormed across the Horizon to join Stan, reporting no discernible changes, save for the quench. Tia went next, then Ariel. The same.

And seeming no worse for it, they adjourned to the house to hash over their latest setback.

• • •

Updates on the quench were not good. TPC estimated several days for repairs. The mood in the living room was already somber when Tia suddenly announced, "Once the collider's back online, I'm dealing with Mom."

The others went quiet, and Ariel tensed. Tia meant, of course, she intended somehow to avert her mother's suicide. The issue had been hanging fire since it became a bargaining chip in Max's ploy to flip the election. Ariel had been dreading this moment. She'd no idea how Tia proposed to accomplish her goal, but Ariel knew her sensitivity in the matter. And Max's callousness.

Max was quick to respond. "Priorities. We do *nothing* till we've got the election in the bag."

Tia seemed not to hear. "I've thought it all out. I have to contact myself in the past and prove I'm from the future. Lay out the whole story for myself—collider, wormhole, Butterfield, *Mom.*"

Max went red, and Stan asked Tia, "But how do you prove to Past you that Future you is really you? That's a tall order, and you're not exactly, how should I say? *trusting* by nature."

"The answer is to include personal details about myself only *I* could possibly know. Things I'd never tell anyone. I've already written the message. Past Tia *will* pay attention."

Ariel asked, "How do you intend to contact yourself?"

"Via my old email address at the time, at MIT."

Stan reminded, "If you're thinking of hijacking Butterfield's browser to email Past you, there's a problem. The Horizon on his end will block it."

"Already considered that. I'll have him forward my message to me when the session's over."

"After *the election*," Max said.

Tia turned to him. "It's safe for me to proceed once Butterfield gets the tape and destroys it."

Max shook his head. "The risk doesn't end with the tape. What if Butterfield reads your email, learns about the wormhole and how we conned him, and takes it to the media? How's the country gonna react when it learns its precious Prophet is a scam? We'll face *another* Big One."

Tia crossed her arms on her chest. "The Lord can forbid Butterfield to read my message. If we can trust Butterfield not to view the Shackleton tape, we can trust him with my email."

"Even if Butterfield views the tape, there's nothing on it to blow our cover. But your email spills *all* our beans. We wait till the election's over."

"The *hell* I'll wait." Tia's face went crimson, dark eyes flashing. "I'll be *damned* if I'm losing Mom again. I intend to be well out in front of that Time-tsunami."

Ariel saw Tia's dilemma. If they succeeded in flipping the election, and assuming they survived it, the resulting Big One it caused would surely change their lives as they knew them. They might never come to know of the wormhole, denying Tia the chance to save her Mom.

"*Think*," Max said. "Assuming Butterfield gets the tape and destroys it, we aren't out of the woods. What if there's another copy? Or Thornton has some other smoking gun? We've got to keep the Prophet in our pocket until Shackleton is declared the winner."

The atmosphere was heating up, and Stan tried to dampen it.

"Believe me, Tia," he said, "we're all for saving your mom. We're going to find a way. But move too soon, and Max is right, it could cost us the election. What if sending yourself that email causes you to quit grad school and go home, and you never wind up here? It was *you* who found the farmhouse and brought us together to begin with, or none of this would've happened."

Tia wasn't swayed, and Ariel feared it would come down to a vote she herself would have to decide. "Let's find a middle ground," she begged. "Assuming Butterfield gets the tape Saturday morning, we'll have him destroy it. We know Shackleton will crush Filby in the debate Saturday night and surge in the polls. If no other tape or problems surface Sunday, let Tia send her email."

"Ariel has a point," Stan told Max. "If Thornton's Council has another smoking gun, they won't wait to unveil it. Not after the drubbing Filby takes. They'll release it Sunday, noon, like before. If we see nothing from them by then, they're out of time. Tia should be good to go."

Perhaps realizing he'd lose this vote, Max locked eyes with Tia. "It's all moot if the quench isn't fixed, but I'll agree to a compromise. Given there's no bombshell from the Council before the polls open Tuesday, you can proceed with Butterfield at the ten o'clock session."

Before Tia could object, Max said, "*Yes,* the polls will already be open. But barring a rout, which isn't gonna happen, the election won't be called till the polls close on the west coast. That's midnight, *Wednesday,* our time—the earliest the Big One will hit. You'll not only have Tuesday morning's session with Butterfield to send your email, but the afternoon to make sure he did. Well in advance of the Tsunami, and with no time for younger you to screw up our Plan."

Ariel's head was spinning. If she understood correctly, the compromise would give Tia ample opportunity to contact her younger self without jeopardizing the election.

Tia wasn't satisfied. "What assurances do I have Butterfield will send my email?"

Max replied, "What assurances do *I* have he won't read it and give it to the media? That's why they call it a compromise."

Stan reminded them, "We still have leverage over Butterfield. *The fire.*"

Chapter 99

Scotty sat alone in his apartment on the couch, Ivy downstairs having dinner with Mrs. Steiner. Ordered by the angel Ariel to lie low, Scotty had passed on a home-cooked meal, relegated to a cup of soup. Also, as ordered, he'd contacted Reverend Thornton with the revised Covenant. And Thornton, rattled by the Lord's threat of doom, had pledged to contact his Council right away. Now with luck, Scotty would soon have the tape in hand, and the means to barter better futures for Ivy and himself.

A sudden weight in his lap broke his concentration.

Come on, let's play.

Scotty had been neglecting his poor pet. Homer could stand some exercise.

"Go fetch me a mousie."

The cat shook its head. *No-no—The Game.*

Scotty blinked. How long had it been since he'd looked in on Scottworld? Anxious, he lugged Homer to the computer and went to the familiar icon of the eye enclosed in a triangle. For a second, he thought it winked at him, then noticed an asterisk appended to

457

it. He'd never seen that before. Clicking on it, he revealed a message from the game administrators:

Official World Record—Infinitiman: 5,492 days,
2 hours, 12 minutes, 2 seconds.

It was followed by an endless list of congrats and condolences from fans and followers. Frantic, Scotty raced to the blue globe, diving through the atmosphere into Times Square—and *chaos.* The streets were teeming with protesters faced off against police in battle gear. Clouds of tear gas, cars afire. He rushed to the electronic ticker to read of turmoil in Pan Europe, civil war on the Continent bleeding into Northern Africa and the Middle East. And now, North America.

Scotty wilted. His once-thriving, prosperous world had sunk into anarchy.

Do something! Homer growled.

Too late. How many times had Scotty seen this terrible scenario play out on other doomed planets? After more than a decade and a half, Scottworld was finished.

Now both his worlds, real and virtual, had collapsed on him. Devastated, he closed out the game and sat back in shock.

Homer pawed him. *Now what will we do when all this Prophet stuff is over?*

Scotty didn't know. If Ivy was right, they might have no future.

There was another link blinking on his screen. *Selfhelpguru.* If ever he needed advice… He opened it to read:

Step # 87: Do not sit idle in the face of adversity.

Swearing, he dragged the icon to the trash, emptied it, and moved on to his email.

Full. Tons of notices from his matchmaker site, *DateMe.* Messages from women the world over, many young and beautiful and fawning to meet him.

Homer perked. *To hell with The Game, dude, you* are *God!*

A false god. These women didn't care about him. They only wanted something from him. Like Kassandra.

Everything rang false now.

He trashed the emails along with his *DateMe* link, and abruptly his phone rang.

He recognized the number, and his heart jumped.

"Reverend Thornton."

"Hello, Scott, I'm relieved I caught you. Great news! The Council's calling an emergency meeting for us to present the new Covenant. This Wednesday, New York City, noon."

The day after tomorrow, here in town. Great news, indeed. Scotty felt the weight lift slightly.

"But there's a proviso." The weight returned. *"They want to meet you. They insist on hearing the Covenant from the Prophet's mouth."*

Scotty sank in his chair. "I can't. The Lord's angry with me. I'm forbidden to leave my apartment."

"Then here's a chance to get back in His good graces. If we're to seal this Covenant in time, I need you at my side."

Knowing how badly the Lord wanted the tape, Scotty stuck his neck out. "All right," he sighed, "make arrangements. I'll clear it with Ariel tomorrow morning."

Once more Scotty felt hope. Assuming Ariel gave him permission to attend, and the meeting went well, he and Ivy's dreams of a new life might yet come true. He *so* wanted a new life.

On his desk, a wrinkled card caught his eye.

Kassandra's unanswered invitation.

CHAPTER 100

For the second time today, Scotty and Ivy sat in front of his computer staring at a blank screen. Ariel had now missed both morning and afternoon sessions—after assuring yesterday she'd stay in touch. A week until the election, and not a single Cosmic rumble or whine.

Ivy asked, "She ever stand you up like this before?"

"Nope."

"One failed Mission, and the Lord shuns us!"

It reminded Scotty of God's pettiness in the bible story, *Exodus*. The Prophet Moses and the Israelites, having fled bondage in Egypt, were left to wander a desert for forty years. Dying of thirst, they begged God's mercy, and God ordered Moses to strike a rock once with his staff to bring forth water. Fearing once wasn't enough, Moses struck the rock twice, and God was so angered by the trivial affront, He condemned Moses never to enter the Promised Land.

And now if Scotty and Ivy were to enter *their* Promised Land, Scotty had to deal with that same, temperamental God. Not forgetting that Scotty, unlike Moses, wasn't a true prophet.

460

Ivy pleaded with Scotty, "What if Ariel's a no-show again tomorrow morning? The Council meets at noon, and you've *got* to be there. That tape's our only leverage, it's our only hope!"

So, defy the Lord, go to the meeting, and pray it wouldn't cost them as dearly as Moses.

Scotty sighed and said, "I guess it doesn't matter if I'm going to hell anyway."

At that moment, a note came shooting under the door, and Ivy stopped it with a foot. "It's time we took a stand," she said. "Enough of this crap—the only Hell you're going to is in Manhattan. And I'm *not* taking no for an answer!"

Snatching up the note, she sprang to the door and left, Scotty too weary to prevent her.

CHAPTER 101

The conference room was packed. A war room prepping for battle. Present were EP&M's principles and executives, the Shackleton presidential campaign director and coordinators, and other special project directors and production advisors. And Kassandra Kraft. The stakes were enormous, air tense-if-optimistic as the long meeting wound to a close.

Kassandra was exhausted. She'd promised EP&M a photo op of Shackleton with the Prophet, and Friday night at Webster Hall was where she intended to do it. A Halloween party wasn't the best venue, Shackleton wasn't thrilled about it. But it was a carrot Kassandra had trusted Butterfield would find irresistible. People sold their souls for tickets. And her instincts had proven correct.

Yesterday afternoon, after Butterfield continued to drag his heels, and Kassandra paced her apartment, and Shonda called obsessively, Kassandra finally caught a break. Butterfield's sister appeared at her door to announce he'd accepted the invitation. With a condition.

"Scotty's not exactly what you'd call a hellraiser," the girl had informed Kassandra, unnecessarily. "You damn-well better bring him home good as you got him!"

Scrappy little shit, that one. And by the look in her eyes, she meant business. Kassandra was so overjoyed she'd hugged the girl, who did not reciprocate.

It was now balls-to-the-walls. EP&M and the Shackleton team were working around-the-clock juggling the candidate's itinerary, coordinating Secret Service protection, and myriad other logistics. It helped that Webster Hall was an EP&M client. Shackleton would have private access to a secured room through a backdoor, all provisions handled in strict secrecy, knowing Butterfield wanted no part of politicians. EP&M would have to spring a trap on him in the manner of Filby's ambush in the City of God.

But unlike Filby's handlers, who'd left the media to document the encounter, EP&M was leaving nothing to chance. No media allowed. Contract videographers and photographers only to record the event. That way, even if Butterfield proved less than cooperative, the public would see otherwise via the magic of computer-edited enhancement. An enormous amount of effort and expense for what would likely amount to just seconds of video.

Invaluable video. The potential return on investment was huge. Last weekend, Filby's brief and questionable encounter with the Prophet was enough to edge him past Shackleton in the swing-state polls. And now with Shackleton facing a Crusade in those states, she badly needed the Prophet Bump.

Franklin Percy rapped his knuckles on the table, rousing Kassandra from her thoughts. Everyone quieted and turned to him, and he turned to Kassandra.

"All right, my dear," he said, eyes grave, "the rest is in your hands. Keep us posted on developments. The slightest thing, I want to know. And anything you need, at any time."

Kassandra mustered her most confident smile, and everyone filed out, offering well wishes.

Shonda was last to leave, paying Kassandra a hard glare.

CHAPTER 102

Mrs. Steiner heard the door to the foyer screech, setting down her paper to check. She was expecting a grocery delivery, preparing for dinner guests Saturday night, worried the ice cream would melt. But peeking into the hall, she was surprised to see Joe Butterfield and a cop arguing.

"…don't want any trouble," the cop was saying, "we got our hands full already."

"The T.O. will be here any minute," Joe told him. "He's got the papers."

"Then we'll just wait for him. You don't go upstairs without my say-so, *understood?*"

Mrs. Steiner poked her head out. "Officer O'Malley, okay if Mr. Butterfield waits here with me?"

Joe didn't ask for permission, heading for her, and the cop waved a blind hand and left.

Joe stepped inside the apartment muttering, "Protect and serve, my ass…" Mrs. Steiner closed the door, and he inhaled. "Got any more a that coffee cake?"

"And coffee," she replied with a wink, heading to the kitchen. "Make yourself at home."

Moments later, he called to her. "These photos your husband?"

"Late husband."

A grunt, and, "You're a shrink, eh?"

He must have seen her bookcase. "No-no," she said with a laugh. "An old interest of mine." She returned with a tray of coffee and rolls to find him seated on the couch, joining him to ask, "So, what brings you here today?" As if she didn't know.

He replied with mouth full, "Ivy ran off and skipped school again."

She poured coffee. "That won't help her college plans. But what can you do, she's an adult?"

"Not yet, she ain't. She's got a choice. School, or juvie."

Mrs. Steiner halted mid-pour. "You wouldn't put that sweet girl in detention!"

He grumbled, and she added, "Empty threats won't get you anywhere."

"How the hell else do I make her listen?" He tossed a half-eaten roll onto the tray. "It's the boy. Hoodwinked her. All that prophecy mumbo-jumbo. I *ain't* gonna lose her, she's all I got."

The man hadn't the first clue about his own son. Scott was adamant that Ivy graduate, too.

Mrs. Steiner suggested, "What if you had a heart-to-heart with Scott. He might surprise you." Joe glared at her as if she were insane, and she reasoned, "If your goal is to keep her in school, Scott's your best bet. Without him, she's nowhere to go but home and school. Scott's your key."

"You don't understand, me and him don't talk. We been at odds forever."

She placed a hand on his arm and smiled. "What if I run interference for you? I can feel him out, see if he won't talk. What have you got to lose?"

The man's eyes narrowed, and he sat back. At length, he said, "Okay, fine. You're friends, maybe he'll listen to you. Make him give her back."

Mrs. Steiner shook her head. "It's not my place to speak *for* you." His face clouded, and she added, "I don't know what caused your rift, but it doesn't have to continue. Keep on this path, you risk losing Ivy forever. Believe me, Joe, you don't want to spend your waning years without the ones you love."

She looked to the photos on her walls, his eyes followed, and she said, "Arty was my only family. Cancer. He put off his screening because of the co-pay, and I didn't insist." She teared. "The mistakes we make and spend the rest of our days looking back in pain and regret. It's not too late for you, but the door is closing—"

There came another screech of hinges in the foyer. The truant officer, Mrs. Steiner suspected.

Joe stood, and Mrs. Steiner grabbed a pen and scribbled her phone number on a napkin, handing it to him. "If you'd like to talk some more…"

He stared at her, at the number, and stuffing it in a pocket, he took his jacket and left.

There came voices out in the hall, and Mrs. Steiner held her breath for the clash about to ensue upstairs. But moments later, the door screamed again, and she went to her window to see Joe and a short man in a suit disappearing into the crowd.

CHAPTER 103

Scotty was without his hoody and staff today. Reverend Thornton had advised he leave them behind for their meeting with the Council. Good advice. It facilitated his madhouse scramble from apartment to cab, where he'd joined up with the reverends Thornton and Melcher. And now, forty minutes later, the three were able to cross the busy sidewalk to the Archbishop's mansion undetected.

A priest admitted them through the front door, leading them up a broad sweep of stairs to the third floor. As they paused at the top to catch their breaths, Scotty looked back on the opulence of the entrance hall below. Unlike anything he'd ever seen. A castle. Walls swathed in ornate wood paneling. The grand staircase alone had to cost more than his entire apartment building.

They headed down a red-carpeted hall, and Reverend Melcher turned to ask Scotty, "This is the Lord's final Mission for you?"

He nodded, if not being completely honest. He wasn't here at the Lord's bidding, in fact, he was disobeying the Lord. This morning, Ariel was a no-show again. And unable to get her permission to be here, Scotty could either forgo this meeting as ordered, and risk losing the tape, or do everything in his power to get it.

But from what he'd learned on the cab ride over, he feared his best efforts today might be inadequate. Reverend Thornton warned that to control the destiny of the tape, they'd have to convince at least six other Council members to embrace the Covenant. Further complicating matters, not all members could make the meeting in person, attending remotely by videoconference.

Scotty felt he was about to face the Inquisition.

The hall ended at an anteroom and tall wooden doors. The priest knocked, and Thornton turned to Scotty, placing a firm hand on his shoulder to say, "I know you're anxious, but have faith. The Lord is with you."

Scotty sighed. If Thornton knew he was here against the Lord's wishes...

The priest opened on a lavish conference room, motioning them inside. The room reminded Scotty of a miniature cathedral. Seated around a large table were six dour men, and behind them, a video wall streaming the faces of four more.

The men at the table rose, and Thornton introduced them. Scotty recognized several, especially the large, cherub-faced man at the head of the table, Cardinal Bartholomew Rand, Archbishop of New York. Rand wore a black and scarlet cassock. The others, including Thornton and Melcher, were in suits.

Rand gestured his new arrivals to chairs opposite the video wall, offering coffee and rolls. They declined, and everyone settled in.

"Thank you for accepting our invitation, Mr. Butterfield," Rand said. "We've been following your ministry with great interest. You've created quite a stir."

Scotty faltered under the Cardinal's gaze. Penetrating. Rand seemed to be expecting a response, and when it didn't come, said, "I wonder if you'd tell us a bit more about yourself, the media has been rather stingy with details."

Scotty squared his shoulders. "There's really nothing to tell, sir. As I've always said, I'm no minister or prophet, I'm simply a messenger. I just do as I'm told."

A man next to Rand said, "You take your orders from God, yes?"

"Not directly. The Lord speaks to me through an angel."

Someone else whispered, *"Like Joan of Arc."*

A wispy-haired man asked, "The angel appears to you? In your apartment?"

"I'm forbidden to say." Scotty's eyes drifted to the chandelier and its thousand sparkling crystals. "But I *can* tell you, if you saw her, there'd be no question in your minds. She's divine. Beautiful beyond words. Silver eyes, golden hair, glowing skin. Angelic in every way."

There were whispers, and Rand asked, "Why did God choose *you* as His messenger?"

"For the life of me, I've no idea. I'm the *last* person I'd pick."

Another man said, "But you're a religious man. A man of God."

"No."

"A prayerful man?"

Scotty shook his head. "I don't even attend church. I was raised Catholic, but lost my faith long ago. To be honest, I never put any stock in religion. Till lately."

There was muttering, and Rand pursed his lips. "As you know, the stakes here are enormous. A great deal hangs on what we decide today. Yet you ask us to accept you and this extraordinary *Covenant* on your word, alone. We'd be derelict not to ask for validation. If we're to believe you, give us a Sign. I ask you now, call your angel, work a wonder for us."

A man at the table seconded, as did someone on the video wall. Another said, "Where's your shepherd's staff? Turn it into a serpent, the way Moses did for the Pharaoh."

Thornton was quick to point out, "Dare we ask the Lord to perform parlor tricks?"

Scotty explained, "Like I said, I have no powers. But you've all heard the Lord's prophecies, and you've seen them come true. Isn't that miracle enough?"

Thornton placed a hand on Scotty's shoulder, asking the group, "How else do you explain the tornado he predicted? The illnesses he's diagnosed? He saved my secretary's life, for heaven's sake. Inexplicable feats, miracles, all." He pointed to his briefcase on the table. "The fact that he knows of this tape is proof he's Godsent."

There were murmurs of agreement, but Rand raised a brow to say, "Of course, he couldn't *possibly* have learned about the tape from one of us."

Thornton's hand on Scotty's shoulder tightened, and the reverend replied, "The truth is obvious if only you'd see. Our faith is being tested. At this moment, our Crusade is descending on the swing states. We must have faith it will succeed. We must put our faith in God." He looked to his briefcase again. "This accursed tape is a pact with the Devil."

The room went deathly quiet.

At length, Rand exhaled and said, "If there are no more questions for Mr. Butterfield, I believe we're finished. I move we recess to reflect and pray over our decision."

Receiving no objections, he stood, leveling cool eyes at Scotty. "Thank you for coming, *Prophet*. We'll get back to you in due course."

It was over so suddenly, Scotty rose in panic. "But-but, what do I tell the Lord? My orders are to bring back the tape."

"In God's good time," Rand told him, and turned to Thornton. "Perhaps the reverend would be so kind as to show you out."

Numb, Scotty watched Thornton grab his briefcase and head for the door, motioning him to follow. They proceeded downstairs and outside, where Thornton hailed a cab. As Scotty slid in the back, the reverend remained on the sidewalk, leaning in, gripping Scotty's arm to say, "I'll stay to press our case. Keep the Faith, son, this isn't over."

CHAPTER 104

Tia and Ariel sat in the living room on the couch, Stan nearby in a chair, all on their laptops. Max was holed up in his room with the door closed, brooding, everyone passing the insufferable time in their own ways. The collider was still down for repairs, no contact with Butterfield in four days. The longest they'd been out of touch with him since they began their dodgy scheme.

Ariel was worried about Max. He'd grown increasingly withdrawn, even for him. The man hadn't the patience to wait for a microwave meal, and this prolonged delay made him antsier than she'd ever seen him. But in fairness, with the election three days away, they were *all* antsy about the Shackleton tape, time running out, team running blind.

There'd been no new news of significance in the archives. It appeared Butterfield had been following orders to lay low. No news of Thornton meeting with his Council, but that was expected, given their secrecy. The deadline for him to deliver the tape to Butterfield was Saturday morning, tomorrow. As things stood, however, the team would have no way to know if he complied.

Suddenly Max's door burst open, and he flew down the hall to announce, "TPC finished repairs, runs resume tomorrow at 10:00!"

Stan and Tia cheered, and Ariel sank into the couch with relief. Back on track in the nick of time, hopefully. Now with luck, Scott would greet them tomorrow with the tape, and it would be on to the election—and into the Great Unknown that awaited them.

But Max began pacing, hands clasped behind his back.

Tia said, "Now what's eating you? We just caught a Hail Mary."

He replied, "What if Thornton doesn't get the tape? We have no contingency plan."

Stan said, "What more can we do now? It's the eleventh hour."

Max halted. He always had a fallback. "We tried carrot and stick with the Covenant. If that fails, I suggest a bigger stick." He paid Ariel a look as if anticipating an objection. "I say we hit Thornton and his Council with the ultimate threat."

Ariel was afraid to ask.

"...A threat no God-fearing Christian can ignore."

Ariel's stomach clenched, and she answered for him. "Eternal damnation."

Damnation went to the heart of Christian sensibilities, a fate no Believer could ignore.

Shutting her laptop, she went to her room and closed the door.

CHAPTER 105

I vy sat on the sofa watching Hawk News, Homer purring in her lap as Scotty took a shower. On screen, a big-bosomed blonde reported live outside their apartment building, asking viewers,

"What's up with the Prophet of Queens? Since his triumphant trip to the City of God last weekend, there've been few sightings of Scott Butterfield. The world's most famous seer is holed up in his apartment. Meanwhile, rumors fly. Is the Prophet about to drop a bombshell new prediction? The country wants to know."

Ivy muttered, "And the Prophet wants to know, what's up with Ariel?"

Four days since they'd last heard from her. It seemed that having passed the divine torch to Thornton, the Lord was done with Scotty. Or maybe angry over the continued delays in getting the videotape— Thornton had called earlier to report discussions with the Council were not going well. The Lord's deadline was but sixteen hours away, and without the tape, Ivy and Scotty had no means to negotiate their fate with the Lord.

Ivy's throat tightened. One way or another, their adventure was nearing an end. The crowds, reporters, and cameras would soon melt away, and she and Scotty would fade back into their desolate little lives to await whatever miserable fate Ariel refused to disclose.

Scotty, at least, had something to take his mind off their worries. Tonight was Halloween, and tape or no, he was attending *Webster Hell* with that vamp down the hall. Ivy could hear him in the bedroom changing into the costume he'd ordered online. She was curious to know what it was. He'd given her only a hint, describing it as, "A fitting way to end my captivity."

At last, his door opened, and he clopped into the living room to announce proudly, *"Ta-dah."*

Ivy's jaw dropped, and she exploded in laughter.

Scotty frowned. *"What?"*

She couldn't stop howling. He was in sandals and a long, red-and-white pullover robe cinched at the waist with a gold cord. In his hand was a cheap, telescoping staff that ended in a curly-cue. And most ridiculous, he sported a long white wig and clip-on beard.

"Who the heck are you supposed to be?" she blubbered.

"Moses, of course!"

Again, she erupted in peels. *"Santa Bo Peep,* is more like it."

But seeing him wilt, she headed over, looking him up and down, trying to stifle her laughter.

"Relax," she told him, "I can fix you." She tugged on his fake beard. "Lose this and the wig, they make you look like a clown." She pointed to the faux staff. "That goofy baton—you've got the *real* thing, use it." And rubbing her chin as if making a finessed call, she finished, "Trade the robe and sandals for your hoody, jeans, and sneakers, and presto, *done.*"

His frown deepened. "Go as *myself?"*

"Isn't that what Kassandra said, come as you are?"

"But it's a masquerade. And I don't want to be recognized."

Ivy sighed. "You've no idea, do you? The hot costume this Halloween is *you.* Trust me, there'll be a hundred lookalikes, everybody drunk or stoned, you'll hide in plain sight."

He seemed unconvinced. But snorting, he retreated to the bedroom, returning minutes later, back to himself.

It was time to go.

Ivy smoothed his hair, and handed him his real shepherd's staff.

"There," she told him, "you look *great.*" Giving him a kiss on his scruffy cheek, she shooed him out the door. "Go, have fun, you earned it. To hell with the Lord for one night. To *Webster Hell.*"

She finally got a smile out of him, and he paid her a thumbs-up, and left.

CHAPTER 106

Scotty paused at Kassandra's door to collect himself.

A *second* date. He'd never had one of those before. House-arrest be damned, he was poised to enjoy a night on the town, beautiful woman on his arm, out in the company of other people.

He'd had his fill of orders. Week after week, scurrying to do the Lord's bidding, anything asked of him, to the best of his ability, at no small pain and cost. Only to be grounded like a wayward child. He recalled from the Old Testament, God had two sides. Kind, loving, and merciful. Angry, jealous, and vengeful. A two-faced God. Bipolar. And so far in his relationship with the Lord, Scotty had mostly seen the dark side. The side that took his mother from him.

He saw no such darkness in Ariel. Simply a messenger obeying orders. Like Scotty. But beyond the dazzle of her eyes was a deep ache he identified with. It gnawed at him. There was something *very* off in all this. Something super*un*natural, and he'd no idea what.

Inhaling, he gripped the shepherd's staff in damp hands and rapped it on Kassandra's door. Suddenly there appeared before him a vision. An angel in a white, strapless, gravity-defying slip of a dress. Black lipstick and eye shadow, white pageboy wig, golden

476

wings, a halo suspended above her head on the prongs of a tiara.

Not an angel of Ariel's distinction, of course, no human possessed such ethereal qualities. And none of Ariel's virtue, either—the dress had revealing gauze cut-outs. But by far, the most gorgeous woman he'd ever met in person.

"You look *amazing*," he told her.

"And you look Prophetic," she said with a wry smile. "I'd invite you in for a drink, but our car's waiting, and it's got a stocked bar."

Grabbing a white shawl and matching clutch, she shut the door, looped her arm through his, and whisked him downstairs and out into the night.

The crowd went nuts. Cops rushed to form a protective phalanx, and Scotty threw his arm around Kassandra, shepherding her to a black Escalade, people lurching and screaming. He slid her into the rear compartment and followed, the driver locked the doors, and they inched away.

"*Damn,*" she gasped. Her wings had been crushed in the scrum, and she removed them, tossing them on the seat. "So much for my angelic side," she said with a grin. And opening a minifridge, she removed a bottle, showing Scotty the label.

Laurent-Perrier Grand Siècle.

He'd no idea, he'd only ever tasted *André.*

The cork took all his strength, and when it popped, Kassandra caught spray. She just laughed.

"Before the night's over," she said, blotting herself with napkins, "we'll *both* be soaked."

An intriguing image.

Chapter 107

Mrs. Steiner sat watching cable news when surprised by a light tapping on her door. She glanced at the clock. Who could it possibly be at this hour?

Switching off the TV, she went to check, peeping through the spyhole, astonished to see Joe Butterfield scowling in the hallway. Next to him stood a cop. She opened, and the cop said,

"Sorry to disturb you, ma'am. Mr. Butterfield here says you're expecting him."

She wasn't, but replied, "Yes-yes. Please come in, Joe."

He did, and the cop added, "He's *not* to go upstairs."

As if she could stop him.

The cop left, and no sooner did Mrs. Steiner shut the door than Joe spurted, *"I want my girl back."* His speech was slurred. "I *ain't* meetin' with the boy. Set me up with Ivy, me an' her."

A tall order, and not something Mrs. Steiner felt comfortable doing. But perhaps this was an opening to help the damaged family on a path to recovery. She took his jacket and directed him to the couch. He sat downcast, knee pumping, looking more bedraggled and forlorn than ever.

Mrs. Steiner excused herself to the kitchen and returned with a glass of milk and plate of cookies, setting them in front of him, taking a seat beside him. He picked a cookie and took a bite. Nodded. Another bite. His knee eased.

Mrs. Steiner asked, "Have you been watching Scott on TV?"

His knee resumed pace. "TV's busted. I ain't here 'bout the boy. What do I gotta do to get my girl home?"

Mrs. Steiner sighed. "What happens if Ivy *does* come home?"

"I ain't gonna punish her, if that's what you're gettin' at. She goes back to school, that's all. She graduates."

"And after that?"

"Community college. Then a job where she can live at home. Lots a kids do."

Ivy had higher aspirations, Mrs. Steiner knew. She said softly, "You think that's what Ivy really wants?"

"She's too young to know. *I* know. *I* raised her."

"Yes, and you raised her well. A bright, capable young lady."

"And I damn well mean to keep her that way. I know what's best for 'er."

Mrs. Steiner folded her hands and sat back. "You know, Joe, even if she does come home, she can't stay forever. Sooner or later, she has to make her own way. Children need to become independent. It's healthy."

From out of nowhere he flashed, *"The hell you know what's healthy for her?"*

Mrs. Steiner recoiled. The man was scary mad. But as fast as he'd erupted, he recovered.

"Sorry, Betsy," he moaned, shamefaced. "Forgive me."

She saw profound pain. A sense of dread crept over her. "What is it, Joe?" she whispered, frightened. "What's *really* going on?"

He looked away, and she placed a hand on his arm. "I only want to help."

"Ya *can't*," he cried, turning back, face dark again. "Nothin' *anyone* can do."

Her heart faltered. "There's something wrong with Ivy?"

Burying his face in his hands, he sobbed.

Mrs. Steiner squeezed his arm. "Neither Ivy nor Scott know?"

He shook his head.

She found herself in tears, too, aghast. "*Nothing* can be done?"

"One thing. Keep her with me. She's safe long as she's with me."

"I don't understand."

He mopped tears with a sleeve. "I, I never told nobody, don't know why I'm tellin' you. Ivy's got the same thing took her mom. She don't *dare* get pregnant."

It took a moment for Mrs. Steiner to put it all together. Ivy's mom died giving birth to her. The girl attended an all-girls school, and Joe wanted her in a commuter college, a neighborhood job, living at home on a tight leash under his watchful eye.

He was protecting his daughter from more than Scott.

"My God, Joe, Ivy's a grown woman. You can't hide her away. And you surely can't hide her condition from her any longer. She needs to be on birth control."

"I was workin' up to it when the boy took her. Like he took her mom from me."

Did she hear right? "You blame *Scott* for the loss of your wife?"

"You wouldn't understand."

She looked to the photos on her wall. "I know the pain of personal loss, Joe. Help me understand yours."

He regarded her blankly a moment, then stared out the window.

She nudged, "What was your wife's name?"

"Rose."

"How'd you meet?"

His eyes went more distant. "High school. She sat ahead a me in math. Terrible at it. I helped her, we got to be friends."

"When did you marry?"

"Straight outta school." He took a breath, eyes softer. "Don't know what she saw in me. But we, we were *happy*. Big plans." Again, he

480

darkened, and his shoulders fell. "But she was Catholic. *Very.* No birth control 'cept the rhythm method, which ain't no method at all. Then suddenly, she's pregnant."

"You weren't ready to be parents."

"We had no money. But Rose loved kids, and I was okay with it. Till it went bad."

"Rose didn't know she had a condition?"

He shook his head. *"Pregnancy-induced Autoimmune Anemia.* Born with it. Ivy, too."

Mrs. Steiner knew of the malady. A very serious threat.

He buried his face in his hands. "Rose had to be off her feet. Quit her waitress job, we're livin' off my lousy wages at a brickyard, all on me, medical bills pilin'. I work all day, come home, cook, wash clothes, dishes. No sex no more, afraid we'd lose the baby."

Mrs. Steiner could feel the heat pent up all these years.

"...The birthing near killed her. They do a C-section, lays her up for months, me takin' care a her *and* the boy. Docs say no more kids, and we live on with a shadow hangin' over us. When finally she recovers, she wraps up in the boy."

Mrs. Steiner placed a hand on his fist—a rock. "It surely put huge stress on your marriage."

"Don't get me wrong, Rose loved me, we worked at it. But what we lost, we never got back. Still, we managed. We were lucky for so long, then..."

"Nothing could be done for Rose?" He didn't have to mention his wife's stand on abortion.

His eyes welled again, and Mrs. Steiner fought her own tears. What the poor man must have endured, marking off the days to his wife's delivery like counting down to an execution. Worse than Arty's final months. Rose could have been saved.

Joe said, "Her last words to me, she made me swear to do right by the kids. I *kept* my word. *I did my best.* But you'd never know it by the boy."

Unable to get over his wife's death, Joe had heaped his bitterness onto his innocent son, resentful of his own child. And now, he saw Scott as a threat to his daughter. The problem was worse than Mrs. Steiner had feared, her hopes to reconcile the family, clouding.

He continued, "Ivy's the image a Rose. Hold their high school pics together, same girl. Seeing her's like seeing my Rose again."

"And you know for certain she has her mother's condition?"

"Her first time a the month, I took her for tests. She's got the gene, all right. I keep up on the research, there's no cure."

"Then we've no time to lose. It's not my place to tell her, but I'll try to get her to sit down with you. They're coming to dinner Saturday night, I'll talk to her."

He stood, blotting his eyes, looking as if he'd shed a great weight. "Much obliged," he said. He took her hand and squeezed hard. "For everything."

And leaving his coffee and cookie unfinished, he grabbed his jacket and left.

Mrs. Steiner closed the door and leaned against it.

What a mess. She wondered if Scotty's angel might be persuaded to work another miracle.

CHAPTER 108

The limo bore Scotty and Kassandra across a bridge to Manhattan, up 11th Street into an older section of the East Village. It stopped mid block before a large, orange-brick building with a theatre marquee. Red neon lights proclaimed:

Webster Hall—Greatest Nightclub on Earth

Lettering on the marquee read, *Oct. 31—Go to Hell.* And queued beneath it, stretching down the block, was a menagerie of wild-looking characters. Zombies, vampires, aliens, monsters, and indescribables. The limo driver opened Scotty's door, and Scotty stepped out into muffled music pumping energy into the night. The champagne made him lightheaded, and he steadied himself with his staff, helping Kassandra out of the car and into her shawl.

As they gathered themselves for a long walk to the end of the queue, two men in sunglasses and suits materialized. The men greeted them by name, and ushered them to a private side entrance under a copper canopy and globe lights.

The doors opened as if magically, the music amplified, and

Scotty and Kassandra were funneled through bouncers and metal-detectors into semidarkness split by laser lights. Before them lay a massive cocktail lounge packed with costumed partiers, its depth lost in fog.

They were led into a lounge past archways and a dance floor jammed with people flailing and pitching at each other in a frenzy, live band in the back. Kassandra smiled and moved to the beat, and Scotty's heart revved. Never had he seen the likes of this.

Abruptly a guy with hands full of drinks turned into Scotty, barely avoiding a spill. They both blinked. The man had longish dark hair and a beard, black hoody, and a walking cane hooked over an arm. Like staring into a mirror. He gave Scotty's shepherd's crook a measured look, grinned and said, "You win, dude, *bad-ass staff.*"

Scotty smiled back. Ivy was right.

Pushing on, they were taken up a wide stairway to another packed dance floor. Cavernous. Four-story ceiling, elevated stage at the back with another live band, balconies overhanging the other three sides. Flanking the stage were giant TV screens streaming live shots of people dancing. Scotty imagined this the club's grand ballroom in posher times.

He and Kassandra followed the men up one more level, and along a long, narrow hall with doors on the right every twelve feet, like a hotel. At one door stood a clone of their escorts, who admitted them into a private balcony with prime view of the stage and floor below. Stairs led down to a railing and a table with hors d'œuvres, set for two. A waiter swirled champagne in an ice bucket. The guards gave the area a once-over, and returned to the door as one man headed out, and two remained to keep watch.

Scotty wondered at all the security.

He sat Kassandra at the table, leaning into her, inhaling the scent of lavender. "This is incredi—" he began, when suddenly above them, a large, glowing object buzzed by.

Scotty gasped and ducked, shielding Kassandra.

Acrobats! *Circe de Soleil*-style performers in dayglow skeleton suits, soaring about on invisible wires. Twenty or more, executing impossible spins, tumbles and interchanges. The TV screens picked it up, crowd oohing and ahhing. Scotty grinned wide despite his teeth.

The waiter poured champagne, and when Scotty looked up again, the acrobats had been replaced by witches on broomsticks, goblins, ghosts, and howling banshees. As the performers wheeled by, they showered glitter and creepy insects.

A plastic spider landed in Scotty's fondue.

Out on the floor below, a caped headless horseman entered on a live black stallion, chasing Olde Dutch settlers with a sword. Then appeared monstrous creatures on long, spindly legs, stalking the crowd, misting fog out their ends. Following them, the biggest dogs Scotty had ever seen. The size of lions, on leashes held by whip-wielding dominatrixes in black leather.

Ivy would have loved it, and Scotty sent her an Instagram. Meanwhile, his glass never emptied, the food kept coming, and he was feeling the effects. Finally, a band started playing, and Kassandra rose with a seductive smile.

"Ready to work off some calories?"

Scotty didn't want to confess he was uncoordinated. But better than proving it, he said, "Not a good idea. I dance like St. Vitus."

She laughed and pulled him to his feet, grabbing his shepherd's staff. And ignoring his pleas, she led him away, informing their sentries at the door, "Off to get sweaty."

On the stairs down, she told Scotty, "The trick is to just close your eyes and move to the beat. Like you're jello, and the music is an earthquake."

They maneuvered onto the packed floor, dodging appendages, real and artificial. Kassandra picked a spot, handed Scotty his staff, and began gyrating. Hard to take his eyes off her, but he closed them.

An earthquake, indeed. The floor bounded under the weight of a thousand ravers, music pounding. Scotty couldn't keep his eyes closed without stumbling, and looked to see cosplay couples writhing nearby. Batman & Catwoman, Mystique & Wolverine. Two roosters, their hair done up in Mohawk-like combs, flapped feathered arms and scratched the ground with clawed, red feet.

Amazing, the effort and expense people went to.

Kassandra shouted to Scotty, "Best costumes win $5,000 in cash."

Suddenly a trio of dancers insinuated themselves between him and Kassandra. A muscular man in a loincloth, and two gorgeous women, one Black, one White, in clingy leotards. A panther and a leopard. The women undulated against the man, all but having sex, and Scotty wondered how they avoided splitting their skintight outfits. Until, peering closer, he gaped to realize they weren't wearing any. Not a stitch, their attire was painted on. And glancing around with new awareness, Scotty spied more such "costumes."

The heat was getting to him, and he navigated to Kassandra, wiping his brow, dizzy.

She shouted, "You OK?" He wasn't sure, and she added, "Wait here," and disappeared.

He was still vibrating when a woman approached. Dorothy from the Wizard of Oz. Pigtails, ruby slippers, stuffed dog in a basket.

"*Oh my God,*" she cried, "it *is* you!"

Scotty froze, and she grabbed him, crying out to everyone in earshot, "*Look, it's him. The Prophet. The Prophet of Queens.*"

People took notice, gathering. A guy in a Hannibal-Lector mask and straitjacket came close, squinting, and Scotty recoiled.

"Too short," the guy decided.

A Bride of Frankenstein agreed. "Too young."

All the same, Alexander Hamilton thought otherwise, and more people collected. Someone tugged on Scotty's beard, another his staff, others pawed and pinched. Just as Scotty was starting to panic, Kassandra rematerialized to snap at the pigtailed woman, "*Back to Kansas, Dotty.*" To the rest, she declared, "Are you nuts! Would a *real* Prophet of God attend an *orgy?*"

It created enough pause for her to spirit Scotty away. She steered him to a darker corner, slipped into his arms, and they slow-danced despite the driving beat. For how long, Scotty wasn't sure, a dreamy blur. Then abruptly, the music died, the lights brightened, and Scotty feared his magical night was over.

But the crowd began to buzz and push toward the stage, and Scotty was surprised to see a runway jutting out twenty feet onto the dance floor. On the stage, the band and equipment had been replaced by a tall, medieval-style, wrought-iron fence bathed in eerie red light, fog rolling through. In its middle was an opening, an archway, crowned by the head of a horned demon, eyes glowing fierce. And high above, suspended in a red spotlight, hung a giant Pentagram marked with cryptic runes. Music piped over speakers, deep voices chanting a dirge.

"What's happening?" Scotty asked, no longer having to shout.

Kassandra grinned. "You'll see. Quick—back to the balcony."

Floating upstairs and to their table, they gazed over the railing at men and women on stage in scanty, demonic attire. The demons wielded lit torches, strutting and dancing provocatively, giant TV screens catching all. Seconds later, Scotty was startled by a white flash in the archway, and the smoke cleared to reveal a muscular figure in Devil's mask and spiked headdress. The demons ceased cavorting to bow to him, as a threatening voice proclaimed over loudspeakers:

"All hail His Satanic Majesty."

The crowd cheered, and Scotty felt his palms moisten.

The Devil folded his arms on his chest, and his minions lit the spikes of his headdress with their torches. Scotty made note of the exits, wondering how the Hall got this spectacle past the fire marshal.

When the demons finished, they took their frolic to the runway, leaping, lunging, taunting and menacing the crowd. Another demon presented the Devil with a crystal human skull, and His Majesty raised it to the Pentagram high overhead as if invoking special powers. He then joined his underlings on the runway, thrusting the skull at the crowd to and fro like a diabolic dowsing tool, evoking squeals and retreats.

Suddenly the skull lit up bright red, and the Devil froze, a hunting dog on point. Above, a spotlight beamed onto the floor to target a young woman cowering in a bridal gown. Beside her, a groom in a tux turned and fled, leaving her to the demons who sprang down to seize her. They raised her up and bore her back to the stage, passing her to their cohorts as the audience howled.

A second spotlight lit up the Pentagram, and it began to descend. The demons presented the Devil with the bride, he held the skull to her again, it went red again, and she screamed again. Scotty's mouth was dry despite gulps of champagne.

The Pentagram came to rest beside the Devil, who pointed a fore-claw at the bride. The demons took hold of her gown and rent it to pieces, leaving the poor woman in nothing but a g-string. She tried to cover herself as the throngs went wild, music and chants swelling, spotlights roving. But the demons forced her to the Pentagram, turned her face-out, and bound her to it hand and foot. The Devil raised the skull, and the Pentagram rose once more, hoisting the helpless victim high above the stage where she hung screaming and thrashing, camera's flashing.

After an agonizing lull, there was an explosion and burst of light and smoke, and the Pentagram was lost to view. When the cloud dissipated, the woman was gone, g-string dangling from a nail as a disembodied voice proclaimed: *The virgin is sacrificed.*

The Hall roared, and Scotty was startled by a hand on his shoulder—a woman in a Harley Quinn costume with two pinkish drinks on a tray. Giving Scotty a lascivious grin, she shoved a drink in his hand, passing the other to Kassandra.

"What's this?" Scotty asked.

"A toast to our night," Kassandra said, clinking his glass.

They swigged. Bitter. But when Scotty went to set his glass down,

Kassandra insisted, "Once more for good measure." They drank again, and the woman took their glasses and left.

The music and dancing started up again, and a waiter brought more champagne. Scotty had had enough, woozy. In fact, giddy. He found himself giggling.

"Come," Kassandra said, standing, extending a hand, "there's someone I want you to meet."

He rose unsteady, spilling his champagne, and the escorts came down to lend a hand. They helped him and Kassandra out to the hallway, and into the charge of a half-dozen more men, who led them a short distance to a lone door. More men awaited, frisking Scotty, taking Kassandra's purse, admitting them into a brightly lit room full of photographers.

Scotty squinted to see an area with gold carpeting and a red, white, and blue-striped loveseat. Behind was a paneled wall and an array of American flags. Nearby stood a woman with auburn hair, facing away, talking to a group of people.

As Scotty and Kassandra approached, the group noticed, and the woman turned...

CHAPTER 109

Ivy sat rigid on the couch, surfing channels with Homer, Scotty snoring away in the bedroom. She couldn't believe what she was seeing. All over TV, breaking news: a short, silent video of the Prophet one-on-one last night with Ellen Shackleton.

Adding to Ivy's confusion, the encounter didn't appear to take place at Webster Hall, but a campaign office—in jarring contrast to the wild videos Scotty sent last night. The news gave few details, simply clips of the two looking chummy. Scotty was clearly drunk. Clear to anyone who knew him. The video never lingered on his face, but Ivy saw the glassiness.

Of course, he'd been set up. Ivy had suspected something wasn't right when awakened at 3:00 last night by a knock on the door. She'd opened on Kassandra propping Scotty against the wall, Scotty wearing an "I heart Shackleton" campaign button.

"We had a ball," Kassandra had said, grinning, handing off Scotty's shepherd's staff. He sniggered and slid to the floor, and Kassandra breezed off. Ivy pulled him inside and tugged off his hoody and shoes. He smelled of alcohol and cigarettes. Dragging him to his bed, she'd rolled him in and left him passed out behind his door, roaring like a semi climbing a hill.

This morning she'd awakened on the couch to his phone ringing, rooting it from his hoody to see tons of calls. Among them, Kyle Heath and Reverend Thornton, who'd left multiple voicemails. She'd resisted checking them, knowing Scotty would be upset. But now, in light of the Shackleton development, she had no choice. The Lord's deadline for the tape was in two hours, and Scotty showed no signs of being back among the living.

She selected Thornton's most recent message:

"I've been trying to reach you, Scott. I'm devastated to tell you, after the Council saw the morning news, they decided against handing over the tape. We need the Lord's help!"

Ivy dropped the phone and pulled Homer tight. Scotty had unwittingly secured Shackleton's future at the expense of theirs. Fat chance now the Lord would be merciful to them, not this vengeful God. No closure for her and Scotty. No explanation for their enigmatic encounters with the divine. Their moment in the sun would end without them learning their fate, or even what was on that damned videotape—

Thunder erupted in the room, causing Ivy to jump. Homer scuttled to the bedroom, knocking the door wide, and Scotty's snores joined the thunder in a duet.

Ten o'clock. Ivy shivered. She and Scotty hadn't heard from Ariel in days, and given the reverend's new message, Ivy was terrified at the thought of facing the angel alone.

She curled on the couch to wait it out.

But as thunder segued to whine, she reconsidered. While she had no faith that the Lord would forgive them, she recalled the conflict she'd often seen in Ariel's eyes. And more important, the *empathy.* By throwing herself on the angel's mercy, might Ivy persuade Ariel to reveal the fate awaiting her and Scotty? And like in the case with little Teddy, might Ariel give them a chance to change it?

Nothing to lose, she opened videochat with trembling fingers, beholding once again that ethereal face. But this time, Ariel looked distraught. Angels perspire?

"Ivy? Where's Scott?"

"Uh, indisposed. It's just me."

The silver eyes grew intense. *"The tape. Did you get the tape from Reverend Thornton?"*

"I'm sorry, the Council refuses to give it up."

Ariel looked more ashen than ever, if possible.

Ivy thought she heard swearing on the other end, and asked, "Who's there with you?"

The angel seemed not to hear. *"What happened last night? Scott was told not to see anyone, talk to anyone. Above all,* not *Ellen Shackleton!"*

"I don't know, I was gonna ask *you*. But I know this much, it *wasn't* Scotty's fault."

Ariel lowered her head. *"The Lord is very angry. The consequences will be dire."*

"What consequences?" Ivy moaned. "What will become of us!"

The angel faltered, her voice sounding scripted. *"Fail to deliver the tape, and you, Scott, the reverend, his Council and Churches—you will all suffer the Lord's wrath... Eternal Damnation."*

Ivy rocked back in her chair. "Oh my God! What can we do? The deadline's in two hours!"

Ariel raised up, cheeks wet. *"The Lord's granted you an extension. Your last. If you value your souls, Thornton must deliver the tape to Scott before our session tomorrow at 10:00. Contact Thornton immediately. He must swear on his soul he'll comply, and Scott must confirm that in person today at our two o'clock. Do you understand?"*

Ivy nodded numbly, and the screen went blank with time to spare. It took a second to get her limbs moving, and she stumbled back to the bedroom. Homer lay next to Scotty, fleeing under the bed as Ivy stormed in.

"Wake up, wake up!" she cried, shaking her brother. "We're in *big* trouble."

Scotty came out of it slowly, grimacing, eyes not in sync. "Whuh?"

"I just spoke to Ariel. If we don't get that tape, and fast, there'll be hell to pay."

She grabbed his face and leaned close, forcing his focus. *"Literally."*

CHAPTER 110

Ariel sat in the tent in angel mode, watching with glazed eyes as Stan probed the vortex with the grabber pole. The image on his laptop showed the inside of an umbrella plant—until Max yanked the antenna from the hole, turning the screen to snow.

Stan protested, but Max snapped, "Forget the damned rabbit's foot, *it's Defcon 1.*"

Ivy Butterfield had just confirmed their worst fears. Thornton's Council refused to surrender the tape. The team expected as much this morning, after waking to a media bomb in the archives. Last night, four years ago, paparazzi caught the Prophet chumming with Ellen Shackleton. Now, even if the Prophet's defiant actions raised Shackleton's numbers, the devastating tape would soon sink them.

Tia barked at Max, "Nice work, Mr. Wonderful. Now what the hell do we do?"

Ariel's moon shot was collapsing. Once so promising, her vision had been hijacked by Max and fashioned into a fraud. A carnival con, with Ariel as shill. She had a horrible feeling how it would end. And finally, her role in this pretense, so wearing for so long, had worn through. She stood to face her friends.

494

"Whatever you decide," she told them, "leave me out. *I quit.*"

Grabbing her laptop, she raced to the house and her room. And changing out of angel mode for the last time, she crumpled on her bed in tears.

CHAPTER 111

Scotty's head throbbed. And not just from a monster hangover. He sat on the couch watching with dismay TV clips of himself in a confab with Ellen Shackleton. Head-to-head, nodding, grinning stupidly with his crooked teeth. An encounter he had absolutely no recollection of.

Ivy brought him a second mug of coffee and more aspirin. "I *dare* Kassandra to show her face," she spit, shoving Scotty's phone at him. "Call Thornton, no time to lose."

Scotty was still working to scrape his wits together. He swilled down the pills and dialed, and Ivy turned off the TV, her hand tight on his shoulder.

A distressed voice answered, *"I'm terribly sorry, Scott. When the Council saw the news, there was nothing more I could do."*

Scotty pleaded, "I was bushwhacked, like Filby did me in the City."

"I told them as much, but their minds are made up. Have you heard from the Lord?"

"I'm afraid so. He's furious. I've bad news, you better sit down."

Thornton moaned and Scotty said, "But there's still hope, the Lord's granted us an extension. You've got till 10:00 AM tomorrow to get me the tape. And you must swear to God you will."

"Or what?"

Scotty had difficulty forming the words. "Or it's damnation for all of us. You, me, Ivy, the Council. The Council *must* listen, or it will cost us our souls."

There came a nasty clatter, Thornton dropping his phone. Scotty feared he'd passed out.

But then came a strained whisper. *"I, I hear the Lord, and I obey. I'll deliver the tape to you personally, first thing tomorrow morning. But I must beg something of the Lord in return..."*

• • •

Two o'clock, and thunder filled Scotty's living room once more. He faced his computer, Ivy at his side clutching the cat. Her anxiety mirrored Scotty's. And yet, their long, harrowing journey might still end well, if only the Lord would swallow His Wrath to grant a last favor.

The whine faded, and yet the videochat window on Scotty's screen remained quiet.

Ivy grumbled, "What gives?"

A minute passed, still nothing. Then up popped that face-of-God icon from the Sistine Chapel, bearded and angry.

"A stupid epistle!" Ivy snapped. "They're *really* pissed this time."

Scotty opened it:

is thornton bringing the tape

Scotty typed:

yes, flying up tomorrow for AM session. insists on face2face w/u, has questions

A delay, and:

the lord will not allow

Ivy cried out to the screen, "Cut us some slack, for chrissakes!" and Scotty typed,

how badly u want tape

A longer delay. As they waited, Scotty noticed Ivy squinting at Mom's plant in the corner.

"What now?" he said.

"I saw leaves moving. There's something in there. *Yuck,* I think you got mice."

"So let Homer earn his keep," Scotty told her. She set the cat down to investigate, and Scotty turned back to the screen to see Ariel had responded.

must have absolute assurance thornton brings all copies

Scotty agreed, confirming there was only one copy, and Ariel replied,

very well
thornton surrenders tape to me in person
tomorrow at 10:00
or you pay with your souls

The link ended, and Ivy said, *"Wow.* You made the Lord blink."

CHAPTER 112

Ariel lay on her bed trying to read, unable to keep her mind on it. Her friends seemed to have gotten the message to let her be, handling the two o'clock on their own. That session had ended an hour ago, and still no one had disturbed her. An indication things went better than expected.

Then came a knock at her door.

Tia popped her head in, and suddenly Stan and Max entered, too, all facing Ariel.

After an uncomfortable silence, Tia said, "Sorry to interrupt, we gotta talk."

Ariel assumed, "Thornton rejected the ultimatum?"

"Actually, no. He's agreed to hand the tape over tomorrow."

Ariel brightened, then darkened. "The catch?"

The men shifted, and Tia exhaled. "Before he'll fork it over, he wants to meet you. See you on screen. He insists."

Ariel glared at the floor, and Max said, "It's no big deal, he's just hedging his bet."

"It's a big deal to *me*," Ariel snapped, feeling her face heat. "I told you, *no more*. And regardless, it won't work. Thornton's met me, he's seen me as I really am. He'd recognize me."

Stan said, "We considered that, and we came up with a work-around. We'll simply adjust the lights and camera aperture till it's too bright for him to make you out."

Max added, "Thornton has no idea what an angel looks like. He'll be awestruck, he'll cough up the tape, and we're done."

Tia said, "Our concern is, he'll recognize your eyes and voice."

Not an issue. Ariel had always been too self-conscious to look the man in the eye, much less speak to him.

Max said. "This is your last performance, we swear. Your curtain call. We get the tape and the election, and Tia gets her mom back."

CHAPTER 113

SATURDAY, NOVEMBER 1, 8:28 PM, QUEENS

"Your meatloaf is deee-lish," Ivy gushed.

"Everything," Scott seconded, helping himself to more mashed potatoes.

Mrs. Steiner smiled, hiding her tension. Tonight wasn't what she had in mind when she'd extended her invitation. She'd planned a relaxed dinner catching up on her guest's adventures, taking dessert over the debate. She and Ivy shared an avid interest in politics.

But that went out the window after her talk with Joe Butterfield this morning. Learning of Ivy's condition, Mrs. Steiner's goal now was to arrange a meeting between daughter and dad—and without disclosing its sensitive purpose. She was uncertain how to proceed. Fortunately, Scott's new friend, Kassandra, couldn't be here. Such a delicate discussion couldn't take place with another party present. Mrs. Steiner bided her time, waiting for an appropriate opening.

She asked Scott, "So, what's Ellen Shackleton like in person?"

Ivy said, "If only he could remember. He was too stoned."

Mrs. Steiner laughed. "Well, you sure stirred things up. Especially for your fans outside."

The chanting and songs were constant, louder than ever.

"That's all about to end," Scott said.

Ivy jumped in. "Reverend Penbrook Thornton's coming to visit us tomorrow!"

Mrs. Steiner was surprised. "Here? In your apartment?"

Scott nodded.

"My goodness, it sounds important."

He nodded again, adding, "Once this is over, we'll have one heck of a story to tell you."

Scott's dealings with Reverend Thornton and the Lord were no doubt sacrosanct, and Mrs. Steiner didn't press. She made a mental note to sweep the foyer.

"So much excitement," she said. "But then what? What will you do after all this, Scott?"

He replied without hesitation. "Look for a job."

"That shouldn't be hard for you now with your celebrity. You'll have your pick."

He sighed. "I'm afraid people will be disappointed to learn I'm *not* what they think."

Ivy brightened. "I know! You can start a church. Lots of bucks in that, look at Thornton."

They all laughed, and Scott said, "That may be our only hope to cover your college."

Mrs. Steiner saw her opening. She turned to Ivy. "So, you've decided to finish high school?"

"That's the plan. I'm still on track to graduate, I haven't missed that much."

"Wonderful. Do you intend to stay here with Scott till then?"

The girl looked to her brother, and he offered, "For as long as you want."

She gave him a hug. "I've been burden enough. Pop can afford me, you can't." She told Mrs. Steiner. "It's time I go home."

The pressure in Mrs. Steiner's chest eased. She'd call Joe tomorrow with the good news.

Grinning, she asked, "Who's up for some cherry pie à la mode?"

• • •

Kassandra sat in her living room surfing news channels, basking in the hot story of the day: the Prophet's surprise liaison with Ellen Shackleton. In the fiercely competitive environment of 24/7 news, networks grubbed for viewers by turning stories into entertainment, hashing, rehashing, dissecting and bloviating. Kassandra's coup was the rage de jour, and she was thoroughly savoring her triumph, when suddenly distracted by voices in the hall outside.

It didn't sound like Butterfield, but she was taking no chances. Switching off the TV, she grabbed her laptop and a glass of wine, and tiptoed to the bedroom.

Butterfield had called and stopped by today, and Kassandra had ducked him each time. He'd left a message on her phone thanking her for last night. To her surprise, no mention of the Shackleton subterfuge. He'd also slipped a note under her door inviting her to dine with him and his sister tonight at that nosey old lady's downstairs. Kassandra couldn't imagine anything duller.

She felt a twinge of guilt. Butterfield wasn't the complete dork she'd pegged him to be. True, he hadn't even made a pass at her last night, but he'd proven wittier and more amusing than expected. All the same, she couldn't face him now, and thankfully she wouldn't have to risk it much longer. With Shackleton's polls soaring, Kassandra was still collecting accolades from colleagues, including Frank Percy, himself. Very soon, she'd leave this dump for an apartment in Manhattan, her position at EP&M now a lock.

Tonight, however, after the most memorable day of her life, all she wanted was to hole up and enjoy the debate.

She went to her nightstand to switch on the lamp, only to see it flicker and die. Damned thing had been giving her trouble. Another annoyance she'd soon dispense with. She gave it a whack, it blinked into service, and she opened her laptop on her bed, livestreaming.

The debate was already in progress. A townhall format before a live audience in-the-round. Shackleton and Filby were perched on stools, separated by a moderator fielding questions.

The styles of the two candidates couldn't have been more distinct. Shackleton was a beautiful woman in her early fifties. Smart blue dress, vibrant red hair, green eyes and warm smile. A polished pro, rising from her seat to engage questioners, looking them in the eye, comfortable, confident. Honest Ellen, champion of fairness and women's rights.

Filby was Mr. Folksy. In his fifties also, laid-back and slack in an open-collar shirt, sleeves rolled to his elbows. Defender of American values. All artifice, down to his staged mannerisms.

A woman in the audience took a microphone to address Shackleton.

"I'm a single mom," she said. *"I work full time as a cashier. But the high cost of childcare forced me onto welfare. What will you do to help people like me?"*

"You work for a large corporation?" Shackleton asked.

"A merchandising chain."

Shackleton nodded. *"We live in the wealthiest nation in the world, yet millions of full-time workers are on welfare to survive. But there's a deeper irony. Did you know the corporation you work for is on welfare, too?"*

The woman puzzled, and Shackleton continued, *"Your company won't pay you a livable wage, so we taxpayers are left to cover the difference with public assistance. Our taxes subsidize your company's low payroll so it can reap big profits. That's* corporate *welfare."*

To the cameras, Shackleton said, *"The answer is to raise the minimum wage till employees and employers are both off the dole. That's how it used to work in this country, and if you elect me president, I'll make it work again."*

There was rousing applause. Then Filby was allowed to rebut.

He remained on his stool, legs crossed, face bunched. *"Ya know,"* he said, *"we're blessed ta live in a nation that values freedom. But these last years, government's been pickin' away at it. Got its hands in everything, tellin' us what to do, tellin' employers how ta run their businesses."*

He faced the questioner. *"What ya really want is a job that pays more. An' ya might have that job now, 'cept ya know where it is? Overseas. People like my opponent here chased it away with rules an' regs an' taxes. You elect me, I'll clear that brush and make the country open for business again, like it used ta be."*

More rousing applause.

It went on, back and forth...

Kassandra awakened to the sound of raucous laughter. She'd dozed off, the clock on her laptop showing the debate almost over. She was confused to see Filby sitting scarlet-faced on his stool while the audience, Shackleton, even the commentator, were howling with laughter.

Quickly Kassandra rewound to see what she'd missed.

A man in the audience was asking Shackleton, *"Where do you stand on teaching Intelligent Design in our public schools? Why Evolution only?"*

Shackleton replied, *"I believe each of us has the Constitutional right to exercise our own spiritual beliefs. But I also believe our public schools are bound by the 1st Amendment to keep out of the religious arena. The courts have ruled that Intelligent Design—Creationism—isn't based on fact, but entirely in spiritual belief. Religion is best taught at home and church."*

There was isolated, but enthusiastic response.

Filby's turn. He inhaled and let his breath out slowly, shaking his head. *"Look at this country, folks, whaddya see? Everywhere, violence, drugs, porn, disrespect for authority. We've lost our way 'cause we lost the Christian principles we were founded on. Ya pull God, prayer an' the bible outta our schools, our public squares, our government, where's our moral compass?"*

Pockets of audience cheered, shouting, *"Amen,"* and *"Alleluia."*

Kassandra watched Filby gather-in the enthusiasm. He rose from his stool, standing tall, voice elevated like a preacher in a pulpit.

"I'm tellin' ya, friends, if we don't change, an' fast, we're gonna lose

what religious rights we got left. A government without God is a soulless creature. An octopus reachin' into our lives, wrappin' its long, cold testicles 'round our necks."

He paused, awaiting his propers, but they didn't come. A split second of dead silence, then sputtering guffaws building into an eruption of laughter. Filby looked perplexed, gaping around for a clue. The moderator finally went to him and whispered in his ear, and Filby turned scarlet.

Kassandra doubled over with laughter.

Desperate to recover, Filby went into attack mode, pointing at Shackleton, crying shrilly, *"Is this what America wants for its leader? A divorcée. A drunkard with an arrest record? A godless carouser and con artist? Is this the Role-Model-in-Chief for our kids?"*

Shackleton's face blanched like she'd been slapped. Eyes blazing, she snapped, *"I never claimed to be perfect. I had a failed marriage, yes. I drove home from a party once not realizing I had too much to drink, and paid the price for it. That much is true, and public record. But I learned from those mistakes, I never repeated them."*

Leveling a fiery glare at Filby, she said, *"The rest of your accusations, sir, are garbage, and you know it. This entire campaign I've put up with attacks from your Super Pacs. Sexist slurs about affairs and disgusting acts of perversion. Cynicism about my Christian faith, my morals. Baseless character assassination—and now you yourself stoop to it!"*

The audience began to react, calling out support. *"You go, girl. You tell him."*

Shackleton singled out a TV camera and marched up to it, right in the lens.

"For the last time," she snapped. *"For the record, my mouth to God's Ear: There isn't an ounce of substance to these charges. My whole life I've strived to conduct myself with dignity and honor."* She turned to Filby. *"I'll happily put my standards up against yours for the country to decide. The same high standards I intend to take with me into the White House next January."*

The assembly roared, and Kassandra finished her wine glowing.

Shackleton had rolled her opponent. And now, coupled with the Prophet's boost and just two days to the election, the candidate appeared on a glide path to the presidency.

Chapter 114

"Look into the camera, please," Stan said.

Ariel sat at the table in the tent, squinting into the lens of her laptop as the klieg lights blazed brighter than ever. Stan and Max were testing iris exposures and light levels to strike a balance between obscuring Ariel's identity and maintaining her angelic aura. Behind her, Tia worked her hair into platinum braids and ear ringlets.

Max cued Stan from a laptop in a corner, "Okay, we're good, lock it down."

Stan cut the lights and Tia mopped Ariel's brow, the electric fans worthless.

"You looked like the Resurrection," Max assured Ariel. "Unrecognizable."

She took his word for it. Max was as determined as she that Thornton not recognize her during this next, crucial session. Their last hope to get the tape. While these charades always upset Ariel, this morning was especially tense as she prepared to face the towering spiritual figure of her youth. Like her friends, she saw no other choice. She was their only hope. Today at noon, four years ago and three hours from now, the Shackleton video had exploded onto the

508

world. Everything the team had been working for, all they'd risked these many weeks, was coming to a head.

And their hopes had grown dimmer with some troubling news this morning. According to the archives, Filby's debacle in the debate last night, which came on the heels of Shackleton's Prophet bump, had dropped his poll numbers even lower than they were in the *un-adulterated* past.

More pressure on Thornton and his Council to air the tape.

There was, however, some good news. Comparing this debate with the original, the team found the videos almost identical, down to Filby's disastrous gaffe. It led Ariel to suggest, "The effects of our time-tampering seem negligible so far. Is it possible we'll get lucky Tuesday, and squeak past the Big One?"

Stan reminded her, "The changes are cumulative, drip, drip, dripping into the pool of Time, damming up. The quakes are getting stronger and more frequent. It can't continue."

In other words, whoever won the election, the dam was going to burst. Damned either way.

Tia mopped Ariel's brow again.

CHAPTER 115

Scotty paced the living room, Homer on his heels, Ivy in the bathroom preparing for the arrival of their guest. Thornton was sending Scotty progress reports on his flight from The City, and Scotty received each with anxious anticipation. He'd lain awake much of the night fearing something would go wrong, sword of Damnation dangling overhead.

A new text on his phone brought him to a halt, and the cat plowed into him.

Scotty called out to Ivy, "The reverend's touched down, he's on his way!"

"Great. I'll be right out."

Homer sat rubbing his nose, and Scotty noticed something in his mouth. A mousie.

Kneeling, he scratched the cat's ears. "Sorry, buddy," he said, "I know I've neglected you. Be patient, it's almost over."

Scotty had been slinging that same old hash for weeks, but this time he had real hope. If Thornton harbored doubts about Ariel, once the man stared into those mesmerizing eyes, he'd hand over that tape faster than he could rattle off a prayer.

Scotty went to his computer to get ready, and Homer followed, jumping into his lap, pawing. Scotty brushed him away, but he kept it up, unusually needy today. Relenting, Scotty wiggled his fingers, and Homer spit out the toy. It felt odd, wetness aside. On closer inspection, *not* a mousie, a memory stick keychain in the form of a rabbit's foot. It wasn't Scotty's, he'd never seen it before.

Ivy came out to join him, and he dangled the foot at her. "Yours?" She puzzled. "Nope. What is it?"

"Not sure, Homer found it."

He tossed it on his desk, but Homer failed to chase it.

• • •

"Close as I can get you," the cabbie said, halting a full block from the address Thornton held in his fingers. The crowd outside the car was thick and rowdy, having slowed their progress to a crawl.

Thornton checked his watch. He'd fallen far behind schedule, and dare not be late for the most important meeting of his life. Closing his eyes, he said a prayer. *Never* had he felt such responsibility and stress. He'd undertaken this trip against the vote of his Council. The worst rift of his tenure, and it had cost him his chairmanship. So be it. He *had* to deliver the tape. And he *had* to speak to the angel.

He had to know.

Thrusting bills at the cabbie, he reached into his suit jacket once again to ensure the tape was still there, and stepped out into the turmoil. Instantly he was recognized.

"*Reverend Thornton,*" a young black woman cried, holding up a baby with a heart-rending deformity. "I beg you, *help my child.*"

Others pressed their own desperate pleas, overwhelming Thornton. Thankfully, the police were on the lookout for him and rushed to his aid, herding him through, mobbed and jostled. He was led to an old brownstone, up the front steps past a screeching door, into a dim foyer.

Cracked plaster, worn linoleum. But clean. A familiar voice said, "Welcome, Reverend, sorry for the rough reception."

Thornton looked to see Scott in the hallway, and a neighbor peeking out her door.

"Sorry I'm running so late," Thornton panted in reply.

They hugged, and Scott ushered him upstairs into a small, threadbare apartment where Ivy awaited. She greeted him with a hug, too.

"Excuse the mess," Scott said. "It's been a tough few weeks."

"I'm honored to be here," Thornton said, recalling Proverbs, 17:5: *He who looks down upon another insults his Maker.* Glancing around, he asked, "Where does the angel appear to you?"

Scott pointed to a table/desk filled with organized clutter, and Ivy went to stand behind three chairs facing a computer monitor.

"Here," she told him.

Thornton joined her to behold a screen of swimming fish. *"On the Internet?"*

She nodded. Scott seated Thornton in the center chair, he and Ivy flanked him, and Thornton felt his heart pound. This was so unlike what he'd imagined. So *fishy.*

And yet, all those miraculous, impossible prophecies...

"Cover your ears," Ivy warned, and did so herself. "Ariel makes a noisy entrance."

Hardly had Thornton followed suit than a terrible thunder rolled through the room, only to be displaced moments later by a plaintive wail. The noises soon lapsed, and the computer screen awakened in dazzling white. Thornton winced, but he did not look away.

He could make out *something* in the brilliance. A cloud within cloud, quickly coalescing into a recognizable shape. Humanlike. But like no human Thornton had ever seen. Impossible to discern clearly, female in form, breathtakingly beautiful. Eyes piercing like Truth, skin aglow as if with internal light.

Scott noted, "She looks different today."

Ivy agreed. "Like she's been holding back."

The angel's eyes fixed Thornton to his seat, and he clutched hands to heart and tape.

She spoke, voice silky, yet tense.

"Good morning, Reverend. I am Ariel, Paraclete of the Lord."

Thornton felt his mouth move, tongue stuck.

"The Lord wishes to know if you've followed his Command."

Thornton got his hands working, fumbling the tape from his pocket. The angel's eyes grew more intense.

"Are there more copies?"

He found his voice. "N-none."

Appearing relieved, she pointed to Scott. *"Then please..."*

Thornton said, "I graciously submit to the Lord." The tape wavered in his grip, fingertips throbbing. "B-but I beg you, one thing more."

The angel frowned. *"The Lord has granted you a sacred Covenant, what more do you seek?"*

It fell so quiet, Thornton could hear the tape rattling in its case. He whispered, "Forgiveness. Please, *I ask the Lord's forgiveness.*"

The penetrating eyes blinked, but the angel said nothing. Thornton pressed, "Many years ago, I committed an unspeakable sin." He lowered his eyes. "The Lord knows, He's punished me severely for it. Yet, He also knows I've lived my life since in penance. I never again repeated my trespass." He looked up. "And now, I ask—*I beg*—absolution."

The angel seemed at a loss, looking around. At length, she said, *"Very well. Yes. You're forgiven. The Lord forgives you. Now please, the tape."*

The pardon was so perfunctory, so anticlimactic, it stunned Thornton. He thrust the tape into Scott's hands like shedding shackles, breaking into tears, sobbing his thanks.

Ivy comforted him, and Scott asked the angel, "What now?"

She replied, *"Nothing more for the reverend. I'm sending you instructions on the disposition of the tape. You must follow it to the letter, without delay. I'll return at 2:00, and if you've done as instructed, you'll be freed of your Missions at last, once and for all."*

An attachment arrived on screen, and Scotty acknowledged it.

THE PROPHET OF QUEENS

Thornton composed himself, and the angel squared her shoulders and seared him with her eyes once more. Then she fixed her gaze on Scott and Ivy.

"The Lord commends you all. Through your faithfulness and courage, you've now ensured a blessed future for your country."

Ivy, silent till now, leaned forward. "What about Scotty and me? What about *our* futures?"

Ariel blinked. *"We, we'll discuss that at our final session this afternoon. I must go…"*

Thornton thanked the angel profusely, feeling the sublime lightness of his purified soul. And as she dissolved back into celestial radiance, he could swear he heard cheering on the other side.

CHAPTER 116

No one said a word as Scotty, Ivy, and Thornton absorbed the moment. Then the noises came and went, and finally Thornton exhaled. Looking a blend of awestruck, elated, and exhausted, he asked softly, "Can I trouble you to call me a cab? I believe someone at home is waiting for me."

Scotty obliged, and texted the police outside a heads-up. Ivy gave Thornton a hug, and Scotty escorted him downstairs.

At the door, Scotty said, "I don't know how to thank you, Reverend."

Thornton took Scotty's hand in both of his, searching his face. "No, my friend," he replied. "It's *I* who thank *you*. You've blessed me more than you'll ever know, and I'm eternally grateful. There will always be a place for you and Ivy in my City."

And seizing Scotty in a bear hug, he released him and ducked outside into the deliria.

Scotty took his time on the stairs. He felt confused and strangely sad. With the madness coming to an end, he should have been ecstatic. Yet nagging him was the awareness that, at just twenty-six years of age, he'd just seen the high point of his life. And would soon see the last of the angel Ariel.

515

Ivy was still at his computer when he returned, her face vexed, arms crossed. The Shackleton videotape sat on the desk where Scotty left it, and as he joined Ivy, he saw open on his computer screen Ariel's instructions for the tape's disposition.

"You couldn't wait for me?" he asked.

She snapped, "The Lord won't let us watch the tape. We're supposed to destroy it!"

"That comes as a surprise?"

"After all we've been through to get it?"

"What do the instructions say?"

Ivy turned to the screen, reading aloud,

> "follow these commands immediately and to the letter
> do not view the video
> take the tape to the kitchen and place in microwave
> heat on high for 74 seconds or until spool melts
> keep fire extinguisher handy
> save residue to show at afternoon session
> do as directed and you will be absolved of further duties
> after which the lord will reveal to you your fate
> and how to change it for a brighter future"

"A brighter future!" Scotty cried, elated and relieved. "*That's* what we needed to hear! And snatching the tape from his desk, he headed for the kitchen.

Ivy chased after him, clutching his arm.

"*Wait,*" she begged, "let's think this through."

"I have. Whatever's on here, it isn't worth angering the Lord."

He pulled free and went to the cupboard, slipped the tape from its case onto a plate, stuck it in the microwave, and slammed the door. Setting the timer for 1:14, he rooted in a cabinet under the sink to produce a small fire extinguisher.

Blowing dust from the gauge, however, he saw it read *Expired*. He told Ivy, "I'll get one from a neighbor. Sit tight, I'll be right back." He paused to lock eyes. *"Give me your word."*

She huffed, but nodded, and he left.

• • •

Soon as the apartment door shut, Ivy grabbed the tape and ran to the living room. She could hear Scotty in the hall knocking on a door. Kassandra's, she suspected. Apparently he got no response, footsteps trailing off, and Ivy switched on the TV and VCR, and shoved in the cassette. She lowered the volume and hit "play."

Her heart raced as an image came up on screen. Dim, shaky. The interior of a building. A large basement, maybe. Ivy could make out a cluster of people at one end, in burgundy robes, hooded. The camera's perspective was waist high, and as it advanced, Ivy saw young women. College-age, clustered around something.

No one seemed to notice the camera forcing its way in. Ivy imagined it was concealed in a purse, also explaining the muffled audio. She heard yelling, cheering, chanting.

Then an unseen woman shouted, *"Who is it? Who's the supplicant?"*

Another unseen woman, presumably wielding the camera, answered, *"Pledge Shackleton."*

"Ha-ha. That pompous bitch. I bet Handsome Dan's got a milk-bone for her!"

The view pushed on through the crowd to reveal a brick wall with a burgundy shield flanked by flaming torches and a coat of arms: skulls, bones, strange symbols, and Greek.

The image tilted down and tracked into an open area around which people were gathered, tittering and laughing. Ivy saw a burgundy blanket spread out on the floor, gold letters in the center that she couldn't make out. Kneeling on the letters facing away was a woman in a hooded robe and Versace boots, hood up. Facing her was another woman in a robe holding a leash. Whatever it tethered was obscured by the kneeling woman.

Some sort of ceremony. As the camera drew near, Ivy heard the woman with the leash intone, *"...to accept you tonight into the bonds of eternal sisterhood. Now, bow and consummate your fealty with the actum humilitatis."*

The crowd began chanting, *"Kiss-kiss-kiss-kiss,"* and the woman on her knees appeared to take a deep breath. Dropping to her elbows, she exposed in front of her an enormous bulldog squatting in a navy turtleneck with a large, white "Y" on the chest.

But it wasn't a kiss she was delivering. Ivy watched stunned as the woman gave a few quick bobs of her head under the dog, and the room erupted in jeers and groans. Then the woman raised up and shook off her hood, auburn hair spilling out. And turning to accept rounds of disgust, she smirked wickedly, defiantly, and the dog came into view again, wagging its tail, sporting an erection.

Ivy recoiled, freezing the video, appalled. She nearly threw up. But quickly she sobered at the sound of footsteps in the stairwell outside. Heart racing, she scrambled to eject the tape, switching things off, rushing for the microwave, flinging the tape inside like it was radioactive.

Seconds later, Scotty entered the kitchen with another fire extinguisher. "Mrs. Steiner to the rescue again," he said. But paying Ivy a look, he frowned. "You all right? You look sick."

"Cat food," she said, waving a hand in front of her nose.

"You think it stinks in here now..."

Ordering her back, extinguisher at the ready, Scotty hit "start." The oven began to hum, tape revolving on the carousel.

Ivy fought the impulse to confess. She desperately wanted to share her revulsion, her outrage, her feelings of betrayal and confusion over yet another lying, soulless, self-serving politician. Ellen Shackleton. The leader America could finally put its faith in. Champion of women, nothing to hide, her mouth to God's Ear.

Not *that* mouth.

Ivy started to speak, but nothing came out. How could she

condemn Shackleton for lying when she herself had just broken her word to Scotty?

And then it was too late. Through the door of the oven, the tape collapsed into black goo, emitting a noxious odor. The chime went off, Scotty removed the plate, set it on the stove under the exhaust fan, and lay a hand on Ivy's shoulder.

"A few more hours," he said, squeezing, "this will all be over."

When Ivy didn't respond, he squeezed again. "What are you thinking?"

She exhaled. "I'm thinking, whatever the Lord's reward, *it's not enough.*"

CHAPTER 117

The moment of truth.

Ariel, Tia and Stan sat in the living room of the farmhouse, monitoring the archives for evidence the Shackleton video was no more. Frozen on their laptop screens was the notorious image of a youthful Ellen Shackleton, in a robe on her knees, smirking. The video had debuted on YouTube four years ago today at noon, two days before the election. But the noon hour had just passed, the image remained, and the team's concern was growing.

Except for Max. He waltzed into the room with a bottle of champagne he'd iced for the occasion, wedging himself between the women on the couch.

"Must you be so smug?" Tia snapped. "You'll jinx us."

"Must you be so superstitious?" he replied. "Next we know, you'll be praying."

Setting the bottle on the coffee table next to four glasses, he leaned into Ariel's screen for a look. And at just that instant, the image of Shackleton vanished.

Profound silence filled the room. Then Stan leaped up and started dancing—the most ungainly thing Ariel had ever seen. She

520

broke out laughing and crying at the same time.

"We did it," he whooped. *"We did it."*

The others joined him, hugging and cheering, and Max broke open the champagne, making a point to pop it near Tia's ear. She was too overjoyed to care.

Pouring for all, Max toasted, "Ladies and gentleman, I give you the moon."

They clinked and drank. It felt so sudden and impossible and incredible.

Wiping away tears, Ariel turned to Tia. "You can send Scott your email now!"

Max corrected, "Not till Tuesday morning. We have a deal."

Tia lost her smile. "With the video gone now, what's it matter?"

"We settled this," Max said. "What if there's another copy? Or Thornton and his cronies have something else up their sleeves? You send your email as agreed. Tuesday, 10:00 AM."

"But if the Council has another copy," Tia argued, "they won't hold onto it. When Thornton fails to release his, they'll release theirs. Surely in the next few hours."

Ariel begged Max, "For all we know, stopping the video could trigger the Big One. If the Tsunami strikes before Tia sends her email, it won't transmit, she'll have no hope of saving her mom."

Stan looked at Max. "Ariel's got a point."

Max crossed his arms, paying Tia a cagey look. "I'm willing to be flexible. Assuming no problems surface by the first run tomorrow, you can send your email then, with one proviso."

Monday morning, a day before the election. But Max's provisos always made Ariel tense.

"...At the 2:00 session today," he said, "we give the Prophet a last Mission. Assuming he destroyed the tape, he goes on TV tonight with a farewell announcement. He endorses Shackleton and orders his followers to vote the straight Democrat ticket."

Ariel was aghast. Had Max planned this maneuver all along? "But we promised Scott *no more Missions.* And it breaks our Covenant with Thornton, he'll be furious."

Max shrugged. "The Lord changed His Mind, divine prerogative. And Thornton can blow a gasket for all I care. Nothing he can do about it without the tape."

Stan asked, "Shackleton will win anyway, why the overkill?"

"It completes our moon shot," Max said with a grin. "In addition to flipping the presidency, we'll pick up both House and Senate. We'll push the Dark Agers out and get our country back, in one fell swoop."

Tia was frantic. "But it's going to upset Butterfield. What if he refuses to send my email?"

"We still have leverage over him," Max said. *"The fire."* He gave everyone a hard look. "If Tia wants to send her email tomorrow morning, the Prophet endorses Shackleton tonight."

CHAPTER 118

S cotty was worried about Ivy. She hadn't been herself since the morning session, hardly touched her lunch. He'd thought maybe she was simply sad to see their Missions come to a close. Now he sensed more, but she refused to talk about it.

He watched her drag to his computer and slump into her chair.

"You *sure* you're feeling okay?" he asked.

She nodded, and he squeezed her hand.

One last session and their lives would return to a semblance of normality, with a better life awaiting them, hopefully.

The noises cycled through, and the angel materialized, back to her usual glow after her dramatic incandescence this morning. Scotty saw sadness in her still. He felt it, too, as he stared into her dazzling eyes for the last time. In this life.

Ariel greeted them, and Scotty responded. But Ivy said nothing, arms and legs crossed.

"We followed your instructions," Scotty reported, holding up the melted glob of cassette.

Ariel regarded it closely, and Scotty thought he heard muffled cheers on the other side.

"You've done well," she told him, "the Lord is pleased. But there's been a change of plans. There's something else the Lord needs of you now."

That old knot returned to Scotty's gut, and he declared, "No more, we've had enough."

Ariel exhaled. "I understand your reluctance, but the Lord insists. You must go on TV tonight and deliver a final announcement. You must endorse Ellen Shackleton and tell your followers to support all Democrat candidates with their votes."

Ivy gasped, and Scotty cried, "But-but, the Covenant!"

The angel lowered her gaze. "You must have faith. The Lord works in mysterious ways."

Ivy snapped, "Nothing mysterious about it. The Lord's breaking His Word. Again."

Ariel raised a hand. "There's something else the Lord wishes you to know, and it's very important. Your lives and the lives of others depend on it."

That had their attention.

"There'll be a fire in your building soon."

Scotty stiffened, and Ivy gripped his arm with both hands.

"In return for your loyal service, and for performing this final Mission, the Lord will spare you. The fire will arise in the bedroom of apartment 2D. A faulty lamp cord."

Kassandra's apartment.

"When?" Scotty croaked.

"Thursday, this week. Remove the hazard, and all will be well."

Ivy's fingers dug deeper, and Scotty felt her tremble. The angel froze him with her eyes.

"Go on TV tonight and do as the Lord commands. I'll return tomorrow morning to confirm you've done as told."

Before Scotty could object, Ariel bit her lip, bid them goodbye, and dissolved. Scotty pried Ivy's hands loose, jumped up, and raced out into the hall. This time Kassandra would see him if he had to bust down her door.

He nearly did. A full minute of pounding and shouting before she finally opened a crack, leaving the chain on.

"*Emergency,*" he cried. "There's gonna be a fire in your apartment!"

Kassandra screwed up her face. "How the hell do you know?"

"I'm a prophet, for chrissakes. Let me in!"

She undid the chain and he rushed inside, straight to her bedroom.

"The lamp," he said, pointing to her nightstand. "The cord."

Moving past him, Kassandra seized the lamp, causing the drawer to open and expose a frayed crimp of wire. It sparked, and she jumped. "*Oh my God,*" she gasped, unplugging it, thrusting it into Scotty's hands like it was a bomb. "*Oh my God.*"

Scotty wound the cord around it and exhaled. "All safe now," he said, and turned to go.

Kassandra stopped him, taking his hand. "I, I don't know what to say," she replied, sheepish. "I haven't been avoiding you, just busy with the election, you know? But I could use a break, if you'd like to stay for a drink."

"Another time," he told her.

She looked surprised, and he pulled away and hurried off.

Ivy was still at the computer when he returned, as glum as he'd left her. She regarded the lamp with relief, and he set it on his desk and headed to the coatrack, grabbing her backpack and jacket, bringing them to her.

"Get the rest of your stuff," he said, "you're going home."

She darkened. "What? *Now?*"

"We're not taking any chances. If the Lord can renege on Thornton, I don't trust a thing He says. I want you far from here. You're going back to school, anyway."

Looking stunned, she skulked to the bedroom while he called a cab, reappearing minutes later in tears. He helped her into her jacket, stuffing cash in her pocket.

She asked, "Are you gonna obey the Lord's last command?"

"I haven't decided, I need time to think." He sighed and took her hands. "Listen, Ivy, I know you're upset, too. I want you to go home and get a good night's sleep. Call me tomorrow from school when you can, and we'll talk."

"Pop took my phone."

"Then borrow one."

Giving her a hug, he pushed her into the hall, and shut the door.

• • •

Scotty paced while Homer observed from the couch. No matter how he looked at it, Scotty couldn't square the Lord's decision to cheat Thornton. How could God break His Word? Then relegate to Scotty the shame of announcing the treachery? On national TV, for God's sake?

From the very beginning of this insanity, the tone of the Lord's demands always struck Scotty as insensitive. And Ariel's angelic attributes aside, she exhibited *un*-angelic traits. Human-like responses, emotional *and* physical. Confusing. Troubling.

Scotty's eyes fell on the photo of Mom on the wall behind his desk, and he went to stand in front of it. His favorite picture of her, pretty and glowing, taken just before her fatal pregnancy. Once again, he relived the anguish of witnessing an intelligent, vibrant young woman sacrifice herself to her God. A God Who continued to push His inscrutable Will on the Butterfield family.

Hearing a noise behind, Scotty turned to see Homer sitting on the desk, staring at him.

Whaddya gonna do, dude?

Scotty frowned. "I can't risk upsetting such a fickle God. I'll go on the news, one last time."

The cat cocked its head at him. *Or maybe you could try showing some balls for once.*

Scotty cocked *his* head, feeling it would explode. "Christ, it's not like I'm dealing with Pop, here! You wanna get me zapped by a lightning bolt?"

Interesting you should mention lightning.

"What?"

Homer licked a paw and began cleaning his ears. *Used to be, people thought lightning was the finger of God. Smiting the wicked, and all that. Except, church steeples got struck all the time.*"

Scotty knew. "Until Ben Franklin invented the lightning rod."

Even then, churches wouldn't use 'em at first.

Scotty knew that, too. "People thought lightning was God's judgment, and thwarting Him would only anger Him more."

Until finally science beat out superstition, and now all steeples have lightning rods.

Scotty exhaled. "Your point?"

Point is, Mom had a lightning rod, too, so to speak. But she shunned it, and lightning struck.

"What the hell are you talking about?"

Birth control. Her lightning rod was The Pill. If she'd used it after you, she'd still be here.

Albeit, Ivy wouldn't. The knot in Scotty's gut tightened. "What's Mom got to do with this?"

Everything. You blame God for her death. Pop blames you. Bullshit. Doncha see? It was all Mom's call. She put her faith ahead of you and Pop. And to this day, it haunts you both, still. Neither of you ever came to grips with it.

Blinking, Scotty collapsed into his chair. How could he blame Mom for following her faith? He buried his head in his arms and sobbed, and Homer placed a paw on his shoulder...

After a time, Scotty dried his eyes on his sleeve, lifted up, and checked the clock. To drop the Lord's bombshell on the evening news, he had to leave now.

Homer paid him another sideways look.

Come on, bro, give it a rest. Let's watch the Jets.

Reflecting, Scotty finally set his teeth, grabbed the cat, and went to the couch.

If the Lord had no conscience, Scotty did. And sliding in with Homer, he turned on the game.

CHAPTER 119

After breakfast, Ariel sat in the living room with the team discussing developments. Or rather, the lack thereof. With less than twenty-four hours till the first polls opened, they'd seen no news in the archives that the Prophet of Queens had thrown his support to Ellen Shackleton and the Democrats. Nor even word of a pending announcement.

It seemed Butterfield had ignored the Lord's orders. Max was furious, but Ariel and Tia were frantic. In order to save Tia's mom, they'd need Butterfield's cooperation. And they'd no way to know how the man's sudden defiance would impact their plan.

Tia snapped at Max, "You pushed him too far, demanding that damned endorsement!"

Max said nothing, and Stan tried to lighten the mood by pointing out, "At least we've seen no trace of the Shackleton video, and the archive polls now show her ahead in the swing states." But then he darkened, too. "On the other hand, we had another quake last night. Big. Six point six."

Was the quake triggered by the video vanishing from history? With the rabbit's foot now lost in the hole, Ariel felt afraid to speculate about

528

anything. Despite a frantic search of the houseplant last session, Stan was unable to locate the flashdrive and its archival data. The team no longer had the means to determine if a Timewave altered their reality, or memories. Ariel didn't trust her reasoning now, and her heart leapt when Max suddenly announced, "We can't wait any longer, we've got to move operations out to the tent and gird for the Big One."

The room went quiet. While the Trapping Horizon offered no protection from the final Timequake, it could shield the team and their memories from its subsequent Time-tsunami.

Hopefully.

Ariel could feel Fate closing in, squeezing them into their bunker. So, they flee to the tent, *then* what? Even if they made it past the Big One and its Tsunami, they couldn't hide inside the bubble forever. Sooner or later, they'd have to brave the new world beyond.

Ariel rubbed her weary temples. She'd mulled this quandary before. But now faced with the certainty of uncertainty, she was gripped with panic. At some point during or after the election tomorrow, their world would change, past, present—and future. And no telling to what extent.

Max said, "We may weather what's coming, we may not. But I want to survive long enough, at least, to know we stuck our moon landing."

He rose, Stan followed, and the two left to prepare the tent for their last stand.

Ariel could hold back no more. Grasping Tia's wrist tight, she said in a quavering voice, "When the wave hits, all we've shared here could vanish. We may never have met, and never will." Her heart trembled. "If you hadn't taken me under your wing that first year, I wouldn't have made it." She burst into tears. *"I'm lost without you."*

Tia grabbed Ariel by the shoulders. *"Listen to me,"* she said, eyes glistening, but voice firm. "You *will* make it. You're a butterfly, *mi corazón.* You've always been a butterfly. Whatever the future holds, wherever you find yourself, it's only a matter of time before you break out of your cocoon and fly. And regardless, there's something I haven't told you."

Ariel wiped her eyes, and Tia leaned close. "That email I'm sending myself? I wrote about *us* in it, too. It's all there—everything that happened here. Our friendship, our hopes. When this is over, wherever we end up, I'll find you, I swear. And that bastard stepfather of yours, I included *his* files in my email, too. Together, you and I are gonna take that bastard down!"

She'd given Ariel something to cling to, and Ariel hugged her with all her might.

Whatever it took this next session, Butterfield *had* to forward Tia's email.

• • •

As the 10:00 AM hour loomed, Ariel assumed her place at the table in the tent, in angel mode for the last time. *Again.* The tent was now packed with bedding and other personal items for their sequester tonight. To ensure the clutter was out of Butterfields' view, Ariel zoomed her laptop camera tighter on herself.

Max was still fuming over the Prophet's failure to endorse Shackleton and her Democratic slate. And with the race tightening just as it had four years ago, he was hellbent on trying again.

He pressed Ariel, "It's not too late to influence the vote. Bat your eyes at Butterfield, work your magic. *Get him on the air with that endorsement.*"

Tia countered, *"My email."*

Tia's email sat waiting in Ariel's outbox. Depending on how receptive Butterfield was to that, Ariel would consider broaching Max's request. If, that is, Butterfield showed this morning. A worry, seeing how he blew off his orders to appear on TV last night.

Soon the noises came and went, the vortex appeared, the hole opened, and Stan inserted the antenna. Max and Tia hovered near Ariel like helicopter parents, just out of camera range.

Ariel was relieved to see Scott emerge on screen. But he was *not* happy. Coiled in a chair with a frown. Alone save for a big, orange cat in his lap, which also appeared to be frowning.

He failed to return Ariel's greeting. She asked, "Where's Ivy?"

"I sent her home. Not taking any chances after the fire alarm."

"But you found the threat and removed it, yes?"

"Yes," he spit. *"And now I want to know what other threats the Lord has in store."*

Ariel bit her lip. She'd never seen him so surly.

"No more threats," she assured. "You have the Lord's Word."

"Like His Word on the Covenant?"

This did *not* bode well for pushing a new task on him. But Ariel had no choice.

"I've a small favor to ask of you. A *personal* favor."

His frown deepened.

"I've something to send you. An epistle for you to forward to another party."

Out the corner of her eye, Ariel saw Max mouthing, *Shackleton.*

She continued, "All I ask is that you *not* open it, and you pass it on right away. Nothing more. It's the last I'll ever ask of you. Will you do that for me, Scott?" And she batted her eyes.

Max was livid, but she ignored him, and Scott ignored her, failing to respond.

Ariel pressed, "I'm sending it now. Please forward it, unopened, to the cc address—"

But as she moved to hit "send," Max reached to block her, Tia tried to block him, and they both struck the laptop, knocking it off the table. It hit the ground and its screen went black.

Ariel met Tia's frantic eyes to answer the question in them.

"I don't know if it went through."

CHAPTER 120

S cotty paced his living room with the cat on his heals, still in shock, disbelief and anger over what he'd seen during the morning session with Ariel.

Abruptly he veered for his computer, dropped into his chair, and replayed the ending for the umpteenth time. The video was blurry at normal speed, but in slomo, Scotty saw the heavens move to expose the corner of a cluttered tent sectioned off by white sheets and bright lights.

A movie set.

He could make out two people struggling with Ariel—a dark-haired man and a purple-haired woman. No one he recognized.

Homer leaped into Scotty's lap. *You got hosed, dude.*

Yes. The qualms he'd wrestled these past weeks had proven out in devastating fashion. All very clear now. The angel he'd come to trust and admire, and her Lord, were frauds. Ariel, if her real name, and her co-conspirators had somehow, impossibly, found a way to forecast the future. Then abused the ability to manipulate Scotty in an attempt to throw the presidential election.

"Why *me?*" he spit. Had Ariel scoured the Internet for the most gullible pigeon she could find? He knew what Pop would say. *What comes a living in a fantasy world.*

He was interrupted by a text. An unknown phone number—a heads-up from Ivy that she was about to call from a friend's cell. She was the only person Scotty could talk to about this insane turn of events, and he badly wanted her input.

Taking the call, he found her upset.

"What happened last night?" she cried. *"Why weren't you on the news?"*

"Because it's all a huge scam."

"What do you mean? What's going on?"

He inhaled and rolled out the story, beginning with his decision last night not to renege on the Covenant—damned glad he hadn't now—and ending with his devastating discovery that Ariel and her "Lord" were no more than elaborate con artists.

When he finished, there was silence on the other end. Then, *"Holy, holy crap! But I don't get it. How'd they pull it off? The prophecies, I mean."*

"A Magic 8 Ball, for all I know. I still can't believe Ariel would do this. She *lied* to me."

A pause, and Ivy said, *"I lied to you too, Scotty."* He heard guilt in her voice. *"There's something I gotta tell you. You're gonna be mad. Yesterday, while you were out looking for a fire extinguisher, I, uh, I sorta watched the tape."*

He felt only a flash of irritation in the scheme of things.

"I'll skip the yucky stuff. Enough to say, those stories about Shackleton's past? They're true. She's as much a fraud as Ariel and her Lord. Probably colluding with 'em, too, I'll bet. That's why they wanted that tape, it would be a slam-dunk for Filby if it got out."

"And if I'd made that endorsement last night, I'd have played right into their hands."

"Well, I say that's exactly what you should do. Go ahead, endorse Shackleton."

He stared at his phone. "What!"

"*I had all night to think about it, hear me out. Yes, Shackleton's a phony and a liar. But so's Filby. I mean, they're politicians, after all. Are Shackleton's flaws any worse than his? At least she's got the right agenda. Those people outside your window, they're hurting, and there are millions of 'em across the country. You think Filby cares? He'll drag us back to the Dark Ages.*"

Scotty was floored. "That's election-tampering. It's criminal!"

"*Look, we don't understand how she does it, but Ariel knows things we don't. For heaven's sake, she knows the future, and she's desperate to change it. What's that tell us?*"

"I can't believe you advocate cheating."

"*What if you knew Filby would turn out to be another Hitler, and you could do something about it? You always said you felt helpless and hopeless and voting was a waste. Well, here's your chance to make a difference. Whatever you think of Ariel now, you gotta admit there's something about her. Maybe her tactics are wrong, but I believe her heart's in the right place.*"

In fact, Scotty couldn't reconcile his former feelings for the woman. All the same, to subvert a presidential election, sway the course of the nation by feigning the Will of God?

"It's moot," he said. "Shackleton's up in the polls, she doesn't need my help."

"*Haven't you seen? It's narrowing in the swing states. Thornton's army is making headway, the electoral count's gonna be cl—*"

She broke off, someone interrupting her, then said, "*Crap, the T.O.'s looking for me. Listen, the way you've handled the madness these past weeks, I have faith in you. I know you'll sort it out and make the right call. Please, just promise me you'll think about it. Please.*"

He promised, she told him she loved him, and was gone.

His wounds felt raw, but Ivy's words weighed on him. Twenty hours till the polls opened.

Suddenly a blinking icon on his computer screen caught his eye. *An epistle.*

CHAPTER 121

S tan, Max, Ariel, and Tia sat side-by-side at the table in the tent, anxiously awaiting the afternoon run. Their last shot at Butterfield before the election.

The morning session had ended abruptly with Max and Tia knocking Ariel's laptop to the floor. While the computer survived, its signal to Butterfield had been cut just as Ariel attempted to send Tia's email. A copy of the message showed up in Ariel's "sent" file garbled and unreadable, and there was no way to know if Butterfield had received the same gibberish. Or how much of the incident he'd seen, possibly endangering their credibility with him.

Tia demanded a redo, but Max was hellbent on Butterfield endorsing Shackleton, and though they'd given Ariel and Stan their solemn oaths not to interfere with the next run, they were still pointing fingers at each other. Ariel was caught in the middle, as usual, shrinking in her chair as she felt her moonshot slipping away.

On the table next to Ariel sat Tia's laptop, open to the *Omaha World-Herald* archives. An obit of Tia's mom. A kind-looking, gray-haired lady with Tia's complexion and eyes. Tia was convinced that if Butterfield had in fact forwarded a legible email to her younger self, Past Tia would have been persuaded by it and moved to save her mom. In which case, the obit would vanish, like with little Teddy. But hours had passed, and the obit remained.

Max turned his laptop to Ariel, displaying a "new" election poll from four years ago.

"Shackleton's lead in the swing states is dwindling," he said, "We need that endorsement from Butterfield. If saving his life wasn't incentive enough for him, let's up the ante. Offer him a million-dollar lottery this time. Hell, *ten* million."

Tia grabbed Ariel's arm. "Twenty, *if* he forwards my email."

Of course, the bribes would go unpaid after the Big One, and Ariel was relieved when thunder ended the bidding. The hole opened, Stan inserted the antenna, and Ariel sucked up her scruples once more. But when she tried to connect with Butterfield, she found his link dead.

She alerted the others, and Max checked her connections.

"The problem's on the other side," he snapped. "The bastard shut off his computer!"

Preventing them from contacting him.

And Ariel from resending Tia's email.

• • •

The afternoon crawled as the team hunkered in the tent sifting the archives for changes in the past. Nothing of consequence. The obit of Tia's mom remained on her screen.

Then shortly after 5:00, Max rocked forward and whooped, startling the others.

"Hot damn," he cried, turning his laptop to show them.

Ariel saw a four-year-old Hawk News promo:

Election-shaking Announcement
from The Prophet of Queens
Live at 6:00

Tia whispered like a prayer, "If Butterfield follows through on the endorsement, he'll forward my email, too."

Assuming he received it.

Time passed like torture till the top of the hour, Tia's obit never wavering. As twilight fell, everyone crowded Max's laptop for a new, four-year-old announcement.

A Hawk News host appeared on screen, seated at an anchor desk.

"Ladies and gentlemen," he said, beaming, *"We're pleased to have with us, Scott Butterfield, better known to viewers as the Prophet of Queens. Mr. Butterfield informs us, this will be his last public appearance. He has a special prophecy to deliver, and it concerns tomorrow's election."*

A headline read: *Prophet Makes Election Pick,* and Ariel's chest felt taut as a drum.

The camera widened to show Butterfield in a black hoody, cowl up, shepherd's staff in hand. A sign he was still on board, Ariel trusted. But he did *not* look in good spirits. Like he hadn't slept in days. And there was something else. A hardness in his eyes and jaw she'd not seen before. Gone was that air of uncertainty he often displayed, replaced by steely resolve.

He corrected the host, "Not *my* prediction." And turning to the camera, he declared:

"The Lord's prophecy is simple: These are dark times, the country is in deep trouble, and we need a leader who can guide us back into the light. The Lord has therefore decided to bestow victory on the best choice for our next president—Republican Senator, Roger Filby."

The oxygen went out of the tent. Ariel felt numb, and Max moaned as if his soul had been wrenched from him. They watched dazed as Butterfield hauled himself to his feet with his staff, and refusing questions, he tossed his lapel mike on the desk and walked off set, leaving the host speechless.

Max's face was redder than the setting sun, and the team went deathly quiet as the enormity of their defeat settled over them. Then Stan began frantically searching the archives, breaking the silence to report, "The prophecy is going über-viral…" He clicked more keys to add, "And the InstaPolls are already moving."

Tia looked like she'd been in a car wreck. Rising with a grimace more animal than human, she turned on Max to scream, "You just *had* to keep pushing him, didn't you? You not only lost us the election, you goddamn sonovabitch, *you lost me my mother.*"

CHAPTER 122

Reverend Thornton sat alone in his office, riveted to a TV. The Prophet had just delivered a profound new prediction, and Thornton couldn't control his shaking. His phones began to ring. He let them go to voicemail, drinking-in the moment. No God-fearing voter in this God-fearing country would dare flout the prophecy. The Lord was delivering on His Covenant, same as He'd saved Alice's life and forgiven Thornton the grievous sin he'd borne these many years.

Tears rolled down his face. He felt overwhelmed and deeply humbled. It was as if God had raised up this unlikely Prophet expressly to help Thornton achieve his dreams. The lofty goals he'd set for himself so long ago were coming to fruition. And now with the Lord's continued blessings, Thornton and his protégé, *President* Filby, would begin returning the nation to rock-solid Christian principles.

A familiar voice came over his answering machine—Archbishop Bartholomew Rand. Thornton detected a more deferential tone to His Excellency's voice tonight.

"Congrats, Brooks. Looks like I owe you an apology, our Prophet delivered on his Covenant after all. I suppose it's time we call a Council

meeting, set our priorities for the new administration. Is next Wednesday here good for you?"

Already it was starting. Rand and the other Council members would be jockeying for influence on Filby. But *none* had Thornton's éminence grise. He, and he alone, would pull Filby's strings. He picked up the phone.

"Yes," he replied, "a meeting. But we'll be holding it *here*, in the City of God."

CHAPTER 123

In the wake of Butterfield's mutiny, the team sat around the tent in silence, a dark night closing in. Ariel watched with concern as Tia grew increasingly sullen and distant. No hope now of seeing her mom again, she'd left the newspaper obit on her screen as a haunting reminder to Max.

At length, Stan spoke the unspoken.

"All our hard work and risks, and we made things worse. If Filby wins by a larger margin than before, he'll pull *more* Dark Agers into Congress. It'll mean even *more* anti-science bills."

"And this time," Max said, "they'll have the votes to shutter TPC."

Dooming their careers here before they'd even started. Four years ago, construction on the collider was far from complete. Were TPC to have shut down prior to the team arriving, it was unlikely any of them would have ever met. Each would have been set adrift on the sea of Time, and of the four, Ariel saw her voyage into the future as most precarious. Fighting panic, she scavenged for hope.

"Assuming Filby wins again," she asked, "is it possible we'll be spared the Big One?"

Stan looked dismal. "I'm afraid the bulk of our tampering hasn't caught up to us yet."

Max exhaled. "Like getting a bill for the surgery that killed you. The tab *will* come due." And then he surprised everyone by suddenly slamming the table with a palm. "But by God, as long as I'm still kicking, I'll be damned if I'm giving up!"

Ariel moaned, "The polls open tomorrow at 8:00 AM. Even if Butterfield turns his computer back on, we can't reach him till 10:00."

"Too late to prevent Filby's election, maybe," Max said, "but we can still clip his coattails. If we can just get Butterfield to walk back his prophecy, we might stop the Dark Agers from taking over Congress—and keep TPC alive."

Ariel had never met anyone as tenacious as Max. She wondered if OCD was fueling it. But at least he was giving them something to focus on besides their imminent demise.

"*Think,*" he prodded. "There's got to be a way to change Butterfield's mind. Surely we can come up with *something.*"

Stan checked his watch. "Get him on air by midday tomorrow, we'd have eight hours before the polls close out West. *Maybe* enough time to salvage Congress, a lot of tight races out there." He turned to Tia. "And we can take another shot at your email."

Max said, "Everyone has his price. We'll offer Butterfield a *hundred* million."

Tia seemed too deep in her spiral to pull out. "He's onto us," she snarled. "He knows we used him, and he's pissed. A bribe will only make things worse."

Stan pointed out, "How could it be any worse?"

Silence.

Ariel said, "There's one approach we haven't tried yet…"

The others looked to her, and she saw a glimmer of hope in Tia's eyes.

"*The truth.*"

CHAPTER 124

The team spent a restless night in the tent, suffering three more quakes, each stronger than the previous. Between the tremors and Stan's snoring, Ariel hardly slept. But Stan and Max had made reinforcements to keep the tent standing tall—hopefully enough to weather the Big One.

Ariel woke before dawn, Stan and Max still asleep. But Tia's bed-roll was empty, and Ariel saw no sign of her. Thinking her in the house making coffee, she rose and slipped into her robe.

Soon as she stepped from the tent, however, she spotted Tia sitting on the porch steps, face awash in the light of her laptop. As Ariel drew close, she saw Tia's cheeks wet with tears, and rushed to her.

"What is it?" she cried with alarm.

Tia rotated her screen to display the *Omaha World-Herald* obits page. Ariel was confused, then felt her eyes bug as she searched the listings for Tia's mom, in vain.

"*Oh my God, Tia,*" she cried, hugging her. "*Oh my God.*"

Newton started barking, and moments later, the men staggered from the tent and stumbled over. Max was near naked, Stan in pajamas, no glasses, squinting.

They stared at Tia's screen, Stan's eyes popped, and he wrapped Tia up, gushing, "Butterfield sent your email after all! *And it worked.*"

Max yawned. "I don't get it. He double-crosses us with Shackleton, but follows through on Tia's email?"

"Makes sense to me," Stan said. "He couldn't go back on his word to Thornton, and he couldn't refuse Ariel a favor."

Ariel asked Tia, "Have you tried calling your mom?"

"Yes. Her number's disconnected. I sent her an email, and it bounced. But I know she's out there, she has a Twitter page now." Showing the link to the others, she took a long breath. "And apparently, so do I. We tweet each other every day."

Max's voice fell to a whisper. "You've got a *Doppelgänger?*"

Stan said, "Please tell us you didn't contact your, uh, your *self.*"

"I tried, but I couldn't get through to me, either." Tia wiped her eyes. "There's a commuter flight to La Guardia at noon. I can connect to Omaha, and be home tonight. I'll send for my trailer later."

Stan froze. "No-no, Tia! You and your twin *can't* meet. *The Law of Conservation of Mass.*"

Conservation of Mass: a law of physics stating that the total amount of matter and energy within a universe cannot change, neither increase nor decrease in quantity by so much as an atom. Meaning, the addition of a *second* Tia to their universe presented a grave dilemma.

Max said, "If you meet, one of you will cancel the other out like a duel. No telling which one will be left standing."

Tia appeared taken aback, only to recover and counter, "Then why do I still exist? There's *already* another me running around out there somewhere, and I'm still here." She pointed to the tent. "It's *not* the Trapping Horizon protecting me, we're on the porch."

Stan said, "I have a possible explanation, but you're not going to like it."

Everyone went quiet, and he sighed. "The many Timequakes and waves we've set off these past weeks? I believe it's thrown the universe into a state of upheaval. We've prodded and stretched the Timeline to the breaking point, stretched other laws of physics along with it—including the Conservation of Mass."

Max nodded. "But it can't continue like this. The universe will correct the instability."

"Yes. The universe will recalibrate Time with a final quake and Tsunami."

Ariel felt panic. "We've got the Trapping Horizon to protect us."

"Only so long as we remain inside it," Max said. "If Doppelgängers are already popping up, it bodes bad for us sooner or later. It says the world has moved on and left us behind."

"What do you mean?" Ariel cried.

Stan said, "It seems we're anachronisms. We've entered the last phase before the Big One. And when it blows, its wave will wipe away all the accumulated glitches."

Including *them*.

Max looked as pensive as Ariel had ever seen him.

He took a long breath and said, "We know now, multiverses *do* exist. Superstring Theory is correct, we solved The Grand Equation."

The elusive, long sought-after Theory of Everything.

He sighed. "Unfortunately, I don't think we'll be around to collect any Nobels."

Tia jumped to her feet. "I've got to pack."

Ariel panicked, clutching Tia's arm. *"You can't go!"*

By her eyes, Tia was well aware of the risk.

"I can't hide here forever, *mi corazón*," she said. "Mom's out there, and whatever time I've got left, I'm spending it with her."

And turning, she went inside the house.

Chapter 125

Kassandra cleaned out her office, chucking her belongings in a cardboard box, swearing under her breath, fighting tears.

Not that she wasn't expecting this, but to have it done so, so *dismissively.* After how hard she'd worked for this damned place, how close she'd come to saving EP&M's ass. A pink slip left unceremoniously on her desk. Franklin Percy hadn't the courtesy to sack her himself, leaving the satisfaction to Shonda.

A guard stood at Kassandra's door, burly arms folded, watching what she put into the box. She was dreading the walk of shame through the office, everyone aware. And of course, Bobby Driscoll wasn't letting her off without a last shot.

He popped his head in her door. "Gotta hand it to you, Kassie," he chirped, "you had me worried for a while. Slick move seducing that Prophet. No way I could compete there."

Failing to draw a response, he leaned against the door by the guard to add, "A little advice, babe, from a man's perspective. Next time you want to hustle a dude like Butterfield, make sure he puts up *before* you put out."

He cackled, and the guard joined in.

Kassandra finished packing and turned, smiling sweetly. "You know, Bobby, I was wrong about you. We've got something in common after all."

He raised a brow.

"...We'll both screw anyone to get ahead."

Snatching the box, she marched out the door, tossing back, "And you can keep your advice. If ever I want your perspective, *I'll stick my head up your ass.*"

She breezed off, and the security guard followed, laughing.

CHAPTER 126

Ariel sat at the table in the tent flanked by Tia and Stan, staring into the roiling vortex before her. Like seeing inside her own head. She'd adjusted her laptop camera to include Tia and Stan in its view this time. Max was perched on a stool in front of the vortex, poised to insert the antenna in the wormhole when it appeared.

No longer was Ariel dressed as an angel. For the first time, she was presenting her true self, hair down, plain blue blouse. In the spirit of full disclosure, however, she'd skipped contacts and makeup.

The election of four years ago was already underway, outcome a fait accompli, according to the exit polls. All the same, the team was committed to slowing down the Dark Age onslaught. If they could somehow convince Butterfield to endorse the Democrats, they might yet keep Congress out of Filby's hands, and save TPC. Assuming, that is, Butterfield showed up this morning. The prospects did not seem good after his recent behavior. And as the wormhole opened once more, Ariel had the sinking sensation it was for the last time.

Max inserted the antenna, then rested its opposite end on his stool to keep it in place. Hustling behind Ariel and the others, he dropped to one knee where he could be seen on camera, too, his hand warm on Ariel's shoulder.

Ariel opened videochat. And to her surprise and relief, there sat Scott Butterfield. Slumped, arms folded across his chest, big tabby in his lap. Maybe he was seeking some closure, too.

"Hello," Ariel greeted him contritely.

He said nothing, taking them all in. His frown deepened.

Anger, or curiosity?

"You've every right to be upset," Ariel told him. "We should have leveled with you from the start. My name is Ariel Silva. These are my colleagues—" she gestured to each in turn, "Tia Diego, Maxwell Bach, Stan Bronkowski. We want to apologize for what we've put you through. Please let me explain."

He dismissed her with a wave of a hand. *"Way ahead of you,"* he said, glancing offscreen. *"I moved my plant. I'm looking at your wormhole as we speak. But I admit, I'm still trying to wrap my head around the time-travel thing."*

Ariel's heart felt leaden. He'd read Tia's email and uncovered their ruse. And now, rightfully resentful, he was going to make Ariel's job all the harder. She pushed on.

"Whatever you must think of our tactics, we know you care about the country as much as we do. Under Filby, things are going to get *very* dark. He's a puppet of Thornton's Council, up to his ears in illegal collusion. If you'd let our hindsight be your foresight—"

"I get it. You don't like the direction the country's headed, and you stumbled onto a way to change it. Except, stealing an election isn't exactly legal, now is it?"

Stan said, "Our goals were honorable. We put our lives at risk."

Tia added, "We made mistakes, yes. There's no precedent for what we faced, no guidelines."

Scott scratched the cat's ears. *"You needed guidelines to act in good faith? And now you're caught in your own trap. A Timetrap, and the clock is ticking. So what becomes of you?"*

"We're not sure," Ariel said. "There'll be a change to spacetime, as we know it. A *big* change. Imminent. We've no idea what, or how to stop it."

Max said, "The way it's shaping up, it *won't* be a survivable event for us."

Scott seemed shaken, and Max pressed, "You backed the wrong horse, pal. Filby is a nightmare. The only way to avoid complete disaster is to save Congress. You've got to go back on the air and tell people to vote Democrat."

Reflecting, Scott replied, *"You've given me no reason to trust you, and I don't. I'm afraid I'm going to pass."*

Strong fingers tightened on Ariel's shoulder, and Max demanded, "What is it you want, Butterfield? A hundred million? *Two* hundred? Price is no object."

The man's response was a stony glare.

Max exploded. "You're making a *huge* mistake. You think life's tough for you now? Do what we say, or I swear to God we'll bring hell down on you and your sister!"

The cat hissed and ran off, Scott went livid, and Ariel moaned.

Max and his insufferable bullshit, always his last resort.

"Enough fire and brimstone, Lord," Scott snapped, spitting the last word. *"I'm done here."*

He stood, bending down to pay Ariel a somber gaze.

"I'm afraid for you and what's coming," he said, *"more than you'll ever know. But for once, let me leave you with a prophecy."* He pointed to Max. *"If you do survive this, Ariel, whatever your future holds, give your heart to this conniving bastard again, and I guarantee you he'll crush it again."*

Ariel blinked. How'd he know about her and Max? It wasn't in Tia's email.

The rabbit's foot.

Suddenly Scott stepped out of the frame, and seconds later his shepherd's staff and Max's antenna came sailing through the hole, clattering to the tent floor.

And Ariel's screen went dark.

Chapter 127

Shortly after the session ended, the team experienced another intense, short-lived quake. Eight-point-four. Followed by another towering, terrifying wave, larger than ever. It passed leaving no trace, other than the weight it added to the team's despair.

As the others picked up the tent, Max slipped outside, returning before he was missed.

"I just got off the phone with TPC," he announced. "My password no longer works, and no one there knows me now. They've no record of my employment."

Everyone stopped what they were doing, tent very quiet.

Ariel whispered, *"You left the bubble?"*

The protection of the bubble extended but a mere ten feet beyond the tent.

Max shrugged. "My memories still seem intact. Including those from TPC."

Stan said what Ariel was thinking. "We're anachronisms, all right. Time's passed us by, the Big One can't be far off."

Tia stopped what she was doing.

"All the more reason for me to go," she said. She'd booked a 12:30

551

flight, bags packed and sitting by the tent door. Stan was driving her to the airport. Cabs weren't available out here, Ariel's car wasn't trustworthy, and Max hadn't offered.

Fighting tears, Ariel seized Tia's hands, crying, *"Please,* take me with you."

Tia's eyes welled, too, and she squeezed Ariel's fingers. "No, *mi corazón,*" she said. "This is something I have to do alone. Stay here till the Tsunami passes, then we'll see."

See if Tia survived, she meant—and if she still remembered Ariel.

Ariel begged, "Let me ride to the airport with you, at least."

"The Big One could hit any moment. Stan's already at risk, no sense both of you."

That was it, then. Ariel would be left to cower here inside the bubble awaiting the great unknown. She preferred Tia's choice to confront the future head-on. At least Tia wouldn't know what hit her.

Tia placed her hands on Ariel's shoulders. "If we've learned any-thing from all this," she said, we've learned it's impossible to predict what will happen. Maybe some of the good we tried to do will reso-nate. Maybe a few butterflies we set loose will land on the right side of history. I have to believe that. I *have* to believe that whatever becomes of us, it won't all be for nothing."

Ariel forced a smile as if she believed it, too. They embraced, and Tia left her with, "I'll call when I get in. *Good luck.*" And she and Stan ducked out.

Ariel watched at the tent door, heart leaden as Stan pulled out of the drive. He stopped to grab the mail, calling to her with a smile, "Hold off on the Big One, I'll be back before noon."

She waved through tears till the truck disappeared, then went to be with Newton. Stan had moved the doghouse safely inside the bubble, but what would become of Newton if something happened to Ariel? She gripped him tight, crying into his fur as the wind picked up, angry thunderheads lumbering in. Ariel worried about Tia's flight.

Max called from the tent, "A storm's brewing, better get inside."

Ariel composed herself, and giving Newton a long squeeze, she returned to the tent.

Max sat at the table facing her with a bottle of sherry and two glasses. He'd shoved her laptop out of the way, making room for Ariel at his side.

"What's this?" Ariel asked, zipping the door flap against the gusts.

"Found it in the pantry the other day," he said, pouring. "I was saving it for a special occasion. The end of the world will do." He added, "Exit polls show Filby and the Dark Agers sweeping it all in a rout. Shackleton hasn't conceded, but I'm sure we'll know when she does."

He offered her the chair next to him. She sank into it, and he raised his glass.

"To the future."

They clinked and drank. Bitter, and Ariel winced.

Max topped her up, and she whispered, "Even with the wisdom of hindsight, we leave the world worse off."

He shrugged. "We gave our best, and came up short. *C'est la vie.*"

She took another sip. Sweeter. "No regrets?"

"Would I do things different if I had the chance? Sure. But the choices I made, I made with the data available at the time. I'm not God, after all." He paid her a wry grin. "Or an *angel.*"

If he was playing her, it felt comforting somehow.

Ariel wanted to ask a question long stuck in her craw, something she'd resisted, knowing the dignity it would cost her.

But with the clock running out, it was now or never.

"Any regrets about *us?*"

She watched his tongue roll along the inside of his cheek. He took his time, then said, "You know, I never set out to hurt you. It just…happened."

Ariel felt a flash of hurt and anger. "Don't hand me that. We both know you grew tired of me. The prudish rube wasn't enough for you."

He spread his hands. "We're all ruled by forces we can't control."

Was he referring to himself, or *her*? Incredulous, she asked, "You're telling me, you couldn't control your libido?"

"That's exactly what I'm telling you."

She set her drink down hard. "Don't try to turn this into a bipolar thing. I know more about your condition than you do."

Back during those painful days, Ariel had strived to learn all she could about the demons of his disorder. An overcharged sex drive wasn't among them.

Max said, "It has nothing to do with my condition. It's my meds."

"What?"

He nodded. *"Hypersexual Dysfunction.* Side effect of the Valpro. It helped my mood swings, but amped my sex drive."

Ariel rocked back in her chair. She knew little about psychotropic medications, recalling his aggressive, self-indulgent behavior that drove her away, and him into the arms of another woman.

"I didn't know at the time," he said. "I found out online, and experimented with my dosage till I found a better balance."

"Why didn't you tell me—not that it excuses what you did."

"By then, things between us had scabbed over."

Suddenly Ariel found herself in a backwash of emotion. Closing her eyes, she swam in confusion and frustration. She was so ignorant about matters of the heart, always looking to Tia for guidance. A part of her still loved the man. The first and only love she'd ever known.

A clap of thunder made her jump, and a strong arm wrapped her shoulders, musky scent filling her with nostalgia. She felt weary to the soul, and he pulled her close to kiss her neck.

It felt so endearing.

He said, "I never stopped loving you, and no Timewave will ever change how I feel."

There came that *look* again. He leaned in and kissed her on the lips, hot, moist. The memories flooded, Ariel weakening.

Outside, the wind kicked up, snapping the canvas. A corner of the tent went slack, and Max disengaged to say, "I'd better snug the rope. Sit tight, I'll be right back."

He refilled her glass, jumped up, undid the door flap, and ran out.

Ariel shook her head, overloaded, unable to clear her mind. But end of the world or not, there was something she *had* to know.

Rising, she circled the table to her laptop, turning her back to the door, bending down to type into *Google Search*:

Valpro: sexual dysfunction

Seconds later she was inundated with results. Foremost was a pharmacology white paper with several lines highlighted, including:

Among the top antipsychotics prescribed to treat bipolar disorder, sodium valproate (Valpro) has no known sexual side effects.

She froze. And before she could recover, she heard the door flap zip closed, Max purring, "I've missed you so, I want you back..."

Hands gripped her hips. Brazen, presumptuous hands.

Instantly, Ariel went from frozen to white hot. Pirouetting, she laid her palm hard across Max's leering face. He fell to the floor, shocked, a red handprint glowing on his cheek. Ariel was just as shocked, she'd never struck another being in her life.

He gaped up at her wide-eyed as she stormed, *"I wouldn't take you back if you were the last man on Earth."*

Which, in their world, he very well could be.

Stan should have been back by now.

Chapter 128

A truce of sorts settled over the tent. Ariel in one corner on her phone, trying to reach Stan, Max in another on his laptop, in a sulk. Outside, a slow-moving squall rumbled as it advanced.

Again Ariel was sent straight to voicemail, again leaving word, "Stan, call me, *I'm worried.*"

She turned to Max to insist, "For God's sake, give me your car keys."

Cheek still red, he replied without looking up. "If Stan ran into his Doppelgänger, there's nothing we can do."

Big One notwithstanding, Stan could already have been erased from existence.

Ariel could take no more. Hoping her car had a few more miles of life, she grabbed her keys, leaped up, and marched for the door.

But as she unzipped it, she was relieved to hear the crunch of gravel in the drive, and rushed out into cool breeze and black skies—only to brake.

Not Stan's truck. Much bigger. *Orange.*

It grated to a dusty stop, and two men emerged. One was huge and had Stan in his grasp, hauling him from the cab by his collar, Stan's face bloodied and bruised.

Ariel moaned and ducked back before they spotted her.

"What?" Max grumbled.

"Those men in the orange truck. *They've got Stan.*"

Max sprang to join her, peering out. "Crap. They beat our location out of him."

"Stan would never give us away," Ariel insisted. "They found our mail in his pickup."

She stole a look to see the men muscle Stan toward the house. Newton began to bark, the men glanced over, and Max pulled Ariel back. She heard the big man snarl, "What's in the tent?"

"Nothing," Stan replied. "Equipment. Storage."

Newton was going nuts when suddenly a gun went off. Ariel jumped, and Newton yelped and fell silent. Before Ariel could cry out, Max muffled her with a powerful hand.

"Not a sound," he whispered, *"or we're all dead."*

The big man told his partner, "Check the tent, I'll do the house. An' hands off the blonde bitch, she's *mine.*"

The porch door slammed, and Ariel shuddered through her tears. At least it appeared Tia had escaped their clutches. Max grabbed Ariel and pulled her to the side, forcing her to crouch.

"Don't move," he hissed, and went to stand by the door. In his hands was the shepherd's staff, and he gripped it like a baseball bat, curved end high as he reared back.

Footsteps approached on the lawn, slowed, and a voice said cautiously, "If you're in there, come out, or I'll shoot."

Max gave Ariel a warning glance and cocked himself. A handgun protruded through the door, followed by a squinting, whiskered head in a ball cap.

"Ah ain't shittin' ya—"

The words ended in a crunch of shattered teeth and bone as Max brought the staff around like a Louisville Slugger. The man dropped the gun and fell out the door in a heap of gushing blood. Max gave him a few more swings, leaving Ariel shocked and nauseous. She feared the man was dead.

"Listen to me," Max told her, picking up the gun, sticking it in his belt. "If we're gonna get out of this, I need your help."

"Wh-wh-what are you going to do?"

"I'm going around to the side of the house. When the bastard comes out, show yourself and draw his attention. He won't shoot if you're not armed, that's not what he has in mind."

"You'll shoot him?"

Max grunted. "I never fired a gun in my life, I'm liable to hit you or Stan." He brandished the staff. "Just stand here in the doorway, I'll do the rest."

And heading outside, he took the fallen man by a foot, dragged him to the side of the house out of sight, and flattened against the clapboard, giving Ariel a thumbs-up.

Ariel moved numbly to the door, heart thundering, thunder thundering, tent flaps flapping. Then the porch door blew open and Stan burst out ahead of the big man and his gun.

Stan saw her, his eyes went wide, and he yelled, *"Run, Ariel, run."*

The big man shut him up with the butt of his gun, and Stan tumbled down the stairs in a tangle. Ariel cried out, lightning burst, and the storm unfurled. The man stepped over Stan and lumbered for her, calling, "Bo, where are ya?" And to Ariel, "Where's your asshole boyfriend?"

Ariel clenched to see Max slip out from hiding and steal up behind, staff at the ready. Her heart pounded triple-time as Max closed, and then he launched like a ninja, bringing the staff down hard on the big man's gun hand. The man howled, his gun went flying, and before he could react further, Max planted his feet, flipped the staff end-for-end, and hooked it around the man's thick neck, pulling and tugging. A cowboy with a roped steer.

But the big man hardly budged. Face dark as the skies, he turned, shook off his injury, and grabbed the staff in both hands. A tug of war. A war Max was no match for, it looked. He was jerked around as if he weighed nothing. Ariel couldn't watch.

Literally.

The ground beneath her began to buck, tossing her back into the tent. She landed hard, wind knocked out of her. The earth continued to heave and rock like a paint-can shaker, tumbling her about. Anything in the tent not battened down toppled and shook to pieces.

The Big One.

How long the quake lasted, Ariel had no idea, rattled senseless. But when it stopped, somehow the tent remained standing. She raised to her elbows, dizzy, panting, aching and fearful as her thoughts returned to the other crisis at hand. Out in the yard, removed from the bubble, Max and the man had ceased their struggle to gape at her. They stood with mouths moving, no sound, not even from bolts of lightning overhead.

And then Ariel saw it. Far off on the horizon, a dark wall of cloud roiling like a dust storm, high as the sky. It approached in a fury from every direction, all the eerier for its silence. A tidal wave of Time to wipe away the old and leave a transformed world in its wake. A world that, despite all their ardent efforts, Ariel and team had failed to save from the Dark Agers.

The wave was more massive by far than previous, and Ariel had no faith the bubble could withstand it. Far worse for the two men who battled in its path. She cried out to Max, not that he could hear. He knew what to expect, letting go the staff, breaking for the tent.

But his opponent had position on him, and as Max skirted by, the man hooked Max's leg and sent him crashing to the ground. Then raising the staff high, he brought it down hard on Max's head.

And Max went still.

Ariel uttered a scream only she could hear. The man started for her, foul grin on his lips, and she moaned, sinking to the floor again.

After a gut-full of wormholes and butterflies, lies and deceits and fizzled moon shots, her world was now completely destroyed. Whatever upheaval this Tsunami brought, she prayed it would come in time to spare her a final humiliation.

And feeling faint, she closed her eyes.

CHAPTER 129

Ariel woke on her back to muffled voices and harsh light. Squinting, she raised a hand to shield her eyes, and her arm ached. She felt weak, disoriented, addled.

"Kill the spots," a woman's voice said.

A familiar voice, in a strange way. Yet no voice Ariel could identify.

The light dimmed, still bright, her eyes slow to adjust. She was still inside the tent on the floor, she could see. Broken equipment and personal items lay scattered about.

She rose to her elbows, pain sharpening her senses, and her mind turned to her friends. The storm and Tsunami had passed, sun glaring. And then Ariel realized—*not* sunlight.

Artificial illumination.

Pushing to her knees, she crawled to the door, confused to see the lawn end at the arc of the Trapping Horizon. Beyond was polished white tile, and ten feet further, dozens of people in white lab coats, staring at her. Behind them was a large array of sophisticated equipment—computers, electronics, floodlights, cameras.

This was *indoors.* Like the inside of an airplane hangar.

Confused, Ariel inched out onto the grass, and the people burst

560

into applause. She was shocked to make out TPC Director, Winston Keller. And to her relief and astonishment, Stan, who looked fully recovered from the blows he'd taken, sporting a goatee and no glasses. He smiled and waved.

Next to Stan was Tia, clipboard in hand, eyes glistening. Her hair was different, again. No longer pink or purple, *un*-tinted, and smartly styled. Max was nowhere to be seen, but beside Tia stood a dark-haired, clean-cut, handsome young man. Ariel didn't recognize him, though he nodded as if he knew her. In one arm he held a big, orange cat. And holding the man's other hand was—

Oh my God...

Ariel trembled. A young woman with pale skin, no makeup, platinum hair pulled back in a loose ponytail. Black-rim glasses, apprehensive silver eyes. And she held a leash.

Newton.

The dog seemed calmer and more under control than she'd ever seen him. He stared at Ariel, then turned to nod at the cat, and Ariel could swear they exchanged winks. The woman passed the leash to the man with the cat, and approached Ariel as far as the Horizon line.

Ariel forced herself to unsteady feet, gaping at a reflection of her own anxiety.

The woman said in a voice familiar-yet-strange, "We've been expecting you. We didn't know exactly when the Big One would hit."

"Where am I?" Ariel asked, overwhelmed. "*When* am I?"

"Where and when you were before, in the tent outside the farmhouse. Except, it appears we no longer exist in the same world. We replaced the house and yard with this facility years ago."

Ariel was incredulous. The things she'd experienced here had never happened?

The woman seemed to read her. "We suspect you inhabit a parallel dimension—presuming Superstring Theory is correct. This is all new to us, too, we've much work ahead."

"But where's Max?"

The woman puzzled, then said, "Yes, yes. I never met Mr. Bach, he works at Hadron."

"And the Tia and Stan I *used* to know?"

The woman shook her head.

Ariel's head was spinning. All her years here had been erased. Never had she felt so alone. The woman was right, this was no longer Ariel's world. She was lost, marooned in time.

Her eyes teared once more, and she saw the same in her twin. It seemed all Ariel's efforts over the past weeks, all the risks she and her friends had taken, were in vain.

Fearful, she asked, "What happens if I leave this bubble?"

The woman lowered her gaze. "Also unknown. It's possible you'll return to the world you left, if it still exists in the multiverse. Or one of us may replace the other. Or something else entirely that we can't yet imagine."

Ariel turned to stare into the tent at the last shattered remnants of her life. All that remained of her now lay broken on the floor.

"What should I do?" she asked, hurting and confused.

"That's a decision only you can make."

"But won't my leaving this bubble put *you* at risk, too?"

The woman looked to the people behind her, who seemed to share Ariel's fear. Facing Ariel again, the woman set her jaw. "I've spent years preparing for this moment. All of us have. But there's no clock, no urgency. It's entirely up to you."

The room grew tense, and the woman's eyes shimmered under the lights. She said, "Whatever happens now, we want you to know we're deeply in your debt. You made our world a far, far better place. If not for you, your brilliance and courage, none of us would be here today."

Another round of applause. It washed over Ariel leaving her more confused than ever. She felt trapped. She'd felt trapped her entire life. Trapped by her family, her religion, her appearance, her shyness. And now, this Trapping Horizon.

It was time to free herself. Whatever her fate, she accepted it.

"I'm ready if you are," she said.

Taking a long breath, she extended her hand to the woman, the woman took it, and instantly everything within the Horizon flashed and vanished.

Ariel, too.

PART FOUR

Chapter 130

"Where do you want us to set up?" one of the cameramen asked Kyle Heath as they removed equipment from the van.

Heath rubbed sleep from his eyes, trying to absorb the scene before him. "Nowhere," he replied. "I want you to roam the area and document *all* of this."

He and his news team had flown in late last night for an up-close look at the phenomena unfolding here in Penbrook Thornton's City. Stories had been going around, but Heath was the first reporter Thornton had allowed in. Another Hawk exclusive.

Their van was parked outside Chapel Mount Park, the town's large commons. When Heath was last here eight months ago, it was a quiet, grassy area, with towering hill. Now it was a bustling tent city sheltering thousands. A sea of neat, white canvass spread out uniformly across the fields like an army encampment.

Busses were unloading passengers and their meager belongings. The same busses that once transported Thornton's Evangelical Crusaders into political battle, apparent from their faded signage. Now bearing people of differing faiths and ethnicities, down on their

566

luck from across the country. The newcomers were met by attendants in golf carts who ferried them off to tents.

Heath's crew headed out, and he took a path toward a very large tent in the distance.

As he went, he shook his head with amazement. Never in his reporting had he seen a homeless shelter like this. The residents appeared healthy and content, greeting him pleasantly as he passed. He saw bathroom and shower facilities with fresh clothing, bed linens and towels. Mobile medical and dental units, playgrounds, ball fields, bookmobiles with computers. And as he neared the large tent, he inhaled the scent of bacon and sausage.

• • •

Reverend Thornton stood at the tent door welcoming arrivals. He was having a *very* good day. Last night, the Supreme Court announced its decision regarding the ACLU's suit to negate the City's charter. In a narrow ruling, the Court sided with the City, and given Filby and the GOP majority had prevailed in the election, there was now nothing to interfere with Thornton's work.

He looked up, pleased to see Kyle Heath of Hawk News approaching. Thornton was expecting him. After months of hard work, the reverend was ready to break some news.

Accepting Thornton's hand, Heath gestured around to say, "My, how things have changed."

"Indeed they have," Thornton replied, "praise the Lord. We've much to discuss."

He led Heath into the tent where there was a buffet and tables filled with people dining and chatting. Grabbing coffee at a beverage counter, the two men settled at a table in a quiet corner.

Heath noted the ring on Thornton's finger to say, "I hear congratulations are in order."

Thornton felt his heart glow. "You'll meet Alice shortly, she's on our itinerary."

"Looking forward to it," Heath replied. "In the meantime, I've a million questions. I wish you'd let me bring in my crew and get you on camera."

"As I said, I don't do on-camera interviews anymore. Our work now is about the message, not the messenger. All part of our Revised Enlightenment."

Nodding, Heath took out a pen and notepad, and continued. "I've heard bits and pieces about the Prophet's Enlightenment. Or should I call him, 'Hermit?' Seven months, and not a glimpse. But he's certainly been busy with new prophecies. The world's flipping out, people are dying to know what's going on."

"To be clear, I've not seen him either, not since his last appearance on TV. But he contacts me now and then to give counsel and assistance."

"Do you mind sharing some of his counsel? I admit, I'm at a loss."

"It's actually very simple. According to the Prophet, most of us have things backwards. The point of religion, he tells us, is to serve people, and not the other way around. The Lord wants us to ease off the proselytizing and lead by example, get out there and make lives better, particularly for the poor and downtrodden."

"And these services you offer here, they're open to *anyone* seeking help?"

"Yes, irrespective of race, creed, politics, or sexual persuasion—no obligation. All anyone need do is contact us or other participating Churches, and we do the rest."

"But how long can you and your associate Churches expect to fund all this?"

"Given the commitment and generosity of our congregants, indefinitely. And I should add, our funds are matched dollar-for-dollar by the Prophet."

Heath's jaw dropped. "Where does the Prophet get *his* funds?"

"I don't know. But I imagine, as they say, the Lord provides."

Scribbling notes, Heath asked, "I understand your Enlightenment cost you followers. When refugees began arriving here, didn't many congregants bail?"

"True," Thornton said. "Some find it hard to disrupt comfortable lives and incomes in service of our less fortunate. Others find the diversity hard to swallow. But like the Prophet instructs, you can teach old dogma new tricks. As people come to realize the success of our program and others like it, more are seeing the light."

Indeed, over the previous months, Thornton and all but one laggard Church on the Council had undergone spiritual overhauls. With guidance from the Prophet, they were resolving moral questions not by reaching for the bible, but by reaching into their hearts and minds. A more compassionate, tolerant reflection of faith tempered by reason—and even science.

Heath paused, took a breath, and said, "I know this is a sore subject, Reverend, but I'd be remiss not to bring it up...your Family Research Institute."

The joy in Thornton's heart faded, and he lowered his eyes. "In my blindness and ignorance," he admitted, "I brought a terrible evil into our City. That wrong has been dealt with, and I'm doing everything in my power to make amends. We've turned the Institute into a Diversity Center, run by my wife."

In fact, since changing the Center and other Church reforms at the urging of the Prophet, the City's plague of troubled youth had plummeted, praise God.

Both men reflected for a moment. Then Thornton rose to say, "Come, I'll introduce you to Alice. Then we'll drop by our subsidized housing development. You can see firsthand some of our on-the-job training...

CHAPTER 131

The Present, Monday, May 10, 9:00 am, Queens

Ivy sat in the backseat of an electric car, gazing out tinted windows at the block where Scotty's apartment building used to be. Well, the building was still there, but it no longer housed apartments. The entire block on both sides was under renovation.

Across the street, the brownstones were being gutted and refurbished, turned into upscale, low-income housing. Empty corner stores were being converted into a medical clinic, a soup kitchen, a recreation center, a library, a continuing-education facility. More such mixed-use construction was in the works for surrounding areas.

Scotty's end of the block was finished, transformed into a mega-complex of offices. Each weekend for months, Ivy had been coming to assist him with his ambitious goals, but today she was here for a different reason.

Her driver turned into an underground parking garage, passing through a security gate, stopping at an elevator. Ivy exited, promising not to be long, and rode up two floors to exit in front of another security gate. Before she could swipe her ID card, a guard inside smiled and buzzed her in.

"Morning, Ivy," he said. "Didn't 'spect to see you on a weekday. No school?"

"Hey, Pedro," she replied. "Not today. Got some travel plans."

She continued to a reception area with several unmarked doors. A woman sat at a desk of video monitors under a sign reading:

No Unauthorized Personnel

"Hey, Ivy," the woman greeted her, waving her past.

"Hey, Tiffany. You seen Scotty this morning?"

"Main conference room. Said to send you in when you got here."

She thanked her and continued through one of the unmarked doors into a spacious area. Tall ceilings and windows, exposed brick, desks, and computers. Half the room was open to the floor below, where dozens of people hummed about in an open-office setting and meeting areas. To Ivy's right was a glass-enclosed conference room. A gilded sign on a wall behind read:

The Rose Butterfield Foundation

Scotty was at a table inside, in discussions with a dozen men and women. A meeting of department heads—a select, sworn-to-secrecy inner circle that administered Scotty's "prophecies." Curled on the table was Homer, the tip of his orange tail in a lazy wag.

Every Monday, Scotty presented his departments with predictions from what he called *The Archive of Things to Come.* He kept the true source of his omniscience hidden from all but Ivy. Scotty hated the title "Prophet," but by necessity, it remained the banner under which he revealed his pronouncements to the world.

Ivy's heart welled as she watched her brother. No one who knew him before he went into seclusion would recognize him today. Trim in a tailored suit and tie. Clean-shaven, hair neatly cut and combed, smiling big, teeth straight and bright. He spotted Ivy and waved her in, and she entered to see a man at the table holding a chart of zig-zaggy lines, trending up.

The man said, "Earnings exceed projections. Our investment portfolio has tripled, stock returns quadrupled. Lottery winnings and off-track revenues are through the roof." He paused to recognize Ivy, who waved a hand of apology and took a seat in the back, returning nods from others. The man continued, "But the big news is our winnings from the basketball brackets. Although after this, we may have to back off on sports a while, Vegas bookies are getting wise to us."

Scotty thanked him and acknowledged a recent addition to the group, an intriguing young woman Ivy had met before, but not yet gotten to know. Nicole LeClair. Dark hair and eyes, gorgeous skin, cool neck tattoo and piercings.

Scotty had gone to great lengths over the winter tracking her to a "gentlemen's club" in New Orleans, convincing her to come work with the Foundation. After a rough start, Nicole had settled in, rising to head a department and proving Scotty's point: given the right opportunities, unaccomplished people could accomplish remarkable things. Of course, Scotty himself was proof of that.

Nicole headed up the Life-Threatening Personal Tragedies Division—accidents, fatal diseases, murders and such. She was charged with alerting those in Fate's crosshairs. Ivy had hoped for a chance to work with Nicole, but that would have to wait.

Finishing her report, Nicole yielded to a woman who oversaw global natural disasters: pending earthquakes, avalanches, floods, fires, and on. Her responsibility was to warn governments and relief agencies well-enough in advance to mitigate casualties and property loss. To ensure the Foundation's warnings received due attention and respect, each alert always went out under the official rubric of *prophet@deiknumi.kyrios*.

Next, a woman reported on preventable mass disasters: terrorist attacks, plane crashes, oil spills, and such. These, however, were issues Scotty chose to deal with personally, and when the woman concluded, she added, "I sent you the latest list with full details."

Scotty thanked her, glanced at his watch and said, "I'm afraid that's all for today. Nice work, everybody, great stuff. We'll pick up when I get back."

As people filed out, Scotty stowed his laptop in a shoulder bag, grabbed Homer, and suggested to Ivy, "We've got a moment, what say we peek in on ground zero?"

They exited the main office, out into a hallway to yet another security gate. Accessing it with an ID badge, Scotty led on to a second, more formidable-looking metal door requiring an iris-scan cued solely to his eye. Ivy heard the sound of heavy tumblers, and followed her brother inside a dark room.

Scotty's old apartment.

"Unrecognizable," Ivy said, amazed. She hadn't seen it in months.

Walls to the next building had been removed to create a large, open space, lots of lab equipment and machinery sitting around in plastic wrappings and tags. The only things familiar were the front window and Mom's umbrella plant, lush and soaking up sun, a living memorial to all that had transpired here. Right of the plant along the front wall was an area cordoned off by barricades, reserved for the wormhole, if and when it reappeared. A video camera on a tripod sat in front, monitoring twenty-four/seven.

Scotty seemed lost in thought, and Ivy had to remind him, "We've got a car waiting."

They returned to the hall, secured the door and sped downstairs to the garage and car. They saw only a few hangers-on and paparazzi outside these days, the madness ebbing at last. Not that anyone would recognize the new-and-improved Scotty, who could now pass in plain sight.

"Airport, please," he told their driver. And closing the privacy screen, he handed Homer to Ivy and opened his laptop, averting it so she couldn't see. He speed-dialed, and a woman answered.

"Morning, Mr. Butterfield. He's expecting you, hold please."

Seconds later, a western drawl filled the compartment. *"Hey there, Scott, how ya doin'?"*

"Fine, sir. And you?"

"Great, great. Ya see the Bureau of Justice crime stats today?"

"Why, no."

"Waaay down, praise the Lord. Perps can't figure out why we're always three steps ahead of 'em—hahaha."

"Great news," Scotty said. "I've a few new items to send you."

"Anything urgent?"

"Nothing you don't have plenty of time to head off. A school shooting, a cyber attack on the Pentagon, a train derailment. And a few political issues you'll want to deal with."

"Send me the skinny and I'll get right on it. Anything else?"

Scotty sighed. "The Lord is *still* not happy with campaign finance reform."

Pause. *"Uh, yeah, Congress is draggin' its heels. Would sure help if the Lord has something on my Speaker of the House. Give him a little goose, ya know?"*

"I'll see what I can do. In the meantime, why not let Secretary Shackleton take a swing at it? She's doing a great job cleaning up the super-PACS."

"Good idea. Yep, the Lord was right 'bout bringin' her aboard, sure smoothed feathers."

"That's it, then. I'll touch base with you next week. Good luck."

"Bless ya, Prophet. Thank the Lord from me an' the country."

"Bless you, too, Mr. President."

Scotty hung up, locking eyes with Ivy.

She said, "From puppet to puppeteer."

"So long as I've got the rabbit's foot. But the more we meddle with reality, the more we change it. Without someone on the other side to update the archives, sooner or later our prophecies will start to fail, and there goes my credibility."

Last fall after the election, Scotty had lost all contact with Ariel. And not a single appearance of the wormhole since.

Ivy assured him, "The new lab will get your Plan back on track."

A Plan for a world where humankind would look into the future to avoid mistakes it made in the present. A world of second chances.

Scotty sighed. "We won't know for three years, not till Talawanda is up and running. I just hope things go well with my meeting today."

Ivy patted his knee.

Their car passed through airport security onto a tarmac where a small jet idled. Formerly Pembroke Thornton's jet, gifted to Scotty's Foundation to assist in its expanding, humanitarian enterprises.

Soon, Ivy and Scotty were soaring above the skyline.

A half hour later, they landed in Philadelphia, cabbing to a university where Ivy had an orientation tour, and Scotty was anticipating an important encounter. Ivy had been accepted here months ago, her school of choice. Pop backed down about her leaving home, despite her affliction. While Scotty's donation to the Autoimmune Association gave hope for a medical solution, what ultimately allayed Pop's fears was Ivy coming out. He was *still* reeling from that.

Money no object now, Ivy would start in the fall as long planned. Though thrilled, she had regrets. She'd wanted to postpone college and work full time at the Foundation.

That caused a squabble between Pop and Scotty. But it got father and son talking and on the same side, for once. Scotty brought in Mrs. Steiner, who got Ivy to capitulate, and Mrs. Steiner also nudged Pop and Scotty into counseling—with her graciously serving as mediator.

A new beginning for everyone.

• • •

Scotty and Ivy arrived on campus, and Scotty was impressed. Grand, stately, picturesque. Everything he'd wanted for his little sister. Ivy seemed impressed, too.

They put Homer on a leash and walked to admissions, stopping outside to hug.

"I'll meet you here after lunch," Scotty said. "Go enjoy yourself."

She paused to regard him closely, leaning in. "Listen," she said, "I know you're anxious about your meeting. But remember, you're the *new* Scotty. *You* made all this happen, you alone."

It didn't help the butterflies he felt.

She punched him in the arm, gave Homer a pat, and strolled into the building.

Scotty stood lost in thought, brought back by a tug on the leash. He looked down to see Homer raise a brow.

Cold feet?

"Lead on, faithful companion," Scotty told him, and they struck out across the bustling quadrangle toward a statue of Ben Franklin.

Students turned to gawk at Homer as they passed.

• • •

Ariel Silva sat in her favorite reading spot, the lawn outside the library under a tree. She was riveted to her laptop and a news story she'd been following.

The Family Research Institute in the City of God had been closed. Somehow, Reverend Penbrook Thornton had come by secret files implicating Ariel's stepfather in a terrible scandal. The FBI had descended on Phil's office and led him away in handcuffs, charging him with multiple felonies. Scores of victims from all over the country had emerged in response to the publicity.

Other surprising news. After all these years, Mom had called! They'd talked for hours, and at Ariel's urging, Mom was coming to UPENN for graduation ceremonies next week. Ariel was *ecstatic.*

She removed her sunglasses to blot her eyes, and happened to notice a well-dressed, handsome young man walking a little dog on a leash. He appeared headed straight for her, no one else in the vicinity. As he drew close, Ariel marveled to see not a dog, but a *cat.* Big and orange. She couldn't help but laugh.

The man grinned back, a warm, wide smile. He stopped in front of Ariel.

"Excuse me, Ms. Silva," he said. "I'm from the Rose Butterfield

Foundation. I wonder if I could have a word."

What an auspicious day. Last fall, a surprise endowment from the Rose Butterfield Foundation had absolved Ariel of all her student debt. This was her first contact with her enigmatic benefactors.

"My goodness," she cried, leaping to her feet. She felt so unprepared, wearing one of her frumpiest dresses. "I'm honored and thrilled to meet you, sir."

"Please, I'm Scott. Scott Butterfield."

She was further stunned to recognize the name. Or maybe it was coincidence. This gentleman bore no resemblance to the quirky fellow she'd seen on TV, the once-famous Prophet of Queens who'd flashed into prominence last fall, only to vanish. Ariel hadn't made a connection to the Foundation until now.

She gushed, "I'm grateful for the chance to thank you in person, Mr. Butterfield!" She simply couldn't bring herself to call him by his first name. "Your foundation has been so generous to me!"

His smile grew. "Our confidence in you was well placed. Summa cum laude."

She felt herself blush.

"Forgive me if I get to the point," he said. "I'm here to present a business proposition we hope will interest you. Our Foundation is building a research facility near the new cyclotron up in Talawanda. Nothing like it anywhere in the world, state-of-the-art. When the collider comes online, we'll be working with TPC on some rather unusual experiments. We'd like you to consider joining us."

Another astounding coincidence. Ariel had recently been contacted out of the blue by a graduate student at MIT she'd never met. The woman encouraged her to apply for a research position at TPC. Ariel had done so, but had yet to hear back.

Mr. Butterfield said, "We'd like to fly you up to see the lab and discuss plans. The position we have in mind is first assistant to TPC director, Winston Keller."

Ariel was flabbergasted. Not an analyst, a full-fledged researcher at the world's most advanced collider, working alongside the world's foremost astrophysicist. Far surpassing any opportunity she could have hoped for.

Before she could regain her breath to accept, she felt a soft tap on her leg.

The cat, pawing her.

She laughed and bent down to pet it, then gasped and jumped back. It had a dead critter in its mouth. *A mouse.*

The cat dropped it, and Ariel saw not a mouse, but a rabbit's foot. A keychain.

Mr. Butterfield hastened to explain, "Forgive me, it's fake. It's a flashdrive. But it *is* good luck. The data it holds has the power to change the world."

Ariel puzzled at him, and saw the strangest look in his eyes. As if he knew her.

Knew her soul.

She glanced down again, and the cat smiled at her.

It *smiled?* She'd never seen a cat smile.

And then it grinned, and said, *Welcome to our new future.*

Manufactured by Amazon.ca
Bolton, ON